Butler, Edward Ruadh :- Swordland

2000668027

Published by Accent Press Ltd 2016

ISBN 9781786150479

# GLOSSARY

## WALES

**Aberteifi** – the fortress commanded by Robert FitzStephen in the modern town of Cardigan in western Wales

**Brecon** – a town in central Wales

**Ceredigion** – Cardiganshire; it was a province in west Wales claimed by the Princes of Deheubarth and Gwynedd as well as the Norman Earl of Hertford

**Deheubarth** – kingdom in southern Wales

**Glamorgan** – kingdom in southern Wales

**Gwarthaf** – cantred west of modern Carmarthen in south Wales

**Gwent** – kingdom in south-eastern Wales

**Gwynedd** – kingdom in northern Wales

**Melrfjord** – Milford Haven

**Pebidiog** – barony around city of St Davids

**Penteulu** – a Welsh warlord

**Powys** – kingdom in eastern Wales

**Rhos** – cantred around Haverford in south-west Wales

**Saesneg** – the Welsh word for English

**Rhys ap Gruffydd** – king of Deheubarth, anglicised to Rhys, son of Griffith. His sons, **Maredudd** (Meredith) and **Tewdwr** (Tudor)

**Striguil** – fortress held by Strongbow which the English called Chepstow, or the 'market place'

## IRELAND

**Banabh** – a village on Bannow Bay

**Bearú** – River Barrow

**Bhanna** – River Bann

**Brehon** – a Gaelic judge or lawyer

**Breifne** – petty-kingdom covering the area of modern Counties Cavan and Leitrim in Connacht

**Brian Bóruma** – famous King of Tuadhmumhain and Mhumhain, and High King of Ireland, who died in 1014; his name is anglicised as Brian Boru

**Carn tSóir** – Carnsore Point

**An Carraig** – modern Ferrycarrig, two miles north of Wexford

**Ceatharlach** – modern Carlow Town

**Cluainmín** – a small Norse settlement between Veðrarfjord and Waesfjord close to modern Wellingtonbridge

**Tir Eóghain** – translated as Owen's Land, it was ruled by the Mac Lochlainn family and their kinsmen the Uí Néill

**Corcach** – Cork; an Ostman city in Ireland built on the 'swamp' after which it takes its name

**Deasmumhain** – Desmond; petty-kingdom in southern Munster ruled by Mac Cartaigh clan

**Diarmait Mac Murchada** – King of Laighin, anglicised as Dermot MacMurrough; his children, sons **Conchobair** and **Eanna** (Conor and Enna) and daughters **Aoife** (Eva), **Orlaith** (Orla), and **Sabh** (Sive)

**Diarmait Ua Mael Sechlainn** – King of Mide, anglicised as Dermot O'Melaghlin

**Domhnall Caomhánach** – Diarmait Mac Murchada's eldest son, anglicised as Donal Kavanagh

**Domhnall Ua Briain** – King of Tuadhmumhain, anglicised as Donal O'Brien

**Donnchadh Mac Giolla Phádraig** – King of the Osraighe, anglicised as Donncha MacGillapatrick, but the family is now called Fitzpatrick

**Dubhlinn** – modern Dublin. It was a *Viking* city on the south bank of the River Liffey built around a 'black pool' from which it takes its name

**Dubh-Tir** – woodland area once known as Duffrey in modern County Wexford

**Eirik Mac Amlaibh** – chief man of Waesfjord

**Fearna** – Ferns in northern County Wexford

**Feoire** – River Nore

**Fionntán Ua Donnchaidh** – Irish warrior, anglicised as Fintan

O'Dunphy

**Gabhrán** – Gowran; a settlement in County Kilkenny

**Laighin** – Leinster; the kingdom ruled by Diarmait Mac Murchada which includes Counties Wexford, Wicklow, Offaly, Carlow, Wicklow, Laois, Kildare and south Dublin

**Hlymrik** – Limerick; city populated by the Danes but ruled, nominally, by the Uí Briain

**Lorcain Ua Tuathail** – Archbishop of Dubhlinn, anglicised as Lorcan O'Toole

**Máelmáedoc Ua Riagain** – Diarmait Mac Murchada's secretary, anglicised as Malachy (or Maurice) O'Regan

**Mide** – Meath; a major kingdom ruled by a southern branch of the Uí Néill. It was claimed by both the Meic Murchada and the Uí Ruairc

**Mhumhain** – Munster, which was at different times ruled by the Uí Briain and the Meic Cartaigh

**Muirchertach Mac Murchada** – brother of Dermot, anglicised as Murtagh MacMurrough

**Oirmumhain** – Ormond; translated as east Munster which roughly equates to modern County Tipperary. A petty-kingdom ruled by the Uí Cinnéide

**Oisin Ua Bruaideodha** – Bishop of the Osraighe, anglicised as Oisin O'Brody

**Osraighe** – Ossory; a people to the west of Laighin ruled by the Meic Giolla Phádraig. Their lands roughly equated to modern Counties Kilkenny and Laois

**Ruaidhrí Ua Conchobair** – High King of Ireland and King of Connacht, anglicised as Rory O'Connor

**Seosamh Ua hAodha** – Bishop of Fearna, anglicised as Joseph O'Hugh

**Sláine** – River Slaney

**Siúire** – River Suir

**Taoiseach** – a Gaelic warlord

**Teamhair na Ri** – translated as 'Hill of the Kings'. Present day Tara in County Meath

**Thing (Þing)** – a council

**Tigernán Ua Ruairc** – King of Breifne, anglicised as Tiernan O'Rourke

**Toirdelbach Mac Diarmait** – petty king in Laighin, anglicised as Turlough McDermott

**Tuadhmumhain** – Thomond; petty-kingdom in northern Munster ruled by the Uí Briain

**Tuaim dá Ghuabainn** – the 'burial mound of the two shoulders' – modern Tuam in County Galway where Ruaidhrí Ua Conchobair had his chief fortress

**Uí Ceinnselaig** – tribe in modern County Wexford, the closest approximation is 'the Kinsella'

**Veðrarfjord** – Waterford; an Ostman city built up the Suir River from a windy sea inlet for which the town is named

**Waesfjord** – Wexford; it was an Ostman town built on mud flats with a name which means 'Wide Inlet'

# NOTES

The '**Fitz**' prefix is the Norman derivation of the Latin 'filius' or 'son of' e.g. FitzStephen is 'son of Stephen'. '**Mac**' in Irish signifies 'son of', as does '**ab**' or '**ap**' in Welsh.

A **miles** (one of a number of milites) is a Norman horseman armoured similarly to a knight but not considered of the same rank.

The **Ostmen** (East Men) were made up of *Fionngall* (Fair Foreigners), the descendants of the original Norse invaders who populated the cities of Dublin, Waterford, Limerick, Cork and Wexford, and the *Dubhgall* (Dark Foreigners), who were Danes and arrived a hundred years later following their conquests in northern England. They became the ruling class in most of these settlements.

Irish families were divided into clans (**tuath**) and septs (**finte**), thus Diarmait Mac Murchada was the King of the Uí Ceinnselaig (*tuath*) as well as the Meic Murchada (*finte*)

# Part One

# The Outpost

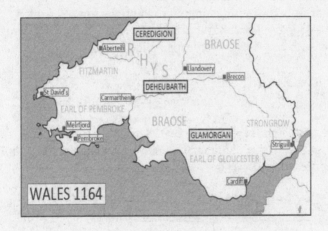

# Chapter One

## Ceredigion, Wales
### April 1164

The cobbled stones of the priory were cold beneath Einion's knees, but on he prayed, murmuring verses to St Padarn as he crouched before the mass of candles. They provided him with little heat or comfort as their flames fluttered, casting a hellish flickering shadow battle on the stone wall of the church.

'Holy Padarn, hear me and bring my prayers to Our Lord so that he might grant me forgiveness for what I must do,' Einion ab Anarawd whispered. He wrung his hands together and then spread them out before his chest, casting his eyes towards the high roof in entreaty. The smoke from candle and torch mingled with the sickly sweet aroma of the honey mead brewed behind the brothers' cells. It caught the light from the small windows, casting wispy spear-shafts of light across the building above the Welsh warlord.

Einion sighed after a few silent seconds of staring heavenwards. He bowed his head and sat back on his heels to think. Had he been expecting a miracle? That was exactly what he had been anticipating, he admitted. This priory was where one of the holiest sons of the Church, St Padarn, had performed his greatest deed. Here was where the great Penteulu Arthwyr, or Arthur the Warlord as the English called him, had been humbled. It was a place where wonders were commonplace and the connection between man and God routine. And yet Einion felt nothing; no marvellous presence of divinity and no absolution.

'I bring a mighty gift, Lord,' Einion appealed again, speaking towards the twelve trembling candle flames above him on the altar, at the same time indicating towards a beautiful

1

coat, expensive and red, by his side. It was just as the stories instructed, just like the one that Arthwyr was said to have stolen from Holy Padarn.

'A mighty gift,' Einion repeated. 'And all I ask for is for one small indulgence.' He licked his dry lips. 'My uncle's life.' Again his eyes flicked skywards awaiting some signal that his proposal was accepted and his immortal soul safe from damnation. But none was forthcoming.

'Rhys stole my throne,' he shouted, suddenly angry. 'I am a warrior! He is nothing but a jumped-up cleric, a stock-taker, not a real leader. He cannot defend our people against these Normans! I can, for I know I can match their evil!' Flecks of spittle caught in Einion's heavy black beard. 'They are an infestation of maggots searching for an open wound, and they smell the blood fresh on Rhys. They are circling these lands ready to invade. The Normans can sense weakness in Rhys, but I can stop them,' he appealed. 'Give me the strength to stop them!'

The beam of sunlight which illuminated the smoke from burning torches wavered above Einion and abruptly shone into his eyes. Perhaps it was just a passing cloud or trick of the light that had caused the quivering beam to settle upon the praying man, but he smiled and nodded his head appreciatively at the flat stone ceiling.

'Alright then,' he said, a smile upon his face, 'but you need more, I understand.' He picked up the red woollen tunic. 'For that most desperate sin, I will promise the same act of atonement that Holy Padarn asked of Arthwyr.' He smiled at the candles. 'I will bury myself in the ground up to my neck for a day and a night.' Einion looked smugly at the ceiling of the small priory and held his breath in anticipation. Nothing happened for many seconds, but then the rows of candles before him began whipping uncontrollably as a sudden rush of divine wind poured through the priory and Einion knew instinctively that his promise had been accepted by God. For a long time he simply inhaled the deific air, tainted though it was with lime from the brothers' vellum baths below. He lifted his sapphire ring to his lips and kissed it. His God had granted him

2

absolution to kill. War and fear and glory would come to his country of Deheubarth. The invaders would die, that he promised God, because it was they, not he, who had caused Rhys' demise.

But as quickly as the feeling of rapture overtook him, it disappeared – to his rear he heard the faint scrape of steel links on cold, dusty stone and his warrior's instincts swept aside his reverie. Einion had heard the sound before and had learned to fear it; the crunch of chainmailed feet on cobbled stone. A Norman had entered the priory and that could mean only one thing – his life was in desperate danger.

Einion didn't move, but inhaled long through his nose and slipped his dagger silently from his belt. Obviously it had not been God's grace, but the draught of the priory door opening so that the Norman assassin could slip inside. He momentarily wondered why his four warriors had not alerted him to the presence of his enemy before realising that his friends were almost certainly dead at the hands of the Godless barbarians from the south. Undoubtedly he was now on his own, but to escape Einion first had to deal with the assassin, the immediate threat to his life. He concentrated on identifying where the newcomer was behind him, his eyes rolling in his head as he listened intently. He did not move save to continue the pretence of praying, mumbling a soft verse in his native tongue. Another scratch sounded just a few yards behind him and Einion knew that his would-be murderer had crept into his killing range. He almost laughed out loud at the Norman's clumsy attempt on his life. With a roar he turned to meet his enemy and stabbed forward with an almighty and much practiced lunge which ripped deep into his enemy's torso and up into his stomach.

'Ha!' he laughed as he looked up into the dying man's face. But it was no Norman. It was one of his own warriors, Walter ap Llywarch. Einion's mind struggled to catch up with what his eyes saw before him: Walter had his mouth gagged by a thick piece of cloth and bound with rope, and yet blood flowed from beneath the gag and down his coarse dull shirt. His tongue had been removed. On Walter's feet had been tied the chainmail stockings of a Norman knight while his hands were secured at the small of his back. He may not have been able to speak but Walter's eyes screamed in pain and begged his warlord to help him. Einion ripped the dagger from his warrior's belly. Warm blood trickled down the blade and onto his hand.

'What?' was all Einion could manage as Walter dropped to his knees, tumbling down the steps into the nave. 'What the devil?' Einion whispered into the smoky, echoing darkness of the priory. Everything was silent except for his own shuffling feet and Walter's heavy, agonised breathing below him. The holy site of St Padarn no longer felt welcoming and safe to the Cymric warlord. His breath misted before his eyes in the frigid cold of the stone church. The flickering shadows cast by the candles and the windows gave ample hiding place for the Normans to hide and Einion felt the cold clasp of ice grip his heart.

'Come out and fight me, you devil,' he screamed, but there was no response to his challenge. He spun around to face the chapel and then back to where Walter lay in the nave. His sword whipped through the air as he turned. 'Where are you? Are you a coward?' he cried and backtracked towards the high altar.

Suddenly his hair was clasped in a vice like grip from behind and a dagger slashed across Einion's wrist, cutting into flesh and severing tendons. The Welshman's bloody blade clattered loudly to the floor before Einion, roaring a battle-cry, could even react. He swung his uninjured arm but missed his hooded assailant, who ducked under his poorly aimed blow. Another surge of pain seared across the ligaments of Einion's left knee, forcing him onto the uneven cobbles as if in prayer. He grabbed at his sword on the floor, but a bare foot slid it away before he got close. In the blink of an eye the knife was at his throat, an odd sensation of warm blood running and cold, sharp steel as it pressed against Einion's windpipe.

'Hello, cousin.' A voice whispered French words in Einion's ear. 'I told you we would meet again, did I not? Did you think I would forget?'

Einion did not answer but quickly perceived how the Norman, bereft of chainmail and silent as a ghost, had tricked

4

him, entering the priory in Walter's wake to ambush him at prayer. 'Prince Rhys will pay good money to have me back,' he said in Welsh.

Sir Robert FitzStephen, Constable of Aberteifi Castle, snorted scathingly at his cousin's proclamation.

'Kill me and it will mean war,' Einion told him.

'And what makes you think that is not exactly what I want?' FitzStephen said calmly. He gripped his prisoner's hair tighter, his knife scraping small hairs from Einion's bearded throat. 'Your men scared off all the monks, so there is no-one to give you the rites,' he stated without feeling.

'For pity's sake,' Einion moaned. 'We are kin,' he appealed as he gripped FitzStephen's forearm with his good hand. But he heard his death in the warlord's laugh and anger overtook him. 'Curse you then, you Norman bastard,' Einion snarled. 'I curse you and all your Godless kind. Before my body is long cold you too will know defeat and death. I swear it on my immortal soul that you will be brought to your knees …'

'Witchcraft,' FitzStephen accused and dragged the knife across his throat. 'May Christ have mercy on your wretched Welsh soul,' he said and kept sawing as Einion tried to curse and struggle, choking on blood and phlegm and fear. FitzStephen kept cutting until his head came away, the last sinews ripping away so that he could cast Einion's body down on the floor of the priory where a pool of blood quickly gathered. The head soon followed the rest of Einion's body as it rolled sickeningly down, step by step, into the nave.

Walter ap Llywarch lay where he had fallen, hidden in the shadow of the altar. The agony from his stomach wound was almost too great to bear, but his hands were still bound and he could not do anything to improve his condition except pray for death or unconsciousness to take him. Einion's decapitated head lay just a few paces away and appalled Walter, but he did not want to move lest FitzStephen remember he was there and deal with him in a similar fashion to his Penteulu. His hollow eyes flicked up to the dark, smoky recesses of the chapel where he could hear the Norman asking forgiveness of his sins.

'St Maurice, bless me,' the voice repeated again and again in the French tongue. 'St Maurice, speak for me,' he whimpered. The knight's voice stopped suddenly and he stepped back out into the light cast by the small windows. In one of FitzStephen's hands was the huge golden cross from the high altar which he had stolen. The Norman pulled down his hood. Tall, beardless, and with his hair cropped short, FitzStephen threw his grey cloak aside to reveal his brilliant gold and crimson surcoat. He looked like the Archangel Michael in all his glory to the gagged man on the verge of unconsciousness.

'It is done,' FitzStephen shouted, his voice echoing around the cavernous priory. Three men dressed similarly to their captain entered the building along with a young Welsh warrior. Walter recognised the boy as Geraint, a cousin of Einion.

'Don't worry,' FitzStephen switched to the Welsh tongue to address the terrified boy, 'I am not going to kill you. I want you to deliver a message to your Prince Rhys.' The Norman knight knelt and picked up Einion's head by his long hair, throwing it to the boy who squealed as it struck him in the chest and rolled down his body to his feet. 'Take that to my cousin and tell him who sent it.' The boy was wild-eyed as the head was forced back into his arms. 'He will know where to find me,' FitzStephen said and turned to his warriors. 'Take him outside and put him on a horse,' he told his men. 'Then we are for Aberteifi and home,' FitzStephen shouted. 'We have what we came for. I have my war,' he added more quietly.

Walter groaned as another bout of pain surged through his body. His heavy breathing interrupted the Norman captain who turned around to look at the Welshman, sprawled on the floor.

'Walter, I had forgotten that you were there,' FitzStephen said. 'Alas, I am afraid that I am going to need my armour back.' The Welshman whimpered once as his enemy stalked forward with his dagger poised to strike again.

### Six months later

The Norman army, gaudy against the greys and greens of rain-soaked Dyfed, marched towards the fast-flowing River Teifi. They strode with smiles upon their faces, the smirks of men who knew that victory was imminent.

'The Lord of Hosts is with us,' Sir Robert FitzStephen shouted at the horsemen and pointed to the black and yellow banner of St David which hung limply above the warriors sent by the Norman bishop. 'You'd better be with us,' Sir Robert murmured as he cast his snarling gaze skyward. 'Now of all times.'

'Tell the Lord to go back to heaven,' a warrior shouted from the midst of his armoured horsemen, 'because we don't need his heavenly host, we have the Devil on our side! His name is FitzStephen.'

The other men-at-arms laughed as Robert punched a chainmailed fist in the air and led the army north across the long wooden bridge between the countries of Cemais and Ceredigion. Behind the cavalry came the ranks of archers and infantry, twice as many as there were horsemen. They laughed and joked amongst themselves as they tried to hide their excitement and terror at the thought of the fight ahead. Yet they were all glad to be free of the boring garrison duty that had so dented their opportunity for plunder and acclaim in Wales. The girls of the town cooed and waved as the dim light danced off the cavalrymen's armour, and boys ran alongside, grasping to touch of the weapons that hung from the flanks of the Norman horsemen. Above, pennants trembled in the wind on lances and spears. The horses seemed to sense the oncoming storm of violence and shuffled nervously beneath their masters.

'I wish this rain would stop,' Sir Roger de Quincy said as he trotted alongside FitzStephen. His courser's hooves knocked dully on the wet wooden timbers of the bridge which spanned the Teifi. 'I don't fancy fighting in this downpour …'

'I wouldn't worry about the weather,' FitzStephen interrupted, 'I need you to stay here at Aberteifi with five milites and a section of archers …'

'Stay?' Quincy interrupted, his nose curled with petulance. 'Why do I have to stay? Why can Ferrand not stay here?'

'Because William Ferrand is going with me and you will learn not to question my orders,' FitzStephen replied in a low voice, waiting until Quincy sullenly nodded his head.

'I know my duty,' Quincy added angrily, clipping his heels to his horse's flanks and riding ahead of the Constable towards the end of the bridge.

FitzStephen shook his head in anger at Quincy's lack of respect and sent a curse through the deluge towards his lieutenant's back. It had been raining on Ceredigion for two weeks; a sticky, constant drizzle that, along with the warm weather, made woollen clothes cling to their owners, itching and uncomfortable. The grey clouds had come in from the east and wrapped themselves around the top of the low Welsh mountains, pouring their contents unceasingly across the already sodden hills. But no matter how much it rained the heavy October clouds did not diminish and the land of Ceredigion seemed cut off from the rest of the Wales, flanked on either side by the leaden mountains and the grey, stormy sea to the west. Rainwater splashed on rocks and ran between the sparse clumps of grass before it was collected by streams and tributaries which wound their way down the hills to join the mighty River Teifi.

But not even the rain could dampen the relish in FitzStephen's eyes. It was six months since the incident at the priory and finally his moment had arrived: the native princes had united and would give him battle! Droplets drummed on helmets, shields, weapons and armour yet victory seemed assured. Had not the priests sworn that in the eleven hundred and sixty-four years since the birth of Our Lord Jesus Christ, no army had ever been so grand? Were the Normans not the masters of Wales? And who could possibly defeat such an army led by that great knight himself, Sir Robert FitzStephen? Surely not this rag-tag army of Welshmen coming out of the hills to the north, he thought. What did it matter that the priests from Deheubarth and Gwynedd claimed that God had abandoned the man who had murdered their heroic captain, Einion ab Anarawd?

'Get your vanguard moving faster, Sir Robert,' a knight in the colours of the Baron of Cemais shouted through the rain. 'We want to get across today,' he yelled sarcastically.

'He is very keen for a boy who has never lifted his sword in anger before,' FitzStephen shouted back. The knight's face turned red and he rode away rather than reply to the insult against his lord. Nevertheless FitzStephen urged his men to greater speed as asked. 'We go north, lads,' he shouted as he reached dry land below the high earthen motte of Aberteifi Castle. 'We go north, for plunder aplenty and Welsh wenches for one and all!' His men cheered and streamed past him towards the road upon which, he had no doubt, they would soon find the rebel Welsh army. The sound of cantering horses' hooves made FitzStephen turn.

'The Cymri have stopped their advance, Robert,' William Ferrand shouted in his direction as he slowed to a trot, surrounded by more outriders dressed in the same gold and crimson arrow-headed surcoats.

'Where?' asked the Constable of Aberteifi.

'Two miles to the north,' Ferrand said as his excited horse fought against its bit. 'They are waiting for us. They are led by Rhys of Deheubarth and Owain of Gwynedd.'

'They are definitely going to give us battle?' FitzStephen sounded dubious, and well he might; the Welsh princes had rarely allowed themselves to be caught in a pitched battle with the Normans. By the same token, the dwindling numbers of FitzStephen's people were too few to risk a head on collision with the more numerous Welsh and were content rather to sally out from their castles to wreak havoc and ravage the land, extending their influence piece by piece and mile by mile.

This campaign was different. All the native princes of Wales had united to take on the murderer of Einion ab Anarawd, and expel the Normans from the land of Ceredigion. FitzStephen smiled when he considered the Welsh horde that approached his small fortress. In his wildest dreams he had thought that Einion's death would have given him the opportunity he had wanted since he had been created Constable of Aberteifi: to draw out his enemy and meet them in battle, Norman lance against Welsh bow. Thanks to Einion's death only one victory lay between Sir Robert FitzStephen and the destruction of the greatest lords of Wales. One decisive encounter and the kingdoms of Ceredigion, Deheubarth, and Gwynedd would lie open to conquest.

'Rhys will stand and fight?' FitzStephen asked Ferrand with a sceptical shake of his head. 'You are sure?' He could not believe that his cousin, his mother's nephew, would take this action. 'You are sure?' he repeated.

'The Cymri are arrayed for battle,' Ferrand confirmed and stared nervously through the drizzle towards the hills to the north where their enemy waited. 'The armies of Gwynedd and Deheubarth have come to Aberteifi,' he breathed out and shook his head. 'It will be a long day, even with the Baron of Cemais' army at our side. I hope you know what you are doing, Robert.'

FitzStephen smiled and nodded his head. In his world, reputation in battle was everything; triumph in battle meant castles to govern land: land supported wheat, wheat fed warriors, and warriors could extend borders. Reputation meant power. The whole basis of the Norman way of life fed off conquest and in Wales was found the last fighting frontier in Christendom.

Shouts in the distance drew his attention and FitzStephen cast a scathing and distrustful look through the rain at the young Baron of Cemais, his neighbour from across the Teifi, who had inherited his father's vast Welsh estates just a year before.

'Spoiled brat,' FitzStephen said quietly – and jealously for, despite his many successes, he was essentially a landless knight. As Constable he held the castle of Aberteifi for the Earl of Hertford, the absentee lord of Ceredigion, and could only hope to become rich through the favour and endowment of land from his liege lord after his service was done. All he could expect for his efforts was the enjoyment of his lord's offices until he retired to some upland estate where he and his sons would struggle to raise crops and defend themselves against the Welsh. He thought of Aberteifi and Ceredigion as his inheritance, but the reality was that he could be replaced as Constable at any time if his lord so chose. FitzStephen was no longer content to wait for either reward or dismissal from the Earl. The time had come for him to prove himself against the two most powerful princes in Wales. He would take a prize for himself, and if God was with him then it would be a Marcher kingdom without equal.

'If the Baron of Cemais stands and fights,' Ferrand interrupted FitzStephen's thoughts, 'then the Welsh will only outnumber us by four to one.'

'We have them then,' FitzStephen said to his friend and circled his courser. 'We have them,' he shouted towards the dark, encroaching clouds. Around him the Norman warriors of the Welsh March cheered through the rain.

Victory was near, Sir Robert FitzStephen was certain.


Bodies littered the street all around him as he deflected another Welsh spear thrust with his shield. FitzStephen screamed as he ducked and swept his sword through his enemy's knee. The man went down screaming amongst the dead, his leg hanging by tendrils of flesh, and FitzStephen wasted no time in claiming his life with a stabbing downward lunge. Chainmailed Normans lay pierced with arrows and Welshmen lay contorted with horrific open wounds. The street of Aberteifi was awash with blood diluted by rain. FitzStephen ignored the horror and panted hard, searching for another enemy to kill.

'Sir Robert,' William Ferrand exclaimed as his men fell in alongside their constable, 'we thought you were dead!' Blood was visible on his spangenhelm as he locked shields with FitzStephen.

'St Maurice was watching over me,' he replied hoarsely.

'Where is the rest of your rearguard?'

'Those that live are back in the castle,' the knight told him indelicately, 'but there were not many that made it back.' He paused and shook his head. 'Quincy said that the baron had fled back across the bridge to Cemais?'

Ferrand nodded and spat. 'And good riddance, I say. He tried to get me to abandon the castle and defend the far side of the river, do you believe that? Sir Roger told me that you were dead and that he was going to follow the baron too. Wulfhere put paid to that; he told Quincy he'd put an arrow up his arse if he saw him on the bridge, so he stayed put.'

'Good,' FitzStephen replied and turned to stare at Aberteifi Castle, white and shining under the weak autumn sunshine.

'We've built a wall in the street,' Ferrand told him. 'I suggest we get on the other side of it.'

FitzStephen nodded and followed Ferrand to the rudimentary rampart erected across the main street through Aberteifi.

'This man says he has a rich ransom,' Robert's half-brother, William, interrupted. Below the esquire, a terrified Welshman was on his knees, his hair coiled around the teenager's fingers and a hunting dagger at his gullet. The Cymri warrior babbled nonsense as the boy held him firm. 'Do shut up,' William snarled in the Welsh tongue and thumped the man on the side with his knee. Under normal circumstances FitzStephen would have taken any ransom to enrich his coffers, but this was not the time to lose even one warrior to watching prisoners.

'Kill him,' he told his brother. William looked up regretfully before finishing his victim, hands flapping in his face as the Welshman squealed for pity from the young esquire. He received none and William dragged another body towards the gruesome barrier of dead men and loose timber which Ferrand had thrown up across the street.

'Shields,' someone shouted suddenly from FitzStephen's left. The Cymri, who had pursued his rearguard back to Aberteifi, once again began their aerial assault and the Normans raised their long, leaf-shaped shields to take their arrows. The occasional grunt and yelp of pain told the Constable that his men were taking damage. The Welsh bows didn't have the killing range of a crossbow, but a good archer could shoot ten arrows every thirty seconds whereas the Flemish crossbowmen that FitzStephen hired could only manage half that number. The archers would make an unholy mess of the Norman chainmail at close range, but they lacked the power to penetrate wood- and leather-backed shields. Every Norman knew the skill of the Welsh bowmen and had learned to fear that ability. To make matters worse, FitzStephen observed more enemy warriors streaming down the hill to the north-east. They would come looking for plunder, to kill men and to rape women.

He had wanted this war, he recalled, and had engineered an invasion of his territory by killing Einion, confident that he could destroy his enemies in open battle. But Einion's uncle,

Prince Rhys of Deheubarth, had prepared a trap and FitzStephen, arrogant as he was, had bumbled straight into it. Rather than the untrained raiders which the Welsh usually deployed against the Normans, he had found armoured and disciplined enemy who had matched his infantry blow for blow in the horror of the shield wall. The Welsh should have broken, should have dispersed into the hills as they always had in the face of Norman force, but Rhys' army had withstood FitzStephen's advance. And the surprises had not finished there; a distant thunder of hooves was as much as Sir Robert FitzStephen could remember of the moment his army, and his dreams for conquest, had died.

He recalled doubting the evidence his ears provided, telling himself that the Welsh did not have armoured cavalry as he had continued to stab and defend in the very centre of the shield wall. But moments later he felt the shudder pass through his army like wind through a field of bluebells, and he had stolen a glance at his right flank where he saw a rout taking place. His ally, the Baron of Cemais, Ralph FitzMartin, was fighting for his life, his men streaming from the hillside and back along the road towards Aberteifi. The Welshmen had ambushed his army using the Normans' own tactics. Then, suddenly, his whole army was retreating, step by step at first but before long they were running, the Cymri on their heels. The Baron of Cemais' men were already on the road in disorder, assailed by arrow and Welsh lance, and the soldiers of Aberteifi had added to that chaos. FitzStephen had been able to keep his fifty household warriors together, and had strung them across the muddy road while his army had fled back to Aberteifi. Only twenty of that rearguard had made it to the fortress alongside their constable. The rest lay on the road, destroyed, like his ambitions.

However, the Welsh were seemingly not simply happy with victory in the field, and had followed FitzStephen back to his castle at Aberteifi. They wanted to rid Ceredigion of the Norman invaders, to pull down the walls of the castle and to destroy the bridge across the Teifi. FitzStephen swore as his shield was battered by the staccato strike of arrows. He had hoped to hold the town until nightfall, denying the attacking

Welsh protection from the inclement weather which he knew was gathering over the sea. But now, with the town about to be overrun, the only thing left for him to do was to withdraw into the fortress and face a siege. FitzStephen did not like the idea of being trapped and he growled angrily at the thought until an arrow punctured his shield, penetrating far enough to cause him to cry out in shock. Unheralded, Einion ab Anarawd appeared in his mind. Before he had died, his Welsh cousin had told FitzStephen that he would face defeat and then death. The Constable stabbed his spear into the soft mud and used his free hand to cross his chest to avert evil.

As he did, William Ferrand tapped him on the shoulder with the butt of his own weapon and spoke in his soft growl of a voice. 'Bastards are coming,' he said simply.

The Constable turned around and followed his subaltern's nod towards the west. He could see two Welshmen at the end of the road, staring and pointing at the Norman left flank with their spears. They turned and shouted at someone behind the houses that FitzStephen couldn't see. But the message was clear: the Normans were about to be assailed in the flank and in force.

'Sneaky bastards,' he exclaimed and turned back to his friend. 'Get your men back into the castle. Secure the gate.'

Ferrand swung his shield over his shoulder and jogged the short distance back to the castle gate. His small troop of warriors followed his lead without the need of an order. FitzStephen then despatched three more of his senior milites in the same direction leaving only a skeleton crew at the makeshift wall of bodies and broken timbers.

'Get your arse moving,' he hissed, grabbing Herluin de Exeter by his hauberk, dragging him to his feet, and pushing him towards the open castle gates, thirty yards behind. He then shouted the order to the last of his men, 'Back to the castle!'

At that second the Cymri began their advance, unleashing their hunting bows, spears, knives, and hatred at the cursed invaders. Frenzied Welshmen hacked through the fragile white-plastered wattle houses to get at the Normans behind the wall. They clambered over the thatched rooftops to get a better-sighted shot. They came around both sides of the castle down the small streets, threatening to cut off the small Norman warband as they withdrew.

'Full retreat,' FitzStephen shouted. His voice was already hoarse from screaming commands on the battlefield. 'Quickly, get back to the gates. Get moving!'

It was a straight foot race through the drizzle. The armoured Normans slipped and slid through the mud, avoiding, at the same time, arrows raining down upon them and the long spears of the men running alongside. FitzStephen held his shield over his head to protect his back from the arrows while urging his men onwards. He stole a glance over his shoulder and saw a lone long-haired warrior clamber over the crude wall and leap after the retreating Normans.

'Keep moving,' he panted. He looked up to see William Ferrand closing the first of the heavy wooden gates, while above him on the ramparts the massive English captain, Wulfhere Little-Fingers, directed his archers against the Welshmen.

A Norman crashed into FitzStephen's right arm and then fell to the floor. An arrow was lodged in his calf. Another man splashed into the muddy ground directly ahead of FitzStephen with a wooden spear shaft protruding from his spine. There was no stopping to help the injured for FitzStephen fancied that he could feel the very breath of the Welsh warriors at his neck, but dared not pause to look. He had fifteen yards to go and Ferrand was waving him on and shouting something inaudible. FitzStephen heard his mailed feet thump the last few steps across the small footbridge that spanned the deep flooded fosse and then he was through the gate where he turned and snarled as he looked at the Welsh horde that screamed and charged towards his castle. They had long, wild hair and beards and were dressed in dull clothes, bearing shields with no devices and wicked short blades like savages from his worst nightmares. Some of the barbarians had mail, others were bare-chested.

'Close the damn gates,' FitzStephen exclaimed. Beyond the defences he noticed a small man pointing towards the gate and, for a brief second before the wooden gateway slammed shut, his eyes met those of the diminutive warlord. The man stood out amongst the enemy for he was dressed like a Norman, complete with a full suit of chainmail, spangenhelm, and surcoat bearing the three black ravens and red lion of Deheubarth. Though he had never met the man, the Constable intuitively knew that it was Prince Rhys, his mother's nephew. The Welshman held FitzStephen's gaze across the body-strewn street before the prince turned to urge his men onwards, screaming commands and pointing directly at Sir Robert FitzStephen.

'Wulfhere,' the Constable shouted skywards.

'Loose!' came the Englishman's answer, followed by the sound of bowstrings striking wooden stocks and ash heartwood.

Ignoring the effect of the arrows, FitzStephen put his shoulder to the great wooden gate and grunted with the effort as he helped two of his men to close them together with a bang. Six of the esquires, led by his half-brother William, dragged up the heavy split trunk and hoisted it above their heads, thumping it into place, locking the two doors together. Green moss on one side showed just how long it had been since the gates of Aberteifi had been required to be sealed. The Constable, hands on his knees and panting, spat on the hay and mud-strewn street inside the castle bailey. Lifting his head, FitzStephen stood straight and groaned as his sore back stretched. Two women were on the roof of the nearby cookhouse pouring water on a flaming Welsh arrow that threatened to set the building's sodden thatch alight, but FitzStephen ignored that small threat.

'Stay ready,' he ordered his exhausted warriors, 'and be prepared to defend the gates to the death,' he said to Ferrand as he leapt onto the bottom rung of a ladder which took him up onto the allure. Despite his anger at the day's events FitzStephen watched with pride as his archers and crossbowmen performed their duty with a mechanical killing rhythm. Stationed either side of the barbican, they worked in twos, with one man selecting a target and shooting while another man loaded his weapon. Then they swapped, continuing the steady stream of murder in front of the castle. Arrows replied from what little cover the Welsh could find.

Striding around the rampart, Wulfhere seemed oblivious to

the danger of the Welsh sharpshooters. He barked a mixture of flowing French and guttural English orders at the crossbowmen and archers. They kept up their steady stream of arrows despite, rather than because of Wulfhere's commands. The old Englishman, one of the few of his people in FitzStephen's service, growled a short welcome in his constable's direction:

'Curse this weather,' he moaned, 'and a curse on loosened bloody bowstrings. Bastard by the garden wall,' Wulfhere shouted abruptly at Ludo de Chester. The archer had his weapon spanned to his mouth in a moment and closed one eye in concentration as he aimed the arrow shaft at the Welshman crouching behind the wooden wall. A second later the arrow flew straight and true and the man buckled and screamed in Welsh as he flopped to the floor.

The Normans loved nicknames, just as their Danish and Norse ancestors had done, and they had shown their acceptance of the English warrior Wulfhere by calling him Little-Fingers. Both of his hands had all the fingers removed to the second joint, tribute to four decades spent fighting in a shield wall.

'They've had enough, cease shooting,' Wulfhere shouted as the last of the Cymri warriors left the open ground before the castle walls and only their insults remained. His men ended their efforts and dropped to their knees behind the palisade, massaging strained shoulders and inspecting red-raw fingers.

'Well, Robert,' Wulfhere said to FitzStephen, 'I hope you are happy.' He flapped a stunted hand at the town outside the castle walls where Welsh insults mingled with the screams of the wounded. 'We are bloody surrounded.'

FitzStephen snorted a sardonic laugh at his words. 'Aren't we always?' he replied. 'For that is the fate of an invader,' he told him. His smile faded as the Welsh victory songs begin in the sodden town of Aberteifi.

FitzStephen stayed on the allure as the weak sun slipped slowly into the rolling Irish Sea, spending an hour walking amongst his men giving encouragement, orders, and defiantly bombastic declarations of their skill in battle. He flippantly boasted about how the Normans would overcome the minor setback of defeat and how the Welsh would again learn how to fear their lances.

'We'll be richer than pious old Thomas Becket when we storm out of Aberteifi and secure all Ceredigion,' he joked to his men, 'and the women? However many you want you will have. And all we have to do is to hold this fortress against that pathetic rabble outside our gates,' he bragged and pointed over the wall at the Welsh. 'Truly, they surprised us during the battle, but they are dullards.' The men all nodded along and even smiled at his banter but FitzStephen could tell that they did not believe him.

In the town beyond the castle walls the screaming had all but finished. The Welsh had taken the spoils of victory; the women of the town and the souls and property of their husbands, brothers, and fathers. FitzStephen listened as the Norman monks in the small monastery on the edge of town sang one of King David's laments. Slowly the song became more fraught and yet quieter until he realised that the Norman monks were being despatched to heaven one by one by the Cymri. Laughter took the place of singing as the last monk died and his song came to an end. In its place another Welsh war song arose.

Standing on the barbican with his elbows resting on a merlon, FitzStephen thought of the past. Rainwater spat off his shoulders as he looked out over the town. Wulfhere had told him that he had been born during a battle, a fight between his father and the Welsh for this very fortress. He believed in his soul that, somehow, his beginning meant that he was born for combat. In any case, warfare and victory had been the only constant in his twenty-eight years. It made the rout all the harder for Sir Robert FitzStephen to accept.

The hideous weather seemed able to find every gap in his armour and soak through his heavy woollen cloak to his back, but the method of his defeat plagued him yet worse. For the first time since becoming a knight he had lost a fight, and the memory of it sat uncomfortably on his wide shoulders. Time and the pressures of the Welsh March had changed FitzStephen from the boy who had served as a page in the household of Robert de Caen during the anarchy of King Stephen's reign to the young, talented knight thrust to the forefront of Welsh politics after he saved King Henry's life at Coed Ewloe seven years before.

*You are only as good as your last fight*, his morose father had often told him when he was a boy and, looking around the wet wooden walls, he could tell that many of his men agreed with that sentiment. Some looked at him with accusatory eyes, attempting to hide their anger when they caught him looking their way. But FitzStephen could not miss those who mouthed silent prayers as they looked out over the palisade at the many Welsh fires springing up throughout the town. The light in the semi-darkness made it look as if a horde sat before their high wooden walls. Had none of his men ever heard the priests preaching about Gideon's torches when he faced the Midianites? Of course they had not, he thought. Few if any of the warriors could read or speak Latin. FitzStephen knew that his men prayed for salvation and cursed them for their timidity. In the story of Gideon, the hero had sent the unwilling soldiers home and won a stunning victory against the invader of the Holy Land. Looking at some of his men FitzStephen wished he had that luxury. Did they not realise that they still held the advantage? There was a multitude outside their gates, yes, but sickness would inevitably spread through the besieging force and their men would get bored and hungry. Desertion would thin their numbers.

Aberteifi Castle had a good well, many supplies, and an adequate number of replacement arrows for the archers. They only had to hold out for a few weeks until either the Welsh returned north or news of the attack spread south. Then his half-brother, Sir Maurice FitzGerald, the King's Constable in Pembroke, would come north to chase off the Welsh. That was real war: patience and good sense. Even after a defeat he would not be beaten. FitzStephen knew that any army could win a battle with bravery and ferocity, but you could not win a war without intelligence and planning. That was the genius of the Norman way of war, he thought. His people could match anyone in battle, and could crush most, but it was their will to dominate that set them apart, and the castle was their ultimate weapon. The English had built their burghs and the Welsh had

19

their hill forts, both of which were designed to protect the people, but a Norman castle was meant to control and intimidate the local populace – to give the few superiority over the many. FitzStephen smiled and decided that there was no way for the Cymri to break into his lair. He had defeated them once again and perhaps that meant his dreams could yet come to fruition. Still, his men's lack of fight made him grind his back teeth as he continued to smile, acting confident for the sake of their morale. Did they not realise that the Welsh were unable to fly over the walls? The enemy didn't even have siege equipment! His cousin, Prince Rhys, might dress like a Norman but he did not know all their secrets. FitzStephen pushed himself away from the barbican walls and walked along the allure where he joined Wulfhere. The Englishman stood stock still, wrapped in a cloak as he watched the town through the rain.

'That was a shit day,' Wulfhere said.

FitzStephen wondered if his friend was talking about the defeat in battle or the weather. Neither would have surprised him. He grunted an affirmative in the archer captain's direction.

'Bloody Welsh have the wind up them now and our boys are battered and scared shitless,' Wulfhere continued. 'But they will hold together.'

FitzStephen nodded and stared out at the town, listening to the drunken Cymric victory songs in the distance. He hated the screeching sound, already telling of the Welsh heroes who had beaten the Normans. FitzStephen despised them all; this was not their country anymore, it was his. His father's people had won South Wales through strength of arms and the Cymri could go to hell if they thought this setback would stop him from taking back every blade of grass that he had once owned in the same fashion. It would be a maelstrom of terror, he promised himself.

'So I hear the Welsh have learned some new tricks,' Wulfhere said, half turning towards FitzStephen and raising an eyebrow as the Constable's chin dropped to his chest. 'They surprised you, and the Baron of Cemais ran for his life. There was nothing you could do but fall back on Aberteifi. You did well to get away with as many alive as you did.'

FitzStephen stood, nodding his head. Though thankful for Wulfhere's words, doubt was clawing at his heart; that his murder of Einion had precipitated the attack, and that his curse had brought about this defeat. He felt for the relic hidden beneath his armour beside his heart.

'I need to organise some food for the archers,' FitzStephen said suddenly and turned to leave. 'Fire the town,' he told the Englishman. 'I don't want those damned Welsh here in the morning.'

Wulfhere nodded and spat over the wall. 'We need more bolts for the crossbowmen, and water as well as the food.' As he spoke, the Englishman turned and looked at his commander, a brute wrapped in steel. He had been around warriors for the greater part of his long life, but Wulfhere had met no one who was more suited to battle than the tall, blond, blue-eyed ruffian. Robert FitzStephen had scars from fighting in the shield wall and from the saddle, and his mud- and blood-covered sword was dented from use and thin from regular sharpening. Wulfhere had known FitzStephen as a boy and had watched him rise from page to esquire, knight to constable, each advance exacting a price from the ambitious warrior.

The Constable whipped off his blue and white conical helmet and, starting from his forehead, pulled his chainmail coif back from his head and onto his shoulders. No Englishman, Briton, or Frank wore their hair so short, shaved from the top of the ear to the crown and down to the neck in the old Norman style. It gave the wearer an odd, unnatural, and intimidating look: half monk, half lunatic. But FitzStephen was proud of his heritage and, unlike others of his kin who had adopted the foreign custom of wearing their hair and beards long, he fastidiously kept his chin clean-shaven and scraped the hair from the back of his head. He had told Wulfhere that the style made wearing chainmail easier as his hair didn't get caught between the circlets of steel and allowed him more manoeuvrability within the hauberk, but Wulfhere knew it was because FitzStephen remembered his father and his fellow warriors shaving each other's heads to give the wild and harsh look that had so scared him and his young friends growing up in the outpost. Many of the younger men in FitzStephen's army had adopted the same practice of cutting their hair in the old style to show that they belonged to the army of Robert FitzStephen. Boys in Ceredigion, too young to wear the gold and crimson surcoat, raggedly shaved each other's heads and dyed their clothes by rubbing crushed flowers into the dull wool to be like their hero.

'That's not right,' said FitzStephen suddenly at his side.

Wulfhere had been daydreaming; the lasting legacy of a long day. 'Eh? What's not right?'

'That,' said FitzStephen from beside him and looking out through the dim light provided by the burning buildings. Wulfhere followed his commander's outstretched arm and saw several women leaning over some of the Norman dead in the streets. Knives flashed in the firelight from the town torches as clothes were torn from the bodies.

'So? They're seeing what they've got on them.' Wulfhere was confused. He had personally watched FitzStephen slice open the shirts of men and women, Norman or Welsh, and even priests, monks, and nuns he had just killed and steal everything they had hidden on their person. The Constable was not a squeamish man.

'No, they're not,' FitzStephen grimaced. 'The saints preserve us.' He crossed his chest without taking his eyes off the scene.

Wulfhere looked closer. It was difficult to see in the darkness but he focussed in on the closer of the twenty or so women. Then he saw it: the blood splashed on the body was not dry but wet. She had cut off the Norman's genitals and was now stuffing them in the dead man's mouth.

'Jesus Christ,' said Wulfhere. 'What are they doing?'

Welshmen, already half drunk on the beer, wine, and honey mead they had found in the town, were laughing and pointing from doorways in the buildings nearest to the carnage. Wulfhere's wide-eyed gaze moved to another woman who he had bought apples from just a few weeks before. She was cutting off a dead Fleming's nose and was stuffing it in another

22

upturned Norman's backside. One was squatting over a fallen warrior and was urinating on his head. All the bodies were being defiled in some way or form by the women. Wulfhere had not realised how much hatred the Welsh had for their Norman overlords. The archers on either side of the Constable began grumbling and shouting at the women, calling them animals and worse.

'You, boy,' FitzStephen said to the nearest bowman. 'Kill one of those bitches.' He shouted at the other men to hold their tempers.

The young archer was a killer, plain and simple, and without so much as considering the morality of his captain's command for a moment he turned, aimed and squeezed down on the crossbow's trigger. His bolt took the woman in the throat as she squawked towards the men under the thatched roof. FitzStephen watched as she fell backwards as the arrow passed clean through her throat to lodge in the mud behind. Her hands went to her gullet as the blood started to pour from the wound, but she was already dead. The remaining women sprinted towards cover given by the houses while the Welsh warriors threw hopeless curses at the wooden walls of the castle from the houses before they retreated indoors to continue their looting and drinking. Nobody in the fortress cheered the death.

'It's just not right,' Sir Robert FitzStephen said to no-one in particular. 'Throw some torches out there,' he ordered an archer, 'and if any of them come back, kill them.'

'They won't be back,' said Wulfhere with certainty. 'Nor will the warriors. That's why two popes tried to ban the crossbow,' he said with pride, clapping the young bowman on the back with his disfigured hand.

More laughter issued over the white wooden walls causing FitzStephen to snort. 'They're all getting pissed as popes in my town on my booze.'

Wulfhere grunted.

'Set the watches. Two hours on, six hours off,' FitzStephen said. 'I'm going up to the keep. I will be back in three hours,' he said. He looked out over the thatched roofs of the settlement, depressing in the darkness and the rain. 'Burn the town,' he said again.

The Englishman turned to the nearest bowman, rubbing what was left of his hands together with glee. 'Time to cook the little Cymri piggies,' he said as the rainwater spat off the end of his nose.

FitzStephen planted a hand on his friend's armoured shoulder. 'Well done today, Wulfhere, my friend. It was the longest two miles I've ever covered,' FitzStephen said of the retreat from the battlefield. Raising his eyebrows, he managed a small smile despite his utter exhaustion. 'I don't think we would have made it back into the castle but for your archers,' he added, raising his voice for all nearby to hear. 'For a lazy bunch of string-plucking minstrels, led by an old *Saesneg* piece of shit, you lads can fight!' Some warriors on the palisade shouted their agreement at his assessment of the archers who, in turn, cried insults back in their direction for the quip.

FitzStephen had already climbed down from the allure when Wulfhere shouted: 'And make sure you get some food down here, you damned Norman brute. I'm starving.'

Serlo de Brecon's plump little wife looked terrified when FitzStephen walked into the cookhouse and asked her to organise some bread and water for the men on the palisade. Under the torchlight he could see that her face was still covered in soot from the thatch fire on the roof but she nodded, accepting her task and disappeared through the building to the castle well which stood behind the kitchens. FitzStephen quickly grabbed a hunk of bread and a cup of water before making his way towards the steps which led up to the keep.

The buildings in the bailey usually looked bright and welcoming with the white lime mortar between the timber frames sparkling under the sun. But after two weeks of rain the damp, discoloured thatch and mud-speckled walls looked grubby yellow, cold, and uninviting. Passing between the hay store and the small bath house, he waved at two boys who peered out of the smithy on the other side of the bailey. The bigger of the two immediately ducked his head below the window ledge while his brother stood up and returned the gesture, pale mouth dangling gormlessly. Terrified cattle collected at the back of their enclosure under the window of the house, Welsh arrows poking out of the mud around them like harsh tufts of coarse beach grass. Next to the smithy was the marshalsea and FitzStephen's courser was easily recognisable as it shuffled amongst the group of rouncies. The horse was muscled and expensive and was the only one munching on hay. He walked over and reached through the fence to stroke the stallion's nose, giving up the hard crust to the hungry horse.

'Good lad, Sanglac. How is your leg, you big fool?' The courser had cost him the best part of six months' income, but he was worth it; small and fast, strong and sturdy, he was the perfect platform for handling his favoured weapons – lance, teardrop shield, mace, and sword. He had even learned to use his crossbow from his back. 'How is he?' FitzStephen asked the esquire who tended to his horse.

'On the mend, Lord Constable,' the boy replied before scampering off into the depths of the stables for a brush to get Sanglac's coat shining again. The young esquire had been with FitzStephen all day, had seen things that should have scared him witless as he had attended to his master's weapons and horses. But here, in the castle, he had simply resumed his day-to-day duties, seeking comfort from the horrors outside in his work. In his youth, FitzStephen had spent time attending to both horses and hounds for his master, and he knew how their companionship and his responsibilities to them could help shield a lowly esquire from the realities of life outside the marshalsea.

FitzStephen took a quick look at the wound where the arrow had grazed Sanglac's flank before saying goodbye to the courser and continuing on his way to the keep. The castle citadel towered sixty feet above him on a man-made hill of earth and stone, commanding the river crossing between the lands of Cemais and Ceredigion. He passed through the inner barbican and began the slow climb up the flying bridge. FitzStephen groaned at the effort of the climb. His back hurt from carrying chainmail which grouped uncomfortably at his shoulders and where it was belted to his waist. His elbows ached from carrying his shield and sword, while his head pounded from lack of sleep.

He coughed, swallowed, and spat to clear the hoarseness from his throat and wondered why he had even bothered shouting orders during the chaos of the retreat from the battleground. His commands had been lost in the din of the battle anyway. His eyes flicked to the heavens where he guiltily hoped that God and the saints were ignoring him. It was not the first time that he had hoped to avoid heaven's notice in the years since his assumption of control in Ceredigion. He paused to catch his breath and watched the silver River Teifi shimmer below him.

He wondered why the guilt of Einion's murder was affecting him so badly. He had killed before, many times, and it had never cost him a second thought. Perhaps the Welshman had indeed cursed him? Such things were well known to occur amongst the strange people of the frontier. The Cymri claimed to be Christian, but their practices and saints were not like those he could recognise. Alien and repugnant, the Welsh were known to associate with ancient spirits and devils that could be sent against good Christian men like the Normans. Einion, no doubt, had been able to draw upon the same evil. The devil had come to claim FitzStephen's soul, as he had his army, just as Einion had directed. The Constable grappled for a touch the vial of the Virgin's breast milk which hung around his neck, but it was hidden far below surcoat, hauberk, and gambeson and barely discernible from the folds of chainmail and stuffed linen.

FitzStephen composed himself and turned to continue his ascent to the donjon. By the time he reached the top of the flying bridge his thoughts had turned away from the world beyond and were focussed on the dark, wet one in which he currently existed. He returned a young guard's nod under the barbican before crossing the open ground in front of the white-plastered keep. The heavy keep door was embossed with ironwork, and FitzStephen grunted in the effort it took to push his way through into an antechamber packed with armoured men. His men-at-arms had taken a battering that day and, unneeded on the wall, were awaiting their constable's orders.

These warriors, above all, did not enjoy being cooped up in a garrison, desiring nothing more than firm ground beneath their coursers and an enemy before them to fight. They all turned to look at him.

'My Lord Constable,' an excited voice pierced the tumble of voices and the drum of raindrops on the wooden roof. A tall, thin, balding man dressed in a pale shift pushed through the crowded warriors from the kitchens and came towards him. The man looked incredibly uncomfortable as he gently urged one armoured and rotund man to move out of his way, earning a contorted frown from the warrior before a reluctant response.

FitzStephen greeted his steward, handing him his steel-tipped spear as he took off his sword. 'Rhygewarch, let's get these men into the hall and get them some food.' With a groan, he removed the long shield from his back and handed it over to his steward. The armament was decorated with the three long red arrow heads on a yellow field, but also had haphazard chips and splashes of blood and mud over much of the surface. FitzStephen, as a knight, could have worn his own colours – a silver star on a sapphire field – but as the Constable of Aberteifi and Seneschal of Ceredigion he was expected to parade those of his suzerain, the Earl of Hertford.

He groaned as he dragged his soaking surcoat over his head and lobbed it through the air to the servant. His cold chainmail hauberk needed even more effort, but FitzStephen eventually got it free and handed it over along with his conical helmet. The hauberk was made up of thousands of steel circlets and was worn to protect his real armour – a thick quilted linen gambeson. Steam rose from the sweaty jacket as it too was removed. FitzStephen turned to see Rhygewarch holding up his hauberk, poking his finger through a hole on the lower portion.

'Are you injured, Sir Robert?' Rhygewarch asked.

FitzStephen had felt the sticky and uncomfortable wound as he had climbed the stairs to the donjon, his damaged and bent mail scratching at the injury and causing it to start bleeding, though he could not remember when the wound had been sustained.

'It is fine, Rhygewarch,' FitzStephen told his steward as he handed over the gambeson, stained pink with blood. 'Bring me clean water and cloth. I'll wash it and ask Father Philip to say a prayer over the wound. Have one of the esquires scrub my armour and try to fix it as best he can. I'll need it again in a few hours.' He looked around the room at the warriors who milled around, awaiting orders. 'Are William Ferrand and Roger de Quincy here?'

'They are already in the great hall,' the servant replied as he handed his lord a fine shirt. FitzStephen threw the woollen garment over his head before buckling it at his waist with his thick leather belt. A swift rustle of his scalp had his short hair in order.

'So what's the plan, Sir Robert?' one warrior asked of him as he moved towards the closed door to the great hall. 'Sir Roger says that we need to retreat across the river.' FitzStephen recognised the man who had spoken. Theobald Laval was one of Roger de Quincy's friends and at his side were a number of other warriors who listened in and added their own nods of approval to Laval's question.

FitzStephen was shocked at the impertinence of the enquiry rather than its content. He stared at Theobald, but neither he nor his friends backed down. The other milites in the room had also gone quiet and were awaiting the Constable's response. Rain drummed on the wooden roof and trickled through gaps in the white walls.

'We'll have some food ready for you in a few minutes, lads,' he pointedly avoided answering the question and food smells were already beginning to emanate from the three doors which led to the kitchen, pantry, and buttery. Theobald Laval gave the Constable an uncivil look in answer as FitzStephen pushed his way past him and into the main hall in the eastern wing of the donjon. It was dark inside, and warm. Heads and skins of hunted animals adorned the walls while simple tapestries retained the heat and cast colourful images of battles from long, long ago back into the room: William the Conqueror at Val-es-Dune and Hastings, Henry Beauclerc at Tinchebrai, and even a faded one portraying Bernard de Neufmarche's victory at Brecon. There had been no great victory to celebrate in almost a hundred years, he thought morosely. It had only been that morning, before his army had marched north, that he had studied the woven depictions, wondering how long it would be before he could commission one made to commemorate his own victory over the Welsh – the great triumph which should have made his name and handed him a kingdom. Now those same images mocked him as a failure and he turned his back on them sharply. In the corner, three of his favourite dogs raised their eyelids, if not their heads, as they noticed their master. One of the dogs' tails wagged, but only for an instant.

Ferrand and Quincy were alone at the far end of the hall perched on the edge of the dais, already eating and seemingly in the middle of an argument. FitzStephen ignored the two men as his hounds had him, and went over to the small chapel where he lit a candle and started a short prayer to Maurice, patron saint of soldiers. In truth the chapel was little more than a table with several candles and a surfeit of religious treasures taken on raids around Wales. Golden crosses, bejewelled icons, and silver cups caught the light from the candles and made it dance on the back of FitzStephen's eyes as he knelt before them. The treasures meant that he could worship his God in all His glory and wonder. They had been taken, rescued even, from the devilish Cymri, and their strange practices. He pulled the vial of the Virgin's breast milk from around his neck and held it between his hands as he attempted to find his words to say before the small chapel.

'Ah, there he is,' said Sir Roger de Quincy as he noticed FitzStephen. 'Sir Robert, join us, please.' Roger stood up and held out an arm to the Constable, offering him a chair as if he, and not FitzStephen, was the lord of the hall.

FitzStephen's eyes narrowed as he continued to pray. His duties forced him to spend much time touring the Earl of Hertford's extensive lands, mediating over disputes and dealing out justice at the manors loyal to his lord. FitzStephen, twenty milites, and a mass of servants and scribes, had spent almost three months before the battle touring the various manors to the north which paid rents to Aberteifi. His journey had taken him to the very extreme of Norman-held territory. Obviously Sir

Roger de Quincy, whom he had left in command of Aberteifi, had become a little too self-important during that last absence. Ferrand did not get to his feet, but simply raised an eyebrow at Quincy's forwardness before turning back to his hard-bread trencher filled with rabbit stew.

FitzStephen stopped praying and looked over his shoulder at the man in the red and yellow diamond surcoat of the Quincy family. Sir Roger was a fine-looking man: tall, dark, naturally strong, and equipped with the best clothing and the finest weapons; his curly hair was combed back from his face while his beard short and neat. In short, everything about him infuriated FitzStephen.

*Sir Roger could charm a trout straight from the River Teifi*, Wulfhere often joked, and FitzStephen did not doubt that this was true. He had added that he believed that Quincy could have crept up on a startled cat and convinced the animal to do the trout charming for him.

'What do you want?' FitzStephen asked Quincy as he returned to the pretence of praying.

'For you to join us,' Sir Roger countered with more than a hint of impatience. 'We must talk about how we make contact with Prince Rhys and negotiate our retreat to Cemais.'

FitzStephen snorted as he heard Quincy's words, but did not turn or open his eyes. 'We aren't going anywhere, Sir Roger. The Welsh will be gone within the week and then life will return to normal,' he replied and attempted to concentrate, thinking only of God.

'Normal?' Quincy spluttered. 'They killed half of your milites and threaten to overrun our walls ...'

'I am trying to pray for the souls of the dead,' FitzStephen interrupted him, 'so if you wouldn't mind shutting up ...'

'You can't ignore that we are surrounded,' Roger exclaimed. 'We must negotiate with Prince Rhys!'

FitzStephen sighed, finally abandoning his prayer, and rose slowly to his feet so that he could look directly at Sir Roger de Quincy. 'Ferrand told me that you were going to abandon your post and follow the baron across the river.'

'They said you were dead. He is a baron ...' Sir Roger

shifted uneasily under FitzStephen's unblinking gaze before the Constable suddenly turned aside without another word and walked towards the doorway to the stone staircase in the eastern wall. Quincy quickly followed him to the foot of the stairs, scattering dry reeds on the earthen floor aside in his haste.

'Where are you going?' he demanded.

'To my bed where there is a delicious little morsel waiting for me,' FitzStephen called back as his feet touched the first steps which led to his private rooms in the solar.

'Damn your floozy, FitzStephen, there's an army outside our very walls! We must come up with a defence ... a strategy ... something.'

FitzStephen stopped in his tracks. Some day he would marry a noblewoman who would add prestige to his family name, a rich dowry, and powerful connections for his political machinations. But for the moment Richildis, a beautiful Norman woman, kept his bed warm and he felt a pang of defensiveness on her behalf at Quincy's words and turned on the step to stare directly at his lieutenant.

'This isn't Jericho, Sir Roger, and the Welsh have neither God's trumpets nor siege towers,' he scorned. 'So if you get nervous, come and get me and I will make it all better.' He spoke slowly as if he was addressing a spooked child. 'Otherwise sit tight and listen to what Wulfhere tells you to do.'

'I won't do anything that bloody savage tells me,' Roger said under his breath. 'He should listen to me, I am a knight and he is no better than a beast of the field.'

FitzStephen sighed loudly, the tiredness and frustration quickly getting the better of him. Roger still stood at the bottom of the steps and FitzStephen deliberately leaned forward, face just inches from his subaltern's head. 'If I want your opinion, Sir Roger, about any man under my protection or the way I command him, I will ask for it,' he said as he held his gaze, daring his lieutenant to respond.

Roger recognised the challenge and stubbornly refused to back down. 'Do you think you are better than me, FitzStephen?' he asked, his voice brimming with caustic anger. 'You're nothing but the son of a spear-carrying farmer who slimed his way under a noblewoman's skirts.' William Ferrand gasped in shock at Quincy's slur and, for his part, Sir Roger looked stunned at the ferocity of the words which had escaped his mouth.

FitzStephen did not react immediately. His low birth had long been a point of resentment, but he had learned to live with it. His father had indeed been a lowly Norman spearman whose viciousness had won him some renown and a Welsh princess for his bed. Oddly it was never that royal part of his parentage that FitzStephen's detractors fixated upon, but the shame of illegitimacy. That, he thought, he could live with. A subordinate's defiance was another matter.

FitzStephen grabbed Quincy by the throat and slammed him onto the nearest tabletop with a crash of wood against chainmail. The piece of furniture was strong though it strained loudly under the weight of the two warriors. Quincy tried to kick FitzStephen and grappled at the hand which pinned him to the table. But the Constable would not let him go and gripped his fist above his head ready to strike downwards.

'One more word and I'll ...' FitzStephen snarled as the doors to the main hall opened and the men-at-arms poured in to begin eating. The first men quickly spotted their two leaders' tussle and stopped in their tracks to stare. FitzStephen lessened his grip on Roger's surcoat and it allowed Quincy to slither free and to his feet.

'You bastard,' Quincy said loudly, holding his throat and pointing his finger at FitzStephen's chest. 'This is not my doing, it is yours!' Roger was red-faced, shocked, and scared by the attack and humiliated in front of the men. 'You lost the battle. I saved the castle,' he accused. 'Those dead men out there,' he swept his finger towards the north, 'they are on your conscience! The Welsh want your life, not ours.'

A growl of support issued from the group of warriors before FitzStephen could answer and it was quickly taken up by a number of other men. Guilt had been circling FitzStephen's mind all day and it left him speechless and frowning. Usually FitzStephen would have gone on the offensive at the first sniff of attack, but now he hesitated. He hated his indecision.

William Ferrand climbed to his feet and started to direct the milites out of the hall rather than have them listen to the fight between the Constable and his deputy, but FitzStephen stopped him with a wave of his hand.

'No,' he told his friend, signalling instead for his warriors to enter the hall, 'come in and get some food into your bellies.' The men trundled into the room and took their places at the tables silently. Seconds later Rhygewarch, unaware that anything had happened, led in the other servants with trenchers, cauldrons of steaming food, and mead for the warriors.

FitzStephen turned and with a last venomous look at Quincy, started up the steps to the solar. He heard Sir Roger complain loudly to Ferrand over the general chit-chat in the great hall. He knew that they would be talking about the disagreement between the two knights and about his failures and probably his illegitimacy. He stopped at the door to the solar, at the top of the curling stone stairs, and tried to tidy his hair which was pasted to his head after being encased in a spangenhelm all day. Richildis was inside and some short dirty words in the English tongue described perfectly what he had planned for her. The language of England was definitely better than French in this instance, and FitzStephen grinned as he thought of the words which Wulfhere had taught him.

In the distance he heard the crunch of burning wood as a building collapsed in the midst of the town. The Englishman had done his job and it was now just a matter of time before the Cymri would be forced to retreat. He smiled when he heard the faraway voices of the panicked besiegers shouting for water, assistance, and mercy. The smell from flaming thatch annoyed FitzStephen's nostrils even in the highest point of the castle donjon and he inhaled strongly with his eyes closed, enjoying the Welsh despair outside his citadel.

The day had been a disaster, but the campaign could still be salvaged. The Cymri would be forced to give up the siege and in the spring Sir Robert FitzStephen would sally out against them and anyone who remembered the Welsh victory would fall beneath his war horse's hooves. The thought left a good feeling in his chest and he opened the door in front of him and stepped through.

'Hello, soldier,' Richildis said as FitzStephen closed the door on a dreadful day.

Rhys, son of Gruffydd, son of Rhys, son of Tewdwr, and descendant of Rhodri the Great of the House of Dinefwr, was angry. He had won at Carmarthen and destroyed his enemy at Llandovery. He had humbled his enemies at Aberdyfi and Aberystwyth, Blaenporth, Pwntan, and Olfagren. He had taken Cilgerran and Llandygwydd without losing a single life, but he knew that he unless he took the castle at Aberteifi he could yet lose everything he had won. He stared at the fortification in the light given off by the burning buildings and tried to calm his seething fury. It took the small man several seconds to steady himself, but the resentment at the Norman success soon passed and he was able to think clearly about his next move.

'Are we under attack?' Ieuan ap Hywel shouted in Rhys' direction. Though unsteady on his feet, probably the effect of copious drinking, the tall warrior had five armed men with him, ready to fight the flames which scorched through the town. Rhys found it difficult to even look at the blaze, such was its ferocity.

'Take your men to watch the gates of the castle,' Rhys shouted over the roar of the fire. 'If the Normans sally out again, raise the warning.'

All around Rhys his people were running in the semi-darkness, carrying their stolen belongings away from the inferno that was spreading from building to building in the town of Aberteifi. Rats fled the thatch and one Welshman jumped over a long line of the vermin as it passed through the streets. There were only sixty or so buildings outside the slick castle walls and almost half were alight, threatening the remaining thatched and wooden homes which stood downwind to the east. But no-one was organising water for the blaze. No-one cared about anything other than their plunder. Screams from the animals still tethered to fences surrounded Rhys but he just stared at the mesmerising flames, considering his options silently in an unblinking daze. Perhaps he could use the blaze to burn down the walls of the castle? Or he could signal another attack! He immediately discounted the latter thought. Night assaults were notoriously dangerous even with sober troops and safe conditions underfoot. He had neither of those things. And anyway, the Cymri chieftain could think of no method to get his men past the deadly archers crouched behind the Norman defences. His attackers would be easy targets as they blundered forward into the darkness, outlined against the flaming backdrop.

Another roof collapsed into the heart of a building and Rhys flinched as the beams tumbled with a crash sending hundreds of fiery cinders skyward. How had the damned Normans managed to get a blaze going with the rain falling so heavily, he wondered. He made a mental note to extract the information from one of the prisoners when the castle fell. If it fell, he thought grimly. It looked so fragile from where he stood in the street, and yet he could find no weak point to attack, no earthwork ready to crumble, and no stretch left undefended.

'Bleddyn ap Gruffydd, come here,' Rhys shouted at a hulking warrior as he dragged a screaming woman through the darkened town. 'I thought I told you to keep watch on the postern gate?' Rhys could picture how a small detachment of devious Normans had crawled down from the keep in the shadow of the castle motte to set the fires and rob his army of the protection of the houses in the town.

'Nobody came through the gate,' Bleddyn asserted to his chieftain. At his heels the screaming foreign woman tried to break free of his grasp and the Cymri warrior slapped her hard across the face. 'The Devil is protecting the murderer FitzStephen,' exclaimed Bleddyn, making a sign to ward off evil. 'He must've set the fire. It is the only answer!'

Rhys shook his head slowly and despairingly. 'Gather your warriors and get these fires put out. I am holding you responsible. Do you understand?' Bleddyn started to protest, but a stern glance from the prince stopped him in his tracks and he took off into the darkness where Rhys heard his orders echo over the flames to the five warriors whom he had brought with him to battle.

The Welsh chieftain knew that the grumbles would grow louder now. They would say that he had not fulfilled his oath to avenge his nephew Einion's murder. They would say that the crusade against Aberteifi had been for naught. But Rhys knew better. He had cared not a jot for Einion ab Anarawd and, if he was being honest with himself, he was glad that Robert FitzStephen had cut his nephew's throat. Einion had been a powerful and popular rival for his own throne in Deheubarth and, despite Rhys' many successes there were those who thought that Einion could have done a better job as ruler of Deheubarth than he. Rhys had heard the debate rage in quiet corridors during the bad days when the Normans were advancing deep into his territory. They had said that Einion was tougher, younger, and stronger than Rhys, bolder in his decisions and more forthright in his opposition to the invaders. Rhys had made his own plans to deal with his elder brother's son, but thanks to the Norman FitzStephen, he no longer had to sully his own soul with the sin of murder.

However, the reaction of his people to Einion's demise had surprised Rhys. Stories of the murder had spread quickly and suddenly his boorish nephew was being portrayed as a saintly Welsh hero cut down treacherously by the bestial devil of a Norman knight. From Lleyn to Cardiff, Welshmen were up in arms at the assassination and Rhys had used the wave of anger to draw support to his cause. He had paid priests to say that it was God's wish that he lead the army and take vengeance for the death of his beloved nephew. And how his people had swarmed to his banner! The holy men had even convinced Owain of Gwynedd to join the offensive; all Wales was united against that most evil and foul murderer, Sir Robert FitzStephen. And suddenly, thanks to one death, his dream of freeing Cymru from the invaders had become a very real possibility.

Rhys said a short prayer for FitzStephen's soul. Everyone knew of his exploits, and bards already sang about FitzStephen's great deeds and his bravery in battle. Rhys had heard accounts about how his cousin had saved King Henry's life at Coed Ewloe when but an esquire, before almost single-handedly beating back a hoard of Gwynedd spearmen to rescue his army on Mona. A few short months ago, before Einion's death, the songs had seemed frivolous and silly to Rhys. But now, in front of the fiery backdrop and with a battle against his cousin fought, the stories somehow seemed more visceral, savage, and territorial. The tales of his cousin's fall from grace were almost as numerous as the songs of his brave exploits. Stories of pillaging, brawling, and murder committed by Robert FitzStephen were told up and down the country. Rhys heard how he would fight against anyone for the right price, were he Welsh, Norman, Dane, Fleming, or Englishman.

Across the street, Rhys watched Maredudd ap Dafydd pull a smoking body from a burning building by its arms and dump it in the middle of the road. He then darted back into the flames, escaping seconds later, his arms laden with several pieces of plunder. Coughing, Maredudd shouted inaudibly at the bullish Owain of Gwynedd who stomped angrily in Rhys' direction. Owain was a brute of a man and his contempt for Rhys was obvious. The Prince of Deheubarth did not turn around to greet his fellow chieftain but the familiar feeling of apprehension arose in his chest whenever he was confronted by this veteran warrior. Rhys immediately chastised himself for the weakness and turned to meet Owain's massive presence.

'Why the hell didn't you post sentries?' Owain demanded in his harsh northern accent. His shoulders were wide and uncovered despite the chill in the damp air that forced Rhys into a heavy cloak. As ever he was accompanied by his seneschal, Cynwrig ab Ednyfed.

Deliberately, Rhys waited to answer for a long time, annoying the impatient Owain. 'I had planned to burn the town when I captured the castle,' he said finally, 'this saved me the bother of wasting firewood.' Rhys glanced purposefully at Owain's foolhardy show of manliness and grimaced like a disapproving tutor. He made sure that Owain saw the look. 'I notice that you did not post any sentries either,' he said.

Owain ignored at the quip. 'The weather's coming in again,' he stated, wiping his nose with his forearm.

'Without the protection of the houses,' Cynwrig spoke for

the first time, 'I don't know how we can keep our men from leaving, especially since they now have plunder to take home.' Owain sniffed and agreed with Cynwrig's words.

In other words, thought Rhys, Owain had all the loot he could carry and didn't see the point of maintaining this siege so far from his own lands. But he could never admit that and had left it to his seneschal to describe the reasons for leaving. Exhausted as he was from little sleep and ferocious activity in the lead-up to the battle, Rhys was in no mood to be civil to the ally who meant to abandon him. 'So you're running away then?' he asked brusquely.

'What is the point in assaulting the castle? To avenge Einion?' Owain laughed sarcastically. 'Let Robert FitzStephen stay in there and rot! We have taken back all Ceredigion but for this small fort!' He waved his hand northwards. 'They are like a tiny pimple on my fat arse,' he laughed. 'We have squeezed the poison juice from them and soon enough they will wither.'

This was the problem, thought Rhys, as he swept rainwater off his brow. Owain and many of his people were only interested in short-term gain rather than lasting security. Just raiders, he concluded with a small shake of his head. Not like the Normans. After they had won a battle the first thing they did was to build a castle from which they could sally again and again and again to ravage the wealth of the surrounding countryside and keep the people under their boot heel. War was a career to the marauding foreigners whereas the Welsh were little more than brigands who slipped across the landscape at night to steal cattle and sheep. Thieves against soldiers, he considered, and Owain was the worst of bandit of them all. Yet Rhys had forged an army of iron from amongst the rustlers and won the greatest victory since Arthwyr had crushed the Saesneg at Mount Baddon. The murderer, his proud cousin, still held the castle, but he would be humbled, Rhys thought, despite his countrymen's shortcomings.

'Go then,' Rhys turned his back on Owain and Cynwrig, 'and take your plunder back to Gwynedd with you.'

Owain realised that he had been dismissed and stomped off into the darkness, with Cynwrig ab Ednyfed in his wake, cursing all soft bookish men of the south.

It irked Rhys that the oafish Owain had taken half the glory simply by agreeing to add his warriors to his own. It had been Rhys' plan to use the hidden cavalry during the battle, and his idea to isolate the Baron of Cemais. His jealousy raged, reminding him of the envy he had often felt as the youngest of six brothers.

*It was my direction of the archers,* he thought, *and my discipline that had destroyed the Norman army.* What had Owain done? Nothing, yet the man from Gwynedd had demanded all Ceredigion north of the River Dyfi as payment for his help. *Bastard,* thought Rhys, *bastard.*

More than anything the prince wanted the invaders gone from his kingdom, thrown back across the Severn and into their own lands. That was his dream. All his life he had heard the stories of the heroes of old; stories that had survived even after the deaths of the men of whose lives they spoke. He wanted the immortality that Arthwyr had discovered, not at Avalon but in the memory of the Cymric people. That great warlord had thrown the English out of his kingdom and ruled as Lord and Master answerable only to God. It was tantalising to think that only the small garrison of Aberteifi lay between him and the rule of Ceredigion. And after that? Pembroke, Brecon, and Striguil were the only strongholds of real note in Wales, and why would they stand where all others had fallen? Owain of Gwynedd was a fine warrior, but the northerner could see no further than the plunder he could carry back across the mountains that encircled his small territory. His banner would fall too and Rhys' raven standard would rise even higher. The whole of Wales could be his! Like his ancestor Rhodri he could be Tywysog Cymru – Prince of all Wales.

Ultimate victory was within his grasp, but first he had to find a way into Aberteifi Castle which lay dark and menacing beyond the firelight, blanketed in smoke which drifted in the small wind of the night.

## Chapter Two

Robert FitzStephen woke with a start. Was it his dream that had awakened him or was there something else that pricked his senses? He listened intently, eyes flicking from side to side in the semi-darkness. Nothing stirred within earshot, but the alertness remained. He used the ball of his palm to rub the sleep and drink from his head. He rolled onto his back upon the palliasse bed.

'What's wrong?' Richildis asked angrily from his side.

'A bad dream,' he replied. St Maurice had certainly invaded his slumber, he remembered, to warn him of dangers yet to come. Einion had been there, and his own father Stephen, and Sir Henry FitzRoy to whom he had been apprenticed as an esquire. His imaginings had been long and confused, but just as he had woken up he distinctly remembered being on a boat drawn over rough seas towards a strange and forested land.

'No more wine and cheese before bed,' he groaned as he stretched his legs and arms to their furthest extreme. He broke wind loudly and Richildis gave him a dig in the ribs with her elbow. He growled cheerfully at his mistress as he leant over and kissed her shoulder in the semi-light. There had been no cockcrow even though light was pouring through the gaps in the shuttered windows of the solar. He supposed that one of the Welsh had caught the bird for a tasty meal during the night. He would have done the same if it was him sitting outside the walls of the castle, bored and hungry.

It had been three weeks since Aberteifi had been put under siege and the garrison had suffered its share of hardship. Five Welsh attacks had been bloodily repulsed with the loss of twenty archers and four milites. But it was the food situation that was becoming most desperate, and he had been forced to halve the daily ration in an effort to maintain his defiant stance.

To make matters worse, someone had been stealing from the stores, and despite Wulfhere's best efforts the perpetrator had yet to be discovered. Nonetheless, FitzStephen still believed that he could last another two weeks before he would be forced into action, but that did not assuage his fears. His best hope was that his half-brother, Sir Maurice FitzGerald, would come north to break the siege, but that seemed less and less likely given that Pembroke was only two days' march away and no sign of help had appeared from that direction. And so FitzStephen prayed that hunger was biting Rhys' men as hard as it was his. He had only shared the true extent of their situation with Sir Roger de Quincy, a feeble attempt to clear the air with his second-in-command. The young knight had seemed genuinely shocked at the news that they were running low on food, and had quickly vanished into the depths of the bailey with his small band of cronies including Theobald Laval.

The supply of arrows was also becoming a problem, but at least the dwindling number could be supplemented by those that were being shot at the castle walls by Rhys' men. Oddly enough, this did not stop the archers from grumbling to Wulfhere, and him to FitzStephen about their seemingly hopeless situation. He could understand the stress under which the men toiled. He felt it himself yet he urged the feeling of peril away and sat up onto his elbows, tilting his ear towards the window beyond the bed drapes. Outside birds were already chirping and it had finally stopped raining. Richildis slept quietly, naked on his left.

He sighed, swung his legs out from under the woollen covers, and pushed open the bed curtains, catching his partially healed leg uncomfortably as he did so. Fully awake now, he pulled on a pair of hose and tied the front. Wandering across the darkened room, he upset a half-finished game of chess on a small table and cursed as pain surged through his injury. Behind him Richildis stirred, stretched, and rolled over onto her side, uncovering her smooth back and bottom from under the blanket. He grinned at his mistress as he pushed open the shutters and looked out onto the castle, his charge. As his eyes adjusted to the early morning light the first thing he again noted was the extent of Wulfhere's fires which had destroyed much of the town close to the walls of the castle, leaving around twenty houses as piles of black ash and scorched struts of timber. Several single stripes of smoke were outlined against the low green and brown countryside showing him that the Welshmen still smouldered in Aberteifi, awaiting an opportunity to burst into blaze of violence.

Nothing looked out of place. *Other than the huge army bent on wiping my small garrison off the face of the earth,* he thought with a smile. He could see Welsh troops at the edge of town talking in small groups or huddled around the dead or dying fires beside the distant watermill. Much of that land had been cleared of forest by his father to stop Welsh rebels from skulking there, and he laughed when he thought what Stephen's reaction would be if he knew his enemies were again using the assart land to besiege *his* castle. The sun was shining for the first time in weeks and FitzStephen had to shade his eyes as he looked at his lands in the distance beyond the town. He could see the sea off to the west and the outline of the mountains to the north and east. All seemed fine in the land of Wales.

As he turned to close the shutters and return to bed FitzStephen spotted something that put the fear of God in his soul – a body was lying in front of the closed gates inside the castle bailey. He looked again and squinted to make sure that he saw correctly.

It was Wulfhere Little-Fingers.

Men were gathered around the motionless warrior but he could clearly see from his armour that it was his friend, the Englishman. Blood was pooled around his head and a dog was sniffing at his hand. He was not moving.

A thousand thoughts entered FitzStephen's head and panic grew quickly in his chest. His eyes remained frozen on the body. Was Wulfhere dead? What had happened? Was the fortress under attack?

FitzStephen pushed his head out the window to shout at the troops in the bailey, but froze when he spotted a number of fully armoured men appear out of the shadows of the flying bridge, move through the upper gate, and out onto the motte compound.

Confused, he watched as Sir Roger de Quincy issued silent orders to some of FitzStephen's own men-at-arms. These trusted men pulled out swords and walked briskly towards the keep.

Too late did FitzStephen realise his danger and it was only as Quincy skirted the wall and suddenly slashed his dagger across the neck of his yawning steward, Rhygewarch, that he truly understood his predicament. Blood arced high in the early morning air as the Constable fully understood that he had been betrayed.

And the enemy were already in his citadel.

'Traitors,' FitzStephen roared down on the fifteen armed men who quite naturally stopped in their tracks as they looked upwards at the source of the rancorous bellow. Sir Roger de Quincy looked up as Rhygewarch's body fell at his feet and went into a death spasm. His eyes locked with the Constable's as he raised his bloodied dagger to point at the door of the donjon.

'Mutiny,' Robert screamed his bellicose roar again, this time towards the bailey where his men stood stock-still in silence. FitzStephen pointed straight at Quincy as he shouted, not caring that the Welsh would also be alerted to the disturbance in the castle.

'To me,' FitzStephen barked at the men still standing around the body in the bailey, but they disregarded his cry. As he hung from the window the archers and milites turned their backs on the keep and on him one by one. He was betrayed.

'Ferrand, bar the door,' he screamed into the household, praying that his lieutenant, who slept downstairs in the hall, had remained loyal to him. As he turned, he crashed into a small chest and sent his vial of the Virgin Mary's breast milk fell towards the ground. Cursing and grasping, he could only watch as the ornate relic smashed, white powdery contents spilling pathetically as gold wire imagery came loose and green glass shattered. A travelling cleric had charged him four months' income when he had come preaching crusade several summers before. He had held the precious vial between his hands as he had prayed every night for six years and now it was gone, and

44

he was cursed.

'Robert,' Richildis whimpered, but got no answer as he crouched on his knees, delicately picking at the fragments of the vial. 'Your soul will keep for now, Robert. It is our lives which are in danger.'

For many seconds he did not speak, but then he gathered himself: 'You are right, where are my weapons?' he asked as he scanned the room. 'Damn it,' he shouted when he remembered having sent them away with poor Rhygewarch to be cleaned. He cursed his vanity and quickly reassessed his position without his weapons.

'Get dressed,' he told Richildis, who was sitting up in the palliasse bed, pulling the covers to her chin as though they would stop a sword strike, 'and hide in the brattice,' he told her. 'I will keep them away for as long as I can.'

'Is it the Welsh?' she asked as the tears started to flow down her face. She knew what would happen if the enemy found a pretty girl like her in the keep.

'No, it is much worse than that,' FitzStephen said, and unsheathed two hunting daggers which were hung on the wall. Testing the weight in either hand, he realised that one was the same weapon which he had used to murder Einion ab Anarawd at the monastery up north. Specks of black blood had dried on the blade and his mind slipped back to the moment he had claimed his cousin's life. Einion's murder had done nothing but strengthen his Cymri enemies and though FitzStephen had got his wish – war with Rhys – he had been bested in battle. He had stood tall when all Wales rose against him, but the treachery of his warriors tore at the very strings of his heart. He had stood alongside them in shield walls and cavalry charges, feints and ambushes; he had drank and laughed with them; faced hardships and threats and challenges, and yet they had betrayed him.

Downstairs there was shouting and the sound of metal on wood rang through the building. Screamed curses and swearing told him that there were casualties. He knew there was no escape from the keep, or from Ceredigion, or from Welsh revenge if he left the fortress.

45

'Who is it?' Richildis asked as she pulled on clothes, tears flowing down her face.

FitzStephen shook his head and despair took him. In the hall the shouting intensified and the clash of steel on steel told him that Quincy's allies were inside his keep. He couldn't think straight but whispered soft, soothing words to the distraught Richildis whom he took in his arms.

'It will be alright,' FitzStephen repeated again and again but suddenly shook his head slowly and brought his hands to his face. The knife which he was holding in his left hand nicked the skin on his forehead, shocking FitzStephen from his wretchedness. He looked at the weapon in his left hand, turning it over in his palm. His father's knife was older than the murder blade and was thin from use and sharpening. He wondered if his was the first blood that it had drawn since his father had held it. He could have benefitted from Stephen's guidance now.

Anger rose in his soul and swept away his self-pity as he considered what his father would have thought of him at that moment. Stephen had been a man who had faced down everything that life in Wales could throw at him to defend the land that, though not his own, he had left to his bastard son. Danes, Norse, Cymri, and Normans had tried to eject Stephen de Ceredigion but he had held on because Aberteifi was his home. He had bled for the land and he had died protecting it still.

FitzStephen had taken an oath to protect this fortress, whatever the cost. Down on one knee before King Henry, he had been made a knight and had promised the Earl of Hertford that he would defend these lands and his castle until his death. He had been young, but he had meant every word and had sworn in the name of the Trinity and St Maurice that he would fulfil his vow.

He had failed God, his king, and his lord. He was cursed. And yet pride would not let him give up. There was still a chance to earn revenge on those who had betrayed his trust and a madness rose in his chest. He would keep his oath by dying in defence of his castle. The thought enlivened his warrior spirit and he gripped and re-gripped the weapons in his hands.

'Let them come,' he growled, eyes closed in anger. 'Let them come.' If he could not hold Ceredigion then he was damned sure that his betrayers would not either. His eyes flicked open as he heard the first footsteps run up the stairs towards the solar. Half-dressed and badly armed, but warmed by his father's memory, FitzStephen snarled and ran to the door to greet his first foe, his knives ready to strike.

Richildis shrieked, 'Robert, please, no!'

William Ferrand was halfway up the steps when he spotted FitzStephen and slowed down. The half-dressed lieutenant had a deep gash in his side and was armed with a sword and a small axe. He had obviously been caught as unawares as FitzStephen to the attack and he leant against the wall of the stone staircase for support.

'I am with you, Robert,' he exclaimed and held up one hand in deference, 'but Roger de Quincy's men are in the hall,' he said as sweat flew off his upper lip, 'and there is no way to get out. John FitzLionel and Maredudd de Guerin are dead.' The warrior's eyes pleaded for inspiration from his commander. 'What should I do?' he groaned as more blood soaked his side.

'Give me your sword,' FitzStephen said gruffly, offering no hope to his man-at-arms. 'Get behind me and protect Richildis. When I fall, please protect her for as long as you can.'

'Sir Robert, we cannot beat them,' Ferrand said without handing over his weapon. 'Quincy has all the men on his side, even the archers. There are ten milites in the hall already,' he pleaded. 'No help is coming for us.' He took a step backwards.

But FitzStephen would not be persuaded. He would not surrender as long as he got an opportunity to kill Sir Roger de Quincy. It had become his one reason to survive and he raised his daggers like cat claws, ready to pounce. Ferrand took another step back towards the hall, as much because of the menace in his commander's eyes as the weaponry in his hands. Ferrand looked at FitzStephen and saw a madman looking for death in battle. He had seen it before. His eyes were demonic and glowed with an urgent desire for blood.

Ferrand spoke slowly and deliberately as if he addressed a child. 'Robert, my friend, my men are dead or gone over to

Quincy. The milites in the bailey are united against you. They are scared and desperate. Quincy has been telling them that we only have a week's food left and that the FitzGeralds of Pembroke have sent a message saying that they cannot come to save us. He said that you are to blame for our predicament, and they believe him.' He took several steps backwards, making sure to keep his sword ahead of him in case of sudden attack. 'They believe him.'

'Does he wish to be Constable?'

Ferrand shook his head. 'I don't know. All I know is that to fight is to die and I cannot die here,' he pleaded. 'You must submit …'

'This castle is my life, Ferrand, and this land,' FitzStephen said through gritted teeth, 'is mine. I will not give it up while I am still breathing. I swore oaths to King Henry, Earl Roger, and my father. I intend to bloody well keep them.'

'Then you will die here,' Ferrand said with a shake of his head. FitzStephen stood immovable with his back to the solar door and watched as Ferrand retreated back down the stairs. The anger surged in his breast but he was not fool enough to rush headlong onto his erstwhile friend's sword. It had gone very quiet at the bottom of the steps and he could not see around the stone corner of the winding stairs so he waited, rigid, for an assault, his father's dagger out in front in his left hand, his own blood-stained weapon held upside-down in his right. He quieted his thoughts and listened for movement on the stairs that would signal the inevitable attack.

Everything went silent.

'Robert FitzStephen,' Roger de Quincy's voice resounded around the stone work of the stairs, 'pray throw away your cutlery and come down here.' Much laughter accompanied his cackling call. 'You will not be harmed. You have my word.'

Ferrand had obviously given Quincy all the information on his impossible situation. Still, his enemy was intelligent enough to know that an animal was at its most dangerous when backed into a corner. They knew they had a rat caught in a trap but they still did not want to attack up the stairs. Not against a fighter of FitzStephen's skill.

'Your word means nothing to me, Roger,' FitzStephen shouted down the stairs, not dropping his guard. 'You are an oath-breaker and a traitor and before I kill you I will cut out your deceitful tongue and nail it to the wall of my castle for the birds to peck,' he said.

Sir Roger de Quincy lost his temper immediately. 'You are a lunatic, FitzStephen! We could never have hoped to hold out against this army. You would kill us all for your pride and stupidity. You drove us to this,' the knight at the bottom of the stairs insisted. 'King Henry himself was not able to beat Prince Rhys. What made you think that you could do it? Your cousin is too strong and your pride too great.'

'You are a coward, Quincy, and all Wales will know it,' he shouted down the stone echoing stairs. 'Lord Hertford will know it and King Henry will know it.'

'Dead men tell no tales,' said Quincy after a few moments, accompanied by growls of assent from his companions. 'I will be the hero who brought this garrison out alive and you will be the disgrace that caused a war to ravage Wales,' said Quincy suddenly and angrily. 'You are a murderer and a bastard not fit to command.'

FitzStephen snorted maliciously and the noise of it was heard at the bottom of the steps. 'I am a bastard, Quincy, a Norman bastard like the William the Conqueror and Richard the Fearless before me. I am from a long line of murderous Norman bastards, Quincy, and if you dare come up these stairs you'll find out just what a murderous Norman bastard can do.' FitzStephen almost screamed his challenge to his enemy. 'Come on, you Angevin-loving scum. Come on, you son of a Tours whore. Come up here and find out what a true Norman bastard can do!'

The only answer from below was the quick stomp of heavy feet on the first steps. He tensed and adapted his stance to the sound. However many men were on the staircase, FitzStephen knew that they would only be able to come up one at a time and the curve of the stone walls would make any swordplay awkward – for them. He doubted Quincy would consider any of these factors. Had he ever had to fight in the close quarters of a castle? Never, he knew.

The first man who came around the corner was Thomas de Cressy, a vicious miles that FitzStephen had disciplined several times for murdering defenceless Welsh women. Cressy crouched and glided up the steps at a quick and steady pace with his spear, couched under his right arm and close to the curling wall. FitzStephen retreated quietly back a few steps and then charged suddenly with his shoulder tight to the outside wall on his right-hand side. He was past Cressy's spearpoint before the warrior even saw him and all the miles could do was roar loudly before FitzStephen crashed into his shield and tackled him backwards down the steps and onto the lance point of his compatriot who followed a few steps behind.

Cressy screamed as the spear punched through his chainmail and deep into his back. The Norman tried to arch away from the blade while behind him the second of Quincy's men, Gilbert de Pevensey, tried in vain to extract his spear from Cressy's back as he too fought to keep his feet. But FitzStephen kept on pushing as the two sweaty warriors, weighted down with armour and awkward with weaponry, stumbled backward down the stairs. Blood splattered all over FitzStephen as Cressy panted, the spear having forced its way further into his back and punctured his lungs and scraped his ribs. But he kept the momentum going with a loud roar.

Halfway down the stairs FitzStephen's attacker dropped his own spear and reached backwards to try to pull out the weapon from his back. His efforts brought both of the armoured men down onto their backs. Cressy screeched in agony. In an instant FitzStephen was on top of them. Unhindered by chainmail or weaponry he quickly scrambled across Cressy's prostrate body to attack Gilbert de Pevensey, who cursed as he struggled to free his arms from beneath his own red shield. He could not react quickly enough before FitzStephen slammed on top of him, pinning the shield to his breast. Slipping his father's dagger inside the neckline of Pevensey's hauberk, FitzStephen said a silent prayer as Gilbert struggled desperately against the weight of the man on his chest. FitzStephen ignored Pevensey's short appeal for compassion and his attempts to bite his hand,

and stabbed down hard into the jugular. Blood poured between the steel rings and Pevensey's eyes glazed over as he died. FitzStephen was already on top of Cressy, and finished him by pushing his dagger deep into the man's right eye and into his brain with a sickening twist.

Panting and sweating, he left the two dead men obstructing the stairwell and shouted down the stairs, 'Come on up here yourself, Quincy, you bastard! Bring your traitor's guts to my knives.' His blood was on fire and he let the familiar joy that accompanied violence and victory wash over him like a gale. He wanted more men to power their way up those stairs, desiring the contest that could only end in his own death. But he would send more to meet the Devil, by God he would. FitzStephen's breathing was heavy through clenched teeth as he took up his position on the stairs ready for another attack.

Both his knees were skinned, as were his knuckles, but otherwise he was uninjured. He did not have to wait long before he heard the men below steel themselves for the attack. Bare-chested, FitzStephen steadied himself on the steps with a deep breath. Picking up Cressy's shield, he threw the guige around his neck and then hoisted both spears. The curve of the walls hindered the use of the long weapon if held in the right hand of an attacker, but helped the defender. To make it easier to use, he broke one spear in half over his knee so it could be used to stab over his shield and into the face of his attacker without impediment.

Suddenly Bernard de Lisieux came around the corner and climbed quickly over the two bodies. FitzStephen roared and launched the longer spear at his uncovered ankles. It skittered across the steps towards its target but he did not wait to see if it struck home, instead he charged down the stairs to meet Lisieux shield to shield. They crashed together with a grunt, faces just inches apart, but this time his opponent was immoveable as his numerous fellows pushed hard on his back with their shields, forcing FitzStephen slowly backwards step by step.

'You bastard, submit,' said a gasping Lisieux. 'You can't bloody win!'

FitzStephen gritted his teeth and struggled back. 'Any time

you're ready to give in, Lisieux, I'll forgive you!' Bernard snorted grimly but both men went quiet as the contact pressure built up between them, requiring all their energy. The Constable chanced a glance at their shuffling feet. Lisieux had no protection on his lower limbs and FitzStephen took his opportunity, raking his shortened spear down Lisieux's shin, tearing the bindings on his legs, piercing his vulnerable foot and slamming the spear into the stone step with a high-pitched crunch. Lisieux opened his mouth wide in agony and screamed loudly as FitzStephen dragged the blade free of his flesh.

FitzStephen saw his chance and did not hesitate as he stabbed his weapon over his shield rim and into Lisieux's open jaw as he bellowed. He felt his weapon strike through bone and sinew, killing his opponent immediately, and he took a pace backwards to let the dead man fall before snarling forward to engage the next attacker over Lisieux's body. He did not have time to steal a glance over his shoulder, but he was aware that he was just a yard from the door of the solar. He was running out of space. Heaving even harder than before, FitzStephen strained against his enemy, hoping again that his advantage on the higher steps would be enough to defeat this next enemy.

Suddenly a lance streaked across the shoulder of his opponent and struck him in the cheek. His spear dropped from his grasp as his hand shot to his face. Blood immediately welled at the wound and FitzStephen growled in pain and anger. He instinctively took another step backwards. His adversary whooped at the injury and pushed even harder. FitzStephen scrambled uselessly against the tide that washed him backwards. His back thumped into the solar door.

Another spear came over the head of his challenger and thumped into the wooden door close to his left ear. Inside the room Richildis yelped. FitzStephen knew he was out of options and summoned his last reserve of strength, drawing his father's dagger from its sheath at his side. Swearing emerged from his mouth like a scream and he reached around the locked shields and buried the knife in the man's neck, simultaneously heaving the spearman away from the door and slipping through. Richildis screamed when she saw him, but he ignored her and braced the door with his shield and shoulder.

'Richildis, get into the anteroom,' he ordered. 'Lock the door and do not open it for anyone.' The small room hid his most prized possessions, but he knew that it would not stay unknown for long. There was nothing else that he could do for his mistress.

'Robert,' she wailed and moved away from their bed, 'I love you.' She closed the door and FitzStephen heard it lock from the inside. With one final look he turned back to the solar door.

'Traitors,' he whispered and panted, 'bastard traitors.'

Their first impact with the door nearly knocked him off his feet as the oak panels jumped inwards but he managed to steady himself and hold fast. More collisions rattled the heavy oak and FitzStephen grimaced as the rim of his shield bumped against his injured face. Then suddenly the pressure relented for a few moments giving FitzStephen the chance to pull a chair over to wedge the door shut further. All he could do now was pray for a miracle.

The first strike of the axe on the other side of the door splintered one of the door panels and might have killed him if he had not moved. The second blow tore out a small chunk of wood close to the latch. A spear tip appeared between the edge of the oak door and the wall of the room and tried to lever the door open. A hinge at the top of the door sprang loose and clattered to the ground. FitzStephen used both hands to power the door shut. But there were too many men on the other side trying to force their way inside.

Blood from his face wound mixed with his sweat and stung his eyes before dripping on his bare chest and feet. He was sliding backwards on the loose carpet on the wooden floor. He was unable to hold the door shut.

FitzStephen was keening now, a steady stream of curses and indistinct words that spilled from his mouth as he desperately fought to keep the door shut. But then they were through the gap, growling and shouting, all shields and steel and colour. FitzStephen fell backwards with the force of their entry and grabbed his shield to take the first strike of a spear. The blow forced him backwards and he landed roughly on his bed, hurting his leg on the heavy wooden frame. His attacker, Herluin de Exeter, fell too and became ensnared in his own shield straps, taking out of the fight for long enough for FitzStephen to force his way free of the tangle of canopy, and deflect another thrust from the nearest foe, Odo of Cirencester. The sudden move threw Odo off balance and sent him stumbling into the corner, where he clashed his helmeted head off a wooden peg upon which FitzStephen's armour would usually have been hanging. The warrior turned quickly and raised his spear again, but FitzStephen didn't give him a second and deflected the point over his head with his shield and, in the same motion, slammed the rim of the willow board into the man's face, noting the sound of the devastating crunch.

'Quincy,' he screamed as he spun around, 'where are you?'

Four warriors were now in the room and FitzStephen went on the offensive, scooping up Richildis' small garment chest and flinging it across the room where it smashed into one man's blood-speckled shield. It was all instinct now, a brawl in the tight confines of the solar. Without thinking, FitzStephen spun around to face another miles who attacked from his right and he raised his shield to take a sword strike. Immediately he felt a spear pierce his left thigh and he yelled in distress, as he shoulder charged the enemy to his front. He turned just in time to meet young Gervais FitzPons' second spear thrust with his shield. The boy, all rage, slid forward to meet the Constable's fist and fell backwards on the floor. FitzStephen lurched away from the bed, unable to find his balance on his uninjured right leg as he sprawled towards the far end of the room and slammed into the wall with a curse.

'Robert!' Richildis screamed and he turned to see his mistress being held by the neck by a bloody-nosed Odo.

'Submit,' Odo shouted. 'Submit or she dies!'

FitzStephen snarled and jumped forward at his traitorous miles. Such was his desire to save Richildis from the sword at her side he did not see Sir Roger de Quincy perched in the smashed doorway. Nor did he see Quincy's fist which reached out and punched him full in the throat. Silver stars appeared before his eyes and he dropped to his knees, gagging and fighting for breath. The fight was over but he managed to raise the shield one last time to defend his head from another sword blow which came from his left.

'No,' Quincy shrieked, 'we need him alive!'

'Fine,' Odo said as he ripped FitzStephen's shield from his hand. 'But he doesn't have to be conscious,' he said as he raised his own shield and brought it down with a sickening thud. FitzStephen crumpled to the ground.

A woman's screams punctured his daze and he rolled from his shoulder onto his back and groaned loudly.

'Bastard,' he coughed, spraying blood and spittle into the air and onto his own chest and the rush-covered floor. It was Richildis' yell which had awoken him and he felt the presence of many men around him, arguing loudly. They all went silent as he spoke and tried to sit up. 'Traitors,' he moaned again and worked his way onto his elbow.

One of the men walked over and violently kicked him into silence. 'Shut … up … you … bloody … bastard,' he swore with each staccato strike. 'I should cut your throat. You've broken my bloody nose!' cried Odo of Cirencester.

FitzStephen realised that only a few seconds had passed since the fight in the solar, though he had been dragged downstairs to his hall. He looked up at his captor, still in full mail and sporting a bloody and misshapen nose.

'I broke your nose?' FitzStephen croaked. 'Well, it's not like I could make you any uglier,' he joked. Odo pulled back his arm ready to strike but was prevented as Sir Roger de Quincy strode cheerfully into the hall from the solar, rearranging his tunic and hauberk at his trouser line.

'The bitch screams loudly enough, eh?' he joked with the miles who stood guard over the Constable. 'It's as if she didn't enjoy it,' he exclaimed with a short giggle.

FitzStephen said a silent prayer for Richildis, hoping that she still lived after the ordeal to which Quincy had subjected her. He finished with a short appeal to God for his soul. He didn't hold much hope for his life. He tried to sit up again but failed and so instead attempted to gauge the damage that had been inflicted to his body. He managed to pull open his left eyelid, which was still wet with blood, but the other would not move because of the severity of the swelling. Naked and bound, he was hurting all over, covered in blood and mud from the floor. Someone had urinated on him but he did not think he had any broken bones. He thought of Walter ap Llywarch in St Padarn's Priory. He remembered Einion's curse.

'Now to the business of saving our lives,' Quincy announced brightly above him. 'Don't worry lads – all they want is the murderer FitzStephen. Pick him up and bring him down to the barbican.' He stomped off towards the door and out of sight. Duly, he felt the armoured hands reach under his armpits and hoist him to waist height.

'Up you get, Sir Robert,' said a voice on his left as FitzStephen hung limply between the two men. 'Oh, Jesu, someone has pissed on him.'

The one on his right gave him a shake but received no answer. FitzStephen heard him turn to ask his friend: 'Maybe he's dead?' He gave him another shake. 'Are you dead?'

FitzStephen managed to peel open his good eye and flop his head back onto his shoulders. 'Still alive,' he managed to croak as the blood seeped between his teeth. He received a laugh and a painful slap on the back from the two traitorous milites.

His feet unsuccessfully scrambled for purchase on the reed-strewn floor as they dragged him out of the keep and down the motte towards the flying bridge. Passing by Rhygewarch's body he could see Roger de Quincy was already halfway down the bridge, walking behind two of his henchmen. FitzStephen felt the anger rise in him and pictured shaking free of his keepers, grabbing a sword, and charging down the stretch of wooden planks to fillet his enemy.

'Don't even bloody think about rushing him,' the guard on his left said as he felt FitzStephen's body bristle and tighten. 'We need you alive so the bloody Welsh can kill you.'

FitzStephen's bare feet bumped painfully off every step as they proceeded down the flying bridge behind Quincy. Blood dripped from the end of his nose as his head dangled and his chin bashed on his chest. After a few seconds he felt the mud and grass of the bailey under his feet. Many of the families of the castle were standing outside their houses watching their lord's appalling demise. All were silent except for FitzStephen's own men who lined the street closer to the gates. As his guards dragged him towards the barbican, the traitorous milites shouted taunts and obscenities at their fallen leader. Mud hit him in the face and chest. His guards laughed along with their comrades until they too were hit by the filth and they shouted at their compatriots to stop. FitzStephen let his chin drop to his chest, exhausted and beaten. Eyes to the floor, his minders dropped him in a pile of hay and tied his hands to a rung on the side of the guardhouse. Left alone, he opened his one good eye and tried to wipe the blood, sweat, and mud off his face with the inside of his sweaty forearm.

Wulfhere's red-spattered body was beside him. His fixed eyes were open and staring at the cloudy November sky. The Englishman's balding head had almost been cut off by a sword strike that had taken him in the back of the neck and shoulder. Under him was the earl's banner which had flown from the keep and now lay covered in mud, blood, and reeds. FitzStephen had no more energy left to cry or rage for poor Wulfhere but sat looking at the grisly mess that had been his friend. He whispered quiet thanks for the older man's loyalty which had brought about his untimely demise. He finished with a prayer to St Maurice watch over the soldier's soul.

'Accept him to your table, Holy Maurice ...' he began but he could not find the words. Still staring at Little-Fingers, he sniggered hopelessly and sarcastically as his thoughts turned back to the disaster. He rolled away from his friend and let the back of his head bump off the wooden wall of the guardhouse. Even though his nose was swollen and stuffed with dried blood FitzStephen could smell the herb garden, just yards away from him behind the kitchen. It was odd that such a delightful sensation wafted around Aberteifi after the horror that had befallen him in the keep. In spite of the mortal terror that threatened to overwhelm him, FitzStephen's one good eye began to close as exhaustion took hold. Within seconds his head lolled and he was asleep.

Sir Roger de Quincy laughed loudly as he kicked FitzStephen between the legs as he slept. His former commander, naked as the day he was born, cried out sharply and rolled away from Roger's next blow making Quincy's companions cackle even more noisily behind him.

'Hit him again,' roared pig-faced Theobald Laval.

'Put it away, FitzStephen,' Roger joked at the unclothed man. 'We like prettier women than you! Richildis, for instance,' he sneered and all his cronies laughed again.

FitzStephen rolled into the foetal position at the corner of the guardhouse and refused to answer his enemy. He steeled himself for further blows.

'What? No jokes?' Roger laughed again and spat on him before stomping off in the direction of the gate followed by his closest conspirators. They each had a swing at their former master as they passed by. William Ferrand, now fully armoured in Quincy's entourage, meekly tramped after the group without looking once at his former lord.

'Pick him up,' Ferrand said to two archers, 'and bring him with us to the allure.'

'Traitor bastard,' FitzStephen coughed behind him as he was hoisted to his feet again and his hands untied.

The rungs of the ladder were rough on his sweaty hands as he climbed onto the wooden palisade which swung away from him in either direction to encircle the fortress of Aberteifi.

'Get on your knees,' Gervais FitzPons ordered him as he clambered slowly onto the barbican. When the knight refused he received a clout to his jaw. Sir Roger de Quincy didn't move as FitzStephen collapsed. He simply stared out over the village chewing on his upper lip.

'What the hell are you doing, Roger?' asked FitzStephen.

'I am getting out of here,' Quincy replied and shaded his face from the sunshine. 'I am getting these people out of here too,' he corrected himself quickly.

'You will hand me over to Rhys? You think that will end the siege?' He shook his head. 'He wants this land, Quincy, not my life ...'

'Jonah,' Roger accused FitzStephen with a finger pointed at his chest, 'that's who you are – Jonah, and I am throwing you to the ocean to save the good men of this fortress and their families.' He said it loudly so that anyone within earshot could hear him.

But FitzStephen knew Sir Roger de Quincy and he snorted back a laugh. 'You don't care a pinch for them, Roger. You just want to save your own skin.'

Roger sighed and, finding Gervais, Theobald, and Ferrand out of earshot, turned towards FitzStephen for the first time. 'You're right – I hate this place,' he confirmed through gritted teeth. 'I hate the weather, I hate the food, I hate the piss-poor wine, and I hate boring garrison duty. I hate the Welsh,' he laughed morosely with a shake of his head. 'I have barely slept a night since coming to Aberteifi,' he spat the name as if the word alone was disgusting. 'I have to get out of here. Death haunts my dreams nightly …'

FitzStephen, who had grown up on the March, had heard the same tale told a thousand times by newcomers to the dangerous frontier, but he felt no sympathy for Quincy. He had come to the March unprepared for the type of war that the Welsh fought. Here vicious bandits and rebels would appear out of nowhere and attack in fury before disappearing into the dawn. Every breaking twig in the dead of night could signal another attack; every howl from the darkness, a new threat. This was the frontier and no one was safe.

'Not how your father described it?' FitzStephen mocked, enjoying Quincy's discomfort.

'Shut up,' Roger said, lashing out with a backhand to his face, but without real conviction. FitzStephen was right about his father. Saher de Quincy's description of war was of noblemen riding through meadows on beautiful chargers, ready to meet on equal terms in warm climes and fight it out like proper knights.

'At least in England noblemen are treated with proper civility,' Roger said. 'They do not choke on blood pouring from arrow wounds and lie dying in the mud as I have witnessed.' Roger paused, his eyes flicking to meet FitzStephen's as a shiver of fear rolled across his shoulders. 'They do not have their throats cut as they kneel in prayer in a monastery …'

'The Welsh cannot get to you here, Roger,' FitzStephen said quietly as if appealing to a particularly dense child. 'We are tucked up safe in the castle …'

'We aren't safe!' Roger interrupted. 'Hasn't Rhys proven that already by capturing the great stone donjon at Carmarthen?' Desperation was visible in Quincy's face. 'What chance does this poor wooden stockade stand if Rhys has already stormed Carmarthen's walls?' he asked. 'It was lunacy to fight on after the defeat in battle …' Roger paused as Ferrand, Gervais, and Theobald climbed onto the allure. 'This is your fault,' Quincy accused FitzStephen as he glanced at his co-conspirators nervously. 'I was forced to act. I saved the garrison. I-I am the hero.'

'You are a murderer,' FitzStephen replied and pictured Wulfhere's body.

'No!' Roger appealed, 'Gervais and Cressy …' he began before Gervais FitzPons interrupted him.

'Are you going to talk to the Welsh prick, or keep talking nonsense to this bastard?' Gervais asked.

Sir Roger de Quincy cast one last angry look at FitzStephen before turning to gaze out over the town of Aberteifi. It was a horror. Decaying bodies still littered the streets and dogs and birds fluttered amongst the carnage, making him want to vomit. Amongst the burnt-out buildings the Welsh had staked twelve severed Norman heads in front of the castle. The eyes had been pecked out by birds, along with the soft skin of the lips and nostrils. Quincy managed to swallow the rising bile.

He put his hand to his cheek and shouted towards the town. 'I want to talk to Rhys,' he called. On the other side of town Roger watched as the Welsh continued to mill about the buildings and no-one came forward to parley. Quincy waited patiently for several more seconds but still nothing happened.

'They are Welsh, Sir Roger,' said Theobald Laval, who joined Quincy and Gervais on the barbican, 'so they probably don't speak French. Maybe you should try barking at them,' he laughed and made the sound of a dog.

Embarrassed, Roger reprimanded himself and switched to Latin. 'I want to speak to Lord Rhys,' he shouted again. 'We have an offer he will want to hear.'

Once more there was no reply so Gervais FitzPons shouted in stumbling English across at the ruined remains of the town. One of the languages must have been understood because just minutes later a number of warriors and priests came forward slowly behind a small, thin man who looked uncomfortable in his lamellar armour. The group stopped below the gatehouse and waited. Behind the man came a standard bearer holding a red and white banner showing three black ravens. They were the colours of Prince Rhys of Deheubarth.

Roger de Quincy paused, unsure of how to continue but the Welsh leader butted in anyway.

'Speak,' he said in fluent French, 'before we decide to wipe your little wooden cabin off the face of the earth. What do you offer?'

'Are you the Lord Rhys?' Quincy had to ask twice, clearing his throat after his hoarse first attempt. He was such a little man, not the warrior of renown that Roger had expected.

'I am the *Prince* Rhys,' said the thin man, who Roger thought looked very odd in his expensive armour. 'Are you my cousin, Robert son of Stephen?'

'Your cousin? No, I am not,' he said with as much force as he could muster suddenly remembering the family connection and fearing that he had miscalculated. It was too late to change tack now. 'I am Sir Roger de Quincy,' he told Rhys, 'and FitzStephen is no longer our leader but a prisoner.' He turned to Gervais and Theobald. 'Get him up,' he whispered, tapping Robert with his toe. Laval looked unimpressed but dragged the naked FitzStephen to his feet and showed him to Rhys. One of the priests crossed his chest at the sight of the murderer, the bogeyman of Welsh children's dreams.

'I will give you FitzStephen in exchange for safe passage back to England,' Quincy shouted towards the Welsh party.

Rhys had been whispering in the ear of one of his warriors but was stopped in his tracks by the unexpected offer. He stood for a long time studying the fortress, Quincy and the bloody mess that was Sir Robert FitzStephen.

'You offer the castle and its constable for your lives? That is all you want?' Rhys seemed sceptical, and well he might. He had not considered for a moment that the soldiers of Aberteifi would hand over a fortress to which there was no obvious line of attack for the Welsh. Not unless they were starving to death or sickness had taken the castle. He could see none of the tell-tale signs of either of those occurrences from Quincy's manner. 'You are lucky,' he told Roger flippantly, 'we were preparing an attack for midday.'

'Ha!' Robert FitzStephen laughed as he leaned over the wall, earning a punch to his kidney from Theobald.

'Get him out of here,' Roger whispered desperately, believing Rhys' lie and fearing that the small warlord would decide to kill them all rather than barter with a defeated enemy.

FitzStephen put up a struggle but his injuries meant that he was no match and was quickly hauled off the barbican and back towards the guardhouse where he was again chained.

'All we want is our lives, Prince Rhys,' Roger pleaded, his fingers wrapping around the pointed wooden defences. 'The fortress is yours if we can go to King Henry's lands. I swear it on the blood of Lord Jesus Christ!' He had not meant to sound so desperate. Changing his demeanour to faux defiance he added: 'Otherwise you will lose a lot of men on our walls.'

Rhys snorted and ignored Roger's bluster. 'Why should I not kill you all? If I let you go will I not have to fight you another day? You Normans gather in Pembroke like vipers ready to slither north and attack my lands. Better that I burn out this snake's nest today rather than let you bite my ankle tomorrow.'

'We are not bound for Pembroke, Prince Rhys,' Quincy told him. 'FitzStephen's brothers are there and they would not welcome us.' He was desperate now and almost pleading with Rhys. 'Let us go and you will not hear from us again.' The sweat was pouring down Roger's back as he watched Rhys slowly consider the truth of his words.

Behind the Norman nobleman, Theobald had returned and whispered to Gervais: 'Buggers aren't going for it. Let's just murder the bastard now. He's in range of our crossbows.'

Roger tensed and whispered back to the two warriors, 'Wait a minute.' He did not want to provoke the Welsh who, even without Rhys' leadership, he knew would surely swarm over the meagre defences.

'Very well,' said Rhys finally, 'you, your men, and their families may leave. But you will swear on holy relics and pain of eternal damnation that you, Sir Roger de Quincy, will lead your men out of Cymru and never return across the great river,' he said of the Severn.

Quincy let out a breath which he had not realised he was holding. 'So you agree to my terms?'

'Your terms?' stormed Rhys of Deheubarth suddenly. '*My* terms are that you leave Wales and never return,' he said angrily. 'That you give me Sir Robert FitzStephen alive and that you go to London and tell Henry of England that he can go and boil his arse in brimstone. Promise to do all that and I will grant you your damned lives and give you safe passage as far as the River Loughor.'

Roger was unused to being talked down to by any man except the hated Robert FitzStephen. Most people immediately tried to please him and almost all wanted his approval and companionship. It especially rankled with him that he was being talked to in this manner by a diminutive man like Rhys, who reminded him of one of his father's clerks, rather than royalty.

'Agreed,' he said through clenched jaw and turned to leave the barbican.

'Wait,' said Rhys stopping Quincy, Gervais and Theobald Laval in their tracks, 'one more thing before you slither away, Sir Roger,' he said drawing out the silence. 'Why did you betray my cousin?'

Quincy considered the question. The truth was that he had been terrified at the slaughter of the battle and daunted by the rumours of Rhys' successes. Blinded by his hatred of Wales and FitzStephen he had convinced himself that he was saving the garrison. But he felt more scared now than he had when FitzStephen was in command. Roger felt that he would be caught out at any time on the lies he had told to the men. In his panic he spun another deceit that had come to him during the night. 'God sent us defeat because we were led by an unholy murderer,' his rehearsed lines silkily spilled from his lips. 'God reached down and washed away our army because we supported the sinner. God cannot be on the side of murderers!'

'But you expect Him to be on the side of traitors?' Rhys said calmly and loudly so that the whole garrison, who had come down to watch the encounter, could hear.

'Treason against a sinner is no sin at all,' Roger replied confidently as many on the wall shuffled their feet uncomfortably.

Rhys decided not to continue the discussion. 'You have one hour to leave the fortress or we will attack and kill you all.' With that he turned and pushed his way between the priests and warriors who gathered behind him.

Behind him, Roger heard Gervais FitzPons exhale slowly through his deformed nose. 'We've slipped the noose.'

Sir Roger de Quincy began smiling for he was leaving Wales at last. He was safe.

The prisoner watched as all the inhabitants of Aberteifi Castle marched out through the open gates below the barbican. Few of FitzStephen's troops could hold his one-eyed stare but those who would were angry and violent, and he had yet more bruising to add to his other injuries. His ten-year-old bastard, Ralph, was the only one who stopped beside his battered father, staring at him with a gormless expression on his grubby face.

'Come away.' Ralph's worried mother Mahel hissed at her son. She was holding little Geoffrey and trying to remain anonymous amongst the throng of people as she frantically pleaded with her eldest son. She had not been happy with FitzStephen since he had shacked up with Richildis, but now she desperately wanted her son to hide amongst the servants in case Welsh revenge would threaten her boys as well as their father. Ralph looked over his shoulder at his mother before turning back to his Robert.

'Goodbye, Ralph,' FitzStephen managed, though his mouth filled with blood almost immediately and forced him to heave.

'Be brave and take care of your brother. Remember that you are from a great Norman house,' he said. 'Find your uncles in Pembroke and remember: a coward dies daily. A brave man dies only once,' he added, rather more dramatically than he had wanted. He wished he had spent more time getting to know Ralph, a good boy who worked hard to please both FitzStephen and his mother.

Ralph nodded blankly. 'Yes, Sir Robert,' he said before blinking twice and running off to join the column that moved nervously into the town through the charred remnants of the buildings. They quickly passed beyond FitzStephen's view.

'Protect my family,' he prayed, 'please protect Ralph and little Geoffrey.'

Richildis' face appeared from under the flap of leather which covered the one of the carts which were going with the Norman column.

'Robert!' she mouthed silently. Beneath the wimple her face was dark with bruising and tears but FitzStephen could do nothing for the Norman beauty now. She cried more tears for him and all he could do was tilt his head in her direction before she was gone with the rest of the army and all of his possessions. He had loved her, he thought, just as he had loved Mahel and countless other beautiful women beforehand. Despairing, FitzStephen wondered if they had really had that much affection for him. He tried to dispel his depressing thoughts but his mood darkened further when Roger de Quincy wandered towards him eating an apple and leading Sanglac, FitzStephen's courser. At Quincy's side was FitzStephen's sword, made by a famous smith in Gloucester for the knight who had trained him, Sir Henry FitzRoy. Quincy noticed FitzStephen's eyes on the sword and began examining its scabbard as he stood at his enemy's side.

'*A brave man dies only once.*' He read the inscription and laughed as he looked down on Robert, bound and filthy at his feet.

FitzStephen looked away, unwilling to suffer his enemy's ignominy. After a couple of bites of the apple Roger gave the core to the small, tough horse. He then began staring at

FitzStephen, licking his fingers.

'I think I will rename him,' his enemy said. 'Sanglac is so old fashioned and these are new times – perhaps a more poetic name that will impress the troubadours at the Angevin Court? Certainly I will choose something so … how do I put this? So damn Norman.'

FitzStephen kept his eyes firmly locked on the ground. How dare Quincy touch Sanglac, he fumed. He had spent years training the horse to ride up to a shield wall without shying away in fear. He hated the loss of his half-brother's sword but Sanglac was even worse. The courser was as important to him as his castle and it was devastating to see him accept Quincy as his new master so quickly.

'Well, Sir Robert, I am sorry it has come to this,' Quincy began again, 'but it was the only way to get out alive from this unfortunate situation. A situation that you caused, I should add.' He raised his hand at two men at the castle's entrance, who removed the cross-beam and pulled open the gates. The archers marched out of the fortress in good order, but gingerly, their hands fingering arrows at their belts as if they expected mischief at any moment. They at least were unwilling to trust the Welsh and FitzStephen felt a pang of pride at their attitude, despite their wanton treachery.

Quincy sighed at the lack of reply and mounted Sanglac, turning him towards the gates. 'Goodbye, Sir Robert,' he said with a shrug, 'we will not meet again in this land, or this life.'

'Where is my esquire?' FitzStephen asked grudgingly and desperately, as though the pain of speaking was almost too great. His young half-brother, William, had not been seen since the confrontation in the donjon.

Quincy's face contorted with triumph as if his words had provoked FitzStephen. He smiled evilly, but then seemed to relent with a shrug. 'He scarpered through the postern gate as soon as they saw us enter the keep this morning,' he said. 'The little bastard will get caught by the Welsh soon enough. And then?' he said dragging his finger across his throat, 'you know what will happen.'

Despite Roger's malevolence, FitzStephen was delighted

that William had got away. He had taught him well enough and the sixteen-year-old would be alright, he decided. His half-brother had been taught to speak the Welsh tongue by Stephen's wife after Robert's own mother's death, and FitzStephen was sure that skill alone would see William safe to Pembroke.

'When my brothers hear what happened here, they will find you and kill you,' FitzStephen shouted at Roger's back. 'And if not, I will not be a prisoner for ever and I will come for you.'

Quincy laughed as her turned his horse towards the prisoner. 'I doubt the FitzGeralds will have much time for vendettas, or for negotiating your release now that Aberteifi has fallen. They stand alone in Pembroke against all the might of Wales.' Roger said. 'Rhys will attack their little fortress come spring and it will fall, FitzStephen, just as Carmarthen, Llandovery, Llansteffan, and Cilgerran have fallen,' he shook his head almost pitiably. 'Me, I will go to my father's house in England, or perhaps our lands in Normandy, so your ghost may seek me there,' he said with a smile. 'Why did we ever come to Wales?' he reflected. 'It never does anything but rain and there is no culture, gold, or silver. How can any man make a fortune here? From coal?' Roger shook his head slowly, the sunshine glancing off his helm and into FitzStephen's eyes. 'No. Better to go to Aquitaine or Normandy and fight a proper battle on horseback instead of running around in the hills with no hope of profit.'

FitzStephen stared up at Quincy, who looked back as if the young man still wanted his approval. The traitor realised what he was doing and changed his tack.

'I have saved the garrison,' he said. For good measure he spat on FitzStephen from his seat in the bucket saddle and kicked Sanglac into life with his heels. FitzStephen watched as his enemy rode through the gates with the last of the Norman men-at-arms, his sword, his dogs, his woman, his sons, and his horse. Soon he was alone in the fortress.

Struggling, he desperately tried to free his hands from the ropes that bound him but the knots were too tight and he had lost all feeling in his hands which had been strung above his head for too long.

'C'mon, you bugger,' he snarled as he fought against the ropes. He let his head drop against the whitewashed wall of the guardhouse when his efforts failed, and said a long prayer to St Maurice, his family's protector. 'Bring my prayers to God and the saints, Blessed Maurice,' he whispered towards the sky, 'save me from this unkind fate. Send providence,' he begged. 'I know that I have not always been good,' he shook his head, his words failing him.

The Norman army was barely out of the gates when two Welsh warriors came through, one armed with a spear, the other with a bow, arrow already on the string. They stalked through the town, ducking into buildings and searching for any Norman chicanery. Once every building in the bailey had been investigated, one of the Cymri jogged over to FitzStephen, chattering in his own language and poking Wulfhere's body with a spear. Shouting back over his shoulder in the same tongue, he signalled for more men to enter the fortress. Moments later a number entered under the barbican. All were heavily bearded and wearing short woollen shirts and cloaks. Over these they had strapped the weaponry and armaments of Norman warriors who had fallen in the fight in town. The steel looked grand against the tribesmen's dull clothing. One of the men wore a fantastic necklace of precious beaded stones which FitzStephen was sure he had seen hanging from a Norman knight's neck before the battle. The gaudy piece now adorned his killer's neck.

'I don't understand,' he said as the Welshman began prattling directly at him, pointing at the keep. But the Norman could not understand his thick accent so he shook his head and shrugged his shoulders. He gasped in fear as the warrior suddenly began hacking with his spear tip at the ropes that held FitzStephen's arms aloft. His limbs fell to his sides as soon as they were free, suddenly painful as the blood returned to his extremities.

More Cymri were coming through the gates with carts and materials. He wondered what all the activity was about and again speculated about what would become of his late father's castle. He had failed Stephen and he sent another short prayer heavenwards in apology.

These thoughts soon left him as he was unceremoniously dragged to his feet and poked with a spear until he shuffled agonizingly towards the gates. FitzStephen snarled at his new guards who cracked him on the side with the shaft of the spear, laughing together as they cracked a joke in barely intelligible Welsh. He cursed angrily in French at the Welshmen and limped his way through the gate and over the footbridge into the village.

Here, before the gates of the castle, was where he, or a trusted lieutenant, had held court once a week. The king's writ did not apply on the March, for one there was no way to enforce his laws, and like all the Marcher Lords FitzStephen had made his own edicts which lurched between the traditions of England and Wales. Court had been the best weekly entertainment and a large crowd had always gathered on judgement days to await his sentences. It was no different today though only one prisoner would be brought before the townsfolk to be judged. And the charges against him were lengthy.

Hundreds of men, women, and children were standing watching as the naked FitzStephen was coerced over the flooded fosse and into the soggy ash-strewn and muddy street. His guard barked something at the crowd and they separated, letting FitzStephen walk forward between the two banks of people, desperately trying to hide his nakedness with his hands. Somewhere in the throng someone shouted and everyone laughed. He knew the joke was at his expense, despite not speaking the language, and he felt the anger rise, but before he could react his guards hit him with their spear between the shoulder blades. He crashed forward onto his hands which were buried up to his wrists in mud from the rain and ash from the fire. He had barely put his hands to the ground before they were kicked from under him and his guards forced FitzStephen to crawl into the town through the filth. The Cymri mocked and jeered his slow progress and his shivering, caused by the cold November weather rather than fear.

It was agony and he fell forward onto his face several times until his guards stamped and kicked him into action. Each time he scrambled to his knees reluctantly and continued his way, too tired to fight them off or even shout. Boys ran up and down the street alongside him, feeding off the excitement and ridiculing the Norman further. He had never been truly aware of the true depth of hate that the Welsh felt for him or his people. He thought that he had been a fair lord – far more even-handed than the greedy local chieftains – but the animosity in the eyes of those in the town frightened him. Madness had taken the Cymri, he knew as two teenage girls dashed out of the screaming throng to spit on his back and slap him on the back of his head.

The crowd divided as he crawled onwards funnelling him towards a large house at the far end of the street where a Welshman called Jasper ap Gethin lived. As he often was, Jasper, who made honey mead, had been away on business in Cemais and Emlyn when the Welsh had attacked Aberteifi. His wife was not so lucky and her naked body lay face down in the doorway of their thatched cottage. Jasper and his wife had lost three children when a pestilence had come to Aberteifi during the summer and FitzStephen wondered silently if the two remaining girls had survived the siege.

In front of the house several men waited like a jury waiting to give their verdict. FitzStephen noted that each one of them had well-fitting armour and weapons, and were arrayed in the Norman style, in the red and white livery of the lords of Deheubarth. One was lazing close to the door with his leg flung over the arm of his chair. FitzStephen wondered if it was his cousin Rhys and if he would be the man to kill him. There was no other way that he could see this scenario ending. He had murdered Rhys' nephew and he had defied his conquering army.

The lounging warrior inclined his head and shouted over his shoulder into the house in Welsh before taking a long drink from his cup. Behind him, FitzStephen could feel the crowd circle around behind him, facing the stage. His guard turned to the crowd and waved a hand to hush them. Their talking slowed from a murmur to a whisper to nothing at all as they anticipated action. Seconds passed before a thin man came out of the house reading a piece of parchment. He was small, dark, and clever-looking, with his forehead wrinkled in concentration. He stepped over the naked body in the doorway without pausing or even noticing it was Jasper's wife. Without raising his head to greet the crowd, the man walked straight up to the prisoner and stood before him, his eyes never leaving the parchment.

FitzStephen bristled and clenched his jaw as he looked at the man before him. It was the same man who had had spotted during the initial fight for the town. On his knees in the cold street, FitzStephen was panting heavily, his lips moving minutely in prayer, eyes open and unblinking and staring at the man who continued to read the piece of vellum. Agonisingly close and threatening, FitzStephen could not help but measure up the man. He was wearing expensive, though ill-fitting, lamellar armour, while at his side was a long sword, too long to his trained eye and it had no dents on the grip. This was no warrior. Behind him, FitzStephen could feel the crowd tense as they waited for the man to react. He could feel their collective menace; they all wanted blood, his blood.

Suddenly the man rolled up the piece of parchment and stuffed it into his belt. He looked down at FitzStephen for the first time. The Norman was determined to meet his gaze with his one good eye, but found it difficult, whether because of his injuries or because of the power of this man, he could decide. He examined FitzStephen quickly before he raised his head and began speaking to the crowd in harsh Welsh which FitzStephen could not decipher. The man's voice was quite high-pitched, but strong like that of a monk used to speaking to large crowds. There was no fear in his tone as he pointed to the Norman at his feet and suddenly snarled at the mob. An unseen member of the crowd spoke back to their lord and several words of agreement from the gathered masses added to the general mêlée of sound. Prince Rhys answered straight away, raising his voice at the end until he was shouting at the crowd, but not angrily – it was if he was trying to convince them to follow his plans. FitzStephen gnawed on the inside of his mouth, desperate to know what was going between them but only able to understand words here and there: *death*, *glory*, and *blood*. Behind Rhys the Welsh noblemen listened intently and FitzStephen's eyes flicked between the men in a frantic attempt to read the situation. Their stern brows gave nothing away.

Then the crowd grunted a reluctant but unmistakeable affirmation of whatever the Welsh leader had decided. For a few seconds there was silence and FitzStephen swept from face to face of the warriors before him. Each set of their eyes were now looking at him with fury. FitzStephen had seen that look a thousand times. It was the grim appearance that every man shared when he desired death of an enemy. FitzStephen began panting again and praying out loud:

'St Maurice protect me, St Maurice protect me,' he panted through gritted teeth. His time was up, he was sure of that now, and he began praying louder, his breath a steamy cloud before him.

Prince Rhys drew his sword and, standing in front of FitzStephen, he looked balefully into his eyes, daring the Norman to plead with him for his life. The Welsh leader did not blink as he hefted the long sword over his head, holding it precariously above his head for the stroke that would take his life. FitzStephen was more angry than terrified but he could not stop himself from staring into Rhys' eyes, willing him to get it over with: 'Kill me, damn it,' he said. 'Come on, you Welsh whoreson, kill me!'

Moments passed as the standoff continued before Rhys blinked abruptly and brought the sword swiftly downwards with a shriek. FitzStephen closed his eyes at the very last instant waiting for the pain and the darkness. But the death blow never came as Rhys purposely buried the weapon in the mud to FitzStephen's left. The Norman heard the sword strike the ground and knew he was alive. Gasping, he fell onto his side, away from the blade with sweat streaming down his face. He had no more energy in him. This traumatic day had truly beaten him now and he was simply calm. He rolled onto his back, caring not whether they killed him or let him live. Either outcome seemed as bad as the other. Around him the Welsh crowd laughed and mocked FitzStephen as he lay naked in the mud, caked in ash and surrounded by enemies.

Rhys was laughing too and leant down beside FitzStephen.

'Hello, cousin,' he spoke in French for the first time. 'I have absolved you for the sin of murder.'

Relief flooded through FitzStephen, and he hated himself for the thanks he murmured to his *saviour*.

'But you are still over-proud, a philanderer, and the product of adultery,' Rhys continued, 'and for that you must be taught a lesson. But as for the invasion of my country,' the Welsh prince said signalling back over FitzStephen's head with a lift of his chin, 'consider us even.' He stood and walked back towards Jasper's house.

The Norman rolled onto his right shoulder and looked back at his father's castle. There was heavy smoke pouring out of windows in the donjon while flames licked the roof of every building in the bailey. The smoke drifted westwards and for the first time he heard the faint crackling of wood aflame.

Sir Robert FitzStephen was twenty-eight years old and everything he had, and everything he had ever promised to become, was gone. Norman rule in Ceredigion had faltered and all Wales lay open to conquest.

# Chapter Three

## *Laighin, Ireland*
## *1166*

Five men stood on the bare hill looking across the heavily wooded valley towards the great fort of Fearna. Their long hair and beards looked ragged as the wicked wind swept westwards, revealing their saffron hose and shirts beneath dull-coloured cloaks. The large stone building in the centre of the rath was aflame and smoke plumed from the reedy thatch towards the sky, where it was lost against the low shapeless clouds. Even the heavy tree-trunk palisade and grassy bank were smouldering and curling grey and white in the heat.

The five watched as fugitives streamed from the fort, down the steep hill, and into the surrounding fields towards the woods. More hopelessly tried to gather their horses and cattle and move them out of range of the fire and the threat posed by the foreign warriors. They would not get far with the rich prizes. But it was not a cattle raid that the five warriors led. This was a venture of vengeance against one man. And now they found that their quarry had fled his lair.

'God damn him!' Tigernán Ua Ruairc snarled. His one good eye shone terrible with rage and spittle foamed down his grey beard. 'Where is he?' he pointed accusingly at Muirchertach Mac Murchada. 'You said he was here,' he screamed. 'Where is he? Where is Diarmait?' The King of Breifne was almost screaming as he stomped across the long green ridge towards his enemy's brother.

Muirchertach shook his head nervously, gesticulated at the rath and stumbled over the words which he hoped would calm the anger directed against him. 'I, ah, he was definitely ... I don't ...'

Tigernán was Diarmait Mac Murchada's most fervent enemy and had sworn to have his revenge against the King of Laighin whatever the cost. His scouts had been the first to get to the fort earlier in the day and had reported back to their king telling him that Diarmait had set his home on fire and had fled; to where they did not know. Tigernán had been unwilling to believe it until he saw the flames with his own bloodshot eye.

'God damn that treacherous bastard. He has gone!' Tigernán screeched the last sentence, his voice almost distraught with rage. 'He is gone,' he wailed like a dog wolf.

'Do calm down, Tigernán,' said the young High King of Ireland, Ruaidhrí Ua Conchobair. The golden adornments at his wrists and neck jangled as he shook his head disapprovingly. How he wished that the old man would act his age rather than throwing a tantrum. Tigernán Ua Ruairc's passion for retribution against Mac Murchada was useful, even understandable in the circumstances; Diarmait had abducted Tigernán's wife fifteen years before, making the King of Breifne a laughing stock throughout the many nations on the island. However, Tigernán's constant tirades about his vendetta against Diarmait did become tiresome after a while. Sometimes Ruaidhrí wondered if his anger against Mac Murchada was all that kept the seventy-year-old Tigernán alive. It was funny that the few times that Ruaidhrí had met Diarmait Mac Murchada face to face he had been immediately reminded of Tigernán Ua Ruairc. He would never admit as much to his ally but both men were so alike, both revelling in argument, invigorated by confrontation and energised by enmity. Despite the Ruaidhrí's words, Tigernán climbed onto his shaggy horse for a better view, craning his neck to its greatest extent, as if he would be able to locate the man who had cuckolded him. He signalled one of his tribesmen forward from the trees.

'Catch one of the fugitives,' Tigernán ordered him, 'and find out where he has gone.'

Ruaidhrí Ua Conchobair held up a long, thin hand to stop the man. 'There will be no need for that, thank you. Think, Tigernán,' he urged his ally. 'Where can he go now that he has burned Fearna?' Ruaidhrí asked, ignoring the anger and

76

snarling energy that exuded from his ally. 'This was Diarmait's only fortress. His people have abandoned him. So where would he go?'

The question seemed to confuse Tigernán and he went silent. He was unused to being asked for his opinion by the clever, young High King who now stared at him expectantly. Tigernán shook his great shaggy head as he considered Ruaidhrí's question. He pointed across the trees that stretched between the hill and Fearna towards the building in the belly of the valley. 'Hiding in the monastery?'

Tigernán's attempted answer received a scornful look from his overlord. 'The Augustinians would not give succour to a man like Diarmait,' Ruaidhrí told his ally. 'They are scholars and would never hide a wolf like him amongst their flock. Remember what he did to the Abbess of Cill Dara?'

Tigernán again struggled with the question. 'To his abbey at Bealach Conglais?' he attempted a second time. 'Or south towards Waesfjord?'

'Ha!' The King of Mide snorted a laugh.

Tigernán turned angrily on the man who had offended him with his scorn. 'Shut your face, Ua Mael Sechlainn, unless you want it slapped off. If you are so clever how come I have been able to thieve so many of your cattle this summer?' The old man coughed as he spoke the last words. King Diarmait Ua Mael Sechlainn snarled and looked as though he would round Ruaidhrí and attack Tigernán, but the High King was fastest and calmed the situation with a raised hand.

'No, Tigernán,' Ruaidhrí said sternly, slapping his thigh like he was scolding his hounds. 'The Ostmen of Waesfjord hate the Meic Murchada and will not give him shelter. He will have to go elsewhere.' Ruaidhrí did not elaborate immediately and an exasperated Tigernán physically struggled to keep his composure.

'So where the blazes is he going to go?' he finally demanded. Ruaidhrí did not answer straight away, ignoring Tigernán's restless squirming and scanning the scene that extended out before him. Behind the smoke from the burning buildings he eyed the line of the River Bhanna, clothed in deep

77

green foliage, which joined up with the River Sláine far to the south and flowed all the way through the Uí Ceinnselaig tribal heartland to the great city of Waesfjord. That fortress was held by the descendants of the heathen invaders, who the Irish called the Ostmen. A ready escape route, but Diarmait was far too canny to allow his people to be surrounded and if he led his people to Siol Bhroin where his only real allies ruled that is exactly what would happen. No, Diarmait would not allow that, Ruaidhrí decided. He considered that his enemy may have tried to escape to the west. His son-in-law was King of Tuadhmumhain and would have given the King of Laighin shelter. That thought scared Ruaidhrí Ua Conchobair. He hated Domhnall Ua Briain more than any other chieftain, for he was his main rival for the high kingship. An alliance between his two bitterest foes was certainly concerning, but as Ruaidhrí looked to the west he knew it was unlikely that Diarmait would have taken that route; the great forest of Dubh-Tir, menacing and dark on the steep slopes of the Black Mountains, Na Staighrí Dubha, was a daunting obstacle to any westward journey. And beyond those natural barriers was the kingdom of the Osraighe and Donnchadh Mac Giolla Phádraig, Diarmait's rebellious under-king. If he got his hands on the King of Laighin, well that didn't bear thinking about, Ruaidhrí thought with a shiver. That way was certainly blocked to Diarmait Mac Murchada. It was to the east that Diarmait would flee, Ruaidhrí decided. From there he would go north into the mountains to where the Uí Tuathail ruled. An assault on that sparse and terrible terrain would be nigh on impossible for Ruaidhrí's alliance, no matter how strong they were. He turned to Tigernán, who had been waiting while his ally observed the terrain.

'They will go towards the mountains, of course,' the High King told him, nodding and lifting his chin in their general direction to the north-east, 'and they will be safe there unless we can get to them first.'

A slow, malicious grin slowly broke from behind Tigernán Ua Ruairc's heavy beard as he began to understand. 'A chase?' he asked happily.

Ruaidhrí Ua Conchobair nodded. 'Kill Diarmait when you find him, Tigernán,' he said. 'He has betrayed my trust too many times. Kill him and anyone that you discover with him.'

Tigernán lifted his chin and barked a venomous yelp of victory towards the clouds. He then shouted at his derb-fine, his closest family and best warriors, who waited unseen behind the bluff of the hill. Hidden amongst the trees was a horde of grey- and black-clothed fighters from all the tribes of Connacht. Several of the derb-fine wheeled their horses around and screamed orders at the army, pointing swords and spears to the north-east. Hardened warriors from the far-off country of Breifne, armed with swords, spears, shields, and slings, detached themselves from the main group and started running through the trees. Armourless, they would be fast over the rough terrain and vicious to anyone that they encountered.

Tigernán turned back towards Ruaidhrí. 'I will go north then. Keep some of Fearna's plunder for me,' he shouted and then he was off, his rugged horse cantering, the one-eyed king bouncing on its bare back, feet gripping awkwardly to the horse's sides for balance. From the dark trees emerged a thousand warriors, most on foot but some, the Uí Ruairc derb-fine, were on horseback.

Ruaidhrí Ua Conchobair turned his back on Tigernán as he and his warriors disappeared beyond his view around the shoulder of the sloping hill and into the depth of the forest. Tigernán would not stop until either he or Diarmait was dead, of that he was sure.

'Why did Mac Murchada burn Fearna?' Hasculv Mac Torcaill asked in his strangely accented Irish. His Ostman forefathers had fought against the armies of Brian Bóruma, the last Irishman to claim to be High King of Ireland. Yet here the King of Dubhlinn stood beside his natural enemies, dressed in heavy links of steel and iron, alongside the latest claimant to be Lord of Teamhair na Ri.

*How times have changed*, thought Ruaidhrí. Back in Brian's time, a century before, the Uí Conchobair had only been in control of a tiny tuath but now only Diarmait Mac Murchada and Domhnall Ua Briain stood between Ruaidhrí and his ultimate goal of the unopposed rule of Ireland. He had already been crowned High King on the ancient hill fort of Teamhair na Ri but he wanted more – to hold the title without challenge and bring the whole island under his rule.

'He burned Fearna because he didn't want us getting our hands on his riches,' Muirchertach Mac Murchada, Diarmait's brother, answered Hasculv's question with a grimace.

Ruaidhrí doubted the accuracy of Muirchertach's response, but said nothing. Both Ruaidhrí and his father had invaded Laighin before and had defeated the Meic Murchada. Yet both had believed Diarmait's promises, forgiven him his many transgressions, and had left him in power. Always, they had been betrayed. But not on this occasion, the High King thought. This time he would kill Diarmait and force Laighin to pay such a heavy tribute that they would be unable to leave their toil in the fields until the day of judgement. They would be incapable of raising a sword against him if their backs were broken by work. Diarmait must have known that the jig was up this time and guessed that Ruaidhrí would place his own man in his seat of power. That was the real reason Diarmait Mac Murchada had burned Fearna – it was a statement which said that Diarmait would rather destroy Laighin than have it controlled by any other man than himself. It was a concept that was alien to Ruaidhrí Ua Conchobair for despite being a successful king who had won countless battles, he was naturally a man who loved peace and wanted to inspire friendliness amongst his subjects; up to a month ago the King of Mide and Tigernán Ua Ruairc had been sworn enemies, but he had made them allies under his rule. In truth, Ruaidhrí had never had to fight an enemy on a level pegging as his political skills meant that he had always been able to raise huge armies from the tribes under his rule. Most of the time he didn't have to fight at all – the majority of chieftains surrendered before the huge power which he could muster. And now Ruaidhrí saw Laighin as another potential ally, strong in warriors, to take on Domhnall Ua Briain and to make his dominance of the island complete, but it would not happen if Diarmait remained king.

'When your brother is dead,' Ruaidhrí Ua Conchobair said

towards Muirchertach, 'you will be King of Laighin.' He held
Mac Murchada's eye meaningfully, waiting for the old man's
answer. Ruaidhrí knew exactly what his response would be.
Muirchertach was the church's price for the disposal of
Diarmait. His ally started to mutter his thanks to his new master
but Ruaidhrí held up a hand to stop him, 'You will be king but I
want hostages and a tribute of two thousand head of cattle every
year. Do we have terms?'

'Two thousand cattle?' Muirchertach stammered. It was a
heavy tribute even for a rich kingdom like Laighin, but there
was no other way that he would ever be king. The law said that
any great-grandson of a monarch could take the kingship if the
derb-fine elected him. However, Muirchertach knew that the Uí
Ceinnselaig had already chosen his nephew Eanna as heir to the
kingdom of Laighin.

Ruaidhrí seemed to read his mind: 'Don't worry about the
derb-fine; they have abandoned Diarmait and I have your
nephews, Conchobair and Eanna, as hostages. With your
brother gone I need someone sensible to lead your people,' he
said encouragingly. 'Will you do it?'

'I will agree,' Muirchertach said quickly, 'if you give me
Conchobair and Eanna.'

Ruaidhrí knew what that would mean for the two young
men. Blinding or castration was the best method to stop
potential challengers to any king's power. Ruaidhrí had used
these techniques himself when his younger brother, Aodh, had
thought to force Ruaidhrí to concede half of Connacht after
their father died.

'No,' Ruaidhrí told Muirchertach, 'Conchobair will stay
with me and Eanna will go to the Osraighe.'

'To the Meic Giolla Phádraig?' The Osraighe were the
traditional enemies of the men of Uí Ceinnselaig, a constant
threat to the security of Laighin, and even a traitor like
Muirchertach hated them.

Ruaidhrí ignored the disgust in his question. 'Donnchadh
requires some bartering power.' He paused and put his hand to
his chest. 'Hadn't I already told you?' he said sweetly.
'Donnchadh will be taking some of Diarmait's lands –

everything west of the Sláine and between the Corock and the Urrin Rivers should suffice. He has been a good friend to me and needs to be rewarded.'

Muirchertach opened his mouth to protest but a single challenging look from Ruaidhrí made him shut it again. Diarmait's brother may have won the throne of Laighin but it had just cost him a third of the Uí Ceinnselaig heartland. Muirchertach knew that things were starting to slip away from him but he was left with no choice other than to accept them. Blinking widely and breathing out deeply he turned back and stared at the burning embers that was the rath where he had grown up alongside Diarmait. It had been a bountiful harvest, thought a thankful Muirchertach, and it would need to be if he was to pay off the heavy tribute demanded by Ruaidhrí and leave him with enough to survive the oncoming winter. He ran his long, bony fingers through his beard. As if the weather sensed Muirchertach's plummeting mood it began to rain. Little spits splashed against the new King of Laighin's face as he looked up to see the lines of dark clouds clash against each other to the east. Then the rain began in earnest. Down on the fields, Muirchertach watched the people of his own tribe try to beat their animals towards the heavy woods that covered most of the countryside. They would have a chance of survival if they reached the woods ahead of Ruaidhrí's Ua Conchobair's army.

Beside Muirchertach, Ruaidhrí Ua Conchobair shouted over his shoulder towards his own derb-fine. Drawing his sword slowly he grinned at Muirchertach and the other kings. 'We didn't come all this way for nothing,' he said with a smile. 'Prepare to attack but ensure your men stay away from the monastery. I won't have that sin on my conscience.' Behind the High King a host of Irish warriors yelled and pushed forward as one like a flocking of birds heading south for winter. They sought blood and tribute from their enemy. Ruaidhrí tapped his heels to his horse's flanks and lurched forward with a smile on his face. He had defeated Diarmait Mac Murchada and Ireland was almost his alone.

Even from a mile away Diarmait Mac Murchada could hear the screaming and he revelled in its sorrow, laughing until it wrenched a harsh cough from his lungs. He could picture the warriors of Ruaidhrí Ua Conchobair streaming down the hill like ants towards the defenceless people of Fearna who had betrayed him, and he cackled a cracked chuckle at the thought of their demise.

His son Domhnall stirred uncomfortably beside him and murmured a prayer. The younger man was restless and nervous, and his father could tell that he did not like hiding from his enemy. His son had only recently returned from his fosterage at monastery of St Caomhan and had picked up some bad habits in his father's opinion.

'Are you angry that I shouted at the friar, or that I didn't go north like you wanted?' Diarmait asked his son.

Domhnall considered the question. 'I'm angry that you burned Fearna,' he replied. 'I'm *uneasy* at going to ground so close to the fortress. Ruaidhrí is certain to look for us here.'

The King of Laighin hissed a laugh in response.

'And the monks are bound to suffer,' he said though under his breath for he knew his father would consider any sympathy for the clerics as a weakness and would scorn him.

Domhnall prayed that his father was right. It was too late to flee, and even if they could Domhnall was not sure where his family could go. Diarmait's friends had frittered away like swallows with winter upon them, and those who had not fled his father's side to support Ruaidhrí Ua Conchobair had stayed away altogether. Diarmait only had a hundred and eighty warriors left and he had arrayed them around the monastery ready to give battle to the death should the need arise. But for some reason, either through trust in God or information that he had not shared with his son, Diarmait was supremely confident that Ruaidhrí would not find him in the monastery.

It started raining suddenly and heavily, and Domhnall watched as the smoke cloud lifted up from behind the tree-covered hill that hid his childhood home from sight. A great alder stood on the grass lawn just yards away and rainwater trickled down the rivets of grey bark and spilled from green leaves onto the stony ground. The two men were standing under the intricately carved triangular stone gateway to the grand Augustinian monastery and the smoke and light from the fire illuminated the great swirling scenes from the Bible that had been carved above the entrance. Depictions from the life of Saints Mary and Aodhán were given life by the dancing flames that engulfed distant Fearna. The great oak door stood open and a smell of hot oatmeal porridge drifted out, earning hungry glances from Domhnall.

'The monks have hidden me when I was at my most vulnerable,' King Diarmait told his son after taking a long slug from a skin. 'Thank God I was good to this holy house when I had the opportunity to be. You should learn from my example, boy. Found a monastery and put someone you trust in place as abbot. Maybe your boy, Domhnall Óg.' He nodded at the teenager who was fighting with his brother, Conchobair, in front of the chapterhouse.

'Ruaidhrí may still come to the monastery,' Domhnall answered, ignoring his father's words. 'We should leave as soon as possible.'

'Ha!' his father scorned. 'I doubt Ruaidhrí would even consider that I would hide here. Our enemy shows the church too much respect. His mistake,' Diarmait added. More screams pierced the austere atmosphere at the stone edifice and Diarmait again chuckled heartily behind his heavy grey beard. He shook his long hair of rainwater. 'They thought Ruaidhrí Ua Conchobair would treat them fairly if they got rid of me,' Diarmait said of his own tribesmen. 'Well that'll teach the traitorous shits.' His voice was hoarse, as though he constantly needed to clear his throat.

Domhnall gave him an anxious look which his giant of a father ignored. Even to his son, Diarmait's features were stern, terrible, unforgiving while his light blue eyes were alive with energy. Domhnall knew what type of man Diarmait was, just as well as those poor people who died amongst the trees. But Domhnall had little sympathy. By refusing to fight, they had forced Diarmait Mac Murchada to flee and the homes of the Uí Ceinnselaig had been left defenceless. Despite his misgivings about his character, Domhnall knew that his father was the only man who could tie together the bonds of the tribe and defend the Uí Ceinnselaig from those who would seek to destroy them. He was strong and sought advice from no man. Domhnall hoped he had that same strength of character, but for now he would be what his father needed him to be: loyal. First the Meic Diarmait had abandoned him to support Ruaidhrí Ua Conchobair, then it was the Uí Gormain and soon after that news had arrived that the Uí Dimmussaig and Uí Faoláin had joined the King of Connacht against their lawful lord. As far as Domhnall knew, only the weak southern chieftains Cearbhall Ua Lorcain and Colmcille Ua Dubhgain had refused to join up with the invading Ruaidhrí Ua Conchobair, but neither had they sent any warriors to protect Diarmait. Worst of all was the perfidy of the Uí Brain. Exiled from their ancient home in the north by the Uí Faoláin, Diarmait had received them with great honour and had given them land to call their own. Yet they had been amongst the first to answer the High King's call.

Just inside the monastery, Aoife and her elder sister Sabh were crying into Diarmait's senior wife's shoulder. When they finally lifted their heads, Domhnall could see damp imprints of both girls' faces left on Mór's expensive woollen clothes by their tears. Domhnall knew that Sabh was probably crying because of the fear of the approaching army, but Aoife was much braver and Domhnall recognized that his youngest sister's tears were for their lost position and possessions, their former lives which were gone.

A rustle of leaves heralded the arrival of Máelmáedoc Ua Riagain. He ran out of the downpour with seven warriors armed with spears and wicker shields. Máelmáedoc trotted up to the two men and panting for air, greeted his king.

'Diarmait,' said Máelmáedoc with a nod, 'I need to speak to you,' his eyes flicked to Domhnall Caomhánach and back to Diarmait, 'alone would be better.'

'Domhnall,' said his father, 'get your boys inside and take Aoife and Sabh to get some grub in their bellies.'

Máelmáedoc gave Domhnall a grin like a victorious older sibling would have done and, as he walked back through the

85

archway into the monastery, Domhnall heard Máelmáedoc and Diarmait begin confiding secretively. He had never liked Máelmáedoc Ua Riagain; he was nobody, a simple spearman from a minor tuath who Diarmait had raised from nothing to be his chief advisor above his brehons and his derb-fine. This should never have happened, and it was one of the indictments that the people of the tribe had placed at Diarmait's door. Every position in Ireland, from king down to farmer, from bard to spearman to slave, was hereditary under the law and Máelmáedoc's usurpation of authority had ruffled many feathers in Fearna, especially amongst the *Filid*, the poets and lawyers who kept alive the tribe's traditions. Lacking their assent, no man could hope to hold the power of the Uí Ceinnselaig without opposition.

Outside, Diarmait barked another laugh in response to Máelmáedoc's news and Domhnall roughly cajoled his sisters, stepmother, and sons through the doorway into the monastic building. The friar of the house, Cillian Mac Giollagáin, stood with some of his brother monks in their dark robes, eager to please their generous benefactor. They all bowed to Domhnall before realising that he was not their king. One of the monks looked hungrily at Aoife who, if anything, looked more beautiful as she angrily swiped the tears from her face. She was embarrassed that the monks should see her cry.

'What?' she demanded of the monk when she spotted him gawping at her. The man bowed his tonsured head and scampered away. Aoife then threw a similar look at Domhnall, daring him to offer her pity for her tears. Instead, he looked up the aisle to the transept and circular chancel where the friar would lead the brothers in prayer many times every day. Beams of light poured in through the high windows and danced off the intricately carved stone curves of the nave. It all added drama to the spiritual setting and Domhnall felt compelled to murmur a short prayer to Our Lady. He thought St Mary's beautiful and he knew that his father was extremely proud of the monastery, which he had built so close to his own fortress. Domhnall's stomach grumbled loudly and he quickly signed off from his message to God with the sign of the cross. Surely, when said in such a place his prayers would be answered and his family delivered from the brink of destruction.

The kitchen was on the far side of the cloister. As he began to shepherd his sisters across the aisle and through the nave in that direction, Domhnall's father called his name and that of Friar Cillian. Domhnall made the move towards the doorway immediately and obediently while the friar stared up at the great silver cross at the far end of the nave.

'They went for it, the stupid bastards,' the King shouted as his son joined him outside. He was delighted and his blue eyes shone below the overgrown grey and unkempt hair. 'Máelmáedoc says they think we have gone north. They have already sent warriors to catch us.'

Domhnall smiled and congratulated his father. 'So what happens now? Are we bound for Tuadhmumhain like we discussed?'

Diarmait stared back at him with a wry grin. 'No, my boy, we are going to a place that they will never ever consider,' he said. He turned on Friar Cillian. 'Tell him what you told me.'

'Yes, of course.' Friar Cillian paused and tapped the ends of his fingers together before starting to speak. 'Last year I was sent on pilgrimage to our brothers of the Cistercian Order in Mellifont Abbey in Aírgialla ...'

'He banged a Norse whore in Waesfjord,' Diarmait butted in and the monk's face bright red in embarrassment, 'in his cell and had to scamper before the bishop caught him.' He laughed harshly. Máelmáedoc politely joined with his mirth.

'Even the Blessed St Augustine himself had a son with Floria Aemilia ...' started Cillian, looking up at the doorway and waving his hand to indicate the stone carving which portrayed the eponymous patron saint of his order.

'Was that before he took his vows or after?' Máelmáedoc asked calmly. Friar Cillian's eyes widened as the layman called his bluff. He looked like a spearman but Máelmáedoc Ua Riagain was in fact a voracious reader, employed as Diarmait's secretary and translator but in reality much, much more.

Diarmait laughed and signalled the Augustinian Friar to continue rather than argue the point. 'Better a whore than a boy,

Friar.'

'Anyway ...' the embarrassed monk started as he attempted to compose himself. 'You may remember that Mellifont was founded by the Holy St Máelmáedoc who, twenty years ago, was ordered by Bernard of Clairvaux to found a church for his new Cistercian Order of St Benedict ...'

'I remember the stories,' said Domhnall, his long wet hair striking his back as he spoke.

'While I was at Mellifont, I was the guest of the old abbot and we grew to be friends,' Cillian continued. 'One night after prayers he told me what St Máelmáedoc had told him: that it had not been a pilgrimage that took him to Rome but a mission to inform the Pope of the degradation of the Irish Church,' Cillian looked contritely at his hands which were folded in front of his dark clothing. He bowed his head so that Domhnall could see the tonsured back of his head. 'And perhaps he was right,' the friar said. 'For too long we had been isolated from the rule of the Holy Father in Rome. For too long we had governed ourselves, making decisions beyond our capacity. Moral and spiritual laxity was ignored and allowed to spread over the years.' Friar Cillian seemed angry at the accusations even if he knew that they were correct. 'Laymen had come to the forefront of many religious houses,' he gave Diarmait a nervous look, 'bishops married and begat children who in turn assumed their positions like mere poets, smiths, or princes,' he shook his tonsured head. 'The good work we were doing was forgotten. That was the report that St Máelmáedoc brought to the Holy Father in Rome,' he continued, 'and Pope Innocent ordered changes to be made. You remember that a Synod was called at Kells organized by the Blessed Máelmáedoc.'

'The four archbishops and the thirty-six sees,' Diarmait answered as he recalled the event. Synods were uncommon and the last one had abruptly changed the entire makeup of the Celtic Church. The upheaval had been felt by everyone.

'Indeed,' the Friar continued, 'but then Pope Innocent went to paradise, as did the Cistercian Pope Eugene, and reform on our island was forgotten. It was only when a Norman of England from my own order came to the Papal Throne that the

Celtic Church was remembered again. Pope Adrian had heard the stories of the decline of the Irish church and even claimed that we had reverted to paganism,' he managed a laugh. 'He wanted change –'

'He wanted our tithes,' interjected Máelmáedoc Ua Riagain.

'He wanted to bring the Church back into the loving embrace of Rome,' Cillian told him sternly, 'and he had just the man to do it. Henry FitzEmpress had brought order to England after twenty years of anarchy and theft from the Church. The Pope *gave* Laighin, Mumhan, Tir Eoghain, Mide – all the lands of Ireland – to Henry and his heirs if he could push through the church's reforms. They say that he even gave him a Papal Bull and an emerald ring to confirm the grant. That was just twelve years ago.'

'I don't understand,' Domhnall said to his father. 'What has any of this – the Synod, Henry of England – got to do with us?'

The King of Laighin smiled. 'Do you remember the story of Mac Con of Munster?' Diarmait questioned his son.

'No,' Domhnall answered.

Diarmait shook his head as he turned towards Máelmáedoc Ua Riagain, 'What type of history are they teaching youngsters these days?' He turned back to his son. 'Mac Con was defeated at the Battle of Cennebrat,' he said to Domhnall, 'and fled to the land of the Scots. He returned later with an army of mercenaries and at the Battle of Magh Macruimhe he won back his kingdom.' He paused and raised his eyebrows expectantly at his son. When Domhnall did not answer, Diarmait continued to speak: 'We will do the same as Mac Con except we are going to England to the royal court of Henry FitzEmpress to seek Norman mercenaries. As you have heard, he has had his eye on Ireland for years,' Diarmait told his son. 'But he has never had the chance to do anything about it because he is always at war with his subjects and the King of the Franks. So in return for warriors, I am going to give him Ireland.' Diarmait was quivering with anticipation, gripping and re-gripping his fists as he gestured towards his son.

Domhnall looked from Diarmait to his secretary to Friar Cillian and back again. '*Give him Ireland?*' he repeated.

'Yes,' Máelmáedoc Ua Riagain smiled evilly, 'we will journey to England to talk with Henry and do homage to him for all of Laighin, just as the Holy Father demands.'

'But ... Henry is a ... a ... foreigner,' Domhnall exclaimed. He was dumbfounded; all the tribes of Ireland had stood behind Brian Bóruma when he led a crusade to expel the Ostmen from the island a hundred and fifty years before. Everyone knew that Ireland had never recovered from that war and Laighin, who had supported the Ostmen, had taken the worst of the damage. Now his father was suggesting bringing more foreigners to the island? Domhnall couldn't understand Diarmait's decision, and he would made his opposition known had not his father interrupted.

'Henry of England or Ruaidhrí Ua Conchobair, what does it matter who calls himself high king?' Diarmait snapped his fingers in front of his son's face. 'Not a tot. But unlike Ruaidhrí, Henry, at least, won't be sitting on our bleeding borders, threatening us with attack every summer. He has other enemies to fight, beyond the sea, and we will be left alone to rule as it was before.'

Domhnall supposed that it was true and opened his mouth to speak but Máelmáedoc Ua Riagain butted in, 'Henry will give us warriors and ships the like of which you have never seen.' The glint in his eyes confirmed to Domhnall that it had been his plan to approach the English King. 'My father helped the Welsh fight against these Normans in his youth. He said that the very earth shook beneath them as they charged and it took five men to take down just one of their horse-warriors. They are the best swordsmen that he ever saw,' Máelmáedoc continued with a grimace. 'But they have one weakness – land.'

'They crave it like clerics yearn for women,' Diarmait joked. Beside Domhnall, Friar Cillian stirred uncomfortably, squeezing his lips together tightly. Diarmait laughed heartily at the joke and Cillian's reaction.

'Mercenaries?' asked Domhnall and Diarmait nodded. 'So we bribe the Normans with the pasture lands of our enemies if they help Diarmait retake Laighin?' His father nodded his head. 'Well that means taking to the sea,' he said with a frown.

Domhnall had never considered leaving his home. He did not want to leave, but if his father demanded it then he would see it through. 'So when do we sail?' he asked.

'We are going south, Domhnall, through the forest of Dubh-Tir to the River Corock,' his father told him. 'Máelmáedoc Ua Riagain has a boat waiting for us.'

Domhnall gritted his teeth. 'Four days' travel? I'll have the provisions and horses ready for first light.'

'Already done,' Máelmáedoc said as he turned and walked away with his bodyguard. 'We leave in five minutes.'

'Five minutes?' Domhnall exclaimed, realising immediately that Diarmait and Máelmáedoc had been plotting this voyage for some time. Why had his father not included him in the plans, he wondered. He opened his mouth to speak but Diarmait pre-empted him.

'You are staying here, Domhnall,' Diarmait told his son, placing a hand on his strong shoulder. 'You are my last son free to help me now that Conchobair and Eanna have been taken prisoner.' He bowed his head to hide his anger. 'I need you here to protect our interests and make sure the people know that one day soon I will return to take back what is mine.' In any other man it would have seemed heroic but, coming from Diarmait, his promise to return to his homeland was simply intimidating, even to his son.

'Diarmait,' Máelmáedoc came back and handed him a monk's robe which he threw over his head. Máelmáedoc did the same. Domhnall looked at them confused until his father's advisor winked at him from underneath the pointed hood of the Augustinian robe. 'Just in case,' said Máelmáedoc.

'We have a hundred and eighty warriors left,' Diarmait continued, also clothed like a monk. 'You will take a hundred and twenty deep into Dubh-Tir where you will hide out and take control of the Uí Ceinnselaig after Ruaidhrí and his army go back to Connacht.'

'I will,' said Domhnall, surprised and suddenly proud that his father had confidence in his ability to lead. He had commanded large raids before but never been trusted with so many warriors alone. He knew he had been set an impossible task but already his mind was plotting how to use the soldiers successfully in the coming months. To conquer the tribal lands of the Uí Ceinnselaig would take a thousand spears, he thought. Re-taking Laighin could take ten times that number.

'Máelmáedoc Ua Riagain, myself, your sisters, and my wives will go to the town of Bristol,' he struggled with the unfamiliar word. 'I have a friend there called Robert FitzHarding. He will help us.' Diarmait pulled the monk's hood up onto his head so that it obscured his eyes. 'God be with you, my son,' he said sarcastically with a malevolent smile and his hands open in prayer, 'or rather, good hunting.' He slapped him on the back and pushed past him into the rain.

Beyond the departing Diarmait, between the tall alders and the edge of the gateway, Domhnall could still see the smoke from the burning hall at Fearna drift over the land of Laighin. For just a moment Domhnall had been convinced that Diarmait knew what was best for his country but the smoke said otherwise. It was indicative of Diarmait's determination to hold onto his kingdom no matter the cost. And now it meant leaving his home and his eldest son behind to become an exile. Domhnall looked up to see Diarmait heave himself into the saddle of a waiting pony and ride off into the trees. With a wave and without a backwards glance, Diarmait Mac Murchada, the deposed King of Laighin, was gone.

## Chapter Four

### *Llandovery, Wales*
### *1166*

'God damn it all to hell and curse the bitch who bred me,' Sir Robert FitzStephen groaned and rolled onto his back as he awoke. Stretching out his legs and arms, he panted sharply and coughed as he lay in his bed. Wincing and groaning he snapped his legs back up to his chest and breathed hard, as though he had just fought all day in full armour. 'I swear that I will never drink again as long as there is breath in me,' he gasped, peeling his eyes open one at a time to let in the early morning light that found the cracks in the window shutters and bed curtains. FitzStephen breathed out forcefully as if it would rid him of his headache which thudded like a sword blow ringing a spangenhelm. The smell of stinking Welsh ale engulfed him and he retched, but nothing came up. He seemed to remember vomiting in the darkness as he had stumbled through the great hall, making his way back to his room in the early hours. *What I would give for some good French wine or Norman honey mead rather than that horrible Welsh muck*, he thought.

The heavy embroideries that hung on the stone walls of Llandovery Castle seemed to spin before his eyes but, with a concerted effort, FitzStephen was able to hoist himself up onto his elbows and so look at the girl who lay asleep beside him, covered by a woollen blanket to protect her against the Christmas cold.

*She looked better last night*, he thought as he examined her in the semi-darkness. She was younger than him, probably twenty-five, rotund with black hair and a pale, slightly unhealthy look. As he turned his head back he glanced at his own sizable belly. He grimaced and he quickly threw the corner of the blanket to cover his lower half, embarrassed at how he had let himself go in the two years since the capture of Aberteifi.

'Oi, you there,' he croaked towards the woman. He was hoarse from singing too many songs with Rhys' warriors after their lord and his family had retired to the solar. He coughed and tried to speak again: 'Hey, time to go.'

The woman stirred but did not wake up so FitzStephen cleared his throat a second time and poked her pudgy, naked shoulder with his forefinger. Again this did not wake her so instead he whistled sharply as though she was one of Prince Rhys' hunting dogs.

'What? What's wrong?' she asked.

Without answering, FitzStephen climbed out from beneath the blanket and, pulling the bed curtains open, wandered naked over to get himself a mug of cider. The coarse liquid was warm but he did not care and drained the mug with two swift gulps.

'It's time to go back to the pantry before they miss you …' he said, pausing awkwardly as he searched his throbbing head for her name, 'Gwen-do-lyn?'

'My name is Gwen,' she stated as she swung her legs over the edge of the bed, shivering against the cold morning air, 'as I have to tell you every time you sober up.'

'Gwen? Surely you are the beauty Gwenhwyfar come back to earth,' said Robert yawning and without sentiment.

Nevertheless Gwen giggled at FitzStephen's gallant reply, oblivious that his habitual charm was shorn of feeling. She pulled her grey woollen shift over her naked breasts as she sat up in bed. 'Well recovered, Sweet Tongue. I suppose if I am Gwenhwyfar that makes you Arthwyr?'

'No, but he is of course my ancestor,' he replied with a wry grin hidden from the woman. He shook his head sarcastically as he remembered Rhys' audacious claim of their descent from the famed warrior. He may have scoffed at Rhys' ludicrous assertions, but FitzStephen privately wanted them to be true. Few could declare descent from such prestigious and noble lineage. Arthwyr's songs were being sung as far away as

Gascony and Languedoc in southern France, encouraged, it was said, by England's queen, Eleanor of Aquitaine. She was the talk of all Christendom since her divorce of the King of France to marry Henry FitzEmpress, the lowly Count of Anjou who had later become King of England. The couple were said to encapsulate the growing fashion of courtly love, romance, and chivalry, revelling as they did in the arts, religion, manly pursuits, and goodliness; a veritable Arthur and Guinevere. Robert had met King Henry and could think of no man less romantic and chivalric than the invidious, squat monarch.

As he pulled on his hose FitzStephen remembered that it was St Stephen's Day and he said a short prayer to acknowledge that great holy man just as his half-brother Bishop David FitzGerald would have wanted. *Drinking on Christmas Day? Having carnal relations with an unmarried woman?* Bishop David would have given him a sermon which would have left his ears ringing. Eleven hundred and sixty-six years had passed since the birth of the Saviour and Robert FitzStephen prayed that it wouldn't nearly so long for his hangover to clear. He made towards the small window to get some fresh air. Behind him, Gwen pulled her leather sabatons onto her feet and stood straight beside his bed. She put her hand on her hip and raised an eyebrow.

'Are you sure we could not just stay here today?'

'I'm going hunting,' FitzStephen said without turning around to look at her. Opening the shutter, he looked out on the morning. It was cold but promised to turn into a beautiful day despite the light shower of snow that swept across Deheubarth. He burped and tasted alcohol, venison, and vomit, so refilled his mug with more warm cider and took a long draught. 'Isn't it time for you to go?' he asked the girl who still lingered beside the bed.

'Can't you leave hunting until another day?'

'*Qui m'aime, il aime mon chien,*' he told her with a shrug.

'What?' she asked. 'I don't speak Saesneg.'

'An old proverb,' FitzStephen said without elaborating or correcting her that it was the French tongue. He opened a small scroll and began reading a passage about St Jerome, hoping that she would get the message and leave. Surprisingly, reading had come quickly to FitzStephen. His teacher, Brother Meilyr, was supposed to have been teaching him humility through God's words, to make him understand his great sins, but those lessons had been incomprehensible to the illiterate FitzStephen and so the monk had begun the laborious study of letters. A study of FitzStephen's soul had never started, for it became quickly apparent to his teacher that any investigation to that end was pointless.

As he read St Jerome's words, Gwen stared at the Norman warrior's back. She liked FitzStephen, and knew she was not alone among Prince Rhys' serving girls in that respect. Merwyn had scorned and reviled the Norman warlord when he had first arrived in Llandovery, two years before, but she had still ended up in his bed just a few weeks afterward his coming. He had not been with Merwyn for a long time now, not since she had given birth to his bastard, Maredudd, and this had allowed Gwen to become his latest fancy. He had been lean when he arrived in Llandovery, Gwen recalled. His years spent fighting and hunting on the Welsh March had turned any of his soft edges into solid muscle. However, she had watched as the subsequent years of inactivity, as well as his fondness for drink and good food, had piled the weight on. All the servants whispered that he liked his drink too strong and too often. Bored, Hywel the steward told them all, bored and going to waste. He had warned them all to stay away from the Norman, though Gwen knew it had not stopped Hywel himself from enjoying FitzStephen's company when at his wine or dice.

Despite his flaws, Gwen thought him a good-looking man, probably inheriting his looks from his famously beautiful mother who had even had a former King of England as her lover. His heavily accented Welsh was endearing too, she thought. He drank, hunted, and joked with the Cymri, and he had quickly learned their songs and poetry. Some of Prince Rhys' noblemen even considered him to be a friend, a surprise after years vying against him across a shield wall. The murder of Einion ab Anarawd was long forgotten, it seemed.

FitzStephen cleared his throat expectantly and continued to

read from the vellum scroll.

'Fine then, I'm off,' she said. 'I'll see you tonight?' she asked as she pulled the dark oak door open.

'Of course you will,' he said, leaving her with a flash of a smile as she left the room. Alone, he immediately let St Jerome's words tumble to the table-top and turned back to staring out of the window, looking down on the bailey and the top of the stone fore-building. The countryside beyond was a patchwork of greens and whites, hills and snow, sparse trees and rivers. He closed his eyes as another wave of nausea hit him. The noises which stirred throughout the household told him that the castle was wakening and that the first meal of the day was being readied. In the distance bells called brother monks to the mid-morning prayers and he inhaled heavily, slapping himself four times in his bearded face in time with the tolling. The stink of lovemaking and alcohol was all over him. He would have bathed, but the Cymri had turned the castle's old bathhouse into a chicken coop. He did not enjoy the thought of a dip in a frozen river and, with a pre-emptive shiver, decided that he would put off his wash for another few days.

He was lost in his thoughts until he spied ten esquires lead a mottle of horses from the marshalsea and into the bailey below him. Immediately he realised that the rugged mounts were being saddled for war and that the esquires' steeds had provisions hanging from their flanks. A raid was being prepared! He sank the remainder of the cider in one and grabbed his clothes from the table. The embroidery at the neck of his red winter shirt snagged painfully for a moment on his beard before it pulled on. None of his former compatriots in Aberteifi would have recognised him now; his blond hair was long and he had grown a full beard. Visitors thought him no different to the other Welsh nobles that came to pay homage to Prince Rhys in Llandovery. His father would have said he had gone native and that thought sometimes made FitzStephen wince. He fixed his shirt at his waist with the leather belt which his cousin had given him. The buckle was brass and heavy and was adorned with a bear design – Arthwyr's symbol. *Would the man never give up*, he thought as he wrapped the long length of leather beyond the buckle to secure it, letting the excess hang down to his knee. From a basin in the corner he wet his hands and ran them through his hair, pushing it out of his eyes and hooking the long blond strands behind his ears.

Outside the shuttered windows, he could hear the horses neighing and whinnying excitedly as they heard their masters' approach. FitzStephen began to hurry. Their leader would be getting his men ready to leave and he did not want to miss them. He was more excited than he should have been at the thought of a simple Welsh raid. He could not help but wonder what their destination would be? Cardiff, Brecon, or Striguil were all within range, but FitzStephen thought that the Flemings at Haverford, or the Normans of Pembroke, were more likely targets. It was so long since he had been allowed the ride to war and he ached to be involved, no matter how small the part he could play. Above him, he heard Prince Rhys and his wife bump around on the oak floor of the solar as they too rose to greet the winter's day. FitzStephen's eyes floated towards the sound coming through the thickset timber floorboards.

Grabbing a heavy dark cloak from behind the door, he stepped out of his room and made his way down the winding stone steps towards the great hall. Twice he stumbled as he forgot the uneven steps in the stairway. The oak door to the great hall felt heavier than usual as he pushed through. Inside castle servants were busying themselves with the readying of the prince's first meal of the day. FitzStephen spotted Hywel the steward at the far end of the room, attempting to coax more life from the fire, and FitzStephen quickly and quietly made his way across so as not to be seen by the servant. His winnings from playing dice with Tewdwr, Rhys' son, had paid off some of his debt to the steward but FitzStephen still owed Hywel a huge sum and the Norman doubted that the bald Welshman would accept any more excuses for non-payment. He crossed to another door on the western wall and forced his way through onto another set of twisting hard steps just as Hywel turned and shouted his name. He did not turn to respond or to stop.

The guardroom was on the first floor above the kitchens. It

was empty as he crossed towards the mighty castle door which divided the main keep from the stone fore-building. No-one expected an attack on the feast of St Stephen and so the main gate was left ajar to allow easy coming and going into the castle. The cold air from beyond soothed FitzStephen suddenly, as it drifted through the iron-embossed door. Ornate and adorned with heavy iron hinge joints, the gate had been blackened with paint by the castle's former castellan, Walter FitzPons de Clifford and his coat of arms still festooned the wall above the door. The portcullis was open too but he could still see the lower edge of the criss-crossed steel armament in the ceiling above the door, hidden between the thick walls. His leather-wrapped feet slapped noisily upon the stone floor as he stomped into the fore-building. A cold wind whipped him as he ducked through the outer door and turned left along the castle wall and down the stone, sloped and icy pathway to the bailey floor. There, he greeted a few men in the group of Welsh warriors who were making small talk while the final preparations were being made before their departure. Jealousy coursed through him as the horses nervously circled with their riders on their backs. He hated not being able to ride out on a raid himself and it was accentuated by the memories brought forth by the sounds, smells and excitement of these metal clad warriors readying themselves for war.

'Tewdwr,' FitzStephen waved to a man in the colours of Deheubarth who had just clambered into the saddle. His horse stamped brightly, circling on the hard ground, as Prince Rhys' eldest son turned to greet his cousin.

'Robbie Boy!' he exclaimed. 'How's the greatest drinker in Wales? I bet you have a sore head this morning?' he asked cheekily.

'Every morning,' FitzStephen replied, matching Tewdwr's smile, 'but luckily we Normans have bellies lined with chainmail.' He slapped his stomach with one hand and caught hold of Tewdwr's horse with the other. 'Where are you headed, cousin?'

'Why? Do you fancy a jaunt at our side?' Tewdwr asked mischievously. 'I'm sure we could make room for you but you might not be able to keep up with us.' With a grin he nodded at FitzStephen's sizable midriff.

The Norman snorted at the levity and shook his head. 'I wish I could go too. I would consider it if you were going north but ...' Robert trailed off.

'But you don't want to run into any of your relatives and have to bash their heads in.' Tewdwr had heard his cousin's stance many times, but did not completely understand it. He personally had no qualms about attacking his Norman cousins or indeed his Cymri kinsmen in Morgannwg, Glywysing, Brecon, Gwarthaf, Pebidiog, Powys, and Gwynedd.

But FitzStephen was a man torn away from all that he knew, abandoned amongst his enemies; enemies who were also family. His life had become a hellish mix of confused loyalties and frustrating inactivity since his incarceration in Llandovery. In England or France, a captured knight was automatically afforded the right of ransom, if he was a nobleman or had rich friends willing to stump up the cash for his liberation. Sir Maurice FitzGerald, Robert's half-brother, had sent an envoy to Llandovery with a very generous offer, but no ransom had come from his lord, the Earl of Hertford, or King Henry of England. That had stung FitzStephen's pride.

In any event, Tewdwr's father had not wanted to release the dangerous Sir Robert FitzStephen back onto the March. The Norman was a man about whom strong men gathered and awaited adventure. Since his fall, the invaders had no-one to lead them and Rhys was not about to hand back that advantage. The prince had no doubt that once back amongst the Normans FitzStephen would continue to have misgivings about fighting his family and, just like before his capture, his Welsh cousins would feel the full force of his revenge.

'So,' FitzStephen asked Tewdwr, 'where are you going? You can tell me. It's not like I'm going to tell anyone.'

To Tewdwr, Robert sounded like one of his younger brothers; hungry for information and longing for the day that they too could share in the adventure.

'We're headed towards Penfro,' Tewdwr confirmed finally, using the Cymric name for Norman Pembroke. 'Miles

Menevensis has been pushing north from Pebidiog and needs to be given a good beating and sent home with his tail between his legs.'

Miles was FitzStephen's nephew, the illegitimate son of his half-brother, Bishop David FitzGerald. His brother's bastard had become a talented fighter since his own incarceration and led the bishop's troops in defence of Wales' most holy site at St David's. He had also become a constant pain in Rhys' arse from what FitzStephen had heard.

'And have no doubt,' Tewdwr raised his voice so that his men could hear, 'we will find the bishop's son and chase him back to St David's so his daddy can make it all better.'

FitzStephen smiled, but listening to Tewdwr's answer made the old hatreds threaten to rise. The Welsh lordling was just a child, yet was leading raids against the Normans for his father while he, a professional warrior, was left to rot behind Llandovery's walls. He quickly swallowed his anger as best he could, 'Good luck, Tewdwr, don't go too hard on my nephew.'

Tewdwr laughed and then waved towards a pretty woman who giggled with her friends from the door of a building beside the stables. She was the daughter of the castle's cooper.

'I had her for the first time last night,' Tewdwr admitted quietly to FitzStephen. 'For luck and all that,' he shrugged and blushed. 'A second-to-none set of legs on her though,' he laughed nervously.

FitzStephen snorted. 'I never worry about their legs. They are the first thing I throw out of the way to get down to the proper business.' The horsemen nearest to Tewdwr overheard the exchange and giggled at FitzStephen's jest, teasing Tewdwr by poking him the arm.

'I heard your little lady has seen more pricks than an archer's target,' he said.

'It's Gwyl San Steffan, Tewdwr,' FitzStephen told the beardless boy. 'Custom insists that you give her a good spanking with holly branches.' Everyone laughed again. Holming was one of the traditional practices of St Stephen's Day when Welshmen would beat their female servants, and late risers, with branches. An odd tradition, FitzStephen, an outsider, thought.

Despite turning even redder, Tewdwr laughed along with his troops and pulled on his chainmail hood, which he fixed with a leather cord at the back of his head. 'Last chance to come with us, Robbie Boy,' he said from beneath his chain mail as he placed his circlet helmet on his head.

FitzStephen smiled and let go of Tewdwr's bridle, allowing his cousin to wheel his horse towards the main gates. 'Perhaps next time,' he said with a forced smile.

Tewdwr ap Rhys shrugged and grinned, happy to be in command. 'Let's get going, lads, we have a lot of ground to cover,' he shouted to his men-at-arms before delivering a final big grin to FitzStephen and setting his horse into a trot towards the gate. His warriors wheeled their horses, the shake of brass and steel trappings ringing like a bell in his memory, the clip of hoof a drum in his chest.

'It's hard to see them grow up and leave the nest,' a voice spoke behind FitzStephen just as Tewdwr disappeared through the gates and into the snow-bound countryside. The voice belonged to Prince Rhys, swathed in a cloak edged with fox fur and a heavy gambeson cap. Small snowflakes flurried down the walls of Llandovery around him, sticking to his beard as he walked gingerly down the walkway towards the bailey floor where FitzStephen stood.

'You didn't come to see Tewdwr off?'

Rhys shook his head. 'We said our goodbyes last night. His mother was tearful and I didn't want to embarrass him in front of the men with a similar episode,' he said with a slight shake of his head, 'and after Maredudd ...' Rhys tailed off with a wave of his hand towards Tewdwr's troop. Another of the prince's sons had been a hostage of Henry of England before he was blinded in a vengeful attack by the King shortly after the capture of Aberteifi. It was a disgraceful episode that went against all the codes of chivalry – codes which Henry was supposed to champion. 'Well, Tewdwr has got his chance now,' Rhys continued with a smile as he stared out over stone walls onto the grassy fields where his son's conrois of shaggy horsemen were slowly following the course of the River Bran southwards. 'Our dear cousin, the bishop's son, has been causing problems around Carmarthen. I would go myself but I think it is time that Tewdwr took on some responsibility.'

FitzStephen huddled his arms around his chest for warmth against the cold wind. 'He has a few sensible men in his conrois that will keep him right. He's confident and is determined not to let you down. Tewdwr has a good head on his shoulders.'

'Let's hope that's where it remains,' Rhys joked lightly. 'It could be you riding out you know,' the prince said as he turned to face the Norman, lifting his eyebrows 'You trained those men. It should be you leading them. I offer you greatness, wealth, and land if you would but forsake your father's people. I offer you redemption for Einion's murder if you will only join your mother's folk.'

'Safety in return for allegiance,' FitzStephen replied quietly, his lips grinding together. 'Salvation for a broken oath?'

'An oath to an absent Saesneg king,' Rhys returned. 'I need you, Robert. I need your skills. I need your experience to win my war against England ...'

'You have had my answer,' he snapped. 'I assure you that it will not change.' No matter how often FitzStephen dreamed about breaking his loyalty to King Henry, it always came back to one thing. 'I won't fight against my brothers,' he told the prince sternly.

'But you will fight your cousins – your mother's people?' The smaller man turned towards him. Reaching up, he put his hands on FitzStephen's wide shoulders. 'You are as much a Cymri as you are a Norman,' Rhys appealed, 'it is in your blood to fight for us. Holy God, will you continue in this horrid state forever? Getting drunk, womanising?'

'I am not Cymri, I am ... something else,' he said, feeling his frustration and anger rise. Rhys' offer was at once tempting and repellent. Simply, Rhys wanted FitzStephen to abandon his loyalty to the King of England and fight for him to free Deheubarth, Dyfed, and perhaps all Wales from the dominion of the faraway despot. FitzStephen could think of nothing he would rather do; he hated Henry of England and would have done anything to hurt him – Henry who had interfered and then abandoned the Normans of Aberteifi; Henry who demanded obedience and offered nothing in return; Henry who had forsaken FitzStephen to imprisonment. He let the now familiar anger rise in his chest. Had he not saved Henry's army on Mona? Had he not saved his very life at Coed Ewloe? Who else could have held Ceredigion as long as he had done in the King's name? What the hell did a man have to do to get some support and loyalty in return from his ruler? His father, Stephen, had been right – you can't trust any of that devil's brood from Anjou. During his time as Constable of Aberteifi FitzStephen had told himself that he was performing a duty for his king, but Henry had not even bothered to offer a ransom for his loyal subject. Henry had abandoned FitzStephen to his enemies. FitzStephen knew that if he fought for Rhys he would be joining the winning side in the conflict. For eighty years the Normans had been carving out lordships for themselves in Wales, but that expansion had come to a shuddering halt during the anarchy of King Stephen's reign and with Rhys of Deheubarth at the forefront of the fight the Cymri had been resurgent ever since.

But could he do it? Could he fight against his own people? The answer came to FitzStephen immediately. Rhys was a good man and he had enjoyed the company of the Cymri during his imprisonment at Llandovery, but he could not join a fight where he could only end up on the opposite side of a shield wall to his half-brothers Maurice, David, and William, and his Geraldine nephews and cousins who served them. His situation was hopeless, frustrating, and all-consuming, and Robert FitzStephen could see no way to escape it. He was surrounded, assailed from all sides by boredom and frustration, guilt and confusion. It was humiliating and he was going mad trying to fill his day, only looking forward to drinking and gaming when the warriors finished their duties. It was childish to be having this resentment pumping through him and he knew he was in a rut, but he could see no way out of it. Disgust kept him from thinking too deeply at his situation while boredom constantly pushed him towards those dark thoughts. An emotional war was being waged inside FitzStephen, one which he was ill-equipped to understand.

Rhys reached out to him. 'Reconsider, cousin!'

'You know what I want,' FitzStephen snarled angrily as he shook off his cousin's hand. 'Let me take the cross and go to the damned Holy Land. Let me fight the Saracens.' This was the last hope. It was a long shot of course, but many footloose and desperate men had crossed Europe to Outremer. Most were younger sons looking for employment, some for religious reasons, but many simply for the excitement, fighting, and opportunity for plunder. FitzStephen's reason was escape, and he was willing to trust in his skills with sword and steed to earn him reward in one of the Christian kingdoms in the east. 'I could do penance for my sins at Rome, Constantinople, and Jerusalem,' he appealed to Rhys' devout leanings. 'I could be forgiven by the Holy Father himself!'

The Prince of Deheubarth was too much of a realist to be influenced by FitzStephen's toadying. 'You know I can't allow you to go without some guarantee that you will not come back six months later to give me problems,' FitzStephen began to speak but Rhys spoke over him. 'I have learned that I cannot trust any Norman, not just you, Robert, and not just because of Einion,' he paused and shook his head. 'And how would you get to Jerusalem? How can you afford such a journey? Do you expect me to fund the voyage? Perhaps you want some of my men to accompany you?'

'I don't want any of your troops,' FitzStephen protested. 'I can borrow money in Gloucester. I know a Jew there who would loan me the money to arm myself.'

'A Jew?' The prince shook his head. 'You should not consort with moneylenders, Robert.' Rhys shook off the snow that had gathered on his shoulders. 'And I am sure you would not take any of my troops deliberately, but many of my warriors would follow you to the Holy Land nonetheless. You still don't understand the power of your name on idealistic young men who think that you, the great knight, will make them rich in Jerusalem on some grand crusade. Tewdwr, my own son, would follow you on your adventures,' the prince of Deheubarth told him as he wrapped the heavy cloak around his chest more tightly. 'I can ill afford to lose any of my warriors at this time, and I still think I can convince you to join me in my adventure.'

'I can't stay here, cousin.'

'But you will nonetheless,' Rhys slapped him on the shoulder and started climbing the stone walkway to the donjon, past a page who struggled towards the kennels with two massive alaunts. Both dogs snarled at FitzStephen as he raised a finger to point at Prince Rhys' back.

'You heard what the priests said during the summer, Rhys. King Amalric needs knights to fight this Saracen General Nur ad-Din and his nephew, Salah ad-Din. They need help now! Edessa has already fallen to the Muslims. I could make a difference in Jerusalem. I could be given forgiveness by the Pope himself, damn you!'

Rhys did not even bother turning around to answer but continued trudging up the steep stone slope towards the main gate. 'I am sure that Jerusalem will stay Christian for a long time yet, Sir Robert. We have been there for a hundred years and my bet is that we will be there for another thousand. God has willed it, has He not?' As he passed into the fore-building Rhys stopped and turned to point his own finger at his cousin. 'And stay away from my serving girls. I can't afford to have any more away from their work having your bastards.'

FitzStephen did not smile. Rhys knew what he was doing if he was still punishing him for his past misdemeanours. His cousin could have locked him up in his oubliette two years ago and thrown away the key, allowing him to die slowly in horrid conditions. He might have executed him back in Ceredigion. But he had done neither of those things. Instead he had allowed him to exist in wretchedness. FitzStephen had been abandoned by his king and his lord, separated from the security of his brothers, betrayed by his warriors, and left as a landless failure. He was adrift and alone. He could try and dull the darker spells with drink, women, gambling, and hunting, but he knew that nothing could dispel those depressing thoughts other than keeping his mind and body active. And what whetted FitzStephen's appetite was the business of conquest, plunder, and the command of warriors.

'*Satan makes use of idle hands*', that was what FitzStephen remembered his brother, David, telling him when he was just a boy, and the Bishop of St David's was right. He automatically dropped his hand to his waist where his sword should have been hanging, but it was not there. He closed his eyes and shook his head. He needed a drink. He needed a woman. He needed something to take his mind off his depressing situation. Instead he turned to an esquire who was crossing the cobbled and muddy bailey holding a saddle.

'Get me a courser saddled,' he told the boy. 'Tell Prince Rhys I am going hunting and he is welcome to join me.'

The stag was the biggest that he had seen in his life. An eighteen-pointer with white muscled haunches that took him through the frosted stream like it was not even there. Up the sandy bank the hart raced, through a gorse bush and out of sight of the pursuing lymers, whose tongues were already lagging out the side of their mouths.

'C'mon,' FitzStephen breathed hard, a lungful clouded before him on the cold winter air. The cloak-swathed Norman pulled on his reins with his one free hand and brought his mare to a standstill on the snowy bank of the stream. Swinging his horse around, he searched through the snow-strewn conifers for his companions. He could not see them, but shouted back to the group of hunters hidden amongst the trees. 'Over here, it's a big one. And it's white!'

A white hart was rare, and possessed a special, almost mythical, significance to the hunter. To catch such a beast was to be considered among the greatest in a famously tough sport, and would give the successful hunter his place in the songs of poets and minstrels in every noble home in Christendom.

The ignominy of defeat, FitzStephen thought, would not taste so foul if it were followed by the roasted flesh of the white stag. He would be lauded for his skill rather than derided for his failures. Yet the animal was proving a difficult prey. Forever moving in circles rather than taking a panicked flight away from the pursuers, he had caught only passing glimpses of the stag's white flank as he gave chase. But he refused to give up.

He swivelled in the saddle and spotted the coloured surcoats and billowing cloaks of Rhys' group as they pushed through the heavy foliage across the small valley. He could hear the men encourage their horses onwards as they fought to defeat the terrain and follow their prey. FitzStephen and the hounds had stretched their lead over the pursuing group quickly, both man and beasts having become lost in the excitement of the sport. The Norman, hood blown back in the wind, had forced the jealously of Tewdwr's departure, and his own dark mood, to the back of his mind. Instead he concentrated on the pursuit of the great stag. Below him, the dogs circled around his stationary mare. Scent hounds all, their noses were close to the hard earth as they sought sign of the stag. His mare pulled on her bit in frustration at the hold-up, but the dogs soon caught the scent and, with a happy bark, forged ahead through the icy water and up through the tangle of branches on the far side. FitzStephen tarried just a moment before he urged his mare over the brook with a double click of his tongue. The water surged up the flanks of the courser, powering against his legs in the shortened stirrups. In battle, he preferred to have the stirrups as long as possible so that he would not lose his seat when striking downwards with a sword or spear. But the pursuit of the hart needed the manoeuvrability and comfort of the shorter stirrup which allowed him to cushion the impact of heavy riding with his knees. The water was both deeper and colder than expected but within moments FitzStephen was encouraging the mare up the steep bank with his heels so that his pursuit could continue.

'C'mon,' he cheered her.

His dogs had gone through the same gap in the gorse and brambles that the stag had used, but FitzStephen was forced to skirt the heavy undergrowth which, even still, snagged at the edge of his cloak. On the other side he jumped a small ditch and both man and horse grunted on the landing on the frozen ground. His horse began her heavy snorting again as she powered behind the lymers. FitzStephen chanced a look over his shoulder and caught another sight of Rhys and his retinue puffing up towards the stream, at least a quarter a mile behind him. Could they see him? He did not particularly care if they did catch up. Rhys was being far too jolly for FitzStephen's mood, more interested in recanting tales from his successful campaign in the south than the business of hunting. The Cymri, while not averse to taking part, did not view the hunt as a serious piece of strategy, more a fun romp of an afternoon. Needless to say, FitzStephen, like most Normans, considered it to be much more than that, and not just because he had little else to take up his time. In its truest form the hunt had eight parts: the quest, assembly, relay, finding, chase, baying, unmaking, and curée. The quest was where the seeker and lymer stalked prey and preceded the assembly when the huntsmen listened to expert advice before deciding how to best bring their quarry down. This was normally done over food, drink, and lots of laughter but FitzStephen had been infuriatingly forced to forgo these important sections by Prince Rhys. The relay part of the hunt saw dogs positioned along the predicted course so as not to exhaust the animals that would eventually chase and take down the hart. The main aim of the hunt, no matter what the beast, was to force the prey to decide that he could not escape and thus would have to turn and fight. It made sense that when that happened the dogs had to be fresher than the hart. Again Rhys had not understood the need for relays and had forced a frustrated FitzStephen to do without the necessary planning, but he was not in the mood to quibble even over something he considered so vital. This was because the hunt proper followed the relay: the finding, when the dogs got the scent of the hart on their nostrils, and then the chase. FitzStephen considered this part of the hunt to be the best fun a man could have outside the bedroom, but it was not the last piece. The baying was when the hart could run no longer and would turn and prepare to defend itself to the death. Usually the hounds were kept away from the scared animal, and the most prominent man from amongst the hunters would creep forward like a gladiator of Rome and make the kill with spear or bow. The hunt ended with the unmaking. Lastly, the dogs were rewarded for their efforts with pieces of meat and body parts that would not be used for the feast.

There were eight parts to the hunt and they were the one set of conventions that Sir Robert FitzStephen had always held sacred. He was a master of the strategy.

FitzStephen and his party had made their way through the forested foothills to the north of Llandovery. The Norman knew the countryside as well as anyone and it was one of his favourite places for the pursuit. Initially Rhys did not allow him out into the countryside alone, lest he escape, and had supplied him with two guards whose companionship FitzStephen had quickly learned to begrudge. He had subsequently ended his rides into the hills. But during the hunt he could pretend that his guards were simply his fellows partaking in good sport. He could pretend he was free and at ease.

Running hard now, FitzStephen could feel that his courser was as keen as he to prolong the chase and he loosened the reins slightly while keeping his leg on, maintaining the mare's speed. Ceredigion had been awful country for hunting; its bare hills had given no natural cover for deer. It had been a good place for hawking, but not for the pursuit. FitzStephen wondered if this stag was from the royal herds originally bred by William the Conqueror in Cheshire. Perhaps it had strayed from the former Montgomery lands around Shrewsbury? He certainly had not heard of any herds west of Hereford.

As he jinked around a small wooded hillock, he momentarily lost sight of the hounds and slowed to a trot while he searched the trees with his ears and eyes. The bow, unstrung at his shoulder, got caught in some branches above him. It gave him a painful thud in the side of the head as it came free and sent a sprinkling of snow down his back. He had become quite proficient with the weapon during his captivity, although he would never have the skill of those who grew up using the bow. He had peppered enough targets to make him comfortable with the massive effort required to draw the weapon. His spear was also proving awkward in the forest and he had to hold it underarm so that it did not snag on the branches which passed him by.

Looking left and right he finally caught sight of the dogs, leaping over the uneven ground to the north, their pink tongues hanging out the side of their mouths. He kicked his horse into action and was after them in an instant. Somewhere ahead was his target and he focussed his mind on the task until he distantly heard a horn blaring behind him. Rhys had obviously lost his trail and was heading east, parallel to the stream which his Norman captive had crossed just a few minutes before. He should have gone back to find Rhys, but he threw caution to the wind and urged the horse over an earthen bank at full pace, squeezing the courser's sides with his knees. FitzStephen's blood boiled and his heart quickened as the excitement of the chase took hold. He vaulted the embankment without breaking step, thumping into the pine-needle sprinkled forest floor with a dull thud before his mare took off into the snow-filled landscape.

'C'mon, girl,' he said again to his horse. The pursuit took him further to the north and west, away from Rhys' group but he was not gaining on the stag as he had wanted. He was escaping.

*Escape*. The word rebounded around his skull as his horse cantered between the trees. Escape. Could he do it, he wondered? England was a great distance to the east but he was armed and had enough rations to last at least a day. After that he could forage for food. He had a bow on his back, for God's sake! Melted snow would suffice for drinking water and he could make a rudimentary shelter with little effort. Immediately FitzStephen pulled the horse to a stop, all thoughts of the white hart gone. His courser snorted, shook her mane, and stamped her feet impatiently.

FitzStephen wiped away the sweat which gathered at the edge of his gambeson cap and looked at the woods around him. Again the hunting horn sounded off to the south-east. He knew Rhys would discover his mistake sooner rather than later, cross the stream, and pick up his path. But FitzStephen could run eastwards before the prince even realised he was missing, giving him a head start which Rhys would never be able to close. He had to move now.

Briefly FitzStephen considered his most recent illegitimate son, Maredudd, still living with his mother Merwyn back in Llandovery, but he instantly dismissed any consideration for her one-year-old bastard and clipped his heels to his mare's flanks. Maredudd would be better off growing up as the cousin of Prince Rhys of Deheubarth than the son of a landless knight struggling to sell his sword to the highest bidder in Outremer. For FitzStephen could see no other future for himself. Still, he thought, the unknown was better than imprisonment.

He kicked his horse into a trot. He knew he had to get some important distance between himself and the tracks left by the hounds. At every moment he feared that he would stumble across Rhys and his followers, and he prepared his excuses for his absence.

An hour passed, and then two as he hurried through the beautiful but deadly landscape. It had started snowing again and though it was still only the afternoon, it became hard to see through the conifers. He rode on, ever eastwards, away from the cloud-blanketed sun.

It was tough on both man and horse, but they forced their way on at a steady trot through the slippery terrain, hour after freezing hour. To his left FitzStephen saw that he was almost past the shadow of Mynydd Mallaen, a mountain which stood alone far to the north. He knew that up ahead was the River Tywi, a tumbling and treacherous torrent through the hills which he still had to cross. But he didn't worry, remembering a score of places to ford the river. However, his rather vague knowledge of the mountainous land beyond the river did worry him somewhat, as did the possibility of finding protection from the weather in the night ahead. He was so involved in this thinking that he was completely unaware that he was no longer alone.

'Sir Robert!' a voice called cheerfully from about twenty paces to the Norman's right.

'Holy Jesu,' Robert dropped a piece of bread upon which he had been chewing. Both man and horse skittered sideways as he tried to ready his spear to fight. But it was just Ieuan ap Hywel, a young warrior whose father owned land south of Carmarthen, estates formerly held by Robert's half-brother, Maurice FitzGerald, at Llansteffan. Ieuan walked out from between the trees leading his horse, a grin plastered across his face. At his hip hung a hunting horn and at his waist, a sword.

'I thought I was going to have to walk home alone,' the youngster with the wispy beard told him. 'I'm glad I ran into you. It's bloody cold, isn't it?'

FitzStephen nodded his head and smiled, 'Truly. Are you by yourself?' He tried to make the question seem as flippant as possible.

'Yes, all by myself,' Ieuan said as he walked over to the Norman. 'Prince Rhys and the rest went over the river to find you but Daff,' he indicated towards his mount, 'stood in an old rabbit warren and hurt his shoulder.' FitzStephen saw that Ieuan's horse did indeed have his front leg rested on the edge of the hoof, keeping his whole weight off the limb.

'Should we wait here for Rhys or make our way back to the castle?' Ieuan asked.

FitzStephen padded over to Ieuan slowly without answering. A year before Rhys had asked him to teach some of his battle skills to his young noblemen, and Ieuan had been one of those men. The knight had been happy to do it, simply to break the tedium of life as a prisoner, and had got the warriors to fight each other using wooden replicas of swords. This, amongst others, was a skill which a Norman esquire would learn during his apprenticeship. FitzStephen remembered a diminutive Ieuan being particularly popular with the other boys, a joker who had made them all laugh heartily when he put an overweight boy on his back to take on Tewdwr and his partner in some piggy-back horseplay. Needless to say all involved had ended up in a pile on the ground in fits of laughter.

'How long since you left Rhys?' Again FitzStephen tried to be as glib as possible.

'About two hours ago,' Ieuan replied, throwing back his hood to reveal his long dark hair. 'They told me to make my own way home.' His eyebrows crinkled as he looked around the Norman. 'Where are the prince's hounds?' Proper hunting dogs took time to train, and were expensive and prized possessions. As if sensing that something was not right, Ieuan's hand dropped to his sword pommel which protruded above the edge of his cloak.

'No,' FitzStephen said as he rolled his spear into the couched position under his armpit. Instantaneously he kicked his horse forward at Ieuan. The Welshman stood no chance to defend himself without a shield and FitzStephen savaged the younger man's stomach with an underarm spear thrust. He had been aiming for Ieuan's throat and a quick death but the uneven roots of the forest made his horse stumble and FitzStephen had missed his target. Momentum took him past Ieuan to the edge of the trees and he abandoned his weapon as he clung to his saddle for balance. Behind him, Ieuan screamed. FitzStephen tried to turn his courser around to finish the murder and silence his victim, but Ieuan's unrestrained horse was in his way and he could not get past. He shouted at the terrified beast but he still would not move so he jumped off his mount and pushed through some trees to get at Ieuan. As he came out through the undergrowth he saw the Welshman on his knees in the snow, blood pouring from the wound. Before FitzStephen could stop him, Ieuan lifted his head and placed his horn to his lips. He prayed that the youngster would be unable to blow the instrument because of his injury, but the note sounded clear and strong, ringing in FitzStephen's ears and causing a dusting of snow to fall to the ground from above. Ieuan dropped the horn to his lap where blood already puddled. The young warrior looked pale and tired but he smiled widely as FitzStephen finally approached with an angry look across his face. 'Pardon me. Must have been something I ate,' Ieuan joked as if he had broken wind. His smile quickly distorted into a grimace as the pain struck him.

FitzStephen did not return the smile, cursing instead. He fancied that he could already hear horns replying across the hills to the west and heralding the resumption of their hunt. He turned back to Ieuan whose eyelids drooped as if in exhaustion.

'I am sorry,' was all FitzStephen could manage as he stole Ieuan's sword and food from his saddle. He could not hold the Welshman's gaze.

'Why did you do this?' the boy asked him. 'You were my friend.'

Robert could not answer, but remembered Einion ab

Anarawd's curse. Another horn blast sounded, much closer than the first, and he leapt into the saddle.

'When they catch you,' Ieuan stiffened with pain, 'they will kill you.'

'I'm sorry,' FitzStephen murmured and dragged his courser's head eastwards. The race was on.

Colour came at FitzStephen from all sides through the darkness and snowfall. The two Welshmen must have been freezing as they waited for him in the mountains and they looked like old men, their beards sprinkled with a mixture of freezing breath and snow. Night was falling quickly but Rhys and his men had caught up with FitzStephen more rapidly than he thought possible.

He had crossed the Tywi and raced eastwards away from Rhys' vengeance, but somewhere in his haste he had gone astray, allowing the Welshmen to catch up with him and his tired horse in the Crychan Forest. His target, the Norman garrison of Brecon, was still at least twelve miles away. The two men who now attacked him must have got in front of him as he wandered listlessly across the freezing hills looking for a mountain pass of which he had heard Hywel the steward speak months before. FitzStephen kicked his horse into a sprint and was away from the two warriors in a matter of seconds. Another horn sounded behind him from the wretched gloom.

He desperately urged his horse onwards. Over his shoulder he could see Rhys and the rest of his companions surging over the brow of the snowy hill and down through the sparse conifers. FitzStephen's horse was one of the best that Llandovery had to offer, apart from Rhys' own, but she had been running all day and was beginning to tire.

A familiar twang followed by a whistle sent an arrow past FitzStephen's head and buried itself in bush just a few paces to his left. He ignored two more shafts that punched through the murky light, and pointed his horse away from the danger and towards a bight in the trees downhill to the south. The wood curled down into the valley for a mile, blocking his course east. More arrows followed him, but Rhys' men were still at the extreme end of their range. FitzStephen was aware that the gradient of the terrain was dangerous but he was too good a horseman to be afraid of the peril. Another arrow went close to his back with a sharp gasp of air and he chanced a look over his shoulder. He was getting away! He dug his heels into his tired horse's sides and she responded once more, white spittle foaming at her mouth.

'Good girl,' he whispered into the horse's ear, having not the breath for anything more encouraging. He chastised himself for not learning the courser's name from an esquire back in Llandovery. The mare, which in his mind FitzStephen now named Fleetfoot, pulled him into the heavy trees which provided him some safety from the aerial threat of the arrows. However, he was forced to slow down because of the heavy foliage which came from all sides. Cursing he took out Ieuan's sword and began hacking at the branches which obstructed his path.

'Keep going, Fleetfoot,' he begged the mare. She shook her head as the branches snagged her face, but still wanted to please her master and kicked forward, using her weight to push aside the soaking vegetation. FitzStephen could hear voices closing in behind him and he again urged the courser forward with his heels. A few seconds later they broke through the undergrowth and they struggled forward from the trees at a canter, FitzStephen eyeing a piece of open terrain ahead, just beyond the treeline.

'Robert!' Rhys' voice rebounded around the wood, but FitzStephen was not going to stop now. He pushed through into the narrow strip of open land which, just ahead, merged with another piece of wooded land. A look over his shoulder told him that the Welshmen had forced their way into the trees behind him but he knew it would take them some time to stumble through the tangle into the clearing. His horse stumbled on the uneven clumps of mountain grass but kept going forward at a canter.

Abruptly, an arrow arched out of the dusk and slammed into FitzStephen's calf. He cried out in shock, but with no armour covering his limb, the missile thumped right through his leg and poked the horse's side through his saddle. It had been a lucky shot, from the edge of the wood where he could still see a young man climbing back into the saddle to pursue him, but it had finished FitzStephen's hopes. Not that he had time to consider this as his startled horse set off in a panicked flight downhill away from the safety of the tree line. Foam and spittle scattered from her mouth and she shook her head angrily at her rider and the sudden pain of the bolt. FitzStephen let his spear fall to the ground as he tried to find purchase with his heels and tug on the reins, but she began bucking irately. Agony scoured through him as the bolt bent and strained inside his leg. Somehow he kept his seat as his tired mount attempted to shy away from the pain in her side. One final body flip shook him free of the saddle and the arrow in his calf splintered as he impacted with the frozen and uneven ground. He screamed in pain and grasped at the wound, his face buried in drifting snow, freezing melt-water chilling the gaps between his gritted teeth.

'Come on,' he gasped and punched the ground. 'On!'

He hauled himself to his feet and managed to stumble a few steps before he lost his balance and had to grab at a small, sodden tree to keep upright. He gnashed his teeth as he drew the two halves of the arrow from his leg, thankful that the break in the bolt was clean and no wood had been left to fester in the wound. He threw the two pieces aside and looked for his mare but she was cantering towards Rhys' horsemen, already halfway across the clearing, urged on by the sight of their quarry's fall. FitzStephen crashed between trees only to collapse on his shoulder on the hard, bare, frozen earth, riddled with tree roots. He knew he was ensnared and cursed his luck and the choices which brought him to this end. Picking himself off the ground with a massive effort, he hobbled further into the woods. His last throw of dice was the hope that he could evade capture until night or the weather inhibited the Welsh pursuit. But as he turned to hobble on he heard the thump of hooves as two of Rhys' horsemen entered the wood. Unarmed and injured he did not stand a chance of fighting two men who urged their horses towards him.

'You murdering Norman bastard,' shouted the first warrior.

Without waiting for the rest of his band of hunters, he clipped his heels to his horse's flanks and jabbed his spear at FitzStephen as he backtracked.

The Norman waited for his adversary to overextend his reach and grabbed the ash shaft and heaved the man forward. The Welshman let go of the weapon and put his hands out to cushion his fall as he slipped out of the saddle. As he hit the ground FitzStephen took two steps towards him and stamped on the back of his head, an unhealthy crunch of bone and snow was accompanied by a mere gasp of surprise from the fallen man. FitzStephen immediately cringed as pain seared up his injured limb, but he steadied himself quickly using the stolen spear and hopped around the stump of a broken tree to evade the other horseman. Seconds later Rhys and his other warriors crashed through the foliage.

'Robert FitzStephen!' he thundered.

Although now armed with a lance FitzStephen did not feel confident enough to take on one warrior, never mind eight and using the spear as a crutch he hobbled off into the heavy trees, blood dripping onto the snow behind him. The Norman knight knew he was caught. He felt the panic grow in his chest, mortal terror. He was being hunted. He knew that the horsemen were coming before he saw them. Snow was scattered from the branches of evergreens as the trotting men followed him. They did not hurry, but came deliberately, stalking the man like they would stalk a wounded beast. And like any animal he was ready to defend himself to the death.

Exhausted, FitzStephen thumped his back into a tree and tried to stand tall. He knew he could go no further and so he turned, ready to fight, and hoping that the first Welshman would pin him to the trunk with his spear through his heart. He was exhausted and the cold air cut his throat painfully as he breathed deeply.

'Come on!' he bayed, urging them to attack.

Gethin ap Hywel was the first to approach and he dismounted, walked up to FitzStephen with a determined look in his eyes and an arrow notched on his bowstring. Slowly he lifted the weapon and pointed it at the Norman's forehead. He was Ieuan's elder brother and he was deathly silent as he watched FitzStephen.

'I should kill you here and now,' Rhys spat the words in his direction as he dismounted and walked between Gethin's bow and FitzStephen, forcing the Welsh baron to lower his aim. 'I should have killed you back at Aberteifi.'

FitzStephen said nothing. He knew then that he was damned, probably from his ill-fated birth to this his unlucky end. His parents' sin had infected him and without God's love he was nothing but a listless spirit ready for damnation. But he knew that he could still choose hell over purgatory. He had already lived a life of captivity and would rather be damned through eternity than caged. In Rhys' fortress he had become a hawk with clipped wings, a lion without teeth. He was a warrior denied a sword.

'Will you submit?' Rhys demanded of him. 'I will not give you another opportunity.'

FitzStephen shook his head and charged directly at Rhys, screaming with rage and desperation, pain surging from his thigh. Gethin's arrow slammed into his heavily muscled shoulder like a hammer blow, spinning him around and sending him crashing into the floor. His spear disappeared into the snow. FitzStephen screamed in pain, his hand gripping the arrow shaft buried in his flesh. He wished for death, yet he knew that he would live and he cursed and pulled himself to his feet to try to lift the spear. His right hand was numb and the weapon slid from between his fingers and back amongst the snow.

FitzStephen forgot the weapon and turned his tongue on the prince. 'Come on then, you whoreson. Finish it, you damned Welsh bastard.'

'Take him,' Rhys commanded his men.

Two warriors approached the Norman gingerly. FitzStephen threw a pathetic punch at one, who swatted the attempt aside and smacked the Norman in his face with his fist. The Norman collapsed to his knees in the snow. Blood flowed freely from his mouth and he said nothing, could say nothing as his hands were tied behind his back by Gethin. He cringed as his weight rolled onto his damaged leg, but that was all.

'The arrow,' he heard Rhys say and then intense agony issued from his shoulder as Gethin grabbed the wooden shaft at his back and gave it several tugs to loosen the sucking flesh before dragging it straight through the wound. The goose feathers scratched the inside of his shoulder like the fires of hell scorched damned souls.

'Did you dislike Llandovery so much?' Rhys stood over him.

'I was a warrior,' FitzStephen replied through closed teeth, picturing Tewdwr's departure southwards that morning. He shook his head, knowing that Rhys, a prince but no soldier, would never understand. 'You turned me into a house pet.'

'You have killed one of my friend's sons. You have probably killed Dafydd,' he indicated to the stricken man who was being tended a little way off. 'Now you will find out how little you are truly worth,' Rhys said and shook his head in disbelief. 'Take that prisoner with us,' he said as he turned to his men with a last contemptuous look at FitzStephen.

They took him back down the mountain, each step wringing another splash of pain from FitzStephen's open wounds. They had not given him a horse and he was forced to walk on the treacherous ground until he had passed out with the pain and had fallen into a snow drift. Then they had thrown him across a horse like a dead man and had walked the last few miles down the valley towards the fortified castle. Ieuan's body had been placed on another horse, wrapped up in his heavy winter cloak, and had made the journey alongside FitzStephen's mount. Grim faces stared balefully at the shivering Norman the whole way down the valley. The snow had turned into hail and it stung the faces of the warriors as the weather whipped across the sad group of men who descended from the heights in the darkness. Eventually they were challenged at the edge of the village which lay under the shadow of the fortress. The guards displayed thorough relief at Rhys' return and sent messengers ahead to the castle. Many noticed the body strapped to the horse, and each looked with growing interest at their lord's cousin, a former enemy, tied up, bleeding, and under guard in the middle of the group.

Stone houses marked out the richer villagers but the vast majority of buildings were made of wood, wattle, and thatch. FitzStephen had his eyes fixed firmly on the tall white-washed stone structure on the hill. They trudged through the small settlement, some of the hunters peeling off towards their homes. One led away Ieuan's body in the direction of the church just outside the town for the rites and burial.

As they traipsed the last few yards towards the castle walls Rhys leaned in to talk to two of his senior warriors. FitzStephen could not hear what they were saying even though he desperately strained his ears to do so. They were discussing what was to be done with him, he knew for sure. But what was Rhys' decision? Would he try him for murder and have him executed? Would he throw him in the deepest corner of the castle and leave him there to rot? Blinding or disfigurations were also common enough punishments but what was to be FitzStephen's fate?

'Kill me or free me, you Welsh bastards,' he shouted through chattering teeth. But no-one even looked in his direction, never mind answer him.

In the castle bailey he was dragged from his horse and for a second he thought that they were indeed going to kill him there and then. He again braced himself for death, determined that he would meet his maker with his head held high. However, they pulled him to his feet and up the steep slope to the door of the fore-building. FitzStephen tried to climb but his leg failed him and he hopped the final few yards painfully.

Rhys awaited him inside the stone building and ordered a servant to strip his prisoner of his cloak. Once this was done the prince removed his own garment slowly, his gambeson cap and fox fur gloves, all of which he handed to the servant.

'Robert,' Rhys started before shaking his head. 'I cannot kill you today...' he tailed off, closing his eyes. 'You have betrayed me. Every chance that I have given you,' he paused and shook his head. 'I wanted you for a friend ... yet again you have proven your untrustworthiness, and that of your entire race.' He looked long into FitzStephen's face but found no regret only anger. 'Put the Norman into the hole.' The last statement was directed towards his two men. Immediately the prince turned on his heel and went further into the donjon.

'Rhys,' FitzStephen bellowed. He knew where he was going and hated the thought of it. 'Rhys, don't do this,' he appealed, suddenly alarmed. Llandovery itself had been a prison for the Norman but where he was going was worse than a death sentence. He dug in his heels as they went under the portcullis and into the donjon proper.

'Wait,' he stammered to the two men who dragged him onwards regardless. He shouted Rhys' name three more times to no avail. 'Kill me,' he shouted. 'Kill me, you damned Welsh coward!' His prison loomed – barely three yards across, a metal grate which covered a chute leading to a room just eight yards wide: the oubliette. Whether the two men were strong or FitzStephen was weak from his injuries and exertions he did not know but despite his protestations he was moving inescapably towards the cell. As he was brought closer FitzStephen fought harder but he may as well have been shouting, like King Cnut, at the tide to turn. The two men threw him against the hard stone wall. One held him there as the other opened the heavy metal grate. He struggled to break free and the first man punched him full in the face, breaking his cheekbone and busting his nose. FitzStephen slumped into the man's shoulder, despairingly tired and devoid of balance. The man pushed him back against the wall and examined his tunic.

'You bastard, you got blood all over my surcoat!' he said as he hit him in the torso twice, left and right, hard.

FitzStephen collapsed to his knees above the gaping hole that was the oubliette. Another punch hit him in the stomach and he doubled over again. One of the two men grabbed him by his hair and forced him onto his hands, staring downwards into the darkness. A smell of decay rose from the depths and engulfed him.

'You see that?' the Welshman shouted in his ear. Spittle lashed across his cheek. 'That's your tomb.'

A foot struck FitzStephen on his back. He fell.

# Chapter Five

### Gwarthaf, Wales
### March 1169

Diarmait Mac Murchada was happy. He knew it could not last of course, but for the moment he basked in his own contentedness and, for almost the first time since leaving Laighin, he wore a smile unforced upon his face. The sun shone high, warming his heavy cloaked back while the wandering wind lifted his long, greying beard to tickle lightly upon his chin. The horse beneath him felt comfortable and Diarmait felt dozy and satisfied as his small company walked through the valley beside the sparkling River Tywi.

Though it was only springtime, it seemed as if the whole of Wales was locked in a beautiful, lazy summer. Butterflies drifted slowly from plant to plant and bees buzzed amongst the armoured men who passed through the forested glade. Just that morning, Diarmait had spotted his favourite bird, a kingfisher, down by the river as he had washed the sleep from his face. He had taken that to be a good omen and thanked all the saints for their favour. If his destination had not been so close and the mission so vital, Diarmait might have stopped and slumbered in the pleasant sunlit country. He had so rarely had the opportunity for peace in his long and difficult life. From his earliest days all he had known was war, grief and suffering. The Norman warriors who surrounded him on all sides reminded him of that fact. He tried in vain to ignore their foreign babble and coarse language by closing his eyes and enjoying the rhythmic bob of his head as his horse juggled his weight across its back. He was fifty-eight years old. Fifty-eight! Few men lived to such a great age, he thought, and few who did had such a daunting future ahead of them. Tilting his chin upwards, Diarmait inhaled long and pleasurably through his nose, imagining himself and his family free and able to enjoy a warm summer at peace in his homeland. The lovely land through which he rode seemed like a haven where one didn't have to feel uneasy, guarded, and fearful of attack. Not that the Norman soldiers around him were unwary; to them this was enemy country and their presence in this beautiful woodland was as alien as an Ostman at a baby's baptism. As Diarmait giggled at the mental image he wondered if that was that a faint whiff of the sea which he could smell on the breeze? Surely not this far inland, he thought, his brow creasing as he tried to identify the scent. No, he had not imagined it! Yet the sea was many miles to the west. He had crossed so many seas since his exile almost three years before that perhaps his clothes still stank of the salty sea spray of the western ocean. From Ireland to England to France and back again to England; Diarmait hoped that he would never have to travel in a boat again. But in his heart he knew that this was not to be his fate. He would make at least one more voyage on the oceans, the most important of his long life. It would be a voyage of revenge, reprisal and reclamation of that which was stolen. The thought of that storm of violence did not daunt Diarmait, but warmed his spirit more so even than the strong sunshine that fell upon his shoulders. A smile curled malevolently into the neck of his rough cloak as Diarmait imagined himself and his sons standing with spears at the neck of those who had hunted him across Laighin and chased him from his home: Ruaidhrí Ua Conchobair, Tigernán Ua Ruairc, Donnchadh Mac Giolla Phádraig, and Hasculv Mac Torcaill; all would die by his hand but only after they had been humiliated just as he had been. He pictured their forts in flames as their cattle were driven south by the victorious Uí Ceinnselaig. A hefty tribute would be imposed on the wretches' successors, he promised, but only after their fathers had been forced to watch their peoples' defeat. Only after his enemies had been maimed to prevent them from taking power again.

This was the dream that had kept him going as he had watched the flames lick his beloved rath at Fearna, the same desire that had forced him to hold his head high while he was begging for charity from Henry of England at Poitiers. It was the same aspiration that had made him make the deal with the warlord Strongbow. And now, with the dream still driving him onwards, it found Diarmait Mac Murchada deep in Welsh territory on a fool's errand.

The bishop sneezed loudly beside Diarmait, disturbing his daydream. Mac Murchada turned and watched his ally, feeling his lip curl in disgust as the priest wiped his nose on the sleeve of his dark robes. Diarmait wanted to scold the man, the way he had done so many times to his own son, Eanna, when he used his sleeve in the same way. But he bit his tongue. Bishop David FitzGerald of St David's Cathedral looked more like a man-at-arms than a man of the cloth, with his broken nose and armour, muscular arms, and cudgel at his hip. Diarmait would have been quite happy to make his way north with just his own warriors, but the bishop and his brother, Sir Maurice, had insisted on accompanying their honoured guest to meet this Cymri chieftain who they claimed could help them. Thus, Diarmait's derb-fine had been left in Pembroke while the small group of the bishop's warriors had followed the Afon Tywi north into Welsh-held territory having sent messengers ahead to warn of their approach.

In the week since their first meeting, Diarmait had built up a stiff dislike of Bishop David. He was not like the Irish clerics he knew such as his brother-in-law, Archbishop Lorcain Ua Tuathail of Dubhlinn. Lorcain had an air of high purpose and bearing as well as a fervent resolve and temper that saw kings kneel and chieftains cower at his judgements. This FitzGerald could not even read or write! And how could a churchman know the law if he had not studied it with his father, uncles, and cousins? David's Latin was dreadful, his Greek worse, and though he claimed French as his first language it was spoken in the harsh Norman-Welsh dialect rather than the high form that Diarmait had learned in his youth.

It was in his first tongue that Bishop David now spoke, barking his questions at three men at the head of their small column wearing the black and yellow arms of St David's

Cathedral. 'How far is the damned castle, boy?' he asked. 'We should have stopped for another night and pushed on tomorrow morning.'

'It is not far, Father,' one armour-clad rider at the front of group replied, 'ten miles, no more.'

Bishop David grunted reproachfully at the man's back as if the warrior had control over the distance that lay before them. Diarmait had noticed that Bishop David was always angry at this one warrior, the leader of the expedition, and, his interest piqued, had discovered that he was the bishop's bastard son. In Ireland this was nothing of note – bishops were still men, and powerful ones at that, and begat sons to carry on their authority – but in England it was seen as some sort of shame. The warrior, named Miles Menevensis, bore the treatment, caused merely by his existence and illegitimate birth, with patience and fortitude that the man from Laighin respected.

Ten miles to go, Diarmait thought, ten more miles to add to the hundreds which he had travelled since leaving Bristol where his family remained as the guests of the portreeve, Robert FitzHarding. Not all his family, he thought grimly; Eanna was still the hostage of his enemy Donnchadh Mac Giolla Phádraig and Conchobair was held by High King Ruaidhrí while Domhnall still struggled to hold his ancestral lands of the Uí Ceinnselaig together in Diarmait's absence. Reminiscences of his faraway sons naturally brought his daughters into his thoughts: Órlaith and Sabh in Ireland with their powerful husbands, and beautiful Aoife, his youngest and favourite, who could have remained safe in Bristol with Domhnall's sons, but had insisted on joining him on his journey into deepest Wales. He smiled proudly at Aoife as she rode at his side. Her long, dark red hair was vivid on her green dress, and he was not so blind as to see how the bishop's warriors watched her with such interest. She was a beauty and, unlike her sisters, had proven canny with his gifts to her. Her herds had grown while Diarmait could only watch as Órlaith and Sabh sold off their newborn cattle to fund extravagant lifestyles. Aoife's livestock and slaves were now under the protection of the Augustinians at Fearna where they would be safe until she could return and claim them.

It had only been a week since he had sold Aoife's hand to Strongbow. He hated how that sounded, but Máelmáedoc Ua Riagain assured him that it was common practice in England, and what other choice did he have? His plans to swear fealty and obtain warriors from King Henry of England had fallen flat on their face during his trip to Poitiers. Henry had proven a guarded, suspicious man who refused to part with a single piece of silver or order one of his lords to send his men to Ireland. Claiming poverty due to his obligations in France, all that Henry had been willing to relinquish was his consent for Diarmait to recruit some of his English vassals as mercenaries. Angry, but armed with his royal licence, Diarmait had sent messages to the courts of all the great men of the kingdom with promises of land to those brave enough to accompany him and help him to reclaim Laighin. But no-one had taken up his offer. He had bribed churchmen to read out his proposition from great pulpits, men to shout his scheme in marketplaces, and troubadour-bards to sing his challenge to drunken oafs in inns throughout the country. Yet no-one had come forward to help him take back that which was his.

He had all but given up when a bedraggled old man – more scarecrow than warrior – and bearing neither sword nor shield had come forward and asked Diarmait to travel with him into the Welsh borderlands to negotiate with his nephew. He had almost chased the man away, but the noble bearing of Sir Hervey de Montmorency had intrigued him and, at a loss on other options, he and a few retainers had followed the ragged knight across the Severn River to the Castle of Striguil. There, he had met Sir Richard de Clare, whom all knew as Strongbow. Diarmait's desperation for followers had been mirrored by Strongbow's yearning for land and wealth and opportunity. Yet the Norman earl had not been fool enough to commit to helping Diarmait without driving a hard bargain. It had only been when the exiled king had offered Aoife's hand in marriage and a claim to his throne after his own death that Strongbow had agreed to help him. It had been a trick of course. The Uí Ceinnselaig would never allow a foreigner to lead them, nor the other tribes permit an outsider to become a king amongst them, but Máelmáedoc Ua Riagain had learned the strange Norman laws of succession through the female line, and had advised Diarmait to dangle the tasty offer in front of Strongbow. And it had worked!

'Ha!' Diarmait laughed out loud, earning a disgruntled look from his daughter.

*Poor Aoife*, he thought as he watched her. He had not yet had the heart to tell her of his pact. The law said that it was her right to choose her own husband, and perhaps she would agree to take on Strongbow. He was rich in land and, even though he was a Norman and old enough to be her father, Diarmait knew that Aoife was ambitious for the power and wealth which he could provide. Bishop David interrupted his thoughts when he coughed loudly, cleared his throat horribly, and spat into some nettles. Diarmait grimaced and swapped a look of revulsion with his daughter.

He had first met the bishop a week previously when, their negotiations over, Strongbow had announced that it would take him at least a year to raise an army to put Diarmait back on his throne. A year! Another, to add to the three long years that he had been absent from his home. Diarmait could not stomach that and on the advice of one of Strongbow's warriors he had travelled to St David's Cathedral in the hope that he could find more daring men to expedite his return to power. He was not to be disappointed. There he had been introduced to the bishop's formidable brothers, Maurice and William FitzGerald. Together the three siblings and were the greatest lords of Norman-controlled Dyfed. Bishop David was the Normans' spiritual leader while his brothers relied on their skill with the sword, command of powerful castles, and a surfeit of kinsmen as ready as they to seek fortune wherever the opportunity would arise.

William, the oldest, had done most of the talking, but it had been Maurice who had impressed Diarmait the most. Quiet, calm, and experienced, he had immediately understood the intricacies facing an army that fought in Ireland. He had also realised that his age prohibited him or his brother from leading such an expedition. The Geraldines, as the three brothers liked to be called, had the funds for the adventure, they had the King's licence, the prestige, trappings, horses, and men, and they certainly had the will to see it through. But they needed a warlord to lead the invasion. Someone they could trust and someone desperate enough to risk his future on the very edge of the known world. If the man they had selected and now sought was even half the fighter that Maurice FitzGerald claimed then Diarmait reckoned that he would have Laighin re-conquered by Yuletide. If he was that good, the exiled king thought, he would have his enemies humbled within the year! And if these Geraldines were not successful, well then Diarmait would need Strongbow's help after all – despite the heavy price that it would entail. His eyes flicked towards his daughter, Aoife.

Like every Norman which he had met, the Geraldines proved to be land hungry. He had never met a people that had such an appetite for conquest, and Diarmait knew some Ostmen! The reality was that he would have promised the moon if it meant that he could have his revenge on his Uí Ruairc and Uí Conchobair enemies, but the brothers had not demanded anything so great for, though the Geraldines were the most powerful Norman lords in western Wales, they did not even own the lands for which they fought and made laws. All they desired were their own estates won by the power of their own swords and not the gift of a distant king who could disinherit their sons with but the sweep of quill over paper. These men were more ambitious than that and, after years of ruling independently of their sovereign lord, none could stomach the interference of King Henry. They wanted to their own kingdom and so Diarmait had offered them one.

'How are you holding up, King Diarmait?' Maurice FitzGerald spoke quietly from his side. It was the first time that the silver-bearded man had made a sound since their midday stop, and Diarmait had quite forgotten that he was riding just at his back.

'Grand, thank you, Sir Maurice,' Diarmait replied hoarsely as the Norman politely asked the same of his daughter.

'I am growing used to travelling long distances,' Aoife answered just as sweetly.

Maurice smiled at her answer. 'I had hoped that you would perhaps tell me about Waesfjord again?' He pushed his horse onto the track beside the father and daughter, ignoring briars and branches which reached out to tug at his legs. 'It is a merchant town?'

'Aye,' Diarmait answered. 'It's the closest port to Wales, safe behind a big wooden wall with its back to a wide estuary. Legally it belongs to my kingdom, Laighin, although the Ostmen have their greasy claws stuck in it now. If you can take it from them, you are welcome to it.'

'And these Ostmen, they are Danes and Norse?'

It was Aoife who answered. 'They are more given to trade than going *viking*, Sir Maurice. I met one of their merchants in Bristol not a month ago, and he told me that business has never been better in Waesfjord. They don't think of war and raiding anymore – only trade.'

Maurice nodded his head. 'Ten shopkeepers with axes in hand may still slay a knight. What about the two cantreds surrounding the fortress?' he asked.

'Two hundred thousand acres of fair farming land,' Mac Murchada lied easily. 'Whatever you wish to grow, the soil will produce.' In truth, Waesfjord was almost an island on a bog. Stony and badly drained, it was difficult to cultivate anything other than tough mountain grass and heather. Even before the coming of the Ostmen, the Gaels had shunned the area, claiming it was occupied by spirits from the underworld who would lead a man to his death. But Diarmait was not about to admit this to his new ally.

Whatever Maurice's reply it was left unsaid when, at the front of the column, Miles Menevensis raised a hand in the air and called a halt to the progress of the small conrois.

'Stop,' he hissed.

Suddenly each of the Normans tensed and searched the shadowed forest for possible threats. No-one spoke. The only sounds came from the jangle of chainmail and the heavy breathing of horses. They had passed into a small glade, shaded and tranquil in the afternoon sunshine. Diarmait leant across and held his daughter by the shoulder.

'I am fine,' she whispered back.

Miles again signalled for silence. Seconds passed as Bishop David shifted uncomfortably.

'What's going on, boy?' It was the churchman who inevitably broken the hush.

'This is where we arranged to meet Rhys' people,' his bastard son replied.

'So where are they?' Bishop David whispered as he glanced left and right, his fleshy bald neck creasing with every movement. 'Bloody late, I suppose.'

Without command a troop of twenty Welsh archers stepped out of the shade and surrounded the Norman horsemen, each with an arrow notched on the strings of their deadly weapons and all pointed at a separate man-at-arms. Like many of the Normans, Miles' mother had been Welsh and he had also married a native woman. He spoke in lilting Welsh towards the archers.

'Miles …' Bishop David began to growl before Sir Maurice laid a hand on his brother's arm to quiet him. A voice called out from the shadows and Miles answered, holding his spear upside down and away from his body to signify that he only had peaceful intentions. His pennant, which showed the black and gold arms of St David, sagged on the heavy gorse beside the track. More seconds passed by in silence before a warrior stepped forward and called out for his archers to lower their weapons. This they did slowly and suspiciously.

'He says that we will not be harmed,' Miles translated the Welsh leader's words. 'We are to follow him. Prince Rhys says that we are free to continue onto his lands.'

The Norman party were now in the hands of their enemy.

'I should kill you where you stand,' Prince Rhys spat across the dais at Maurice FitzGerald, 'you and your … your,' he grasped for an appropriate word as he swept his gaze towards Miles Menevensis, 'despicable nephew.'

The Welsh warriors seated in the main body of the main hall in Llandovery bellowed their agreement at their prince's threat, baying for Norman blood to be spilled on the rushes which carpeted the stone floor. There were enemy in the Cymri midst and they wanted to tear them limb from limb.

Maurice said nothing. Instead he stared directly at Rhys with a hint of a grin at the edges of his mouth. He didn't even stand up. Rather he slouched against the low table by a window with his arms folded over his red and white saltaire surcoat. In contrast, Miles Menevensis growled, but had the good sense to say nothing, happy instead to scowl at the Welsh nobleman.

'I have room for more Norman troublemakers in my oubliette,' Rhys announced. 'I mean no offence to you, Lord Bishop,' the pious prince added quickly to David FitzGerald who sat cross-legged in a wooden chair massaging his bare feet. The bishop's stiff leather sabatons lay on the ground below his seat where he had discarded them. Having just rubbed his dirty feet with his hand, David leaned forward and picked up a piece of bread, examined it thoroughly before tearing a lump away with his teeth as if he was safe in his own palace in St David's. The Norman leaders, as well as Diarmait Mac Murchada, were on the dais at the top of the hall with Rhys, his son Tewdwr, and two of the prince's kinsmen. Sunlight poured in through a huge, elaborate window above the top table, casting blue, green, and red light over the noblemen. Two churchmen sat on Rhys' left but largely ignored the conference between the leaders. They had offered their sycophantic welcome to Diarmait, but when they discovered that this particular king had neither riches nor estates and was thus unlikely to offer any gift to their religious houses, they fell silent and quietly bowed their heads over their bread trenchers, eating their fill of mutton and sipping generously at their ale.

Below the dais, Hugh de Caunteton sat with Maurice's nephew, Walter de Ridlesford, surrounded by a number of irate Cymri warriors. Both Normans maintained a hard, proud veneer as they picked at their trenchers, avoiding their mugs of ale. They were in the lions' den and could feel the resentment from warriors who had lost friends and relatives to their swords over the years. With the two seasoned warriors sat a couple of younger men who ate hungrily and drank liberally, seemingly oblivious to the umbrage taken to their presence. One of the youngsters was an esquire to Miles Menevensis and was trying to hide his excitement at being included in the journey to Llandovery by concentrating on the food before him. He was Ralph, son of Robert FitzStephen, and had begged his cousin Miles to allow him to travel with him on this mission when all other esquires, even Miles' sons, Dafydd and Philip, had been left behind in Dyfed. The other was a tall and broad-shouldered youth named William who sat with a jolly look on his face. Alone of the Normans he nattered away with the Cymri warriors in their own tongue, completely at ease amongst his supposed enemies. He was Robert FitzStephen's half-brother who had escaped Aberteifi Castle following Sir Roger de Quincy's coup. It had been nearly five years since he had laid his eyes on his brother and he, like Ralph, had changed massively, always trying to emulate the image they had stored in their minds of their famous kinsman. At only eighteen years old William was already making a name for himself as a warrior of great potential in Maurice FitzGerald's conrois.

'Oi, Welshy!' shouted Walter de Ridlesford across the table in William's direction. As diffident as a destrier at dinner time, Ridlesford had used a variation on William's nickname, *the Welshman,* to attract his comrade's attention. Walter also used the moniker scornfully, not at William, who he treated like a son, but for the benefit of the Cymri warriors who hated the label *Welsh.* In the English tongue it meant *foreigner* but the Normans had also adopted it as their name for the native people beyond the Severn. 'Where is Robert?' Ridlesford asked as William swung his legs back under their table from his conversation with their enemy. Ralph raised his head from the food at the mention of his father's name and scanned the room again for the man who he had last seen humiliated, naked, and bleeding on the day of Aberteifi's fall.

'He's not here,' said William with a shrug. 'Those good fellows,' he indicated with a leg of mutton towards the Welsh warriors seated at the bench behind him, 'say that something happened in the mountains two winters ago and Robert was imprisoned in the oubliette. They haven't seen him since but suggest that maybe Rhys moved him to another fortress. They wouldn't say more.'

Ralph looked anxious while Ridlesford ran his hands over his bald skull and cursed the Welshmen for their lack of Christian values. Civilised people did not imprison captured knights. They were supposed to treat them with honour and comfort.

'Bollocks to these bastards,' said Walter.

Hugh de Caunteton, leaned over and, in no uncertain terms, told the two warriors to be quiet and craned his neck to listen to the animated conversation going ahead on the dais where Rhys was on his feet again accusing Maurice of cruel acts against his people.

'... Llansteffan where my people tell me that you have burned and pillaged since Yule. So tell me again why I would choose to talk,' he said signalling to some of his men to sit, 'and to keep my men from killing each and every one of you – including your twice-damned brother, Robert?'

Walter, Ralph, and William swapped glances as the Welsh prince confirmed that FitzStephen at least still lived.

It was Bishop David who answered Rhys. 'The King confirmed my brother to those lands of Llansteffan, *Lord* Rhys,' he said, his mouth stuffed with oatcake.

'What the King gives, God can take away, *Father* David,' Rhys sneered. 'And Our Lord seems to favour the Cymri these days.'

'Maybe if your troops would stand and fight rather than running scared into the hills every time my troops get near them,' Miles Menevensis said. 'You Welsh are bloody cowards,' he added causing Tewdwr and Rhys' other noblemen to leap to their feet and began pointing across the table at their foes, shouting accusations and abuse in equal measure. Bishop David jumped up to support his son while Walter de Ridlesford added his voice to the clamour from the belly of the hall. Maurice FitzGerald, sitting beside the window, remained quiet but allowed a small grin to pass across his face as he watched the war of words ensue.

It was Diarmait Mac Murchada who stopped the heated exchange by slamming his trencher against the wall, scattering food everywhere. Taller than everyone in the room by a head, he screamed a bellow that resounded off the walls like a battle cry and slammed a fist onto the table top, making it bounce on the stone floor. With all eyes upon him, he settled himself back into his chair calmly.

'We are here to talk about Robert FitzStephen, not your petty grievances,' Diarmait said quietly, forcing every ear to concentrate on his words. His blue eyes flashed and his hoarse voice pumped out a melodic accent for all to hear. 'I do not care if we get this man or not – for my great expedition I already have the support of Strongbow,' King Diarmait let the powerful name sink in while all the men around the table settled themselves back into their seats, 'but at least let us talk about the subject at hand instead of arguing like children.'

'Strongbow,' Prince Rhys breathed the name slowly. It was tough to find a place in Wales where the name was not feared or respected. Where he moved men died. 'He has agreed to go to Ireland?'

His son, Tewdwr, leant down and whispered in Prince Rhys' ear: 'If Strongbow's is considering going to Ireland maybe we should think about sending some warriors? There could be something in it for us. I could lead them ...'

Rhys scowled and shook his head. His son had raised a good point, however. A man of Strongbow's stature would give credibility to the expedition across the ocean. His involvement would draw Normans away from the Welsh March and over the sea. It could give him the opportunity to defeat his enemies while their numbers were thinned. Perhaps there was something that was to Rhys' benefit in this meeting after all, he considered.

'I am launching a mighty endeavour to regain my kingdom,' Diarmait told the Prince of Deheubarth. 'Not a raid, not a heist – an invasion. My friends,' he indicated towards David and Maurice, 'have agreed to come to my aid ...'

'... but they trust no other to lead their army than Robert FitzStephen,' Rhys guessed the end of Diarmait's sentence. 'I have a prisoner of that name.'

Diarmait grimaced. 'We will need as much of the summer

135

campaigning season as is left to retake the lands of the Uí Ceinnselaig and perhaps a year to secure Laighin. I must have this man *now* if I have any hope of securing my kingdom this year.'

'Robert FitzStephen is a dangerous criminal,' Rhys warned.

'Perhaps, if you are not willing to release him, we should leave and come back in a fashion less fitting to noblemen than honourable negotiation,' Bishop David said. The threat of attack with all the power of Pembroke and St David's did not have any effect. Rhys remained unmoved, his fingertips dancing as he considered his enemy's words.

'When the Normans invaded your father's kingdom many years ago,' Diarmait began again, 'he called to me for help and I provided warriors. Norse seamen and Irish kern came from my lands to save his. Your strength now is built on that friendship. How disappointed would your father be, Rhys ap Gruffydd, to know that you betray his friends by denying them but one man for a similar adventure across the sea?' Diarmait's strongly accented French was mesmeric and silence followed his short speech.

'Robert FitzStephen comes with a high price,' Rhys retorted quietly, 'even to my father's friends.'

'There is swordland available for every warrior who accompanies me ...' Diarmait began only to be interrupted by Rhys.

'We will continue these negotiations in private,' he told Diarmait. 'Everyone out, except, of course, for my honoured guests.' The warriors in the hall groaned but acquiesced and trundled out of the hall, many carrying their bread trenchers and mugs of beer with them. Rhys watched them go.

'When will Strongbow make his journey to Ireland?' Tewdwr asked excitedly from behind Rhys' tall chair.

'I thought I told everyone to leave,' his father growled.

'In truth,' Diarmait answered, 'Strongbow dilly-dallies like an old woman in Striguil, promising much but risking little. It could be a year before he has his army prepared.' He shook his head, betraying his impatience. 'I need warriors *now*,' he insisted, lifting his heavy lids to look at Rhys ap Gruffydd.

'What assurance would I have that if I hand over Robert today, I won't end up fighting a Pembroke supplemented by him and his warriors tomorrow?'

'I thought we were all friends and loyal subjects to King Henry?' Bishop David asked. 'Are we not friends, cousin? So why would we ever face each other across a shield wall?'

Rhys sneered, turning to Diarmait instead asking for an answer to his question.

'I can promise you this,' Diarmait began, 'I will never leave Ireland again and Robert FitzStephen will be sworn to my service and the service of my sons. You may treat it like one of those "death or glory" ventures I hear so much about from your minstrels.' Diarmait coughed a chesty chuckle.

The Cymri nobleman simply pursed his lips. He was concerned that the lure of land in Ireland would prove too great for his own ambitious warriors. Better, he thought, to have Diarmait thin the ranks of his Norman enemies: Pembroke to the west, Strongbow's Striguil and the Braose lands at Abergavenny, than his own. If Deheubarth was to enlarge its borders to an extent enjoyed before the Norman invasion then his principality would have to fight those strongholds. If Diarmait could encourage some of those turbulent invaders to go to Ireland it would be just as good as Rhys killing an army, but without any risk to his own troops. And all it would take was to release one man.

'Tewdwr,' he signalled to his son, 'bring our *guest* up from his room. Let's see what Robert has to say for himself.'

Aoife stared at the oaken doors as if her eyes could penetrate the wooden boards through sheer will and allow her to be included in the negotiations beyond. The dusty tapestries billowed and sighed in frustration as the feeble spring wind found the cracks in the forgotten masonry of Llandovery Castle. Frowning as her attempts proved forlorn, Aoife listened instead to the male voices inside the hall crescendo and then fade. How she wished that she could be beside her father as he and his new allies talked of war and of the future of her homeland. To be told to wait in the anteroom outside the hall like a scolded child was embarrassing, but the condescending attitude of the servant, who had brought her a small trencher of food and had ruffled her red hair, was utterly abhorrent to Aoife. She had cast aside the stew despite her hunger, daring the woman to admonish her for the act of petulance. Despite her family's penury, Aoife remained a princess of the Uí Ceinnselaig and that noble birth and bearing was evident as she had stared down the unfortunate servant until she had scuttled away towards the castle kitchens. That she was left alone while the men conducted the business in the hall was another shame to add to a growing list, and all had common origin: Diarmait Mac Donnchadh Mac Murchada. She loved her father like any good daughter should, but all her life's ills found their source in him and his intractable greed. Not that she thought his ambition a sin – far from it – but simply she was sick of her father reaching too far and falling well short of his target. A king, like everyone, had a role to play in society and Diarmait had failed in his duty because of his insatiable need for power. He was a dreamer and his imaginings had lost Aoife everything – her home, her brothers, her position, and her wealth. All their absences hurt, but she was not sure which upset her most. She recalled how, when she was sixteen, she had received a small herd of twenty cows and one bull from her father. He had also given her three slaves to care for the animals, just as he had her elder sisters when they had come of age. Órlaith and Sabh still had those same small herds, whereas Aoife now had two hundred livestock and ten slaves who sold butter and milk in Waesfjord on her behalf. There were richer women than she in Ireland, but few who did not have to share her fortune with her husband. And yet she had little hope of recovering that wealth, or hope of an advantageous marital match with a man of equal royal status. She was almost twenty and few daughters of provincial kings remained unwed at that age. Aoife's face burned in embarrassment as she thought about that indignity. She knew her sisters and cousins would not forget it. They would gossip about her in her absence and make jests about her. And all the while Aoife was unable to do anything to change her circumstances.

Angry foreign voices swapped insults inside the room, causing Aoife to again look at the door at the end of the corridor. She could identify a few of the words as they were thrown across the great hall of Llandovery by the French speakers, but the Welsh tongue was unrecognisable to her. Soon, the word war quietened and Aoife released the breath she had not realised that she was holding. Why her father required more warriors in addition to those that Earl Strongbow had promised to provide, she did not know.

Aoife sighed and climbed to her feet, bored and alone in the corridor. She did not like the castle of stone, and had yet to find herself inside one such building which made her feel comfortable. It was warm and summery outside yet in the keep of Llandovery there was a piercing chill. Her father's stone house at Fearna had never been so cold, not even in the depths of winter, and the smell of rising damp and mould coming from close by assailed her nostrils. A castle was a cage, she decided; a cold, dank, smelly cage. And to make matters worse it was a cage which gave the impression of security. She had been guest in many fortresses since her family's exile from Laighin five years before, and she promised that she would never reside in such a horrible place, not if all her father's dreams came true and they won back his place at the head of the Uí Ceinnselaig. That said, she had always enjoyed the view from the roof of a Norman keep, and rather than remain on her sullen vigil before the hall doors, she made for the winding stone stair and the roof.

Her leather sabatons, bought for her by the merchant Robert FitzHarding in Bristol, could find little purchase as she climbed upwards through the draughty stairway, but she hoisted her heavy skirts in her arms to make the ascent less of a labour. Nevertheless, by the time she had passed the solar door on the floor above she was already damp with sweat. Inside she could hear women's voices and she caught a glimpse of the insipid lady of the castle, surrounded by her servants, as she passed by without stopping. Lady Gwenllian did not seem angry to have been left out of her husband's negotiations – in fact she looked content to be surrounded by the chit-chat and gossip rather than mediation and arguments which took place below. Not for the first time, Aoife felt anger at being forced by her father and his new Norman friends to either accept the company of these women or to exist in solitude. The daughter of the exiled king turned her back on the solar door without a second glance.

There was no-one on the roof and Aoife thanked the Blessed Eithne and Sodelb for granting her privacy as she stared out over the sun-banked mountains, steeped in yellow flowers and trees heavy with leaf right to the horizon far above. Aoife clung to the battlements as the warm wind whipped through her Norman headdress, and she reached up to tear the veil from her brow and release her dark red locks of hair. During her first days in Poitiers, she had created a small scandal at the royal court when she had appeared in the presence of the English king with her head bared. It had been in the heat of the Frankish summer and her new clothes had been constricting, but it had taught her everything that she needed to know about a woman's role in English society; that one was to be quiet and unopinionated, sedate and modest. In Ireland a woman had a job within the household, but in royal court she had watched the work of a wife being done by her husband's steward. Aoife felt angry on behalf of all those women who were treated like brood mares rather than as partners who could share the burden of power with their husbands.

The three river valleys seemed to stretch upwards and away from the castle like open arms ready to embrace the exiled king's daughter. Below the high motte, she looked southwards to the low roof of the Norman church and the fields beyond where people toiled. She knew they were monks for they were all that remained in Llandovery during the spring and summer months. The rest had taken their flocks and herds into the hills where pastures were plentiful and Normans few. A wave of sadness overtook Aoife as she stared out over the green fields and hills. The mountains to the west of her home at Fearna were more distant, but somehow the scene before her prompted thoughts of her Uí Ceinnselaig homeland. She swiped a tear from her cheek and blamed the small wind for causing it to appear. Angrily she turned her back on the countryside and made for another door that would take back down into the depths of the tower. She did not know where she was going as she skipped down the stair passed many doors, the skirt of her Norman gown light as it caught on her heel. The light green wool provided her with little heat as she made her way down, and she wished that she had one of the thick cloaks she had made under her mother's tutelage. She had been able to rescue one of her patchwork mantles when her family had fled Fearna, but the garment had been soaked during a rainstorm in Poitiers and then forgotten when the family returned to Bristol to the house of Robert FitzHarding.

Lost in her thoughts, Aoife suddenly realised that she had missed the door which would have taken her back to the great hall. She had no mind to return to that lonely vigil and rather than climb up the stone steps again, she kept going downwards into the belly of the castle. It was dark and the smell of damp continued to surround Aoife. The long stair was brightened only by a single window above and came to an end before another closed door. Distant voices above her, perhaps one of Rhys' servants making his way to the kitchens in the bailey, or a warrior on the battlements, was the only noise that she could hear. Aoife leant forward and tested the door. The latch was not locked and though it scraped the dusty floor loudly, it swung open easily to reveal a cellar packed with stacked barrels. With only the light from the little window to guide her, Aoife stepped under the lintel and into the cold room. It was barely twenty paces wide and as she tip-toed further inside, she paused as she heard rhythmic breathing coming from behind the barrels. Aoife was not so naïve that she could not guess what was happening on the other side and she stopped in her tracks lest she be discovered and mistaken for spying on two lovers in the throes of passion. She could not bear the thought of such an embarrassing situation and, as quietly as she could she turned to leave.

'*Sydd yno?*' a man's voice called out in Welsh before Aoife had taken one step. His voice was hoarse, and his manner suspicious and angry, and no wonder, Aoife thought, considering the activity which she had interrupted.

'I'm sorry, sir,' she babbled in French and made a move for the door. Aoife could feel her cheeks burning with humiliation.

'Wait,' the man replied in the same tongue as Aoife scampered through the door and back onto the stair. 'Are you a Norman?' he called, more distantly than before. 'Please wait! Don't leave me alone down here,' the man managed before the cellar door closed behind Aoife. She galloped up the stairs and quickly darted through the door to the floor above. Leaning against the wall, the princess of the Uí Ceinnselaig breathed deeply and calmed herself. Two servants, one of them the women who had offended her earlier, entered the gatehouse from the fore-building and Aoife immediately stood tall, her chin proud and hands clamped together as the pair stopped close to her and stared anxiously in her direction. Neither could speak Irish or French, and nor could Aoife make herself understood in their native tongue. They babbled a few words before realising the futility of their attempts and continuing on their way.

Aoife allowed herself to relax and examined some of the embroideries which adorned the walls. She had barely begun when the noise that had so embarrassed her in the cellar began again. Strangely, it came from somewhere close-by and Aoife, now angry at being put in such an inappropriate position, stormed in its direction, determined to scold the man for his impropriety. The noise led her to a small grate in the floor, barely the width of Aoife's outstretched arms, and through it she could see the sides of a chute. At the bottom, she could see a man punching the air as if in a fight with an unseen foe. She watched as he jabbed the air just in front of him with a vicious power, his long blonde hair and beard waving wildly as he moved from side to side. Before him were iron bars leading, she realised, into the cellar from which she had ran minutes before. It was a prison, though who the man was she could not tell. Nonetheless, Aoife watched him as he furiously fought, his hands a blur as he sent stroke after stroke outwards against a foe unseen.

'If you are attempting to fight your way free, I think you will actually need to strike your cage,' she joked suddenly.

The man came to a halt immediately, breathing heavily from his exertions. He tucked his matted hair behind his ears and looked upwards at her through the iron bars of the grate. His stare unsettled Aoife, but just as she was about to leave, he finally spoke: 'You have no idea how long I have waited to hear someone speaking French.'

'What did you do to end up down there in this …?'

'Oubliette,' the prisoner told her.

'So how …'

'Murder,' he told her plainly and bowed his head.

Aoife scowled at the man, believing him to be trying to scare her. 'Liar,' she accused. 'If you were a murderer they would either have hanged you, or you would have paid the honour-price for the crime and been freed …'

'Perhaps I had no money,' he interjected again.

'Stop interrupting me when I am speaking,' Aoife told the man, though she earned only a giggle of laughter as recompense. However, when she turned to walk away he barked a desperate apology.

'I'm sorry, don't go,' he appealed. 'I apologise, wholeheartedly. I have been down here for too long and I have lost my manners – I don't even know how long I've been down here, for no-one is permitted to speak to me.'

Aoife considered leaving the man to his lies and his unhappiness. However, having explored most of the castle she knew that she had little choice but to return to waiting for her father or to join Prince Rhys' wife in the solar. Neither option interested her in the slightest.

'Are you still there?' the man's voice, full of desperation, echoed through the hatch in the stone floor.

'Yes, I am here,' she told him with forced exasperation evident in her voice.

'Thanks be to God,' the man said. 'I apologise again, Madam, I forgot my …'

'… manners, yes,' Aoife interrupted, a hint of mischief in her admonishment. Thankfully, the prisoner understood her small joke and smiled. 'It is spring,' she told him, 'of 1169.'

The man breathed out slowly. 'Then I have been down here

for two years.' He bowed his head and shuffled out of the light which tumbled down the shaft to the oubliette. For many seconds he did not speak.

'Are you Norman?' Aoife asked.

'I was,' the man said sadly from the darkness. 'But to be Norman is to be free – to be beholden only to your lord and the men under your command. I am a silenced sword now, nothing more.'

'You are certainly a sullen one,' Aoife remarked, earning a caustic snort of laughter from the man. 'I have lost my freedom too,' she told him. 'It was taken from me, but I committed no crime.'

'Then you have my sympathy and prayers that one day you will be able to revenge yourself on the person that wronged you,' he told her. 'Actually, I retract the last part,' he corrected himself. 'I will pray instead that you simply find your way home, Madam.'

Aoife scowled. 'The life of a man is very different from that of a woman,' she told him 'I suspect that I will never go back to the place that I call home. My father has sold me, like a cow, to a man that I have never met, an old man, in return for soldiers. My father thinks that I do not know about his plans, but he can't hide this from me.'

The prisoner climbed to his feet and stared up at the princess. 'The same thing happened to my mother,' he said. 'I think that she found happiness for a little while, though I suspect not with my father. He was a hard man to like.'

'My sister used to tell me how hard she prayed so she would become a good man's principal wife. She did not pray for wealth or good harvests or for our family's health. She prayed that she would not be a lesser wife, and I mocked her. She was taken from her home and delivered to the bed of a stranger. The only familiar faces belonged to her three slaves. But at least she was treated with respect. She told me the same would happen to me. From what I have seen of your Norman ways, I think I would be better throwing myself from the battlements.'

'I don't think that need happen to you,' the prisoner told her. 'Not every woman needs a man to command her.'

Aoife did not reply and neither spoke for many minutes.

'What is your name?' she eventually asked, but before the man could answer the noise of mailed feet and harsh voices sounded on the stone steps above her. They quickly passed by the door beside which she crouched and she looked down the chute into the oubliette to where the prisoner stood in the shaft of light.

'They are coming for me,' the man whispered. 'Oh God, they are coming for me,' he said, his voice full of fear. The noise of metal hinges scraping against stone issued up the chute to where Aoife stood, followed by the stomp of many feet in the cellar below.

'What do you want?' the prisoner shouted into the darkness as the metal bars of his cage were dragged open and men stepped into the cell with him. As Aoife watched the Norman backed away from the Cymri warriors who attempted to grab him by the arms. He fought back but he should not have. Punches rained down upon the man and he was soon overcome and dragged from the oubliette, kicking and screaming in the Welsh tongue.

'Leave him alone,' Aoife shouted down the chute. She did not know what the men wanted with the Norman, but he was the only one, apart from her father and Sir Maurice, to have spoken to her since they had arrived in Wales, and she feared for him. Soon the noise of his fight passed by the door and Aoife ran over and swung it open just as the man passed.

'Leave him alone!' she shouted again in the French tongue at the men but they just laughed and their leader, the Welsh prince's son, forced her off the steps.

'Go ... away,' the Welshman said in faltering French.

'No,' the Norman appealed from the steps above. 'Please, girl, please! Whatever happens, tell my brothers that I was here and that I am sorry. My name is Robert FitzStephen. Find my brothers and tell them to pray that my soul finds eternal rest.'

Aoife's last sight of the bearded prisoner was of his desperate eyes appealing for her help. But she could do nothing as one of the Welshmen stood in her way on the stair.

'No,' the Cymri warrior said. 'No.'

Walter de Ridlesford, Hugh de Caunteton, and the two youngsters, William and Ralph, were all that remained in the main body of the hall and they exchanged nervous glances as they stared at the tangled remains of the man they had last seen five years before. Robert FitzStephen was so heavily bearded that they barely recognised him as he was held between two Welsh warriors in the doorway to the great hall. Clothed in little more than a brown shift and torn hose, his kinsmen could see a thin body wrapped in skin and sinewy muscle. His feet were bare and they made a distinctive slap as he was moved further into the hall towards the dais.

William the Welshman looked at the man but did not see his brother. Instead he saw a shaggy-haired wretch. In an instant he knew that this man held little of the swagger and confidence that had been such a part of his brother's personality.

'Robert?' William asked of the skeletal man who approached the table, screwing up his eyes at the light which poured into the room. Hugh, Walter, and Ralph all stood as FitzStephen advanced close to them.

'William?' FitzStephen replied, his brow creasing in confusion. His younger brother stood staring at the shambling mess that had been his hero and who he had not laid his eyes on in so long. He nodded slowly but could not find the words to greet his brother. Walter de Ridlesford had no such problem with his old friend's desperate condition and pushed the two Welsh warriors out of his way as he threw his arms around FitzStephen's shoulders and battered his back with his right arm. Ridlesford then punched his cousin hard in the stomach.

'There's more meat on a bishop's table at Lent than on you,' Walter said before hugging him again. Bishop David scowled at the joke.

'Robert?' William asked again, disbelieving.

FitzStephen nodded nervously. 'What is happening?'

'We are here to get you back, you dope,' Ridlesford laughed.

'Get me back?' FitzStephen seemed confused by his cousin's statement and did not join in his mirth.

'The enterprise,' Ralph blabbed in answer to his father's

question. The esquire was lost somewhere between anger and happiness at seeing the man who had left him alone, who now looked at him without any paternal recognition.

'Robert,' Prince Rhys growled across the hall and immediately FitzStephen turned away from his kinsmen to look at the figure silhouetted against the coloured window. 'Come up to the dais and greet your brothers. They have a proposition for you.' FitzStephen looked angrily at the man who had put him in the oubliette and he felt hatred course through his bones. He tapped William reassuringly on the shoulder before approaching the dais, his eyes locked on Rhys. Beside him, FitzStephen noticed Tewdwr's fingers dancing on the hilt of a dagger in his belt. He was ready to strike should the need arise.

Miles was the first of the Norman leaders to greet FitzStephen with a strong grip upon his forearm. He was followed by a smiling Maurice and then by Bishop David who scolded FitzStephen on his sinful indiscretion which had led to yet another bastard, Maredudd, to whom he had been introduced to earlier in the day. 'Another bastard, Robert? Another?' he exclaimed. The bishop then introduced his brother to Diarmait Mac Murchada. Few Normans, English, or Welsh were as tall as Robert FitzStephen, but the thin King of Laighin towered over him.

'Are all the men of your country as tall as you?' FitzStephen's voice scratched his throat, forcing him to cough and gave him time to consider what was going on. He was not really sure where Laighin was nor what the strangely clothed man was doing alongside his brothers.

If Diarmait seemed shocked or disappointed at FitzStephen's appearance he did not show it and just grinned at his question. The fact was that the King was thrown off by FitzStephen's build just as the Norman was of his; Diarmait had met many of the brood that were the descendants of Princess Nest by her many lovers – FitzGerald, FitzHenry, Carew, and Barri – and all were short, stout, and dark-haired. But here was a trim, tall, and fair man who looked more like an Ostman from Dubhlinn or Veðrarfjord than the Normans he had met in Wales. Something about the prisoner also reminded Diarmait of himself as a younger man; the blond hair, blue eyes entwined with desperation and ambition.

'I am tall, even for an Irishman,' Diarmait said in answer to Robert's question. 'Before we begin negotiations I want to know if you are the right man for me,' he stated.

'My Lord?' asked a confused FitzStephen.

'I must know everything,' the King continued. 'Tell me about your life. Have you seen much war?'

FitzStephen looked around the room for support, finally settling his eyes on Maurice. His brother gave him the smallest nod. 'I have seen nothing else,' FitzStephen said and shrugged. 'War and life? What is the difference? What is this about?' he asked his half-brother.

'Just tell him what he wants to know, brother,' Maurice urged with a small smile.

FitzStephen shook his head and thought back to his childhood. 'I served Sir Henry FitzRoy at Wallingford and I saw some action during King Henry's attack on Mona ...'

'"*Saw some action?*"' Miles Menevensis blurted out with a sarcastic laugh. 'He saved King Henry's life and the whole army from the screaming horde of Gwynedd –' he told Diarmait Mac Murchada.

'And then I was rewarded,' Robert butted in as if the memory of his glory under Henry of England's banner pained him, 'by being made Constable of Aberteifi. I served the Earl of Hertford in Ceredigion for seven years.'

'Adequate,' Diarmait said and nodded to Bishop David.

'Wait,' FitzStephen said, turning to his brothers, 'what are you all doing here? Tell me what is going on.'

Bishop David began to recount the story of Diarmait's journey and Robert's place in it. FitzStephen sat amazed, drinking only water as he listened first about the Irishman's exile, before the bishop described the political situation in Ireland, finishing with the conditions of their negotiations with Rhys so far.

'So who has agreed to make the journey?' FitzStephen asked the group as he shook his head in disbelief at the amazing turn of events. He was visibly shaking with excitement. Was this it?

148

His two years of praying in the oubliette rewarded by God with freedom? For what else could this news mean? Would he be sprung from prison and given command of an army? Or had he finally succumbed to madness and this was some grand flight of fancy as his mind collapsed? Nonetheless, he felt something rise in his chest. It was a feeling he had not experienced since the day he was knighted by the young King Henry; that he was on the brink of something momentous.

'The FitzHenrys are with us as usual,' Miles Menevensis told him. 'William de Barri's two boys are keen, and obviously Walter de Ridlesford and Hugh de Caunteton will stand with us. The other knights of the March will only follow our banner to Ireland if you commit to leading it.'

FitzStephen nodded. 'Might I see King Henry's licence?'

Bishop David quickly clicked his fingers at one of the priests who had accompanied him north. The man produced a copy of the document and handed it over nervously to the prisoner. FitzStephen examined the seal which showed the two swaggering lions of Anjou. The animals on the wax badge sent disdainful glares at FitzStephen. Henry's symbol made him angry as he uncurled the crisp folded parchment, allowing the seal to dangle from the bottom.

'Henry, King of England, Duke of Normandy and Aquitaine, and Count of Anjou,' he read aloud, 'to all his liegemen, English, Normans, Welsh,' he paused and scowled, 'and Scots, and to all other nations subject to his dominion, sends greeting. Whensoever these our letters shall come unto you, know you that we have received Diarmait, Prince of Laighin, unto our grace and favour, wherefore, whosoever within the bounds of our territories shall be willing to give him aid, as our vassal and liegeman, in recovering his territories, let him be assured of our favour and license on that behalf.' FitzStephen studied the letter silently a second time to make sure that he had got the correct meaning of every single word. 'Does anyone trust Henry's word?' he asked.

'Not one little bit,' Maurice spoke quietly from the window ledge, 'but the licence makes it legal, and with all due respect,' he nodded towards Diarmait, 'that is our king that you are talking about, brother.'

FitzStephen snarled suddenly and aggressively at his half-brother. 'He discarded his allegiance to me easily enough; abandoning me in Llandovery ...' he stopped suddenly and closed his eyes to bring calm learned in solitary confinement. 'So I consider my duty to Henry finished too,' he said quietly before turning back to the document in his right hand. 'But what other option do I have?' he asked. 'To stay here and rot? Rhys will not countenance my going to the Holy Land and he will not allow me to stay in Wales unless I fight for him. It is to Ireland or to death in his oubliette.'

The room went silent for many seconds and the hush was only broken when Prince Rhys closed his eyes and breathed out slowly, shaking his head in sadness. 'If he leaves Wales, I will release him for the same price which you offered to pay five years ago,' he nodded towards Maurice FitzGerald. 'But he must swear it on the Holy relics of St David that he will never come back.' Rhys was small of stature, thin, and bookish, but he looked indomitable. Even surrounded by the famous warriors, no-one contradicted his proclamation. 'If he stays in Wales, he will remain here as my *guest* or he will fight for me. The choice is his to make.'

Everyone turned to look at Robert FitzStephen.

He knew that he wanted to go with them – for any of the children of Nest a tomb was better than a prison. But something was holding him back. Without intending to do so, FitzStephen's eyes locked upon those of Rhys and he could not take them away. He was a hawk stuck in a cage, he knew, and Rhys was his keeper. The Welshman had utterly defeated him.

'I will make it easy for you, Robert,' the prince said as he climbed from his chair and sat down beside his cousin. 'Who are you?'

The question caught FitzStephen by surprise. 'What do you mean?' He could feel sweat beginning to form on his forehead and anger rise in his stomach.

'You have told me again and again that you are not one of the Cymri. True?' Rhys paused, waiting for FitzStephen to answer. Receiving nothing he tried again. 'You call yourself

Robert FitzStephen not Robert ap Stephen.'

'I am no Welshman,' he said defensively, not fully understanding where Rhys, his tormentor, was taking him. His eyes searched the room for support.

Rhys barely heeded the conformation. 'Are you English?'

'English?' he shook his head. Only the serfs of the field claimed that nationality or spoke that tongue, and then only ever amongst themselves.

'Just because Jesus was born in a manger, it doesn't make him a heifer,' Walter de Ridlesford joked from the body of the hall.

'Then you must be Norman?' Rhys said, ignoring Ridlesford.

'My father said that we were Normans,' FitzStephen replied, 'but I've never been to Normandy. Perhaps I still am a Norman.' He shrugged his shoulders.

'So who are you?' Rhys' eyes swept around the room, taking in all the men left in the hall, asking them the same question. 'Who are you? Henry FitzEmpress has abandoned you here,' he said as he turned and looked at David, Maurice, and Miles. 'He has abandoned all of you to your fate.' Rhys let the statement sink in. Not one of them tried to argue against his blunt assertion. The prince turned back to FitzStephen. 'This will be the last time I offer you the chance to join me, cousin. But for your mother's sake I implore you to fight for the land of your birth. Despite everything you have done against me, I still want you to help free Cymru. Fight for us and free Deheubarth from Henry of England!'

FitzStephen, despite his imprisonment, was tempted and the Welshman knew it. Rhys had used many tricks, offers, and threats to tempt him to join his cause, but nothing had got close to breaking his resolve. But the prince could see FitzStephen struggling. Pride, desire, ambition, fear, an outsider's yearning to belong, all the emotions poured into his mind at once.

'So who are you?' Rhys broke the silence in the great hall of Llandovery.

Shocked by the suddenness of Rhys' question, FitzStephen raised his chin and looked at his cousin. Behind him was the wall of the Norman-built castle; strong, steadfast, and stable. To FitzStephen a castle signified order and the rule of law. Suddenly he realised that this was what he craved most – order in an otherwise unpredictable world. The Church promised that it would unite all Christendom in its warm embrace but FitzStephen knew that the meek would never inherit the earth. However, equipped with a sword, a courser, and a castle, a strong man with the will and the skills to dominate could seize a piece of land and bring it to order. From the shaped stone to the dusty tapestries, his eyes flicked around the faces in the room: Maurice encouraging him with his deep, thoughtful eyes. *Come to Ireland*, they said, *take the chance*. Next to him David sat picking at a bread trencher of venison, and beside him Miles smiled encouragingly at him as if he recognised the pressure under which FitzStephen struggled. Miles' grin offered support and constancy.

FitzStephen's eyes finally settled on Diarmait Mac Murchada, the exiled king, whose face gave nothing away. But his lightning-blue eyes flashed unblinking across the wooden table at him. They seemed to invite and repel FitzStephen at the same time. They told him that he had one last chance to prove his courage, one last chance to prove his character – that anything was possible. FitzStephen was enticed. And what a prize he offered! A hundred thousand acres for his own use; not held for some lord or king, but swordland – a huge domain ready to be claimed by anyone with skill in war and maintained by his ability to provide plunder to his followers. If Henry of England and Prince Rhys were trying to close the Welsh frontier then Robert FitzStephen would open up a new front in Ireland. And in that mysterious place he would be at the top of the tree, not just lord of farmland but also of a huge town with good trading links to England, Wales, and beyond. It was more than tempting.

'So tell me, Robert, who are you?' Rhys asked as the silence again began to stretch throughout the room.

'I am …' FitzStephen started but seemed to not be able to find the words to describe what he felt in his soul at that moment. 'I am an invader,' he said finally. 'My father was at the forefront of our invasion of Wales, my grandfather took England,' he shook his head, eyes on the table in front of him. 'Perhaps it is right that I am the invader of Ireland, for war is all that connects me to my forefathers.' From any other man it would have been a ludicrous statement but each of the noblemen, kings, princes, and knights, duly nodded along with the sentiment of the unshaven and half-starved wretch dressed no better than a beggar. 'At any rate, I am done with Wales,' he told Rhys. 'Or rather it has done with me. I must find my fortune elsewhere.'

'We could have freed all Cymru, Robert, and been remembered in the songs of our people,' the prince shook his head. 'And perhaps I will still do it,' he bowed so that his chin touched his red surcoat. 'You are free, cousin. Go and find your fortune in Ireland. My father told me it is a most beautiful place; harsh and untamed, but beautiful.'

FitzStephen nodded to his cousin and jailer, unsure of whether to thank him or scream at him. He suddenly remembered again the stories his father had told him of the famous Norman hero, Robert Guiscard, after whom he was named. Robert the Fox; Robert the Cunning; a younger son of a minor knight who had risen from nothing, carved himself a kingdom in a faraway land and founded a dynasty that still ruled vast estates in Italy, Sicily, and Antioch. But even Guiscard had served the Pope, he thought as he walked around the vast table towards the King of Laighin and knelt before him, taking Diarmait's worn hands in his own tattered, dirty paws.

'Lord King, before you is a poor man, who has defeat and dishonour in his past. I am bastard-born and a murderer. I embody sin.' He bowed his head. 'But once I was a great warrior and lord of battles,' FitzStephen looked up into the Irish king's blue eyes, 'and I swear it on St Maurice's great spear, I will succeed in returning your lands or I will die trying. And all I want from you is a promise that you will be true and loyal to me in return for that service. I can ask no more as you have offered my brothers a mighty prize.'

Diarmait looked at FitzStephen and remembered himself as a younger man. He had been desperate, brow-beaten, and defeated by his enemies after the death of his father and brothers. But he saw the same depth of determination in the Norman and not even the rags could hide the muscle that would provide prowess in battle. Ambition pumped through this man, Mac Murchada thought. The Irish king jerked his head back and barked an unexpected laugh.

'Stop being miserable, young man, and get up off your knees.' Diarmait leant forward and pulled him to his feet. 'We are never truly defeated,' the older man said, 'but nor should we ever truly think ourselves victorious. We are born, we fight, we win, we lose, we recover, and then we die. That's life so don't pretend it is too complicated.' Diarmait nodded to Rhys who stared momentarily at FitzStephen before marching out of the great hall. The Norman watched him go but could not bring himself to speak. Instead the Irishman walked him towards the oaken doors.

'Look at me, for example,' Diarmait continued, 'I am a penniless exile now, but I was a king of the most beautiful and bountiful country on God's green earth, and I mean to be again. But to do it I will need men like you and your brothers.' He removed his hands from FitzStephen's shoulders. 'So I ask you this, have you the skills to help me retake Laighin? Have you the spirit to see it through to the very end?' They were on the steps and as they spoke and wandered into the fore-building below the massive FitzPons crest and the main gate.

Pulling open the gates he hauled FitzStephen into the bright sunshine where they were met by the most beautiful girl that Robert FitzStephen had ever seen. He could only stare at the woman, astonished by her loveliness. Her red hair was unfurled and glittering in the sunshine.

'Father,' the woman said to Diarmait Mac Murchada before turning to look at the man at his side. 'This,' she said as she looked FitzStephen up and down, 'is the man you came all this way to get?'

'He is, daughter,' Diarmait nodded and turned to his new ally. 'I have found the warlord that will take us home.'

FitzStephen nodded to Diarmait but his eyes were only for Aoife. 'I will do it and I will not fail,' he told her. 'You are going home.'

Diarmait cackled and his blue eyes shone. 'Then I have found my taoiseach.'

The fighter was free and Ireland was his target.

# Part Two

# The Frontier

IRELAND 1169

# Chapter Six

## *England*
## *April 1169*

There was no sudden change to tell Sir Robert FitzStephen that he and his half-brother had moved into the Jewish Quarter, but within a few hundred yards all but the most downtrodden of merchants had disappeared from view. In a city famous across the kingdom for its iron-working and leather-crafters, it became apparent to the mounted Norman warrior that some time had passed since he had seen any sign of any tradesman amongst the quiet hovels. Nails, armour, horseshoes, mattocks and spades, arrows, utensils, anchors, and all manner of iron tools had been on display outside every other house back towards St Peter's Abbey, but FitzStephen could not remember when he had last seen an iron-worker's abode as they rode east towards the patched Roman wall. They may have left the Welsh frontier behind, but within the ancient city they had found another border between two warring peoples.

'Why would you need to find a Jew?' the Sheriff's bailiff asked, spitting on the cobble and grass road to underline his feelings on the inhabitants of the city. Some of the spittle struck FitzStephen's horse's hooves, making the rouncey bounce uncomfortably away from the balding soldier.

'I wouldn't talk to them at all if it wasn't my job,' the man claimed as he stared suspiciously at the two chainmailed warriors. 'They killed that boy last summer, you heard that?'

The tall Norman warrior lied and shook his head, repeating his request for directions to the house of Yossi the Moneylender. Even in the twelve years since he had last been to the city it had changed enormously and FitzStephen had become lost in the confusing little streets, which peeled off in every direction between the dirty thatched houses and tiny wooden shops.

'They crucified him in their temple, little Harold, that's what I heard,' the bailiff continued unabated. 'Then they all fed on his flesh in their synagogue.' The man looked at both horsemen for encouragement but received none from their stern-featured faces. 'Well, I don't have to tell you that the sheriff told us to keep an eye on them,' he continued in Robert FitzStephen's direction.

Robert's companion, Sir Maurice FitzGerald, had heard all about the blood libel case brought against the Jews of Gloucester and had told him of it on the long road from Pembroke, just one in a number of stories to get FitzStephen up to speed with recent events. The boy's remains, Maurice had told him, had been found in the river with a hundred cuts and the signs of Christ's crucifixion on his hands, feet, sides, and head. The Jews, of course, had been blamed for the death, and an unsuccessful case had been brought before the sheriff. The morbid distrust between the opposing citizens of the city remained with the peace ostensibly held together by the small band of royal bailiffs.

'Yossi the Usurer?' FitzStephen asked of the sheriff's man again. His French had become heavily flavoured with lilting Welsh and sounded foreign to the man of Gloucester who stared at him distrustfully. He knew little about the turbulent fighters from the frontier, but what he did know made the bailiff uncomfortable. None were more dangerous or untrustworthy than the men who scraped a living from un-Christian and violent conquest on the very edge of the kingdom.

'Well, I suppose you two know what you are about,' he finally said, obviously disappointed at FitzStephen's unwillingness to chat in the street. 'But I warn you, keep your eyes open. You can't trust them Jews,' the man said again before acquiescing to Robert's request with a shrug. 'You keep dead ahead for a hundred yards and then take a right into the Jewry by Job the Goldsmith's shop. You'll have to ask again and no doubt the penny-pinchers will want paying,' the bailiff said with a sniff but did not move off. When it was apparent that neither FitzStephen nor Maurice was going to offer him recompense for his trouble, he continued on his way back into the city cursing the two troublesome men from Wales and all cheapskates who associated with damned Jews.

As the bailiff tottered off, FitzStephen clicked his tongue to get his rouncey moving and followed Maurice down the road away from the city proper. His new lease of life had been somewhat dulled by the stuffy city atmosphere. He had spent just one frantic week in Pembroke overseeing the preparations for the adventure but, with their numbers almost doubling thanks to news of his release, it had become clear that the brothers would need extra materials and workers if their enterprise were to be the success of which they dreamed.

'Are you sure we should not get more silver?' he asked his older half-brother. 'We may not get another chance.'

'Forty marks should be enough, brother,' Maurice said as he dusted off his white surcoat, resplendent with the red saltaire of the Geraldines.

FitzStephen grimaced. It was hardly a fair price for what his family offered, he thought, but if you conspire with Jews what should you expect? The journey across South Wales to Gloucester had given him the opportunity to reacquaint himself with horsemanship in the lovely soft land bathed in a beautiful spring. Sixteen warriors had ridden with Maurice and FitzStephen through Carmarthen, Kidwelly, and Cardiff into Gwent – or Wentland as the English called it – to Striguil, Strongbow's fortress. There they had stayed a night with Maurice's jovial nephew, Raymond de Carew, before making their way across into the soft rolling countryside of England. Camping overnight in the Forest of Dean, ten miles to the west, FitzStephen had again dreamed of the oubliette. In the small world of his prison he had prayed for little else other than freedom, but now that he was liberated he could not stop returning to his captivity. His confessor had told him that there was only one rationale for his unexpected liberty: God had forgiven him for his many sins perpetrated during his rule of Ceredigion. FitzStephen was not sure whether he believed that he deserved forgiveness, but he was determined to live up to the chance given to him, and to a Norman that meant only one thing: triumph by conquest.

Gloucester was a city which FitzStephen thought he knew as well as any man. He had spent many years there as a page in the household of Sir Henry FitzRoy during the wars between the Empress Matilda and the usurper Stephen de Blois. The city had been built by the Romans, occupied by the Anglo-Saxons and now, under the Normans, had become the biggest and most important settlement in the west of England, the last major town before the Welsh March. Gloucester fed the needs of the warring barons who scraped a living from the land beyond the Severn in the old Norman fashion. The city had become rich by feeding the unremitting conflict to the west.

As he and Maurice walked their horses through the streets, FitzStephen suddenly recalled the day when the Earl of Gloucester had brought the captured Stephen de Blois, the usurper of the throne, back to the city. FitzStephen had been a scared child brought to Gloucester by his father to serve in the earl's household, but the jubilation of the people had been infectious as the sad figure of the defeated king, blond hair and beard untidy and his hands bound, sat in a cart as the people of the city taunted him. All had believed that the war was over and the Empress Matilda, Henry of England's mother, would be crowned Queen. But fickle fate had intervened and just months later Sir Henry FitzRoy's brother, the Earl, had been captured in a poorly thought out attack on Winchester. The civil war had continued on and off for another thirteen years, and that time had been the making of Robert FitzStephen as a warrior as he progressed from page to esquire to knight under the tutelage of Sir Henry FitzRoy. It seemed such a long time ago, he thought, but it had made him the man he was today. Or the man he had been before his incarceration, he supposed. He shook loose another suffocating image of the oubliette and looked at the houses which surrounded him.

Back in the main market place of Gloucester, around the docks and St Peter's, every street had been teeming with people. The quayside had been all hustle and bustle, a sea of cloth tents covering tables full of wares brought from around the West Country, but the steamy, suffocating marketplace between the walls of the old Roman city and the crowded banks of the River Severn had been almost too much for FitzStephen. It was the opposite in the areas between the Jewry and those of Gloucester's Christians. Not that any right-minded person would come out of their house when two well-armoured Normans from the frontier were in the streets, FitzStephen thought with a smile. The surcoated warriors were killers and bullies known up and down the island of Britain for the horrors which they left behind, and few would have anything to do with the misfits from the dreaded land of Wales.

'Job the Goldsmith,' Maurice said suddenly, looking up at the sign hanging above a small house on the riders' right with a small hammer pictured on it followed by two sets of script in English and Hebrew lettering. He pulled his horse into the side street and FitzStephen fell in behind him. For some reason both men fell silent as they walked their steeds through the smelly little thoroughfare. All that was audible was the thump of hooves and the tinkle of each man's chainmail armour against steel weaponry.

Further into the Jewry there were more people. Most were Jews, FitzStephen could tell by the oddly pointed yellow and white hats which the men preferred to wear, and they looked up at the two warriors warily before scampering away. FitzStephen realised that he knew these streets, and he began to remember the ways and strange customs of the sons of Israel.

'How many Jews are there in Gloucester?' Maurice asked quietly as he watched a group of young men on the far side of the square climb to their feet when they saw the two Normans enter.

'Three, perhaps four hundred?' FitzStephen guessed, thinking back to the wedding he had attended in this very square twelve years before. 'Certainly even when I was last here there were enough for the locals to be wary.' Maurice hummed a response while FitzStephen ran his hand over his bare chin. All trace of the beard which he had grown during his imprisonment had been shaved off, and he had cropped short his blond hair in the old Norman style, admittedly more out of hygiene than style. The unusual haircut, shaved chin, and colourful surcoat marked FitzStephen out as a danger amongst the long-haired, bearded, and dull-clothed Englishmen and Welsh. Amongst the Jews, the alien looking Norman garnered the same reaction.

'Now where?' asked Maurice.

Caerloyw was the name which the Welsh gave Gloucester and it meant *Bright City,* but today there was no hint of why they had given the walled town this beautiful name. To FitzStephen the whole world seemed dark and suffocating as the tall buildings, sometimes as many as two or three storeys high, cast their shadows over the little street. But up ahead the pleasant, little sunlit square opened up before FitzStephen and he was able to compose himself. Jews were trading goods in their own style in every corner. Bizarre smells hit FitzStephen, foreign scents which he could not identify. Many of the people in the square stopped whatever they were doing and turned to look at the strangers in their midst. One woman screamed and lifted her son into her arms before running for cover in a house.

'Lords,' a voice said loudly from the brothers' left. It belonged to a man who was surrounded by a large group of youths all dressed in similarly extravagant clothes and yellow caps which tapered to a high point. FitzStephen immediately felt a familiar dislike rise in his chest. Twelve years before, he had known the ratty-looking man with the protruding teeth and sharp nose. They had not been friends back then and he doubted that the mutual dislike they'd felt would have dissipated from the other man either. But FitzStephen's face was shrouded in shadow from the surrounding buildings, and the man did not recognise him.

'You are lost, perhaps?' The Jew's polite question covered an underlying threat that the two Normans were anything but welcome in this area of the city. Relations between the Christian and Jewish residents of Gloucester had never been poorer and young men on both sides sensed the unrest and patrolled the edges of their respective territories looking for trouble. Robert FitzStephen could see some of the young men fingering weapons hidden beneath their robes.

'Shmuel ben Yossi,' FitzStephen replied, stepping his horse out of the shadow, 'it is nice to see that you are still the helpful boy that I remember.'

Shmuel's lip curled in disgust as he revealed his face. The other men in his group sensed their leader's mood and tensed excitedly, ready for a fight.

'You,' was all Shmuel could stammer.

'Yes, me,' FitzStephen replied evenly. His horse fussed below him. 'But point me to your father's house and we can reacquaint ourselves there rather than in the street.'

'You are not welcome here,' Shmuel snarled, 'take your lies and go back the way you came. We want none of your sort of trouble.'

FitzStephen ignored the threat. 'Your father's house?'

Shmuel snarled, drawing a small knife from inside his sleeve, and charged forward just as his companions' hands grabbed at his shoulder to stop him. Two men on horseback could easily have cut them all down.

'You bastard,' Shmuel wheezed as he slashed his knife back and forth at FitzStephen's armoured leg, but far enough away to have no hope of injuring the Norman.

A single voice rang out above the clamour: 'Robert, my friend, you have returned. And in better shape than last time I saw you.' The voice belonged to Shmuel's father, Yossi ben Ysaac. A philosopher, moneylender, doctor, and, twelve years before, an unlikely friend to a young and badly injured knight on the make called Robert FitzStephen. He had been brought to Yossi by Walter de Ridlesford when the war wounds contracted in battle on Mona had begun to fester and the blood poisoned. In the beginning FitzStephen had refused the Jew's aid, which was so unlike the help he had received from the Hospital of St Sepulchre in Gloucester where prayer was the main remedy. As he worsened he had finally relented and the two had become close friends as his condition slowly improved under the Jew's care. FitzStephen's transgression with Yossi's daughter-in-law had forced him to flee and had kept him away from the city for many years. Nevertheless, FitzStephen leapt down from his horse and pushed through Shmuel's gang, landing a bear hug on the old man which left Yossi reeling backwards, laughing and scolding FitzStephen. Shmuel stared daggers into the Norman's back. Ignored, Maurice kept his hand on the pommel of his sword and an eye on Yossi's son.

'Are you quite done with this effeminate show of happiness?' Yossi told FitzStephen as he broke clear of his hug. 'Might we rather go to my house and get some food?' Still smiling, he turned towards his son. 'Shmuel, you are not giving these men bother, are you?'

'No, Father,' he started through gritted teeth, 'just reacquainting myself with an old *friend*.'

Yossi preferred to ignore his son's sarcasm as he signalled to Maurice to follow him. 'Good boy. Your mother and I will see you on the morrow.'

FitzStephen walked beside Yossi while Maurice rode, leading his brother's rouncey alongside him. They left his son and his companions behind and walked through the square with people still watching the dangerous outsiders.

'It has been some time, Robert,' Yossi said after he had been introduced to Maurice.

'Indeed it has,' he replied. 'I thought time healed all wounds,' he said with a glance back over his shoulder at Shmuel.

'Some wounds are deeper than others,' the old moneylender told him with a sympathetic smile. They walked on in silence for a few paces and FitzStephen looked around, the smell of burning oak bark from the nearby tanneries strong and vaporous. He was surprised to find that many of the homes in the Jewry were grander than those of the rich burgesses in the west of Gloucester. Even more surprising was that Yossi's new house dwarfed every other in the vicinity. It was by far the biggest on the street, more a fortress than a house, and blessed with a large walled courtyard in the front where many people continued their day's work. FitzStephen felt a sudden surge of contempt and jealousy that Christians all over England experienced towards the Jews. They lived lavishly in these great mansions, buying up more and more land while Christians failed to meet their loans and lost their homes. To make matters worse, the moneylenders also had a stranglehold over the monastic houses to whom they had made loans for building work, including the recently built Benedictine house of Llanthony Secunda, just south of Gloucester. It was mortgaged up to neck like so many others, giving the Jews power over the Christians and put their immortal souls in jeopardy.

'Welcome to my home,' Yossi said as three servants ran out to take the horses. Their master did not take off his hat as he entered the building, but Maurice quickly swept his gambeson cap from his head. A body lay on a table in a room to the left of the entrance hall.

'My brother,' said Yossi, indicating to the corpse. 'We are not permitted to bury him on Christian soil so we must take him to a Jewish plot of land in the shadow of the Tower of London.' Yossi laughed suddenly. 'I have been putting it off because it is a long trip and he is poor company now.' His laugh faded out quickly with a slow shake of his head. 'It is very sad,' Yossi said after a moment's silence. 'You look trim, Robert, though a little pale, so I assume you have not come to me for medicine. You have never asked me for advice, so I assume you have come back to Gloucester for money.'

'That and your upbeat company, Doctor,' he teased.

'Well, I am glad that you came to me rather than Miles le Riche. He is a very bad man, no morals at all,' Yossi said seriously of another Jewish money-lender in Gloucester, shaking his head. 'Like Aaron of Lincoln, if you don't pay him on time he would chase you all the way to Ireland for the money,' he said with a laugh. FitzStephen and Maurice both visibly baulked at the mention of the country across the sea and swapped hurried glances. 'Ah-ha,' Yossi said, 'perhaps you believed your endeavour across in Ireland was a secret?' Yossi arched his grey eyebrows in amusement. 'Not with that king of yours shouting it from every roof top, I think.'

'It was no secret, Doctor, but we had not realised that word had spread so far,' Maurice said quietly.

'King Henry has given his licence to help this Diarmait so what have you got to worry about?' Yossi asked as the two men looked fretfully at each other, considering the news that their enterprise had spread far and wide. 'Ah, I see,' the doctor continued, 'King Henry's mind can be changeable of course. So I take it that you are in agreement with the Archbishop rather than the King in their great argument?'

'An argument?' FitzStephen asked and immediately regretted it as Yossi launched into a ten-minute description of how the former friends, Archbishop Thomas Becket and King Henry, had been in dispute about the supremacy of the State over the Church for nearly a decade. Eventually FitzStephen shrugged his shoulders in answer. As a knight on the March of Wales, London politics had never interested or affected him.

'I'm not on bloody Henry's side, so I am on the archbishop's, I suppose,' he said to shut Yossi up. During his imprisonment, FitzStephen had built up a firm hatred of Henry FitzEmpress; it was irrational, uncontrollable, and based solely on the King of England's abandonment of him to his Welsh prison. His distrust of the Angevin king and his noblemen was all-consuming.

Yossi looked disappointed that FitzStephen had no better argument, but Maurice quickly intervened: 'I believe that the King's motivation for overcoming the power of the Church is honourable, perhaps misguided, but honourable. The Church is,' he paused, 'no longer simply interested in men's eternal souls, they require power over their mortal lives too.'

'And their pockets,' FitzStephen added.

Yossi's loud peal of laughter startled both Normans. 'Ah ha, I see that you are a politician, Sir Maurice,' he said, 'and politics are but a short step from the noble art of philosophy which is where my heart truly lies. It is true! I am not just a simple usurer and doctor.'

FitzStephen groaned. He knew what was coming.

Ignoring him, Yossi beamed at Maurice. 'Have you read any philosophy, Sir Maurice? No! Well we must remedy that now.' He strode off through his home throwing a hand in the air to indicate that the two Normans should follow. 'As well as philosophy, I also read astronomy and poetry, but my particular skill is in exegesis,' he continued and rhymed off several of his interpretations of the Torah which had been well received in educated circles. The doctor pushed through a door and into a library filled with scrolls and parchment. 'As an expert in usurious proclivities and various mercantile pursuits I have been able to procure many texts from around Europe for my library.' He picked down a tightly bound scroll from a shelf with obvious reverence. 'Surely you have heard of the Admirable Doctor, Sir Maurice?' Yossi looked very dissatisfied when Maurice raised his shoulders and eyebrows to indicate his ignorance. 'Abraham ben Meir ibn Ezra,' he said with deep respect. 'Some uneducated men,' his eyes flicked to FitzStephen, 'call him Abenezra and he has written some of the greatest arguments and commentaries on the Torah. I helped a little during our time together in Dreux,' he added quietly, perhaps hoping that Maurice would enquire after details of his assistance. He was let down but unfolded the scroll across a table in the centre of the dusty room anyway. 'This is Yesod Mora Vesod Hatorah – *The Foundation of Awe* in your savage French tongue …'

'We have important business, Yossi,' FitzStephen reminded the bearded old man.

'It will keep for a few moments, Robert.'

FitzStephen rolled his eyes and drifted out of the conversation between the two older men. Instead he studied an old map made by a Greek several centuries before. Ireland was but a blip on the corner of a Europe dominated by Italy, Spain, and France. But to FitzStephen the island meant much, much more than those great kingdoms – it was a second chance for success after his failure in Wales; somewhere he could prove that he was just as good as any man. Yossi's map was old, obviously a copy of an earlier map and the work of a great mind. It was if the mapmaker was trying to bring together all the knowledge of world and what he thought of those far-flung places. Ireland looked like one of the particularly vicious pieces of flint that was sometimes found in the countryside. Long rivers punctured the island to its very core and he could see why the Norse and Danes had loved to raid the country and had finally settled there. Their longships could sail from every corner of the island and bring terror right to the interior. His eye quickly drifted to the south-east corner of the island between two mighty rivers. That was Diarmait's tribal territory, the lands of the Uí Ceinnselaig, and though the map was made long before it had been founded, FitzStephen knew that the city of Waesfjord was in the utmost southern corner, closest to Wales. That was his target, his prize for helping Diarmait: rule of Waesfjord and two hundred thousand acres to divide between his brothers and cousins. Not for the first time since his departure from Pembroke, he thought of King Diarmait, already across the sea in Ireland. The exiled King of Laighin had sailed ahead to prepare the ground for FitzStephen's invasion and had taken an unlikely ally in the figure of eighteen-year-old Tewdwr ap Rhys. FitzStephen was jealous, impatient, and angry at the possibility that the younger man, who he had trained to be a warrior, was again leading the life that he wanted.

'Yossi, please,' the Norman appealed to his host as an obviously bored Maurice listened politely to his argument about the Book of Joshua.

'... how the trumpets could have brought down the walls of a city –' The Doctor stopped when FitzStephen issued his urgent plea. 'All right, all right,' he said. 'You have found Ptolemy's map, I see. So impatient to go to Ireland! Why? I cannot understand,' he shook his head as he set down the scroll on a candle-lit table. 'I have read that it rains incessantly, that the women fight in battle and look no different to their husbands.'

'I don't think that is true,' the Norman said. His mind drifted to the lithe, red headed beauty that he had spotted as Diarmait left from the dock at Pembroke. It had only been a moment meeting of their eyes, but that last memory of Princess Aoife still haunted FitzStephen and he fancied that he could still see the charisma, energy, intelligence and courage dancing across her eyes as she held his gaze for just a split second before boarding the ship to Ireland. Since their conversations at Llandovery, he had not been in a position to talk to her but in his mind she was a confident and opinionated woman, free in ways that Norman women were not, and to think of her made his heart rise in his chest. 'I had not heard that their women are any different to our own, Doctor,' he said to the Jew.

'Well, Pliny is not always to be believed,' Yossi admitted as he sat down and pulled some fresh sheets of parchment from a drawer. 'But let us get down to business, Sir Robert. How much do you need?' He picked up a quill, using his thumb to examine the quality of the tip.

FitzStephen swapped a glance with Maurice. 'We have nearly four hundred troops, infantry, archers, and mixed cavalry, but some still need remounts,' he shrugged. 'We also have workers who need to be paid for building ships and weapons. Food, materials, medicine are all expensive, and we will need some silver for bribes.'

Maurice interrupted, 'Mercenary Flemings are also rather more expensive than I would wish.'

FitzStephen shook his head at Maurice's continued opposition to his engagement of the men from Rhos. He was one of the few Normans who respected the poorly treated immigrants from flooded Flanders.

'But forty marks should cover the whole expedition,' Maurice said. If he was expecting this huge figure to be met with surprise he was wrong.

'Indeed, forty should cover it all,' Yossi nodded at the sum. He scratched the amount into a column on the thick vellum. 'And as collateral for the loan?' he locked his eyes on FitzStephen.

He and Maurice looked at each other. They had only one thing to offer Yossi if their expedition was a failure.

'Carew,' Maurice said, 'a thousand acres and Carew Castle.' It was where David, William, and he had grown up, given to their father Gerald when he had married Princess Nest, his and FitzStephen's late mother. Maurice bit down on his lip. 'You will have a princess' dowry as your warranty. Agreed?'

Yossi licked his lips. Carew was ten miles to the north of Pembroke and on the frontline of the Normans' fight against the rebellious Welsh – not the safest bet in a country robbed of its greatest knights to follow FitzStephen's banner to Ireland. On the other hand, he considered, there was always some rich Norman fool willing to part with his money for land no matter where. And if that failed he could always flog the estate to some Holy Order of monks. It was a property worth the risk, he decided. 'Agreed,' Yossi said. 'It will take me a day to collect the money together. Will you eat with me tonight?'

FitzStephen smiled politely and nodded, glad that the deal was done. King Diarmait Mac Murchada would never know how close he had come to calling off the expedition, but now, with Yossi's help secured, the adventure to Ireland was back on track.

'Do you know a good armourer?' he asked the Jew, 'and somewhere that I can buy a good courser?'

'You are expecting a fight?' Yossi ben Ysaac asked.

'In Ireland?' replied FitzStephen, 'definitely.'

The night was still and cold as Yossi watched FitzStephen and Maurice lead their horses away from his house. In his hand the candle flared wildly as the meagre wick and molten wax combined and sparked.

'Goodbye,' the Jew shouted at the two Normans, 'and good luck,' he added with a small smile, barely more than a wrinkle of his lips. It had been enjoyable to reminisce with the Norman, his charge for a few short months over a decade before, but the deal that he had made was all the better. He waited until the two men had disappeared into the darkness and the clamour of Gloucester. 'Shmuel?' he then called.

His son slinked out of the dark doorway. 'Father?'

'You heard everything?'

'I did.'

Yossi did not turn to look at him. 'So?'

Shmuel shrugged as he joined his father in the light cast from the entrance. 'I have made my enquiries. It was a good price for Carew Castle.'

'So you think that they succeed in their adventure across the sea?' Yossi asked with a smile. 'Or perhaps you wish to have a castle and live like a great lord like Sir Robert there?'

Shmuel scowled at his father. 'I wish that Robert FitzStephen would die a hundred deaths, I wish his every endeavour fail, and his crops turn to dust. If that leads to our ownership of his lands,' he shrugged, 'then all the better. He stole my wife and forced me to send her away. I wish him great harm.'

'Yet you did not think to attack him in the streets as he left my house,' he nodded his head at the gates of his compound through which Robert and Maurice had departed. 'The Normans are but two and your *friends* could easily make it look like an accident.'

'If my friends were involved, no one on earth would think it an accident,' Shmuel replied. 'Fortunately for them, people will have seen them come into our area and we Jews have enough trouble as it is. I do not want the sheriff's men poking around our business. Not even if it led to his death.'

'That is more like the thinking I require in my business partner,' Yossi replied and threw his hand onto his son's shoulder with no little pride. 'No more anger. No more running off into the darkness with a blade in your hand. Those days are done?'

'Yes,' he replied with a glower.

'Good boy,' he patted his son on the arm as he turned to look at him. 'But that does not mean that we cannot have our revenge on that Godless savage.'

Shmuel blinked and did not answer. 'You mean it?' he stumbled. 'I admit that I am shocked. I thought you liked him.'

'Do you think I could like a man who cuckolded my own firstborn? A man that accepted my hospitality and then threw it back in my face?' Yossi spoke calmly but Shmuel could tell he was on the edge of fury. His long beard quivered. 'Yet civility costs me nothing and I will exact a high price from FitzStephen in recompense for the slight on our family.'

'How?'

'By using my brain,' he replied. 'This is the only way for our kind to survive in this place.' He began to stroke his long grey beard and looked up at the stars which punctured the meagre light from the town. He waited for his son to speak.

'They have our gold,' Shmuel said, 'and we have the deeds to Carew,' he paused and licked our lips. 'Do you want me to rob them?'

'No. But if FitzStephen defaults on the loan then we can sell the castle off,' said Yossi, 'and for a lot more than what they asked for.'

'So how do we make sure that he defaults? How do we make sure that he will fail in his plans in Ireland?'

'I would be inclined to wait,' his father replied, looking up at his son. 'No, do not look so shocked, Shmuel! Ireland is a long way away and not even the might of Rome could conquer it. So the castle may well fall into our hands given time and patience.'

Shmuel shook his head. 'That is not revenge. Hadar ...' He stopped and breathed in deeply. He had not said his wife's name in many years. 'She deceived me and FitzStephen betrayed your trust. I do not want him to taste even a moment of success. I would sail across the sea myself and warn the men of Ireland of his approach if it denied him but a single smile.'

'I don't think that will be necessary.' Yossi frowned. 'He has taken our money and within the week will have spent it on those things he requires to do his fighting and conquering.'

Shmuel breathed out in anger in frustration.

'But that,' Yossi said with a smile, 'is the trap. Once the money is spent he cannot get it back. So if his enterprise was to, I don't know, be prevented from leaving port by some unforeseen circumstance, then FitzStephen would find himself in a very difficult bind.' Yossi smiled at his son and walked back through the door. Shmuel followed.

'You have something in mind, don't you?' When Yossi didn't answer his son continued to badger him. 'Please, Father, tell me your plan.'

In response, Yossi led his son from the antechamber towards his brother's body in the room opposite. 'It is such a shame that we must send Uncle to London with only strangers to care for his body.' He kept his hand on his son's arm as he stroked his dead brother's hair. 'Better that one of his blood travel to the Tower and bury him with his people ...'

'Father ...' Shmuel interrupted but Yossi held up a hand.

'And perhaps while he was there my kinsman could pay a visit to a friend of mine who has the ear of the King.' Yossi reached inside his heavy robes and produced a pouch full of coin which he handed to his son, who looked at it shiftily. 'I didn't say he was a good friend,' Yossi joked as he looked down at his brother, 'but he is one who will listen to a poor Jew with information that he can use to his advantage.'

'And what is to his advantage?'

'A share in the spoils of the sale of Carew Castle,' Yossi said with vigour and gripped his son's arm. Shmuel nodded his head as his father pushed the purse into his hands. 'His name is Hubert Walter, a priest and a Baron of the Exchequer. You will find him – or rather he will find you – in the shadows at the Palace of Westminster. Tell him that FitzStephen plans to subvert King Henry and make himself King of Ireland.'

Shmuel raised his eyebrows. 'Is that true?'

'Who knows?' Yossi said with a shrug, 'but Hubert will convince King Henry of its truth. The King will not allow another to threaten his power. He has enough problems with the Franks and Scots without another rival rising to power on his western shore. He will stop FitzStephen from departing and then –'

'He will default on the loan,' Shmuel interrupted.

'And then we win.'

Shmuel tested the weight of the gold in his hand. 'Ruining FitzStephen and his brothers will not bring Hadar back, but it will suffice for now. You want me to go to London tomorrow?'

'No my boy, you will leave tonight,' He laid his hand on his brother's head. 'We deserve vengeance for this wrong, and luckily for us vengeance can be easily bought.'

Tewdwr ap Rhys was dead. Richard de la Roche brought the news, and his five battered men-at-arms, back from Ireland in a merchant ship bound for Bristol. Diarmait was devastated, Roche told FitzStephen in his deep voice, and had taken up hiding in a monastery outside Fearna with his family. There he brooded and plotted against one and all. There he waited for the coming of FitzStephen and for the violence to begin.

'It is a country of contrasts, Sir Robert,' Roche told the knight from Ceredigion as they stood in the bows of the moored ship in Melrfjord sound. 'It has rich soil but few good farmers.

Forests dominate the almost the entire island but they do not try to build castles.' The Fleming shook his head in disbelief. 'The warriors are naturally brave but they have no training or discipline. The churches are packed with riches and students while their warriors are few. They are virtually leaderless but nearly indomitable. It will not be easy to put King Diarmait back on his throne,' he said as he shook his head, 'even the Danes have given up trying to conquer these stubborn Irish.'

'What of Waesfjord?' Robert asked.

'I know not. We landed well to the north of the city,' Roche said, 'though the way the Irish talk of it, Waesfjord may as well be impregnable.' He then recanted the story of Tewdwr's death. The boy had gone ahead to Ireland with Diarmait and Richard de la Roche, without his father's permission or many warriors, and upon arrival had led a small sally into the north of Laighin against an enemy called the Osraighe. It had been little more than a skirmish at a place called Cill Osnadh, and their aim had been to rustle some cattle.

'However,' Roche said, 'the locals were many and we were few, they were well prepared for our approach and they fell on us with animal savagery.' He bowed his head. 'Crazy eyed and naked as the day they were born,' he said. 'It was terrifying. Nevertheless, we fought them off. Young Tewdwr was our only casualty. A throwing spear took him in the throat as he marshalled our line to meet their charge.' He wiped a hand down his face. 'His life was extinguished before his body had even hit the ground. We buried him there and retreated. After that I took charge. I sought out Diarmait's son, Domhnall, who had been hiding in a forest near his home and together we took back Diarmait's fortress at Fearna, but there was no plunder to be had so I brought the men back here on a merchantman out of Dubhlinn.'

'And Diarmait?'

'Forced into hiding for fear of attack by more powerful of the tribes around Fearna,' Richard said. 'He was confident that the Augustinians would protect him.'

FitzStephen blew air out between puffed cheeks as he listened to the tale. The sun's morning vapour had already begun to creep over the land to the east and the Welsh headland, which guarded the mouth of the Cleddau estuary, was already starting to appear out of the distant dark. Robert directed his short prayer for the soul of Tewdwr ap Rhys towards the sun. He had been a brave man who was in heaven ahead of his time. He would have to send someone north to tell the mourning Prince Rhys the tale of Tewdwr's brave demise. Perhaps he would even employ a bard to write a tune to remember the Cymri nobleman. FitzStephen did not want to send a warrior to Llandovery and lose a sword at this late stage, but manners required that he send someone of rank and he could not bear the thought of his cousin hearing of Tewdwr's death from any other source, no matter what had gone between them in the last years. Maybe he would send that chattering priest Nicholas, he thought, even though he doubted that the cleric would tell the tale nearly as well as a fighting man.

Richard de la Roche yawned and FitzStephen dismissed him to his bed, leaving the Norman alone on the ship which rocked slowly in the shallows of the river. His Flemish friend had done the right thing by bringing his men back to Wales and FitzStephen had immediately taken the older man's oath of fealty. Roche, who would accompany him back to Ireland on the next day's tide, had also brought news from Diarmait of a suitable landing place for FitzStephen's invasion, an island in the mouth of a river in the extreme south. To that end the Fleming had also brought an Irishman back with him, old in years and wise in the oceans between Ireland and Wales; a good guide to the island which had been selected for the Norman bridgehead. The Irishman had spoken little since he had arrived except to declare that, following a thorough inspection, he believed the Norman-made ships capable of making the dangerous voyage across the sea. According to a grimly gleeful Fionntán Ua Donnchaidh, the coast around Waesfjord was treacherous and even cursed by dangerous and cruel spirits and it would take a man of his own substantial skill to safely navigate the Normans to Ireland.

'So don't think about giving me any orders or I will lead your whole army onto rocks,' he had told FitzStephen and the

Norman believed him. Every part of Ua Donnchaidh's face seemed craggy and sunburn from sea spray and reflected sun while his eyes were constantly screwed up from a lifetime staring at the same sparkling seas. The effect was a continuous toothy smile-grimace across his face which made him look like he was laughing at everyone. The wiry little man might well have been, FitzStephen considered. Fionntán had also told him that he had fought against Robert's father, Stephen, when Gruffydd ap Tewdwr of Deheubarth had returned to Wales from exile, and that was when he had learned some of the French and Welsh tongues. His reason for helping his old enemy now was unknown to FitzStephen and Fionntán's mocking face gave away nothing.

Yossi's money had been well spent in the few weeks since FitzStephen and Maurice had returned from Gloucester. Six ships had been ordered from the Norse shipwrights who plied their trade at Melrfjord. FitzStephen looked down across the quayside at his fleet: the *Arthwyr*, the *Dragon*, and the *Saint Maurice* were seaworthy while the *Nest* and the *Saint David* were yet to be launched. Those two beached ships lacked only masts and would be used to bring Maurice de Prendergast and his Flemings to Ireland the day after the main landing by Robert and his Normans. The shell of an as yet unnamed ship was beginning to take form and would eventually be used to take Maurice FitzGerald and his reinforcements across the sea a month after the first landings. In addition to finishing the last ship, the workers were cutting down a vast swathe of forest for timber that would be shaped and cut so that FitzStephen's brother could bring the basis for a castle across the sea. The timber would be sequenced and bundled for a quick and easy assembly in Ireland. Everything they needed to survive was to be brought with them. Nothing had been left to chance.

'You fight a battle,' he remembered his father's lesson as a child, 'and then you build a castle. Then you ride for a day, fight again, and build another castle.' It was the Norman way of war and he knew that advice was as true today as it was back then.

The *Arthwyr* bumped thickly on the waves against the beach

and FitzStephen rocked with her. Beside the bulbous ship was the *Saint Maurice*. She was to be captained by Richard de la Roche alongside Walter de Ridlesford and Renaud de Caunteton. Beyond that was the *Dragon* under the command of Robert's nephew, Miles Menevensis, and the Gael, Fionntan. Each ship would carry about a hundred and twenty men, plus supplies and horses.

Sunlight burst suddenly over the land of Dyfed, warming FitzStephen's face, and he closed his eyes, releasing a smile. Through his eyelids he fancied that he could see the blurry red outline of the peninsular on the far headland. It was but a black silhouette in front of the bright sun. FitzStephen could not have hoped for a more beautiful last day in Wales. Quickly he considered his future which lay over the distant horizon in the land of Ireland. What would he find there? Cleanly shaven and clothed in chainmail and surcoat, FitzStephen once again looked like a Norman knight ready for battle. But something was different in his soul. It seemed like all his life had been preparing him for this moment; the few instants of learning at his distant father's side in Aberteifi, as a page watching the great Earl Robert de Caen, as an esquire to the brave, if foolhardy, Sir Henry FitzRoy, and as the Constable of Ceredigion with Wulfhere Little-Fingers beside him. He realised that for all his life he had been working for another man's glory, but now he felt that he was fighting for himself, for his family's prestige, and for a merchant town called Waesfjord. He could almost see the prize in his mind's eye; a settlement with many ships in the river port and traders milling around the marketplace. Well-ordered fields ran away from the town walls and the land was heaving with crops and animals. And above them all was a castle of stone, dominating the river, estuary, and land. FitzStephen opened his eyes and sniffed a small laugh. He was getting ahead of himself and decided that his thoughts of Ireland could wait until the following day when the tide was at its highest. He should enjoy his last day in the beautiful land which he had called his home.

The warming sun had not yet cleared the misty vapour which lay over the fields and birdsong and frog-croaking lulled

179

his mind as he thought of all the old stories about his homeland. He wondered if men would sing and talk of his part in the Norman story in Wales in years to come. Perhaps he would be remembered as a story to scare children. He was shocked to find that he actually quite liked the idea. He thought about the mottle of lordships in western Wales known as *Little England*, a country which he would never see again. Beyond Pembroke was a tight ring of Norman fortresses defending southern Dyfed from the independent rule of Prince Rhys. One of FitzStephen's sons, Geoffrey, was now stationed in those castles. As page to William FitzGerald's wife in Carew Castle, Geoffrey would be afforded a comfortable lifestyle before becoming an esquire and learning to be a miles. It was a good life for a mere bastard, he thought. He was himself an illegitimate son and knew from experience how difficult life could be when people preferred to think of you as an affront to God and His Church. FitzStephen sniffed away the long-forgotten subject and turned his back on the sun. It was all bandit country to the north of Carew, where Welsh and Norman mixed and fought and died. And amongst those warring lands was his home, Aberteifi. FitzStephen had not realised how much he loved the country of Wales and its petty politics, warring barons, and belligerent chieftains. How much he would miss its rolling countryside and high hills! It did not matter to him that most of the people of this country hated him and all his kind; this was his country, conquered by his father, and he was leaving it forever for an unknown future in Ireland.

There and then he decided to take a journey out to the headland at the mouth of the river to look across the sea to Ireland. Turning on his heel, he jumped down onto the shingle and sandy beach from the *Arthwyr* and trotted back towards the small town. Seashells snapped and shattered beneath his leather sabatons as he crossed the strand to his new courser. The small, stout horse had been his first purchase in Gloucester, and he had named him Sleipnir after Odin's eight-legged beast because, like his mythical namesake, the courser was incredibly fleet of foot. Climbing into the saddle he looked one last time at the estuary before turning Sleipnir northwards through the settlement. At his side was a new sword with its grip made from white shark skin which, its creator had told him, would give him an advantage if he fought in the rain.

Meiler FitzHenry, his nephew, was one of the few out of his bed and was eating porridge from a carved wooden bowl which he had bought in the small Norse town. When Meiler saw his uncle he jumped to his feet, knocking over a stool in the open-walled kitchen tent.

'Good morning, Uncle,' Meiler cried, his voice nervous and slightly too high-pitched for such a squat and capable youngster.

'Meiler,' FitzStephen said, turning Sleipnir to greet him, 'you are up very early.' His nephew babbled something about horses needing to be fed but FitzStephen wasn't really listening. Meiler's father, Sir Henry FitzRoy, had been, like Robert, an illegitimate son of the famed *Helen of Wales*, Princess Nest of Deheubarth, though Meiler's grandfather had been no less than King Henry I of England. Meiler was therefore one of King Henry's closest relatives, but he had never even met the King of England. Like FitzStephen he was considered a troublemaker and a law onto himself. Nonetheless, Meiler had served Henry FitzEmpress in France before returning in squalor to Wales, where he found that in his absence his lands had been overrun by the rampaging Welsh of Deheubarth. Castles that had once been deep inside Norman territory now lay in Welsh hands and lands long tilled by Norman farmers were now used as pastures for the roving Cymri. When Meiler had appealed for his cousin King Henry's help his entreaties had been met with silence. His story was the same one told by the Barri brothers, Walter de Ridlesford, and the Caunteton family, the Barretts, the Codds, and the Russells. Their failure in Wales had made them all desperate to succeed in Ireland.

'Could you do something for me, Meiler?' FitzStephen asked him.

'Of course,' his nephew said immediately, eyes twinkling at the possibility of responsibility.

'Take charge of loading the ships. I am going for a gallop.'

Meiler nodded with a smile and repeated FitzStephen's

orders. 'Load the ships, going for a gallop. Got it,' he said, obviously delighted at the small responsibility placed on his wide shoulders. 'What will I tell everyone? When will you return?'

FitzStephen shook his head and beamed. 'When my horse is tired? When I see the ocean? Who knows!' With that he kicked Sleipnir into a trot through the village and whooped.

It was good to be free.

It was after midday when FitzStephen was challenged at the edge of the small town of Melrfjord by two Flemings in the colours of Richard de la Roche. Like their commander, whose family came from a town in the southern coast in Rhos, their French was spoken with the clipped Germanic tones of their flooded homeland. The two men guarded the small gap in a hastily thrown up palisade designed to protect the hundred or so tents. Flags and emblems of the more senior knights crowned several positions on the wooden stockade, whilst behind it the tents were plain and grey against the blue sky.

Most of the men who would follow FitzStephen were considered brigands, trouble-makers, and failures by those outside Wales; dangerous men who disrupted the peace installed by good King Henry. Most had become wandering vagabonds, willing to sell their skills in war to any lord who would feed, house, or promise them plunder. But FitzStephen knew better. These men were exactly what he wanted – warriors who would do anything to follow the sons of Nest and their offer of more land than they ever believed possible.

While the small, tented town was almost empty, apart from the Flemish guards at the gate, the beach was awash with people and materials which were being loaded onto the ships. FitzStephen quickly passed through, pausing only to leave Sleipnir with a smith to re-shoe, and went down to the waterside. Except for the horses and the men, everything was being put on the ships so that the army could move on the early tide.

'Sir Robert,' Meiler FitzHenry shouted at him from beside a donkey which dragged a cart with forty suits of scale armour towards the *Saint Maurice*. The chainmail rang as it travelled along the rough path. 'Where the hell did you get to?' he asked. He was confident now, having been put in command of greater men and older cousins by his uncle. 'Everyone was worried.'

FitzStephen doubted that very much but greeted Meiler cordially. 'I threw a shoe on my way to the headland. Is everything going well here?'

'As it could be,' Meiler confirmed. For a man-at-arms he was a stickler for minutiae, and he had carefully organised the supplies and materials for the trip showing no small amount of enjoyment and fulfilment in the task. 'Not there!' Meiler suddenly shouted at a serf who was trying to store twice-baked bread on deck of the *Arthwyr*, 'put in the hold, you idiot! One splash from a wave and we lose the whole lot.'

FitzStephen realised he was not needed on the organisational front and, leaving Meiler shouting at the serf, pulled off his surcoat and shirt to begin helping the men loading the ships. White, wrinkly scars and war wounds appeared as he tensed the muscles on his chest and arms. He was assisting two brothers from Devon called Scurlock to load sheaves of arrows and bolts into the *Dragon*'s hold when Philip de Barri found him later that evening.

'… and so Earl Strongbow married Roger de Quincy to his only daughter because he claimed that he was a warrior of repute,' the elder Scurlock, Amalric, told FitzStephen, 'but William Ferrand was ridden with guilt and contracted leprosy from praying for forgiveness all day in a monastery where they treated the diseased …'

'Sir Maurice wants you to come up to his tent,' Philip interrupted Scurlock. 'Bishop David is saying Mass before tonight's feast.'

FitzStephen groaned internally. David's sermons were notoriously long with much shouting and banging of tabletops, but he knew it would be bad form and a scurrilous start to the campaign to not give thanks to the Lord with his brothers. He bade goodbye to the Scurlocks, throwing his surcoat, shirt, and sword belt over his bare shoulder and walked back up the sun-blanched beach. He sent the enthusiastic young Philip ahead of him, back up to the Norman camp to herald his approach. As he walked up towards Maurice's tent he threw on his shirt and rearranged his surcoat and belt, dusting off the dirt picked up from his afternoon's work. He steeled himself in preparation for David's Mass, wishing that he had thought to have got himself some food before coming up to the tent. As he was thinking this he spotted them: three men-at-arms wearing the King's livery of two contemptuous golden Angevin lions on a crimson field. The warriors were eating from bread trenchers in the dining tent where he had discovered Meiler early that morning. Some impulse made him turn back and take a different route to Maurice's tent. Immediately confused and alarmed at the presence of royal agents in their camp and, he felt a cold sweat begin at his back. He quietly circumnavigated another shelter and ducked into Maurice's tent where an animated argument was going on.

'You cannot be serious, Sir John!' It was not often that Maurice raised his voice, but FitzStephen could see from his elder brother's face that he had already been shouting at the knight before the top table for some time. 'We have spent money of our own in good faith that we had King Henry's licence to go to Ireland.' In his hand Maurice held a copy of Henry's proclamation complete with a wax seal and ribbon which dangled for all to see.

'My Lord Constable ...' Sir John began before stopping to acknowledge FitzStephen's entry. The tent went silent as he entered and looked at their unwanted visitor. He knew Sir John de Stafford by his yellow and red decorated livery which was famous throughout England. He was a tall, thin, grey-haired man with a short, neat beard who had made his name fighting against the Scots. Now, with age taking its toll and a gammy knee from a battle long ago, he had, ironically, become one of the King's favourite couriers. The implication of using such an important knight as his messenger on this occasion was not lost on FitzStephen: King Henry meant business.

'Sir Robert,' Stafford greeted his host with the smallest of nods and winced from the old war wound in his leg. 'I was just telling your brothers of my mission. I come on behalf of King

Henry.'

FitzStephen felt his lip curl. Obviously there was no Mass as Philip de Barri had suggested, but FitzStephen suspected that Maurice, sensibly, had not wanted to worry the other warriors at the harbour with the news of the arrival of the King's messenger.

'The Justiciar, Richard de Luci, sends me to you with his greetings,' Stafford continued. 'You, Sir Robert, are summoned with horses and arms to attend upon the King in Aquitaine. You must present yourself to the King in Poitiers before Midsummer with any troops under your command.' Sir John bowed his head. 'I believe that you will garrison Chinon Castle through the winter.'

'Chinon?' one man shouted angrily. 'How can the King go back on his licence?' Soon all those in the tent were shouting at Sir John.

FitzStephen could not believe his ears. Everything that he had hoped for was evaporating before his eyes. A decree from the King of England may as well have been issued from the mouth of God himself. 'In short,' he raised his voice to calm the room, 'the King has decided to retract his licence?' The anger threatened to rise in FitzStephen. 'What of Maurice, Sir John?'

'The King gave no orders as regarding the Constable of Pembroke,' the knight said evenly, 'though I do not doubt that he means him to remain in Wales at his proper station.' He raised an eyebrow in Maurice's direction. 'Henry's orders were directed only to you, Sir Robert.'

Wind billowed the door of the tent, sending a shiver through the small group of men who were trying to come to terms with this revelation. FitzStephen barely noticed Miles and Walter de Ridlesford threaten and barter with Sir John who, hands in the air, denied that there was any way out of the situation. Bishop David took up the tête-à-tête with Sir John, but FitzStephen was barely listening.

'If you think we are about to give up on our most Holy Crusade to return Ireland to the See of Rome then you are sadly mistaken,' David boomed, his outstretched arm pointing beyond the flapping tent door which faced east. 'We have made a solemn covenant with Our Lord ...'

FitzStephen interrupted his brother halfway through his religious tirade by laying a hand across his arm. 'And what if we ignore King Henry's decree?' he asked. The gathering immediately fell silent. Most understood the gravity of his declaration. 'What if I do not care what that lying Angevin bastard commands?' he asked again.

John de Stafford laughed briefly, searching each face for a similar reaction. He realised quickly that the warriors of the March were deadly serious. He held up the document bearing the King of England's seal for all to see. 'King Henry's word is law in this land.'

'No,' FitzStephen replied, dragging his sword from his scabbard and stabbing it into the grass before Sir John, 'this is the March and here the sword rules.' The English knight took a small step back from the quivering weapon.

'Sir Robert,' he said, 'please be serious. No-one ignores a command from Henry of England! Don't mistake this king for one like Stephen de Blois.' He held out a finger and pointed at FitzStephen's chest. 'This king will never forgive you if you go through with your plan and he will stalk you like a beast wherever you attempt to flee. Henry does not forget and he does not stop to offer mercy.'

FitzStephen shrugged, his eyes meeting Maurice's across the room. His brother nodded encouragingly. 'So Henry will declare me an outlaw,' he replied. 'I wouldn't be the first and certainly I won't be the last. And I, at least, will be beyond his grasp in Ireland.'

'But what if you do not succeed, Robert?' Bishop David asked. 'It will not be our necks on the line but yours, brother.'

'We will just have to make sure we do not fail. And you can truthfully say that I left against your will.'

Stafford was appalled at the knight's words. 'This is madness,' he said quietly. 'Don't you see what Henry is doing?' he said. 'He remembers the stories of Robert Guiscard and Bohemond; mere knights who became kings. He remembers the stories of his own grandfather, Fulk; a mere count in France, but a great monarch in Jerusalem. His councillors tell him that he should fear a rival Norman kingdom on his doorstep. He fears that would destabilise his empire. Henry will not allow you to threaten his power.'

FitzStephen looked on unmoved. 'I seek no crown.'

'And why do you think he stamps royal authority on every nobleman?' Stafford continued unabated. 'He and his cronies write laws that suffocate and strangle any dissenting voice and make all subservient to his word.'

FitzStephen wondered what decree had caught in Sir John de Stafford's throat. He wondered which law had made him acquiesce to the King's power, but he did not stop Stafford's speech.

'He does it because he is fearful of his subjects,' Sir John continued. 'He is scared of you, Sir Robert, because you may succeed in your venture and become a threat to his empire.'

FitzStephen began to laugh. 'Henry of England – scared of me? Sir John, I thank you for bringing me this message and you may inform our faint-hearted monarch that I received his words.' FitzStephen inhaled sharply, 'But also tell him this – I was his loyal subject until he abandoned me to imprisonment. I consider my allegiance to him over only because he forgot his fidelity to me, and because of that I feel no compunction in ignoring his decree and going to Ireland against his wishes. Like our family's protector, St Maurice, I will not bend to the cruel commands of an over-powerful monarch. Tell him that, Sir John.' David and Maurice smiled at FitzStephen's invocation of the story about the Roman soldier who refused to worship the Emperor Maximian as a living God and was martyred for the Christian faith.

'I assume then that the offer of fifty marks from the treasury would also meet with your refusal?' Sir John de Stafford asked. Walter de Ridlesford whistled at the sum but FitzStephen simply shook his head.

'Some things cannot be bought for any amount.'

Stafford sighed and bowed his head. 'I will pray that you never fall into King Henry's clutches, Sir Robert, or he will tear you to pieces like a terrier with a rat in his teeth. You will understand that I am charged to stop you at any cost?'

FitzStephen nodded in response and Stafford continued: 'So I will go to Gower and get William de Braose's help. It could take me three days to return with his warriors,' Sir John said with a smile.

'Thank you, Sir John,' FitzStephen bowed to his peer, realising that Gower was only a day's riding to the east and that Stafford was allowing him the chance to get to sea.

'I can't say that I am not a little jealous,' Stafford said after bowing to the bishop and the Constable of Pembroke. 'Good luck, Sir Robert, and to you all.' He pushed his way out of the tent to begin his journey back towards the Gower peninsular to the east.

Inside the tent was quiet as they waited for the King's agent to get out of earshot. Then suddenly every man in the room began talking loudly.

'FitzStephen, you are mad, just like your father,' said one agitated voice. 'King Henry will eat us for breakfast!'

'No, he's right! To hell with the Angevins,' another called.

It was FitzStephen's voice which boomed for silence. 'We now have a new enemy,' he told them. 'He is the King of England.' Several in the room visibly wilted at his words. 'Any man who follows my banner to Ireland will probably never be able to return to England, Wales, or any land controlled by Henry FitzEmpress.' He gave every man present a moment to think on their probable exile and the forfeiture of their estates, meagre though they were. 'The King is a man who does not forgive,' FitzStephen continued, 'and time will not temper his thirst for revenge over those who resisted him. I am willing to take that chance because the glory and prize in Ireland is so great. But I cannot speak for every man so if you feel that you cannot stand against the King, I will understand.' Some men groaned angry growls at the thought of giving in to Henry's threats while others shared secret, silent looks to friends of a like mind that they should get out of the dangerous position in which they found themselves. 'And those men may remain here and continue the fight against Prince Rhys with my brother, Sir William,' he continued. 'But tell me, how successful has that fight been of late? How many men has Henry sent to help his

188

loyal knights in Wales? How long can we continue the fight before we are driven back across the Severn?' Many growled their agreement and hatred of the Welsh leaders who had pushed them back into the last recesses of the southern coast. FitzStephen gritted his teeth. 'It won't be easy, but in Ireland we will have a king who will stand beside us in battle, not behind plotting how to get his grubby hands on the prize for which we have fought,' he said. 'And we will have land; two hundred thousand acres and the city of Waesfjord!' He let the vast quantity of land sink in. 'And there will be the prospect of more to any man brave enough to take it.' The Norman leaders nodded their heads in assent. 'So I am asking you to follow me to Ireland despite the hostility of a jealous king,' FitzStephen said, 'and claim your fortune and the gratitude of an appreciative monarch. Hardy men of Wales, let us leave this land behind and forge a new frontier in Ireland!'

The commanders cheered FitzStephen and his vision for the future. They may have been considered troublemakers and bandits in the kingdom of England but they were also the true heirs of the Northmen and their equal in boldness and daring. They all revelled in the desire for land and conquest. It was the same drive which had taken their ancestors from Scandinavia to France, France into England, and England into the Welsh lands beyond. And now it would lead them to the very edge of the known world; to Ireland.

The cheering gradually abated. 'We leave for Laighin on the morning tide.' Sir Robert FitzStephen, son of a Welsh princess and a lowborn Norman knight, was adamant. Sir Robert FitzStephen was going to war and to find his fortune.

# Chapter Seven

## *Wales*
## *May 1169*

It was still dark as the Normans began loading the last pieces of equipment onto the three ships which would make the daunting crossing to Ireland. It promised to be a beautiful day for the voyage but the men worked in almost silence. Water sloshed on the shore and the workers whispered reverently just above the sound of water fizzing through dark shingle. Many of those who would travel westwards had never even been to sea despite growing up on the Welsh coast and they feared the great ocean which bounded their little land. Above them, Fionntán Ua Donnchaidh stood on the *Dragon*, leaning on the steering oar and sneering sarcastically as he watched the Norman army struggle up the pine gangplanks with supplies. The tired men threw angry looks at the old mariner, but he just watched them and offered no assistance as they dragged the animals into the boats and hobbled them in the belly of the vessels. Nor did he help secure the sea chests or ox-hides covering the provisions. Fionntán's mind was on the weather and the tide.

'Get up off your lazy arse and help us,' Amalric Scurlock finally snapped and shouted in Fionntán's direction but the Irishman just spat over the side of the *Dragon* in answer, scaring two gulls who circled in the hope of stealing some morsel of food.

Fionntán tossed the birds a scrap of bread and then returned to his smirking vigil, much to Scurlock's irritation. The Irishman was still unsure of the Normans. He was a man of the Osraighe, the tribe who lived to the west of Diarmait's, but when his pretty young wife had been stolen by the nephew of King Donnchadh Mac Giolla Phádraig he had joined the Meic

191

Murchada in the hope of gaining vengeance over the man who had cuckolded him. He had never expected that his retribution would bring him so far from his homeland to act as a guide for this rowdy bunch of warriors.

Fionntán wondered what effect such a small number of men could have against the vast multitude that stood against Diarmait. Sure, the Normans had horses and armour – but all Gaelic noblemen were horsemen, and the Ostmen had armoured shirts and weaponry just the same as that of FitzStephen's men. What would these mercenaries bring to the table that the Ostmen had not, Fionntán wondered? It was not that he was not impressed with the Normans, on the contrary he had never seen a better prepared force, but there were just not enough of them to make even the smallest dent in the horde available to Ruaidhrí Ua Conchobair.

He had watched the Normans' training over the last few days. To his mind this had largely amounted to the milites and esquires battering each other with sticks and carrying each other into a maul of piggy-back fights. And what, he wondered, could the men-at-arms possibly learn from attacking stationary wooden targets from horseback with their lances? Fionntán did not deny that the mercenaries were tough, but he could not imagine how the horsemen and the archers would work in the middle of a battle when faced by ten thousand screaming warriors from Connacht. They would surely be overrun.

'Fionntán,' FitzStephen greeted him cordially from the landward side of the ship. 'We are ready to get the men on board. Then we can depart.'

The Irishman at the steering oar sniffed. 'If you say so.'

'You don't?'

Fionntán grimaced. 'Do you Normans dress like that so it makes it easy to see you in the dark?' He nodded his head at Meiler FitzHenry who, wrapped in his red and yellow surcoat, tripped as he led an unloaded mule away from the ships. Fionntán rasped a laugh. 'Or maybe they blind you to your surroundings. Bloody stupid for a warrior to dress like you lot do, if you ask me.'

'Nobody did,' FitzStephen replied tersely, causing Fionntán

to snigger as if the Norman had made a joke.

'Those horses will not survive the journey,' the Gael told FitzStephen matter-of-factly. 'I've seen it before. They get sick, can't vomit, and that is that.'

The Norman captain grimaced, but nodded his head. 'I'm aware of the problem – it's the same when they get grass sickness. My brother, Maurice, knows of an old remedy made from valerian, ginger, and skullcap, which should keep them docile while we cross …'

'There are fine horses in Ireland,' Fionntán told him. 'You should leave these ones here. I'll steal you a few. You'll hardly need them anyway.'

FitzStephen looked up at the Irishman as he leisurely hung from the steering board. 'I'd rather leave every shirt of armour and all our shields behind than those animals,' he told him and laughed at Fionntán's disbelief. 'We Normans value those animals, and our castles, like the Ostmen value their dragon-ships …'

'You both need to find a good woman,' Fionntán joked.

FitzStephen sniffed a laugh. 'The sea was the Danes' highway,' he continued, 'but we have discovered how to spread our war inland …'

'I suppose that makes you twice as dangerous?' the Irishman joked, but FitzStephen did not answer. Instead the Gael watched the shambolic Normans on the beach as they tried to steady their drunken horses and to walk them into the bellies of the ships, where they had fashioned pens for the animals. It was chaos and as inauspicious a start to a campaign as any he had ever been involved in. Fionntán considered that success had never been more unlikely.

'You are putting a great deal of trust in your horses, Norman,' he told FitzStephen, 'but perhaps you are hoping that your men's gaudy dresses will blind our enemy before battle.'

Robert simply grimaced. 'Just get us to Ireland safely and quickly.'

Fionntán laughed at FitzStephen's anger and spat a long stream of spittle over the side. He knew that these Normans, despite their captain's bravado, were just mercenaries and were as such likely to leave Ireland if the pickings became slim. They were just too few and did not understand the momentous task which opposed them. He shook his head and sighed in resignation that this would prove another false dawn in his quest for vengeance.

'We'll have little over an hour before the tide gets too low to leave,' the Irishman told FitzStephen.

'... and I'll have the army in the ships in half that time,' the Norman interrupted and marched away up the beach to assist one of the men whose cob refused to go up the gangplank and into the ship.

In the end it took an hour for the rest of the army to be loaded onto the boats by which time the sun was fully in the sky and Fionntán was again complaining about missing the turning tide. Muddled amongst the men in the ships were goats, chickens, and lambs to sustain the army at their bridgehead on the southern Irish coast. The coursers, hobbled in the belly of the ships, were already getting agitated and snorting loudly. To make matters worse Bishop David, encouraged by his young cousin, Father Gerald de Barri, insisted on giving a lengthy sermon in Latin to the troops. Recently returned from his studies in Paris, the priest nodded along as David extolled God and the Lord Jesus to send heavenly power to their swords and give them victory over their enemies. Most of the men could not understand the ecclesiastical tongue and the rest could not even hear his voice above the noise of the gulls, wind, and lapping water.

All the warriors laughed when Walter de Ridlesford farted loudly and whispered that it was 'heaven scent'. Father Gerald ignored the blasphemy and continued to beseech the now bright heavens, asking the powers to send the army a divine strength on their crusade to bring order to the Celtic Church and a return to the rule set down by Rome. Both Bishop David and Father Gerald were advocates of a strong Welsh archbishopric and so the See of Canterbury was derided for a few minutes before he returned to mentioning the many evils of the Church across the sea: lay investiture, simony, and clerical marriage. For some, his mention of an assured place in heaven was ample payment for the dangerous journey across the sea for many of the warriors. The bishop finally signed off his prayer with an appeal to St Christopher for safe passage. Fionntán crossed himself sarcastically, saying his Irish 'amen' rather too loudly for Bishop David's taste, and the churchman scowled at the foreigner. The Irishman ignored him, turning towards the sea and throwing a silver coin into the water as an offering to the old gods, nymphs, and spirits who really held sway with the oceans. David pretended not to notice the pagan gift.

'Father, I seek your blessing,' Miles Menevensis said loudly as he leapt from the bishop's side and knelt before his father. The old bishop looked flustered and embarrassed at Miles' public outburst and rather than lay his hands on his son he simply cast a quick cross in front of his bowed head before turning on his heels and stomping angrily up the beach without another word. It was left to Maurice FitzGerald to lift his forlorn nephew to his feet and embrace him. Miles was long used to being rebuffed by his father in public and private, but he had felt that there may have been a change in his father's feelings towards him at the beginning of this dangerous undertaking. However, he collected himself quickly and shuffled towards the *Dragon* to join Fionntán who, for his part, didn't say a word of spite to the Norman. Miles hoisted the gangplank into the ship behind him and ordered forward twenty serfs who heaved the long ship into the surf using their shoulders and ropes as well as long, thick poles which wedged it free. After just a few seconds, the ship skidded off the shingle and was afloat in a few feet of water. Horses whinnied aboard and Fionntán shouted orders as the ship drifted slowly out into the river. Oars extended on either side of the *Dragon* but they were hardly needed as the ship glided on the current towards the distant sea. A gruff shout from Richard de la Roche sent the English serfs wading towards the *Saint Maurice* where they proceeded to force the second ship into the depths of the river. Roche's commands could still be heard over the noise of man and beast, creaking wood, straining rope, and the splash of water.

FitzStephen watched from the beach where he stood beside

his half-brothers, Maurice and William. 'So do you think they will remember this date, the second day of May 1169, as the beginning of something important,' he asked, 'something that changed the world?'

William FitzGerald, the eldest of the Geraldines, looked puzzled. 'It is only the last day of April, Robert.'

'I thought it was the first of May,' Maurice said quietly turning to look at his brothers. They all were silent for a few seconds before bursting into laughter, the nervous tension broken.

'I suspect history will remember our endeavour, if not the correct date,' laughed William, 'and who knows? In a thousand years the world may still be talking about the actions which we take today. Don't forget that we are going to one of the most learned civilisations in Europe, one which Charlemagne himself respected. Our efforts will, no doubt, be captured in words and illuminated in colour and travel beyond the borders of these little islands to all the great courts of Europe.' William grinned and waved a hand southwards. 'Maybe they won't get the date right but the effect will be felt everywhere …'

Maurice and FitzStephen looked at each other and smiled as their pompous older brother continued without noticing that they were no longer listening to his long-winded lecture. William was a learned man but rather prone to the dramatic. He had been placed in a monastery after he, his younger siblings, and his mother were kidnapped by Owain of Powys. There he had been taught the classics and educated as a churchman before being released to his father in Pembroke. William had always held his literary knowledge in high regard, and liked to show off at every opportunity.

'Remember the three hundred Spartans at Thermopylae long ago,' William continued. 'Our army are but a few more in number than they, and face no lesser odds. The name of Leonidas lives on even to this day.' He stopped to consider his own words, nodding seriously as if someone other than he himself had uttered some astute wisdom.

FitzStephen, who had never heard of Leonidas, breathed out through puffed cheeks, eyebrows raised. 'Easy, William, I only got into this for the money.' He joked, but of course there was much more to it than that; family prestige and a warrior's pride primary amongst them.

'Time to go and make history,' Maurice said raising a sarcastic eyebrow at his elder brother, who scowled, realising that he was, as usual, the butt of a joke.

FitzStephen nodded and embraced his older brothers. 'One month,' he told Maurice, referring to the reinforcements the older man was to bring across the sea. 'By then I will have Waesfjord or be dead before its walls.'

His half-brother nodded. 'I will pray to St Maurice for the former. God be with you, Robert.' He shook his hand.

'Goodbye,' he said, climbing into the ship. William called forward the serfs who began using poles to lever the ship into the river. Some entered up to their waists on both sides and shoved and hauled at the boat which gradually began to float away in the deepening Cleddau River.

'Wait, please!' a voice shouted from high up the beach. A beggar was running down the shingle bank towards the ship which was quickly drifting further into the river. 'Sir Robert, wait!' the vagrant yelled again. Normally FitzStephen gave alms on a Sunday and special saints' days, but he had no time for generosity now. The ship was leaving.

'Try the monks in Pembroke,' FitzStephen shouted at the beggar. The man looked like he was sixty, if he was a day, but was surprising in his speed, running towards FitzStephen at a gallop, unencumbered by armour, with his tattered cloak pummelling out behind him. His head bobbed up and down on his shoulders like a cat as he ran and for the first time FitzStephen noticed that he had a sword held out from his body by his long, thin arm. Who was this desperate old man, he wondered?

'Are we waiting or what?' Meiler FitzHenry shouted from the steering oar at the other side of the ship. Already the men on the river side were sliding the oars out through the oarlocks and into the water, dragging the boat deeper into the river. FitzStephen grimaced, more so because he was interested in finding out whom the man was, rather than out of concern. Still the old man ran towards the *Arthwyr*.

'Wait, wait,' was all that he could manage due to his exertions. He was closer now and FitzStephen could see his long, grey, dank hair flopping around at his neck. Above that was a balding dome; his sparse hair was scraped back from his fading hairline with sweat. FitzStephen did not like the look of the man. He looked desperate and feral and did not blink as he hit the waterside. He waded out towards the boat and FitzStephen had to fight down the urge to beat the old man back into the water with an oar but, a moment later, the vagrant had grabbed the sheer-strake and had nimbly hoisted himself out of the small surf, throwing his long legs over the side into the ship.

'Who the hell are you?' FitzStephen demanded angrily of the old man who lay on his back, gasping for air, in the middle of the *Arthwyr*'s deck. All eyes had turned to look at the man before FitzStephen's bellow sent them back to their toil at the oar. Meiler took the lead and began issuing orders as his uncle knelt beside the gasping and wet old man. 'I can't use a beggar with a stolen sword where we are going and I don't like the look of you,' FitzStephen told him. 'So tell me why I don't drop you in our wake?'

The man's throat rasped and fear showed in his rheumy eyes, but he still managed to compose himself. 'Because I come on Earl Strongbow's business,' he said. It was enough.

FitzStephen tried to wrap his head around the statement and climbed back to his feet. He couldn't believe that a nobleman of Strongbow's reputation would send a person such as this as his messenger.

'Your name?' he enquired.

'Sir Hervey de Montmorency. The Earl's uncle,' he sneered and breathed deeply, showing his rotten teeth to FitzStephen as if his name won any argument. He was not a man who could be thrown over the side without serious repercussions. Nor could they pull back to shore without being left behind by the other two ships. He would have to come with them, though FitzStephen felt certain that trouble would come of the decision. He did not like the look of Hervey de Montmorency.

'Fine,' FitzStephen said, though his disgruntlement was easy

198

to see, and signalled to his men to continue rowing. They pulled the *Arthwyr* into the river channel behind the already distant *Dragon* and *Saint Maurice*.

A Norman soldier, who had previously sailed between Wales and Dubhlinn, had taken Meiler's place at the tiller and he aimed the ship south and west towards the entrance to the estuary. A seasonal south-easterly wind blew across the ship but they kept their sail stowed, preferring the control of the oars in the confines of the estuary. As his men began to get their rhythm, FitzStephen reached down and pulled Montmorency to his feet by his gnarly hand. The nobleman said nothing, not even a small gesture of appreciation for FitzStephen's assistance. Sir Hervey reminded him of a hungry old wolf who would do anything to steal a lamb from the farmer. His very presence seemed to unnerve the warriors close to him.

'Bouchard de Montmorency?' asked FitzStephen of the newcomer.

'My brother,' Hervey said, flashing his ugly and triumphant smile. Hervey's sibling was famous throughout Europe: the Lord Constable to the kings of France, arguably the most powerful man in the Frankish kingdom after the King. However, FitzStephen considered as he looked Hervey up and down, the English branch of the family seemed to have fallen on hard times in comparison to their kinsmen. Hervey resembled a tramp more than a rich and venerable member of the French nobility.

'What business has the earl sent you on?' he asked.

'My nephew wishes me to observe your little enterprise, Sir Robert,' Sir Hervey said glibly as he huddled himself into a nook in the bows, his cloak wrapped around him like bat wings as he wrung water from his clothes.

'My little enterprise?' FitzStephen repeated with an angry nod. 'My deal with Diarmait does not concern the Earl Strongbow,' he replied, a finger pointed at Hervey's chest. The Frenchman sneered at his outstretched digit but did not interrupt. 'And nor does any crown,' FitzStephen continued. Half the lords of England were aware that Strongbow had been offered great lands in return for his help putting Diarmait back on his throne, but less knew that he had also been promised the hand of Diarmait's daughter and a claim to her father's kingdom through her.

'Who said anything about a crown?' Hervey coughed.

FitzStephen smiled and shrugged as if it was no concern to him. 'Most men wanting passage to Ireland would have to pay for it,' FitzStephen said, happy that Hervey visibly blanched at the mention of money. He began stuttering that he had no money, but that his nephew would make *him* pay for his ungentle conduct towards an old man. As the threats began to tumble from Hervey's mouth and become more unseemly, FitzStephen silenced him with a wave of the hand.

'Make yourself comfortable, Sir Hervey,' he said, 'it is a full day's travel to Ireland, but you will be treated well.' FitzStephen smiled as he turned his back on the old man, something he would rather not have done. For some reason Sir Hervey reminded him of his former lieutenant, Roger de Quincy, not in looks of course, but some air of desperation and ambition was similar to the man who had betrayed him during the fall of Aberteifi five years before.

Water sloshed noisily at the bows and the *Arthwyr*'s oars splashed heavily into the Cleddau. Ahead of them both the *Dragon* and the *Saint Maurice* were pulling their sails up as they passed into the western sea. FitzStephen took his place at the oar alongside his younger brother, William the Welshman, and looked back over the river towards the northern bank where he spotted a pair of frolicking otters as he heaved the pine oar.

Some of his men were already being sick over the side. Meiler FitzHenry was one. He vomited down Walter de Ridlesford's shield, which hung along the ship's rail with all the others. Meiler threw an accusatory look at his uncle, groaned, and was sick again. FitzStephen had not the heart to tell his kinsman that the river was likely to be calm in comparison to the sea. Behind FitzStephen and William was Philip de Barri who, having grown up on the coast, loved boats and shouted abuse at those who were sick over the side. Meiler attempted to fight back with words, but it only encouraged more vomit to rise from his stomach and he contented himself with flapping a rude sign in Philip's direction with his fingers. Philip laughed at the gesture, chatting incessantly about times spent on the open sea between his father's castle at Manorbier and the Gower peninsular. Meiler turned green at the tales of their exploits and heaved again.

It was a hard slog at the oars but the *Arthwyr* slowly pulled out between the headlands that guarded the entrance to the Cleddau. A strong current rocked the ship making Meiler groan. Wind from the south-east buffeted the boat and seemed to sweep them northerly towards the headland but no one panicked. FitzStephen gave swift orders to stow the oars and plug the oarlocks for the sea journey. He signalled to two of his milites to raise the rectangular linen and wool sails by the halyards and then he strode across the deck adjusting the rigging to maximise its effect. The boat lurched over onto the starboard side as he let the port braces out and pulled those on the starboard side tight.

'Keep her in sight of the *Dragon*,' he called to the sailing master as he loosened the sheets on the other side of the ship allowing the wind to fill the paunch of the sail, pulling the *Arthwyr* away from the headland and into the ocean. FitzStephen allowed a smile to break across his face as water sprayed and the ship rolled in the heavy sea. In the distance he could see the bright sails of the *Dragon* and *Saint Maurice* blown taut by the wind. He crossed his chest and mumbled a short prayer to St Christopher and St Nicholas. He heard Montmorency snort contemptuously, but when he opened his eyes to challenge the old man, he appeared to be fast asleep amongst the ox-hide-covered sea chests.

The *Arthwyr*'s sailing master was easy on the steering tiller but the horses noticed the shift in speed of the ship and began neighing loudly and stamping their feet. Some of the men went down into the belly of the boat to comfort the small, tough coursers as the ship turned north and west, aiming between two small islands which lay just a mile off the Welsh coast.

'That's Skokholm,' the shipmaster, whose name was Archambaud, said with a nod towards the more southerly island, 'and that's Skomer,' he said of its twin.

'It looks like they are covered in snow,' a bleary-eyed Meiler said as he wiped his chin on his sleeve and stared over the side.

'It's birds,' FitzStephen told him, and soon they could hear the squawking of thousands of seabirds perched on the cliffs as the *Arthwyr* glided by. Here and there FitzStephen saw little dark alcoves where puffins and pufflings had their holes.

'Oh God, please make them stop that racket,' Meiler groaned, his chin resting on the rail of the ship and his hands pressed against his ears. 'Or if somebody could please just kill me, that would also suffice,' he said as he pulled the cloak over his head.

Archambaud laughed at Meiler before turning to FitzStephen. 'You could tighten up the starboard braces there, Sir Robert,' he told his commander and watched intently as he performed the task with the practiced hand of a sailor. 'You've spent some time around boats?'

FitzStephen nodded. 'A long time ago, but it's all coming back to me,' he said with a grin. A look from Archambaud encouraged more information from FitzStephen. 'I sailed with the fleet to Mona from London when King Henry invaded Gwynedd…'

Archambaud grinned. 'I remember the campaign. My brother and I marched with the young Earl of Chester's men. We didn't see much action, but I recall men talking about a young esquire who made his name during the fight at the Vale of Ewloe …'

'A stupid esquire,' FitzStephen said as he tested the strength of a backstay above his head. However, a small smile broke across his face. He remembered the fight in the beautiful woods of Ewloe, confused and vicious, as a snarling army of Welshmen fell upon King Henry's small flanking force. Little had made sense to FitzStephen who, having stumbled upon the fight by pure accident had waded in with no thought for his own safety. Somehow he had lived and somehow the Welsh had retreated when faced with but a handful of Norman horsemen. Somehow from the horror, King Henry had emerged unscathed and had rewarded his saviour, then an esquire, with a

202

knighthood.

'A stupid esquire,' he repeated, 'but he learned a lot on the sea journey.'

Before long the crew of the *Arthwyr* had nothing but water and clouds in front of them and FitzStephen walked back and forth through the ship, chattering to the men who huddled together for warmth. Their captain was not cold and he climbed the ladder up into the platform onto the afterdeck so that he could see more. Looking back at St Bride's Bay he fancied that he could see Roche Castle, painted white and tiny in the distant bay above the sand and the sparse trees.

*This is it*, he thought. If everything went to plan this would be the last time he would see Wales. He sniffed forcefully and slowly. To the north along the coast he saw the dark shadow of St David's Cathedral and the misty cliffs of Ramsey Island. He sighed wistfully, but he knew that he had no future in the land of Wales. Within two hours Dyfed had disappeared behind the ship and beyond the waves. Ireland had not quite appeared in front of the *Arthwyr* as she rode the grey sea behind the other two ships which intermittently appeared over her bows.

The journey was largely uneventful except for a mild panic amongst the men when they spotted a great fish, six times as big as a man, beneath them. It was swimming towards the boat seemingly ready to pounce and drag them down into the depths with its great mouth wide open. Men jumped up and grabbed at spears to attack the predator if it came to close, but it did not strike, rather passing below them, its mouth still wide open. The men quieted down as it passed and FitzStephen noticed their sailing master grinning from ear to ear at the disquiet and he ventured over to talk to him while the jumpy Normans kept a careful vigil just in case the monster from the deep returned.

'Why are you laughing?' he asked Archambaud with a grin.

'Basking shark,' the pilot said with a smile and pointed his thumb at the sea to the north. 'It has absolutely no interest in the *Arthwyr*. I don't know what it was after for his dinner, but I am certain it is not us.'

The wind picked up into the early afternoon and FitzStephen stood in the bows of the ship as the white spray came off the grey sea and splashed his face. It awoke his seafaring spirit and he whooped at the horizon as the *Arthwyr* rode high on the long waves. Because of his position at the front of the ship, he was one of the first in the boat to see a black blur on the horizon to the north-west.

'It's a mountain in the middle of Diarmait's country, Laighin,' Archambaud said when FitzStephen approached and questioned him about the peak. 'It's somewhere inland though I've never set foot on it. You aim for that and you come to Waesfjord,' he said.

'Best keep a bit to the south then,' FitzStephen said. 'We wouldn't want to alert them to our presence or our intentions. Nor do we want to run into a bunch of Norsemen,' he said with a raised eyebrow. 'They would see us as an easy target,' he added, flapping a hand at Meiler who continued to hang over the side though he was now panting and had an absurd grin across his face as if the worst was over. Apparently his body had not forgiven him for going to sea and he retched again, groaning as each wave of nausea struck him.

'Have you ever been to Waesfjord?' FitzStephen asked the sailing master.

'Aye, years ago I was part of a crew out of Chester,' he confirmed as he joined FitzStephen, leaving Philip de Barri at the steering oar. 'We went up the Irish coast between Dubhlinn and Corcach selling Gascon wine. Then we brought back Norse shoes, weapons, and pots to Chester, traded that for dyed-wool and from there went back to France for more wine. A good little earner,' he recalled with affection.

'What's the town like? Is the bay easy to traverse?'

Archambaud paused and held onto the side as a sudden swell of sea rocked the ship. 'If you are asking whether you think I can take the longfort of Waesfjord by ship, Sir Robert, I would say that it is impossible.'

FitzStephen grimaced, proving to the sailing master that his commander had indeed hoped to take the town through an amphibious assault.

'The bay is wide and mudflats surround it,' Archambaud told him. 'They would see us coming from miles away and launch a fleet that we could have no hope of fighting at sea.'

The Norman captain left it at that and sat down with his back to the platform and closed his eyes to think. The sun was still high in the sky and his mind flickered slowly between the thoughts of the past and his daydreams of a trader's town with a castle to call his own. He quickly dropped off to sleep and dreamt of glory.

Archambaud shook FitzStephen awake by the shoulder. His eyes flicked open immediately, but his mind struggled to catch up with his actions and he grabbed the steersman by the arm fiercely and gripped it tight. His first thought was that night was falling, yet he knew instinctively that he had slept for only a few hours and it could not yet be midday. He looked past Archambaud and saw a heavy cloud coming from the north. A violent squall was approaching, dimming the bright sunshine of the day. The ship's sailing master said just one word to bring FitzStephen to full awareness: 'Ireland.'

The Norman got to his feet, his damp cloak fluttering away from him in the stiff wind, and he grabbed onto the pilot's shoulder and the port side sheer-strake for balance. The grey ocean rolled and spat flecks of white in the air. Beyond the bows was only a vast expanse of water, and a red sail less than a mile distant off the steerboard side.

'Trouble,' his sailing master said. Most of the men on the boat still slept, wrapped in their cloaks and unaware of the danger, but Sir Hervey de Montmorency seemed to sense the tense atmosphere and appeared beside the two men.

'The *Dragon*, the *Saint Maurice*, where are they?' asked FitzStephen, his mouth dry from sleep.

'We lost them,' the seaman told him. 'The sea became rougher and they must have gone south much earlier. I am sorry, Sir Robert. I should have taken the steering oar back from your nephew sooner.' He bowed his head and FitzStephen did not admonish him.

'Don't worry,' he said, slapping a hand onto Archambaud's arm, 'There was always a chance that this could happen.' He reached into a sea chest and pulled out a piece of red cloth which he handed to an esquire and pointed to the top of the mast. Seconds later Robert's star pennant was removed and a banner with a black raven unveiled. It was the symbol of the Dubhgall – the dark foreigners; the Danes, the Ostmen of Ireland.

'I can't do anything about the weather but I can take us south,' FitzStephen said, eying the angry clouds to the north. 'How long will it be before that squall hits us?'

'No more than two hours, though it could still miss us entirely,' Archambaud said as he swung the *Arthwyr* south away from Waesfjord. FitzStephen turned his attention from the weather and their pursuers towards a third threat which had appeared from the west – the remorseless and dreaded Carn tSóir Point. Fionntán had told him of the dangerous waters which they were now entering and had said that they, and the lands on the coast, had been cursed by an enchantress. It was a graveyard for ships, a tangle of outlying rocks, cross tides, moving sandbanks, shoals, and even thick and mystifying fog and their present heading took them straight into them. FitzStephen stole a glance of the red sail coming out of the north and bit his lip. The Ostmen were not deviating from their interception course. Either they had not been taken in by his ruse or, more worryingly, they did not care and would attack their own kindred without conscience.

Sir Hervey turned to Archambaud. 'Can we outrun those heathens?'

The seaman shook his head. 'No sir. The wind is with us but they will not be carrying as much weight.' He indicated towards the deck packed with objects, men, and animals. Behind them the Ostmen vessel burst high through another wave, scattering sea spray in wide arcs around its prow.

'And eventually, when they get close enough, they will steal the wind from our sails,' FitzStephen added. 'Keep us going south and west, Archambaud,' he said and walked over towards his sleeping brother and laid a hand on his shoulder to awaken him. 'William, get to the front of the ship and keep your eyes open,' FitzStephen told him. His brother was famous amongst the Pembroke men for his good eyesight, a talent that went along with his expert handling of a bow.

'What am I looking for?' William asked as he rubbed the sleep from his eyes and smacking his gummy lips together.

FitzStephen shrugged. 'Anything that could cause us problems,' he said. 'Waterspouts, whirlpools, or sea monsters … anything that these cursed waters can throw at us. We must be ready.' His half-brother looked fearfully at him but trotted up the deck without any further questions.

The chase continued for another hour with the Ostman ship gaining quickly on the ever rougher seas as they headed towards the turbulent landmass that was Carn tSóir Point. FitzStephen could not help but think back to Fionntán's talk that the area was cursed and he wished that he had the chattering Father Nicholas on board so that he could avert the evil with prayer. As he made his way back down the *Arthwyr*, he woke each his milites and quietly warned them to the danger approaching from the north. They milled around the deck, readying weapons but leaving their armour stowed in the sea chests. Everywhere horses were panicking and fighting against the leather straps which bound their legs.

FitzStephen climbed up into the afterdeck and watched the ship that chased him. He felt useless. Was his adventure doomed to end before it had even begun? If the *Arthwyr* never arrived at their arranged base camp, he knew that Miles Menevensis would take control, but devoid of a third of their warriors they would not stand a chance of putting Diarmait back on his throne, or of storming Waesfjord. The Ostman vessel was so close now that he could see the bearded faces of the pirates eying up the fat foreign ship as she ploughed across the sea. They waved their axes, shields, and swords above their heads but were silent over the shout of the sea. FitzStephen promised that he would die before allowing himself to be imprisoned again and to that end he had put on his chainmail. He would rather cast himself into the ocean with a prayer to St Nicholas than live in chains again.

'They will catch us,' Sir Hervey said as he arrived silently at his side. 'Are your Welshmen ready for hand-to-hand fighting?' He cast a glance over the seasick troops and animals in the puke-ridden belly of the boat.

FitzStephen scowled at the condescending Frenchman. 'We won't have to fight them,' he replied confidently.

'This tub cannot outrun them,' Sir Hervey returned.

The tall captain ignored the insult to his ship and stomped away from Montmorency.

'You, you, and you,' he signalled three archers huddling beneath a cloak in the body of the ship. 'Find two other bowmen each and join me below the afterdeck. Bring your weapons.' The three men frowned at their commander but climbed out from under their cloaks and followed his orders. FitzStephen had already made his way back up the boat and was staring at the longship which streaked its way effortlessly through the waves. There were only three ship lengths between the Danes and their target now and he could hear the catcalls and mocking laughter. Time to teach them a lesson, he thought.

'Are your bowstrings dry?' he asked the nine bowmen who crowded behind him below the wicker afterdeck. All the men nodded their assent.

'Right then,' he continued calmly, 'we are going to let them get close and then we pepper the deck until they pull away,' he held up a hand to stop a question from one of the men. 'I know the sea is rough but the distance will be minimal. Shoot fast and aim just above their sheer-strake. Understood?' The nine archers nodded. 'You men may be all that stands between us and their axes so make your shots count.' He chanced another look from beside the steering oar. The Ostman captain had brought his ship up wind of the *Arthwyr* and, despite the distance between the two she was already stealing wind from the flapping sails of FitzStephen's ship.

'They will come on our starboard side,' Archambaud warned, 'and try to take out our steering oar so we are unable to manoeuvre.'

'We wouldn't want to lose that in waters like these,' said FitzStephen as he had another thought developing in his mind. What if this vessel returned to Waesfjord, or wherever she was from, and reported that they had seen a Norman ship bearing warhorses and archers? Would the Ostman town be ready for their attack? Or worse, would they discover the Norman landing place and lead an army to assault their camp? He knew he had to either chase the Danes off now, or lure them south and somehow make sure that every man on the longship never found their way back to their longfort.

'Here they come,' shouted Archambaud looking over his right shoulder from the steering oar.

'Get ready,' FitzStephen growled in the archers' direction before turning to the sailing master. 'Now! Take us to starboard,' he shouted and began hauling at the rigging.

'God help us,' shouted Archambaud as he pulled the tiller into his belly, sending the *Arthwyr* northwards into the path of their pursuers. Cries of panic sprang from the Ostmen vessel as the captain screamed for evasive manoeuvres to avoid hitting the Norman ship. The surprise move had sent many of the enemy warriors sprawling on the deck, and FitzStephen did not give them a chance to get back in order.

'Up onto the afterdeck,' he shouted at the bowmen. 'Go, go, go!' he yelled as the archers stumbled up the small steps one at a time. FitzStephen arched his head over the side and watched the damage that the arrows were causing as they strafed across the Danes on deck. The snap of bowstrings was like a minstrel's most beautiful song to his ears and he watched as warrior after warrior dropped with the goose-feathered shafts protruding from their faces and chests. More struck the side of the ship and stood tall as the longship rode high on the waves. Indecision took hold on the longship as their captain tried to decide whether to push home his attack or to slink off like a defeated wolf with his tail between his legs. Every second that went by more men died on the red-sailed ship as more arrows flew across the grey sea to pulverise them. Finally, with Danish blood visible on the deck, the captain pulled away to a safe distance to the north.

'Port,' FitzStephen shouted, 'take us south-west!'

The steersman pushed the oar away from him and the *Arthwyr* swept away, her sail billowing to take the full pull of the wind again. For many seconds FitzStephen could not speak as he hauled at the sails, setting the sheets to catch the maximum amount of wind and drag the *Arthwyr* south. Behind him, the men who had made ready for battle at sea applauded the archers. Meiler FitzHenry smiled and cheered their success and was sick again.

And it was just then that the squall from the north hit the *Arthwyr*.

It was quick and it was violent, wind whipped the vast sail and rain ripped across the deck. No-one aboard the ship was asleep now as the *Arthwyr* rolled from side to side, the rigging straining under the wind. FitzStephen's face burned as the freezing rain slammed against him but he loosen the sheets and braces so that the sail would not be ripped free. His commands went unheard and his knuckles froze and banged on the sides of the ship as he and several other Normans bailed for their very lives. Seawater poured into the *Arthwyr*.

'Robert!' William the Welshman's voice somehow pierced the weather. FitzStephen ran, jumped, and fell before making it to the front of the ship where his brother hung over the side.

'What? What do you see?' He shouted through the rain at William though he was only a metre away.

'I saw a disturbance in the water directly ahead.'

Staring out over the rough sea through the rain FitzStephen struggled to see what his brother had spotted. 'What is it, a whirlpool?'

'There,' was all William could shout, nodding dead ahead of the boat and clinging onto the rail for dear life. Behind them Archambaud screamed orders at men, ropes thwacked against wood, and sails billowed and ripped under strain from the sudden squall. Cold wind and water hit FitzStephen's face and he bashed his chin painfully off the wooden sheer-strake. Straining and shielding his eyes with a hand he could see nothing. He was just about to turn around and scold his brother when he espied a white swirl of water where a wave crashed skywards. Rocks, he thought, just above the surface and partially hidden by water. He turned on his heel and cupping his hands around his mouth, he shouted towards Archambaud at the helm.

'Rocks, swing away, now!'

Somehow Archambaud heard his shout over the roar and just in time the helmsman pushed hard on the steering oar and sent the ship southwards again, the wind blowing them dangerously sideways onto the port side. Water began pouring into the ship and, as the men began bailing with their hands or whatever vessel they could find to get the water back to where it was supposed to be, FitzStephen hung from the ropes controlling the sail. Horses screamed in fear and no-one could be spared to quiet them. For a few minutes there seemed no way that the *Arthwyr* would survive. FitzStephen swung from the starboard side, looking down on his men, and listened as rocks scraped the stern section but somehow they were blown clear. Silence took the ship as the men bailed and toiled and shook with fear, totally enraptured with the awesome power of the ocean. No-one cheered their success at missing the rocks.

'Keep bloody bailing,' Archambaud shouted as he battled with the steering oar. The squall kept them at their honest toil for many more minutes. FitzStephen ignored the helmsman's order and with difficulty clambered up onto the afterdeck. There, he watched a ship of Danish warriors die. They had been following the Normans, no more than a quarter of a mile back on a parallel course, a little to the north and watching, always watching for a mistake. They had spotted the evasive action of the Norman boat, taken it for the panic of landlubbers, and raised a cheer. Their captain had turned their boat southwards and had ordered his warriors to prepare for battle, and this time no arrows could assail them with the wind so treacherous. Bearing down on their terrified prey they had grabbed for ropes, hooks, and weapons. And in their haste and desire for the prize not one of them had spotted the rocks between their bows and the *Arthwyr*'s inclining stern.

Later, when they were safely ashore, Fionntán would tell FitzStephen that the Tuskar Rock had claimed more souls than all the wars of Brian Bóruma combined. He informed him that the rocks were a well-known obstacle to which most sailors, Irish, English, and Ostmen, gave a wide berth and he supposed that in his efforts to take the *Arthwyr*, their captain had fatefully forgotten the menace of Tuskar and had paid a fatal price.

As he watched from the wet afterdeck of the *Arthwyr*, the red-sailed ship crashed into the rocks, her bows rising up just like it had hit another wave, but FitzStephen could see the carnage inflicted to the keel of the craft and everywhere the planks of the ship splintered under the ragged rocks of Tuskar. Even through the slashing rain the screams reached to the *Arthwyr* which was pulled south by the tide and the strong wind. The Ostmen would not be a threat any more, he knew.

As if to mock the dying men the squall suddenly passed overhead, leaving only a bright shaft of sunshine, a rainbow mirage, and a swirling easterly wind. Eventually the bailers were called to stop by Archambaud and they slumped exhausted on the deck of the *Arthwyr* in the bright sunrays. To a man they panted hard and shivered because of the cold wind and their soaking clothes. Steam rose from their backs and heads. The *Arthwyr* kept going south-west for another four hours around a fence of islands called Oilean na Sailte. Archambaud insisted on giving this next death-trap a wide berth, much to the despair of the exhausted men who sought the safety of land. By the time they pulled their bows north they only had two hours of daylight left and FitzStephen stood at the front of the ship, staring north, where he was joined by the pilot.

'Who has the steering oar?' he asked much too sharply. FitzStephen was still raw about Archambaud losing the rest of the fleet and worried that they too had encountered difficulties.

'Your brother and cousin are fighting over that honour,' the sailing master said. FitzStephen turned and saw that Philip de Barri was on his arse holding his stomach and cheek as though he had been punched while William the Welshman was grinning in the slowly fading light with his hand on the tiller.

'Is it safe?'

'We have clear sea ahead of us until the bay, Sir Robert.'

FitzStephen didn't push and looked off to the west where he had spotted a light, seemingly rising out of the sea itself. Was it more Danes? A falling star? He was not sure that he liked the omen of a star, his symbol, falling into the blue sea.

Archambaud interpreted his concerned look quickly. 'Don't worry, my Lord. There is a long peninsular that comes out into the sea and at the end of it there is a monastery with a tall tower. The brothers of St Renduane keep a fire burning through the night to warn seafarers of their dangerous land mass. They call it Hook Head.'

'They could do every sailor a favour and put a light out on Tuskar,' FitzStephen replied. 'And our destination, where is the island?' He could not remember seeing Hook Head on any of Yossi's maps back in Gloucester.

'Straight ahead, Lord, Banneew Bay.' Archambaud put the tips of his forefingers together to make a rectangle with his arms. 'The *Arthwyr* is in the wide bay below my wrists,' he said. 'On the west bank is the land called Siol Bhroin with Hook Head at the end.' He nodded towards his left hand. 'The island lies just off the land of the Uí Bairrche on the eastern shore. We will be there in two hours at the most. The worst is over.'

Sir Robert FitzStephen snorted a laugh. 'No,' he said as he turned and looked out over the grey sea. 'The worst is yet to come.' He stared northwards. Ireland was looming and a storm of violence would surely follow their safe arrival. The worst was definitely not over.


'They call it Banabh,' Richard de la Roche told FitzStephen. Over the small body of water the two men watched the armed milites stream through the village, killing where they had to and intimidating those that might prove useful into compliance. 'Bloody odd name if you ask me,' Richard continued and bit into the hunk of bread. One man screamed as he attacked Walter de Ridlesford. One expert sword stroke took the villager's throat and his life, and whatever possessions he was attempting to protect Walter also seized.

'Banabh,' FitzStephen grunted the unfamiliar sounding word, 'how many are in the village?'

'Ten, maybe twelve men capable of bearing arms,' said Roche, 'except that they have no arms to bear; unless you think they can do some damage with their fishing poles.'

FitzStephen smiled softly. 'Then maybe you should be more worried than me,' he joked, nodding at Roche's odd crest on his surcoat which showed three red salmon.

Richard returned the laugh. Both were still exhausted from the traumatic crossing and the last-minute preparations in Wales, but now that they were here in Ireland they felt impatient to get the expedition started. FitzStephen's men were already busying themselves getting the defences ready while Walter dealt with the villagers. The plan was to remain on the island until they could join up with Diarmait's army and until that happened he knew that he would be vulnerable. The island rang to the sound of spades striking earth as they dug out a shallow ditch and raised an earth wall on which they would set up a crude timber palisade to defend their camp. More were stripping branches from the small number of tree trunks they had cut down on the northern end of the island and some had already been chopped into points and dug into the earth at an angle to defend against any attack up the island from the south. After just a few hours of daylight, their camp was almost finished. The men from the *Arthwyr* had grumbled when they had been ordered to build the wall, tired as they were, from the hard slog on the oars which had taken them into the bay against the creeping tide.

The island was no more than half a mile long but the north-eastern side had a good harbour surrounded by small cliffs which provided good protection for the three ships. FitzStephen had been relieved to see the *Dragon* and the *Saint Maurice* already beached and, having greeted his kin, had joined the rest of his army as they slumped exhausted where they sat on deck and slept below the darkened sky. A small inlet carved by the weather allowed the army to easily move all their gear up to the top of the cliff the next morning and from there they had the best possible view of the bay. The island was not the greatest place for a defensive battle, but FitzStephen doubted that it would ever come to that: the cities of Waesfjord, Veðrarfjord, and Cluainmín were all far enough away so as not to be immediately aware of their presence. However, he knew that the longer they remained the more chance that they would be discovered.

'Do the villagers have much food?' FitzStephen asked

Richard de la Roche as he shifted uncomfortably in his armour. The weather was fine and the sun was shining off the small waves which lapped up the beach as well as his chainmail.

'Bugger all, but I can round them all up and put them to work on the defences,' replied the Fleming. 'It's about all they are use for.'

FitzStephen shook his head. 'I need you to leave with your men and find Diarmait,' he told him. 'He must know that I have landed. Urge him to speed, Richard. Make sure he knows that we need to press forward before the Ostmen know we are here.'

Roche nodded. 'Two days to get to Fearna and the same to get back. Assuming that Diarmait doesn't know we are here already, it could take three more days for them to get their army together.'

'You leave immediately, Richard,' said FitzStephen as he yawned. 'Make sure and go far enough northwards to avoid Waesfjord before you cross the big river.' He did not yet know the names in the foreign tongue, but Roche was aware of the River Sláine which ran from the Ostman town northwards through Diarmait's territory right to the fort of Fearna which was the Meic Murchada capital.

'I'll be back in a week,' Richard said with a nod and stomped off to collect his warriors.

FitzStephen remained on the waterside. He looked past the Norman ships and over the small inlet to the beach where the small group of fishing boats and houses were gathered. No defences, he thought. No warriors and no fear of attack. The threat from raiders was obviously significantly diminished in this part of Ireland. Diarmait had also assured FitzStephen that the local lords were loyal to his rule, and so he had sent messengers to Colmcille Ua Dubhgain and Cearbhall Ua Lorcain with small gifts to encourage them to leave him and his men alone while scavenging the area for food. Walter de Ridlesford had been the one who had met with the chieftains and FitzStephen was content that they would have understood the none-too-subtle message that the giant, bald warrior would have put across.

Stretching his back, FitzStephen turned to go back up the

beach to the camp to help his army dig the defences, but he was caught unawares when he was confronted by Sir Hervey de Montmorency standing just five paces behind him, looking out of the top of his eyes menacingly at his back.

'Saints alive,' FitzStephen exclaimed.

Strongbow's uncle was looking as downtrodden as usual; a hungry wolf, scrawny and desperate, all shoulders and large, suspicious eyes. He did not smile at FitzStephen's surprise. 'I will be going with Roche to Fearna to speak to King Diarmait about my nephew's plans for his arrival,' he instructed. 'I will require some of your men to accompany me.'

FitzStephen's laugh was sarcastic. 'All my men stay here.'

'Remember to whom you are talking, FitzStephen. This isn't the alehouse,' he said. 'I am a nobleman and you will remember your manners when you speak to me.' Sir Hervey had purloined a crossbow from somewhere and he gently fingered the weapon's trigger as he spoke.

FitzStephen didn't blink. 'And you should remember that this isn't the royal court of France.'

Hervey looked like he might continue the argument but suddenly turned and walked away from him without a word.

FitzStephen sighed in frustration. He should have avoided confrontation with the Frenchman, but there was something he did not trust about the Earl Strongbow's uncle.


Máelmáedoc Ua Riagain galloped his horse towards St Mary's Monastery. Thick white foam spilled from the sides of the animal's mouth and sweat poured from the man's brow as they thundered through the valley below the old fort of Fearna.

'Out of my way,' he shouted as he bounced on the horse's bare back. The monks stepped out of his path as his legs flew out from the flanks for balance. He abandoned his mount at the intricately carved doorway of the monastery and sped through the cloisters where a service was taking place. He didn't care that he disturbed the mumbled prayers and humming praise. He brought news which he believed would please his king so much that he would reward Máelmáedoc with more riches than he had ever known.

'Where is Diarmait?' His shouted question boomed around the heavy stone walls of the monastery. Before him thirty hooded monks on their knees tried to ignore Máelmáedoc as they swayed and muttered their supplications towards the huge cross at the other end of the large room.

Finally one monk at the front of the throng slowly stood and pulled his hood back from his head. It was Diarmait.

'It is not necessary to shout in this place, Máelmáedoc,' the King said, his hoarse voice carrying over the chanting.

'A Norman army has landed at Banabh,' he hurriedly shouted to him, 'the time to retake your place at the head of the Uí Ceinnselaig has come.'

For a second Diarmait could not speak, and simply stared at his counsellor. He rounded suddenly on the monks of St Mary's with a glare.

'Stop your bloody wittering,' he hissed and began pushing through the field of stooping men. 'Tell me more,' he commanded of Máelmáedoc.

'Over four hundred armoured men in five ships have landed,' his secretary said excitedly, shaking his head as if he did not know what to say first. 'They are speaking several different tongues including French and Flemish.'

Across the sea of bobbing, hooded heads, Diarmait signalled for Máelmáedoc to join him in a large anteroom adjacent to the nave. He pushed between the Augustinians and through the door. Inside Diarmait's daughter, Aoife, stood up from her book and looked at her father, and then his secretary who followed him.

'Who leads these foreigners?' Diarmait Mac Murchada asked as he shut the door. Máelmáedoc still panted from his efforts in racing north and did not bother to acknowledge Aoife's presence. He did not see that her sharp eyes took in every detail that went between the two men.

'They answer to Robert FitzStephen,' said Máelmáedoc. 'His man, Richard de la Roche, is coming back to Fearna as we speak.'

'Oh yes, FitzStephen, of course.' Diarmait sounded disappointed. Somehow he had thought that his herald might be

217

telling him of the coming of Strongbow rather than the mercenary knight from Ceredigion. 'Well,' he told his daughter who listened intensely at his side, 'it is still an army. The time for pretence is over.' Diarmait stood and cast off the monk's cloak which disguised him. Beneath was a saffron robe of mustard yellow which marked him out as a nobleman of Ireland. He turned to his daughter and winked before putting his hands on Máelmáedoc's shoulders and smiling at him. 'Thank you. This is good news indeed.'

Máelmáedoc smiled back. 'There is more, Lord. A man is with Roche by the name of Sir Hervey de Montmorency. He is Strongbow's uncle and comes bearing his greetings.'

'Strongbow's uncle?' he said. 'That is interesting indeed, but one to decipher after we take back our throne. Get Domhnall,' his king said with a huge smile. 'And raise the kern, Máelmáedoc. We are going to war.'

Energy flashed across the Diarmait Mac Murchada's eyes as he perceived that which he had long desired was close at hand; the madness of war was returning to his homeland.

Sir Robert FitzStephen was bored. He slumped on his elbows watching the reedy bay, his blue and white livery resplendent against the earth and timber palisade which surrounded his army's camp. Nine days had passed since he had landed at Banabh and no word had come from King Diarmait or Richard de la Roche. His defences had so far been tested by little other than seagull droppings and it seemed that the clandestine Norman landing had indeed remained secret from the powerful Ostman cities of Veðrarfjord and Waesfjord. Yet until the King of Laighin arrived he knew that he would continue to feel tetchy and uncomfortable.

He had taken to exploring the island – anything to get over the endless boredom of guard duty – and had discovered an old, tumbledown fort. He had considered moving his army behind its ancient walls. However, he had come across some standing stones with peculiar notches etched on each side and had abandoned the idea, sure that an ancient evil was present in the eerie and windy place, torn ragged by the sea salt spray. Instead his army had remained in their small and hastily constructed enclosure above the cliffs. He wished something supernatural would spring to life – at least it would end the boredom which plagued the Norman camp.

From his place behind the timber wall, FitzStephen watched a large group of birds, oystercatchers and curlews, as they fought in the shallows.

'They will never find anything for their dinner if they keep making a racket like that,' Fionntán Ua Donnchaidh said from beside him. The Gael nodded towards the birds. 'They always fight amongst themselves when they find a good spot for feeding.'

FitzStephen smiled. 'It's not the birds I was keeping an eye on,' he told his ally. 'Look who's eyeing the birds up for his dinner.' He pointed a forefinger to where he had spotted a small fox in the long grass, gazing at the battling birds. The sly predator had taken advantage of the disorder to get close to his prey. Part of FitzStephen urged the devious beast to make a run for his target in the shallow sandy pools, but the fox was content to creep closer and closer to the warring waders, never taking his dark eyes off them. Suddenly, when he was just a few feet from the birds he attacked, bursting like a red blur from the shallows at the nearest oystercatcher. FitzStephen laughed as he watched the disappointed carnivore as he was left with a mouthful of oystercatcher tail feathers as a squawking mass of birds leapt into the air above him and flew northwards.

'Keep trying, my friend,' he told the animal.

'They always do,' Fionntán grumped and went to find something more interesting to occupy him.

The whole landscape of Ireland was suffocating and small to FitzStephen. Except for the island and the coastline, which had been almost totally cleared by years of harsh winds off the sea, the whole countryside seemed to be cloaked in thick and impenetrable greenery. He had taken the *Arthwyr* upriver into the interior and had been shocked when he discovered that the vast expanse of trees got even more stifling as he went inland. There seemed to be no break in the vegetation as far as the eye could see, except for some bare hills about ten miles to the east.

No roads penetrated the forest and heavy undergrowth made any journey on the mainland tricky to say the least. It was, the warrior considered, either the best place for the Normans to hide out or the worst place to be ambushed.

The men, even though they were used to garrison duty in Wales, were having as bad a time as their commander at breaking the monotony. The army was now six hundred and fifty strong, and the leaders were having problems keeping all those men occupied inside the temporary fort. Only a few trusted men were allowed onto the mainland to scout the area, and this had been resented by the Welsh and Flemish when Normans had been invariably chosen for the duty. Already FitzStephen had been forced to discipline two men, a Norman archer and a Flemish infantryman, after a fight over the score in a game of football. The small encroachment still simmered under the surface in the camp, and he knew that it was only a matter of time until the frayed nerves of both peoples exploded into yet more violence. The tense atmosphere had been compounded by the rebelliousness of Maurice de Prendergast's mercenary horsemen who refused to stay on the island and constantly tried to break out and have a look around the countryside. To these men of war, a 'look around' could only end in theft and killing. Prendergast was, like Richard de la Roche, another Flemish mercenary, promised plunder and payment by FitzStephen on Diarmait's behalf. He had arrived at Banabh the day after the rest of the army in two ships with just over two hundred men. The Fleming was a thin, pious, and serious man who cared about just two things: the good standing of his soul and the provision of wealth for his troops. He was also a brilliant and instinctive warlord, who constantly derided himself for taking pride in his skill at his violent vocation. Three mornings before, FitzStephen had discovered Prendergast and his horsemen missing from the camp. After talking to the Irish boatman from the village he quickly ascertained that the Flemings had gone several miles upriver.

'*Creach*,' the boatman had said in his native tongue, meaning cattle-raiding and pointed north up the bay towards a small Norse settlement called Cluainmín.

FitzStephen and fifteen horsemen had raced after them catching up just a few miles short of Ostman territory. It turned out that the Flemings had heard that lead ore had been discovered and that the Norse were minting their own silver behind their small walls. It was a target too good for the raiders to ignore. He still feared that their being in Ireland would be discovered and that one morning they would wake up to find a fleet of longships descending on them or an army of Ostmen approaching from the mainland. FitzStephen and his troopers had shepherded the angry Flemings back to Banabh where the bad feeling between Prendergast's mercenaries and Robert's Norman and Welsh troops grew day by day. FitzStephen knew that if Diarmait did not come south soon he would find the discipline of the camp begin to deteriorate. His warriors needed action and they desired plunder. He also knew that their presence would not go unnoticed by the Ostmen forever and it was just as he was thinking this that he heard a shout from behind which forced him to spin on his heel.

'Sir Robert!' the voice screamed frenetically.

As he stared over the tents and the wall of the camp, over the low sand-strewn dunes of Banabh, FitzStephen gulped down a gasp of alarm. An army was approaching the camp. He leapt down from the allure and began running. Skidding around a tent, FitzStephen narrowly avoided a man who poked his head out to see what all the noise was about. A trumpet sounded to the east where the army was coming over the brow of the hill and walked down towards the fishing village. Maurice de Prendergast came from his left and fell in beside him.

'Who do you think it is?' the Fleming asked, his French still flavoured by his forbearers' Germanic roots.

FitzStephen vaulted over a shield which lay propped against a stool, cleaning abandoned with the threatening approach of the army. 'I don't know,' he replied. 'The scouts I sent would have warned of the approach of the Ostmen.' He clambered up onto the eastern palisade, knocking men out of the way so he could get a look at the approaching force. 'How many are there?' he asked to no-one in particular.

'Five hundred,' Philip de Barri answered instantly from his

side. 'They are mostly infantry. No standards,' he said as Fionntán silently appeared and stood beside FitzStephen.

'It is Diarmait,' the Irishman said dismissively, wiping his nose on the sleeve of his leather armour.

'You are sure?' asked FitzStephen. The Irishman nodded to answer his question and casually bit into an apple. Years spent staring at the horizon from the steering oar had somehow stretched his vision. Fionntán claimed he could see a flea on a horse's back at two hundred paces, but could not identify the vegetables in a bowl of stew on a table in front of him.

Sure enough, moments later FitzStephen espied the red and white fish livery of Richard de la Roche amongst the grey and white mass which was the Irish army. Many of the Normans would laugh at Roche's odd surcoat that reminded all of his family's Flemish origin on the shores of the Great Northern Sea and FitzStephen had joined in the good-natured banter, but now he joined with the other joyful Normans and cheered its sighting for it signalled the arrival of Diarmait and his army at Banabh. The Norman adventure on the isle of Ireland could really begin.

Diarmait Mac Murchada bear-hugged FitzStephen like a brother and waved to the cheering Norman army, beaming in pride as would a father towards his children. Only a small number of men from the Uí Ceinnselaig had crossed to the island with their king, but the Normans still cheered the Gaels' arrival. Four nationalities now made up the army and stared on as their leaders greeted each other; Robert FitzStephen and King Diarmait, Maurice de Prendergast and Domhnall Caomhánach, Richard de la Roche and Máelmáedoc Ua Riagain. Hervey de Montmorency looked on malevolently at the King of Laighin's favourable reception of FitzStephen.

Diarmait held up his hands for silence and spoke in French to the gathered mass of four hundred. 'Welcome to Laighin, my brave warriors! We have many enemies to defeat but we have an army of the greatest warriors of Wales and I do not doubt that we will be victorious.' He gave them time to nod along and growl their assent. 'And when we do recover my kingdom and secure her borders, whomsoever should wish for horses, trappings or chargers, gold or silver, I will give it to them!'

They cheered Diarmait and he waved and grinned. Behind the Norman, Flemish, and Irish leaders, a gust of wind suddenly whipped up the bay and the standards of the leaders, which had hung loose from the white tents, thrashed abruptly and violently. FitzStephen signalled to Diarmait to proceed inside the tent where a feast had been speedily prepared as the Irishmen made their way across to the island by boat. The King leaned in towards him as they passed under the flap of the tent and whispered to the Norman commander: 'For those who return my kingdom, I will enfief them, soil and sod.'

'You are most welcome, Lord,' the Norman said as he poured a mug of wine for the King of Laighin.

'I am also glad to see you, Sir Robert,' Diarmait stood back and looked at the Norman knight, large hands gripped on his shoulders. 'And I am glad to find you well-fed and cleaner than the last time I saw you! Although I think you suited your beard,' he laughed at FitzStephen's newly shaven face.

Bald Walter de Ridlesford slapped his cousin hard on the back of the head before Robert could answer. 'He's ugly whatever his hairstyle, Lord King.'

'At least I have some hair,' FitzStephen rubbed his shaven patch on the back of his own head where Walter had caught him. The Laighin derb-fine laughed a few seconds later when Máelmáedoc Ua Riagain translated the jest into their tongue, however, Diarmait's secretary did not share in their mirth.

'Get some food in here,' FitzStephen called through the gap in the tent wall. Several esquires entered with bread trenchers filled with rabbit stew, steaming fish, and various birds hunted amongst the reeds of the bay.

Diarmait laughed at the sight of the boys and turned to FitzStephen. 'I'll have to sell you some slaves to do your cooking. It is not right that you force these boys to cook for you!'

FitzStephen shook his head. 'We Normans don't keep slaves, or permit the sale of them on our lands,' he warned before sensing that he may have offended his ally. 'In any event,' he stuttered, 'it does the esquires good to perform lowly tasks.' He was interrupted while the Cistercian monk, who FitzStephen had convinced to come with his army, said a prayer in thanks for the plentiful food. Though his supplies were dwindling quickly due to the lengthy stay on Banabh Island, FitzStephen felt that he was required to honour King Diarmait's arrival with a great feast.

The King of Laighin took his position at the centre of the top table and began eating as further high-ranking soldiers filed into FitzStephen's own tent. Diarmait was flanked by FitzStephen and Domhnall Caomhánach, while Maurice de Prendergast sat beside the younger Irishman, and they manfully struggled to converse in a mixture of Latin, French, English, Welsh, and Irish about the food they were eating.

Prendergast held up a chunk of lamb and said, 'Mutton with honey,' encouraging Caomhánach to repeat the words before trying, 'Sheep or lamb, oui?'

Domhnall nodded seriously as if the two men were discussing a particularity of the Bible. 'Scheeporlamwee,' he offered with a smile and held up a pigeon breast.

'Nein, nein,' Prendergast said with a shake of the head, and pushed Domhnall's hand back onto his trencher. 'Sheep in English, but lamb if it is young.' He made baby sounds to emphasis his point, confusing Domhnall for a few seconds before the Irishman nodded, turning to Diarmait and whispering that he believed the foreigners to be touched in the head. Diarmait laughed bombastically at his son's levity, rotating towards FitzStephen who sat with Richard de la Roche on his left. Hervey de Montmorency, seated beyond Roche, strained his ears to listen in on the conversation.

'So, Sir Robert, our first step will be to attack the city of Dubhlinn,' he stated and began eating again.

FitzStephen let the salt between his fingers drop back into the jar before him as he evaluated Diarmait's declaration. 'Lord King,' he began, 'we must secure our position, and yours, first. Here, on Banabh, our situation is uncertain and until we take a fortress I will have to divide my forces to defend our backs.'

Diarmait's lightning blue eyes flared momentarily in anger

as FitzStephen questioned his order, and he said nothing for a number of seconds. 'The greater threat to Fearna is from Dubhlinn,' he said quietly but with force. 'The treacherous whelps have always been a menace and until they are conquered I will feel their axes at my neck.'

'All the more reason to attack from a place of power, Lord King,' FitzStephen chanced. 'If we take one of the southern towns we can hold it against any enemy. We can also get men and supplies from Wales easily. Fearna is inland and, even if we can take Dubhlinn, from what I have been told the city's walls are too long for nine hundred to defend.'

Diarmait ground his teeth together. 'The Ostmen murdered my father when I was just a boy. They humiliated him, mutilating his body and buried him in the same grave as a dog. I want them dead,' he hissed. It was difficult to cool the fire in his blood but he emptied his mug of French wine, forcing himself to enjoy and consider the taste, swirling it around his mouth slowly before he swallowed with a gasp of pleasure. 'I want them dead,' he repeated but with less force.

'And I must secure the lands you promised me or my men will return to Wales ...'

Hervey de Montmorency chimed in, 'My Lord, the Earl, would do as you command, King Diarmait.'

'Strongbow can do what he wants when he gets his backside across the sea,' FitzStephen replied. 'What keeps him anyway?'

Montmorency ignored FitzStephen's question. 'If you are not able to bring Dubhlinn to heel, what use are you to King Diarmait? This is worse than when you lost Aberteifi to the Welsh ...'

FitzStephen fumed at that, but Mac Murchada held up his hand to quiet his warring allies. 'This is not helping,' he said, and turned to the younger man. 'You are sure that you cannot take Dubhlinn?'

FitzStephen was sure of nothing except that to attack the biggest city on the island would be a disaster. 'I might be able to seize it,' he answered, 'but we would quickly lose it again and my army along with it.'

Diarmait snarled in disappointment. 'I assume you mean to

take Waesfjord then?'

'It is the obvious target, Lord King,' he replied. 'Waesfjord is close to Wales and to my brothers. It lies in your own territory and it is the nearest immediate threat.' He bobbed his head eastwards.

'The men of Waesfjord will serve as an example to others then,' Diarmait said.

FitzStephen nodded as Maurice de Prendergast took up the narrative. 'Waesfjord is also the further from Ruaidhrí Ua Conchobair in Connacht, and news of our enterprise is less likely to reach him if we take that city than if we attack Veðrarfjord or Dubhlinn,' he said. The King nodded though still seemed dissatisfied as he pulled apart the bread trencher and bit into it. FitzStephen too began eating in silence while Hervey de Montmorency abandoned his chair and began whispering vigorously in Diarmait's ear out of FitzStephen's hearing. The Frenchman gave Richard de la Roche an awful lip-curling sneer as the Fleming interrupted his conversation:

'Lord King, would you tell us more about Waesfjord? On the way here one of the sailors said it had been cursed by a sorceress.'

Domhnall and Diarmait swapped a glance over a steaming bird pie. It was the older man who spoke quickly and with humour in his voice, 'An old storyteller's tale for the fireside, Sir Richard, nothing more.' When it looked like Roche would press his interest, Diarmait continued. 'They do say that it is cursed by a witch who lived out on Carn tSóir Point. You have heard of that malevolent place from your crossing, I believe.' FitzStephen looked at Fionntán whose eyes darted to meet the Norman's before returning to his food. 'The storytellers say that the sorceress was in love with a brave prince from my own people called Garman Garbh, and that she made a spell to ensnare him for herself, killing his true love and their children so that he would live with her forever,' Diarmait continued. All around the tent were listening in on the King's story. He cackled briefly. 'She must have been one ugly, haggard old bitch but she made herself appear beautiful to him and he fell for it. Anyway, either her powers began to wane or she must have begun to truly believe that he loved her, but she let her hold over him diminish.' He shook his head. 'Well you can imagine what he thought! He was unaware of the years that had passed between them and as soon as he was able he fled her abode for his home. But when he got there he found that everyone he had ever known was long dead of old age. So he raised an army and marched against his former captor. Understandable really,' he said as he forced another handful of fish into his mouth. 'At the same time the sorceress discovered that Garman Garbh had left her home on Carn tSóir. Realising her terrible mistake she flew into a rage and made after him,' Diarmait continued. 'She met Garman Garbh's army at the rock which stands to the north of Waesfjord. Seeing that he had come to kill her she used her powers to destroy the army one by one. Hundreds died and soon it was just the sorceress and Garman Garbh left on the rock, surrounded by the bodies of his army. Weakened due to a hundred cuts, she tried to convince him to return to her bed, to let her enchant him again, but he could see the crone that she was and refused to be a prisoner again. In a terrible rage she cursed him and all the lands around him. Using the last of her powers she picked him up in the air and cast him from the rock towards the bay. But Garman was strong and she was weakened, and he grabbed a hold of the sorceress' dress, hauling her into the water with him.' Diarmait shrugged and took a swig from his cup. 'They died,' he said and returned to his food.

After a few seconds a low growl came from the other side of the tent, 'The bitch sounds like my wife,' a Norman said. The place erupted with laughter, breaking the tension which had arisen.

'Ever since that time the area around Lough Garman, the bay on which Waesfjord stands and all the way to the sea, is said to have been cursed and haunted by the ghosts of the witch, her lover and his army,' Diarmait said to Richard de la Roche. 'But it hasn't turned out too badly for the Ostmen.'

'Until now,' FitzStephen whispered.

Hervey de Montmorency allowed a cough of contempt escape his lungs. 'And how will you take the longfort,

FitzStephen?' he demanded. 'How can your horsemen scratch their way into their fortress? It has never fallen to any attacker you know.'

'Not even to me.' The King of Laighin winced at the memory of his attempt on the Ostman town just eight years before. He had not been able to 'scratch' his way into Waesfjord but had sat before its walls until hunger had driven his army back northwards to Fearna. 'But I am interested to know how you will succeed where I failed,' he said as he turned his eyes on Robert FitzStephen. 'Will you make an attempt by sea?' he asked as Hervey began whispering into his ear again.

FitzStephen shook his head as he swallowed the dregs of another mug of wine. 'We have five ships and they will have ten times that number; granted, they are mostly merchantmen now, but they can still carry warriors. We would be surrounded.' He snapped his fingers to stress the swiftness of their defeat should they try to attack the town that way.

'So by land, then,' Diarmait said. 'But how?'

FitzStephen did not answer for many seconds.

'The same way that Garman Garbh did – by taking the fight to them,' he told the King.

# Chapter Eight

Eirik Mac Amlaibh was the chief man of Waesfjord. He held no crown and was of little family, but money was all in the merchant town. Eirik was merely a businessman; a successful one, yes, but a businessman nonetheless. Just a year had passed since he had stood under the linen tent on the muddy quayside before all the people of Waesfjord, man and woman, and had been elected to command by the Thing, the parliament of town burghers. Petty disputes and disagreements, perhaps the odd murder or theft – that was what he had thought he would have to preside over during his period in office. He had thought that it would be easy and that bribes, power, and favour would flow into his coffers and enrich him. But now there was a threat to his city and it made him feel ill at ease.

Word had reached him of an army arrayed to attack his town. Perhaps *army* was the wrong word. *Rabble* was a better description of the force which the Vestmen of Laighin would put against his walls. Disorganised, unruly, and unarmoured, they could stay outside his walls like so many other armies had before them. Waesfjord had never been taken and it would not fall under his command either, he was sure. Eirik sat in his longhouse, the biggest inside the settlement, and tried to ignore the bustle of people who waited outside for their cases to be heard. He yawned and wished that they would all go away so that he could have time to think about his town's situation. The reports from the traders said that the new men were armoured like all Norse and Danish warriors but with strangely shaped shields, triangular rather than circular. Probably from Cluainmín, he considered. It was not beyond the realm of possibility that the King of Laighin, Diarmait Mac Murchada, had hired some Danish warriors from Hlymrik to fight for him.

Who else could they be?

Of course, Eirik had heard about the exile of Diarmait, but he had not realised that the old fox had returned to his lair in Fearna. Had he known, Eirik would have expected Diarmait to bring his army south and demand that Waesfjord do homage to him, hand over hostages and tribute, or face the possibility of attack. Eirik giggled at that thought; he had been away in the land of the Franks the last time Diarmait Mac Murchada had attempted to capture Waesfjord, but he had heard the stories of his humiliating defeat before the town's walls and did not doubt that it would be the said outcome should he attempt the same. If anything, Waesfjord was stronger than it had been since Diarmait's exile, stronger than anything Laighin could throw against her high walls. So why should Eirik do homage to Diarmait? Why should he and his friends stump up silver and cattle and slaves to pay for peace, he wondered. Even with the support of Cluainmín, the Uí Ceinnselaig could never hope to conquer his people!

Suddenly a new political map emerged in Eirik's mind with the Irish clans doing homage to the power of Waesfjord rather than the age-old hierarchy of the Ostmen going on bended knee before the Gaelic petty-kings and chieftains. And all it would take, Eirik thought, was to show his bellicose neighbours that the townsfolk were not only the commercial power in the region, but that they had military supremacy too. Battle always brought risk, but to a merchant like Eirik risk was no different to opportunity. He had taken chances before and come away much the better for it, so why not this time?

At any rate, Eirik was an ambitious man who knew that his town's control faded just five or six miles in every direction from Waesfjord Bay. This could be a great opportunity to expand their territory at the detriment of Cluainmín and Diarmait Mac Murchada and, at the same time, secure more slaves from amongst the survivors. The men of the town may have put down their piratical ways in the centuries before to become merchants and traders but Eirik knew that it would take little to turn his people from mild-mannered wheeler-dealers into the invincible warriors which their forefathers had been. *A scourge* was what the people of Europe had called them, and time had not dulled the battle-axes of the Northmen. Eirik imagined leading a fleet of ships to attack Cluainmín, blood red sails coming out of the morning sun, dragon head snarling at their enemy, and painted shields bumping off the hull in the sea spray. And who would his warriors find there but old men, women, and children as their fathers and brothers bumbled their way across the land towards his town walls.

*No*, he thought, to weaken the defence of Waesfjord would be stupid and he immediately chastised himself for letting his imagination run away with him. Reality was all. What did the men of Waesfjord have to fear from a rabble of Vestmen and the small number of warriors that Cluainmín could put into the field? Good sense told him that he should sit behind his timber stockade and wait for the army to waste themselves upon his walls. But this too presented problems. The English wine trader, Hengist, a man of Bristol, had come to him in a panic after hearing the rumours of the approaching army, claiming that he would be leaving the city on the next tide before his business was complete. Eirik had convinced him to remain, but even then Hengist had fled into the bay where his ship now lay under anchor, ready to flee at the slightest provocation. Soon, more traders would hear about the Irish army and threaten to take their wares and money to other ports. Waesfjord, and by extension, Eirik, could stand to lose a fortune.

What he should do is send out the army and hit the invaders head on as they moved into his territory, he thought. Trade could continue in the town like it had never been threatened and Eirik would be a hero who had saved his people. Sagas would be told about the great warlord who lifted his axe in defence of his city. No longer would he be embarrassed by his father's humble beginnings – he would be a hero! Eirik tapped his mouth with his forefinger thoughtfully. The opportunities that could come with victory were alluring: they could destroy the growth of a market rival and Waesfjord would inevitably become even wealthier. The Cluainmín men had been minting their own coins too and if Eirik could take possession of that …

He licked his lips in anticipation of the vast wealth, and

stared out of the east-facing door of his longhouse. His gaze swept out over the town which dipped away towards the bay. Many merchantmen were beached or secured to posts sunk in the muddy bay of Lough Garman while small figures flitted between them. Beyond his small garden he recognised the løysing Ivar Arnarsson and his blonde wife argue with a visiting Icelander over some gold trinkets the trader had brought from the city of Jorvik. Elsewhere, more traders displayed their merchandise in front of their houses; bone-workers made combs, whistles, gaming pieces, and needles, leather-workers paraded shoes, scabbards, and satchels. Silversmiths made jewellery of all kinds, blacksmiths made weapons and tools while turners and coopers displayed their wooden wares to the many people who milled through the town.

Eirik mulled over the military decision that was before him. There was such a great deal at stake and the final decision rested upon his shoulders. He refocused his eyes on the town beyond. The great earth and timber wall, five times as tall as a man, flanked the activity of the town on all sides. How Diarmait Mac Murchada could be so foolish as to try to attack this longfort, Eirik thought. Waesfjord had never fallen, Waesfjord would never fall.

'Oi, Hrolf,' Eirik called to his man outside the door.

A bearded face ducked under the mantle. 'Eirik?'

The old trader flicked his eyes towards him, 'Call the Thing together. We must decide if we will go to war.'

His warrior nodded and disappeared, but Eirik knew it was only a formality to ask the permission of the town assembly. His people would go on the march again, and great songs would be sung of their victory over Diarmait Mac Murchada.

Five ships burned on FitzStephen's order. Black smoke plumed high into the air above the trees and announced to anyone within twenty miles that there was mischief abroad in Ireland. However, the destruction of the ships was not for the benefit of the surrounding chieftains or the Ostmen, but for his own army which marched away from the island at Banabh. FitzStephen was telling them that there was no escape from Ireland, nothing

232

but victory would suffice. No more hiding or intrigue. War.

Over a thousand men were now under FitzStephen's command. Five hundred were Diarmait's clansmen, undoubtedly brave but ill-disciplined. Some were noblemen, of a fashion, on horses; however, most were infantry simply armed with slings, javelins, or spears. Diarmait called the infantrymen *kern* and most had little more than wicker shields and spears. FitzStephen had thought their lack of armour odd, but Diarmait had told him that his people disdained chainmail rather than being unaware of its benefits. Manoeuvrability was everything to the brave men who were under the command of Diarmait's son, Domhnall Caomhánach. Many in the kern had caked mud into their long hair and dried it onto their foreheads to act in place of helmets. All the men of Wales had laughed at their new allies' savageness, but Diarmait was immensely proud of his countrymen and so FitzStephen did not partake of the mockery despite thinking that, should he ever need to fight them, the Gaels would be easy prey for his horsemen and archers. Hervey de Montmorency rode with the King, not for the pleasure of Diarmait's company, who he thought lacking in manners, but, FitzStephen was sure, to whisper in the King's ear against him.

Three hundred more of the army were Welsh, Cornish, and Flemish archers and crossbowmen, the greatest marksmen that the frontier had to offer, their skill developed in a century of skirmishes and ambushes between the antagonistic peoples of South Wales. At fifty yards the arrows of the Welshmen could mangle chainmail made by any smith in Europe, but only the crossbow could puncture a well-made shield. Richard de la Roche had tried to stop FitzStephen from employing his natural enemy, the Cymri, but the knight had observed their skill in action first-hand and knew that whatever came against his army in Ireland he would need that talent. Pulled back to the chest and aimed with one eye closed, the yew or ash staves and arrows had cost FitzStephen a fortune, but he knew that it was worth it – each archer could shoot up to twenty arrows a minute at a distance of over a hundred yards. These were the men that could win a simple knight a kingdom, he knew. Commanded by Richard de la Roche, despite his issues with the Welsh, many of

233

the archers also had swords, short axes, and daggers for hand-to-hand fighting and, more likely, murder. At their waist was a quiver of a hundred arrows. Three cartloads more followed the army pulled by stolen Irish cattle. A fourth cart carried scaling ladders and several lengths of heavy timber which FitzStephen had ordered shaped back in Wales. Diarmait had asked the use of the twenty-foot lengths of wood, but FitzStephen had refused to tell him. Some secrets were best kept even from his allies.

Alongside the Welsh archers were the Flemish crossbowmen led by Miles Menevensis. They could only shoot about half the number of quarrels that an archer could, but it took a lifetime for an archer to learn to use their weapon and any man could be taught to competently use a crossbow. It was widely known that the crossbow was invented by Satan but most of the crossbowmen rubbed manure on the ends of their quarrels so that if they made any contact with their enemy, they would cause a festering of the blood – just to make certain of death in the event that the Devil was busy elsewhere.

Walter de Ridlesford also commanded two hundred infantrymen who were heavily armed with swords, axes, maces, and spears. Again, some had chainmail but most had just leather jerkins or thick padded linen gambesons to defend them. On their heads were the spangenhelm, the cone-shaped helmets complete with a nasal guard. They looked no different to their Norse or English peers and had the same arms as their contemporaries except for their distinctive leaf-shaped shields. Ninety horsemen were similarly armed to the infantry and were employed as outriders and scouts for the army. Mostly made up of lightly armed esquires and hoblier-archers, they were led by Maurice de Prendergast, who was also FitzStephen's second-in-command.

At the heart of FitzStephen's force was a single conrois of forty heavy cavalrymen. Maces, short-handled axes, and swords hung at their sides and bumped against their horses' flanks. But the main weapon which each of them carried was the lance. It could be held over arm and used to stab down or throw into a crowd of men. Like FitzStephen, these milites wore fully fifty pounds of armoured hauberk which covered the whole body of the cavalryman. Only his face was left open. Their horses were strong and manoeuvrable but not big so that the men would not be unseated when cutting down on an enemy infantryman. Some, like FitzStephen, had livery of their own or wore their lord's, but most simply wore their chainmail open in the early summer sun, shining like the scales of fish, and bound at the waist by a heavy buckled belt. They all followed one banner, the silver star on the blue field, which hung from the tip of Sir Robert FitzStephen's lance.

The army which left Banabh stretched for a quarter mile from front to back and followed Maurice de Prendergast's vanguard eastwards, away from the barrelling smoke which clung to the island. Waesfjord was their target, fifteen miles to the north-west over high hills. It had been suggested at the feast that they would go north and follow the bend of the River Corock towards the Norse town, but FitzStephen had refused, realising that the route would take them too close to Cluainmín, upriver from their island camp. As an alternative, Diarmait had suggested that the army hug the coast and attack the town from the south through the land known as Forthairt. FitzStephen had agreed to this course and they had left for their target before dawn. Riding through the flat land beside the sea had caused few problems and FitzStephen was enjoying the journey beside Albrecht Cullen, a warrior in Richard de la Roche's employ.

'… it is beautiful countryside,' the Fleming babbled. 'I could happily make a manor here, after we beat Diarmait's enemies, and get me a wife here and one back in Rhos.' He scratched his big ears. 'It does remind me of Flanders,' he added wistfully.

FitzStephen was sure that Cullen had never seen Flanders, which was a flooded flat land if Richard de la Roche's account was to be believed. But he did not stop the man talking about his future prospects in Ireland. It was good that more men were planning for their lives in this land.

It took until mid-morning to get the army just five miles up the coast to the first obstacle on their path – an impassable river which ran south into the bay. Domhnall Caomhánach had taken the lead as the army marched inland for a couple of miles towards a settlement called Dun Cormaic where they could successfully ford the river. The little mottle of hovels was on the far side of a deep ravine with long sloping sides through which the river ran amongst the thick trees.

It was just FitzStephen urged his palfrey to follow the Laighin vanguard that the screaming began.

The scream of the dying told Eirik Mac Amlaibh that his two thousand-strong army had successfully ambushed their enemy at the bank of the river at Dun Cormaic. Though he could not see the front line, a howl and the clash of steel on steel followed by the grunt of exertion told him that the two masses of men had come together in battle. The leader of Waesfjord looked to the sky and prayed to St Ivar and St Michael the Archangel that his fight was righteous and that those holy warriors would bring his appeal for victory directly to God.

Eirik had hidden his men amongst the thick sycamore and oak trees on the eastern bank of the high ravine. There, they had waited for the vanguard of the enemy army to splash out of the deep river crossing and onto the steep slope of the riverbank. It was only then, when they were at their most vulnerable, that he had ordered his warriors to form shield wall and advance slowly downhill towards the unsuspecting Gaels who struggled upwards in their soaking robes. He espied a rock and clambered onto it so that he could see over the helmeted heads to where two armies snarled and stabbed and perished.

'Kill them,' Ingólfur Andersson shouted as he brought his axe down on another Irishman's head. Blood, bone fragments, and caked hair flew through the air. Eirik cheered his brother warriors.

Forty enemies had died in that initial clash of arms while another fifty of Diarmait's tribesmen stood in the depths of the river. Despite their obvious disadvantage, Eirik was shocked that the enemy continued to attempt shrieking assaults up the bank to where the axes of the Ostmen made mincemeat of their puny weapons, and every thrust of sword or spear was stopped by shield or chainmail shirt. Diarmait's men fell backwards in agony with open wounds and obstructed the path of their compatriots behind, allowing the Ostmen to step forward and swing their battle-axes, inflicting yet more damage. The shield wall which faced them was impregnable but still the valiant men leapt from the river in attack. Battle-axes swung two handed, ripping arms and legs from the enemy soldiers. The bearded faces of the Ostmen grinned through clenched teeth as they carved men apart from shoulder to torso.

'Push them back into the river! This land is ours,' Eirik Mac Amlaibh exclaimed from his vantage point.

'Slingers,' Ingólfur shouted as rocks the size of fists began to fall amongst the Waesfjord men. One rock landed close to Eirik but, for the most part, the bombardment had no effect on the warriors sealed in mail and crowned with iron helms. Within minutes, the Irish bodies were piling high and the Uí Ceinnselaig taoiseach finally called to his men to retreat back to the western bank.

As they fled, Eirik led the triumphant hollering. 'Go back where you came from, you Vestmen bastards.' He grinned and raised his hands to salute his warrior townspeople. Eirik knew that there would be more to face but this small victory was to be enjoyed. He supposed that with this defeat, Diarmait would send forward his new collaborators from Cluainmín. The long forgotten excitement of the bloodlust had risen in the chest of the old trader, and he relished the crash of shield on shield. He had chosen an unbeatable position on the high eastern bank. What could Cluainmín bring to the battle that he had not seen before?

Eirik laughed out loud. All the land to Banneew Bay would be his and all his people would rejoice with him in glory.

Sir Robert FitzStephen leapt into the saddle of his courser and began issuing orders. The vanguard of Diarmait's army was pouring back through the sycamores in disarray, some with gashes and wounds open and horrific.

'Miles,' he shouted towards his nephew, 'get your men down to the river, but do not engage. Do *not* engage,' he repeated sternly. Miles nodded and began issuing his orders to crossbowmen. They then followed him as he vaulted down the hill into the trees. Seconds later a horseman burst through the treeline and pulled up beside FitzStephen. It was Domhnall Caomhánach. Blood poured from a cut hidden beneath his saffron robe. He spoke in Irish to King Diarmait who, accompanied as ever by Sir Hervey de Montmorency, reined in alongside the two men.

'Ostmen from Waesfjord,' the King translated his son's words.

Nerves showed on Domhnall's face but Diarmait just stared at FitzStephen expectantly and the Norman realised that the King wanted to see his new mercenaries in action. FitzStephen squared his jaw, nodded to Diarmait, and turned his courser's head towards the valley where the noise of war rang clear. He tried to tell himself that he was excited at the prospect of a battle, unexpected though it was. Just six weeks before he had been a prisoner in a Welsh oubliette without a future and now he had an enemy he could fight. That thought rang around his head and suddenly another emotion crept into his body, emanating from his belly. It was a sensation he had not felt for many years but he identified it immediately – self-doubt. The army's advance towards Waesfjord should have been undetected, but obviously something had alerted the Ostmen to his army's location and the enemy now had a position of strength on the far bank. He paused to think, aware that Diarmait still watched him, judging his every move.

*You fight a battle* – his father's words, spoken to him during childhood, came back to him – *then you build a castle*. The sentiment comforted and calmed FitzStephen. Simplicity was the Norman way and a plan quickly came to him. His mind made up, FitzStephen raised his hand to bring Richard de la Roche to his side.

'Robert?' the Fleming asked as he approached. He too was nervous.

'Hide amongst the trees with Miles,' he told him. 'We shall handle this in the old Norman way and lead them to you.'

The Flemish commander grinned from beneath his thin, greying beard and began issuing orders to his company of archers.

'What will you do?' Diarmait asked FitzStephen, his eyes

darting to watch the archers as they disappeared into the trees. Hervey de Montmorency was at the King's shoulder and stared through suspicious, narrowed eyes at his rival.

FitzStephen ignored Hervey and addressed his master, the King of Laighin. 'I will destroy the Ostmen,' he said simply though his confidence belied his true state of mind.

Diarmait seemed contented and nodded his head slowly in consent before urging his pony towards where his son's vanguard assembled and licked their wounds.

Hervey, however, could not resist another remark. 'Yes, good luck, FitzStephen. Don't let King Diarmait down like you did King Henry at Aberteifi.' His broken-toothed grin was off putting, but FitzStephen didn't have the opportunity to retort as Walter de Ridlesford jogged towards him and took hold of his bridle.

'Where do you need my men?' he asked.

'Keep them ready, Walter,' FitzStephen replied, 'you are the reserve.' Ridlesford looked devastated that he would not be involved in the fight and stomped back towards his troops to deliver the bad news, his bald head reflecting the hot sun which poured through the heavy foliage.

As FitzStephen trotted over towards his conrois, he heard the Ostmen begin singing their battle songs of victory down in the ravine. The music was interspersed with terse shouts that he supposed were profanities which cursed their enemy's timidity. FitzStephen smiled, for the men of Waesfjord were about to feel the full force of the Norman way of war. His men were already in the saddle, horses circling and snorting, as they too felt the excitement build.

FitzStephen held up his hands to stop the activity. 'Men, are you ready to earn King Diarmait's pay?' Led by the older men in the conrois they shouted assent. 'Then follow my standard down through the trees and into the river,' he said. 'Keep your horses moving and watch for when I make my move.'

As the men passed back his orders, making sure everyone understood the plan, FitzStephen pulled his chainmail hood up from his shoulders and over his head where he bound it with a leather drawn string at the back of his skull. His son, Ralph, ran up to him with his helm and lance, both crowned with a blue and white plume. FitzStephen took the flat pot helmet from his son who looked up at him looking for thanks. He offered none and Ralph was left standing beside his father, looking up like a dog waiting for a morsel of food from his master's hand. FitzStephen fixed the helmet onto his head, securing the masked iron defence with a leather strap under his chin before accepting his lance which he held aloft above his head, steel tip pointing towards the enemy.

'Are you ready?' he shouted, and his milites snarled their affirmation.

'Then follow me.' FitzStephen swung Sleipnir around and trotted him through the trees above the river. He could hear his own heavy breath beat off the inside of the steel face mask and the rattling chainmail did nothing to cover the nervous pulse which rose throughout his body. Above it all was the roar of the Ostmen's song. FitzStephen had to duck as the branches slashed past him, but he could see Richard de la Roche's red and white surcoat up ahead. Even through the small eye slits which obstructed his sight, he could tell that the Fleming was nervous.

'I count two thousand,' Roche said with a grimace as FitzStephen approached. 'They see us but are waiting for us to attack.'

'Well, I wouldn't want to let them down,' FitzStephen replied, happy that his helm hid the nervous sweat which poured from his brow. 'Stay ready,' he told his friend as he clipped his heels to Sleipnir's flanks.

'Be careful,' Roche whispered after his captain.

The trees became less dense towards the riverbank: mostly bushes and undergrowth, and FitzStephen was able to see the coloured circular shields of the enemy lining the opposite river bank. The nameless stream was just twenty paces across and beyond it he could just see the hovels of Dun Cormaic. He immediately saw that it was indeed a good place to ford as the gravel bottom was just a foot or two below the trickling surface. The Ostman victory song suddenly turned into a din of abuse as they spotted FitzStephen at the head of the Norman advance. Shouting and crashing of weapons on shields erupted from their

240

lines as the line of forty horsemen divided either side of their captain and lined up, facing the Ostmen across the expanse of the river.

'Hold,' FitzStephen shouted, listening as his order was reiterated down the line by the senior milites. Before him, bodies floated in the shallows, caught on vegetation and discarded weaponry. Diluted blood mingled with golden pebble and black water.

Already some of the Ostmen were in frenzy and had jumped into the river, throwing aside their shields and shouting challenges to the Norman horsemen who waited on the western bank. The men of Waesfjord already had blood on their blades and were filled with a lust for more. They screamed insults and urged their brothers to the great deeds of their fathers.

'Steady,' FitzStephen shouted, straining his voice so that he could be heard. His horse beneath him struggled against the reins which he held in his left hand. 'We hold! Disciplined men of Wales.' The longer that FitzStephen held his men back, the more defiant their enemy became. Young Ostmen jumped out of the shield wall and into the shallows of the river. They were overcome with the blood fury.

'Fight me, you cowards,' one man screamed in the Nordic tongue before switching to that of the Gaels. His compatriots gnashed their teeth and tore the chainmail from their breasts like the berserkers of old, daring the iron-wrapped invaders to fall on their line. They threw down their shields, hefted their axes, and clashed their breasts with fists.

'Look, I have no armour. Fight me if you dare,' another man, a duck hunter from the Waesfjord Bay slobs, shouted as he cast his shield across the river at the enemy. 'I'll kill you all!'

'Hold!' shouted FitzStephen as his own men started to snarl at the Ostmen's defiance. 'Hold!'

Behind the Waesfjord army, Eirik Mac Amlaibh looked around at his warriors for answers. 'Horsemen?' he shouted at the bearded and helmeted men alongside him. 'Who are these horsemen?' He had to shout to pierce the hullabaloo made by

241

the warriors on the bank of the river.

Covered in blood from the earlier massacre, Ingólfur Andersson shrugged to answer his chief. 'They are armoured,' he said, 'so they must be Danes or Norse. Or else the Vestmen have finally developed brains and put on armour.' He laughed at that unlikely conclusion. Around him many men joined in his amusement.

Eirik did not like that he now faced horsemen when he had been expecting to fight an undisciplined horde on foot. At worst he had imagined taking on a shield wall, but the sudden appearance of cavalry had brought about a dramatic effect on his own forces. More and more of his soldiers splashed into the water challenging their foes to single combat, or were hurling abuse in the Nordic and Irish tongues. 'I don't like this,' he told his chief men. 'We should get those men out of the river,' he added with a whisper.

'I don't see what difference it makes that they are on horseback,' Ingólfur said confidently. 'We outnumber them by fifty to one and they have to cross the river to get to us! It is laughable that they would even try,' he said, indicating across the river with a flippant wave of his hand. 'Look at these colourful fools; they are scared of us!'

Eirik decided that his companion, more experienced in warfare than he, was probably correct and smiled as Ingólfur laughed loudly. 'I would not attack when faced with the flower of the youth of Waesfjord,' he said, safe behind the pulsating Norse lines, 'and they will not either.'

It was an unfortunate statement because just as he said it, the horsemen vaulted into action, smashing into the already rippling river and thrust across at the Ostmen. Eirik could only watch as the men in the river, maddened with the battle-fever, waded out to meet the horses and were cut down by the glittering spears of the horsemen, steel blades striking through chainmail and into neck, lungs, and throat. Within a few heartbeats, thirty Norse bodies joined the dead Irishmen already floating face down in the beautiful river, and the enemy surged ahead again towards the warriors amassed in battle order on the bank. In the blink of an eye, the horsemen leapt from the river and met two thousand

Waesfjord warriors with shields locked and axes poised to strike. But the Normans did not close the gap between the two forces, preferring to prod and hassle, stab, and retreat out of reach. Water swirled white below them as they thrust down before sweeping their horses away, leaf-shaped shields covering their left sides and that of their horses from Norse retaliation. They whooped and cat-called as they bled the front rank with a hundred cuts.

In their midst, Sir Robert FitzStephen ripped his lance from an enemy warrior's neck, taking half the man's throat tissue with it, and stabbed another through the elbow. His pennant was flush with blood and ripped where one of the Ostmen had tried to pull it from his hand.

'Keep moving,' he shouted at his comrades and stabbed downwards again. Another man charged out of the Norse lines, an axe above him ready to strike. FitzStephen calmly pushed his courser forward and into the man, not even bothering to lift his shield. Half a ton of horse meat pummelled the man onto his back before FitzStephen forced Sleipnir onwards to stamp on the man's body; the distinctive crunch told him that the warrior below had broken bones. He quickly swung his horse around ready to take on his next attacker but there was no-one within arm's reach. Instead, he wheeled his horse away from the Ostmen and quickly assessed the state of his cavalry. Up and down the line the remaining Normans intimidated and probed the enemy to frenzy. It was time, he thought, to finish the battle and destroy the enemy.

'Panic, panic!' he shouted and his call was duplicated up and down the Norman line. FitzStephen raised his standard and kicked Sleipnir into a retreat back across the river. 'Panic, panic!' he continued. It had been no more than three minutes since the Norman cavalry had crossed to attack and yet a hundred Norse bodies lay on the bank of the river; fathers, brothers, uncles, sons, friends, and comrades of those left alive on the bank. And those men had been moved almost to madness by the Norman cavalry's harrying.

Behind him, all FitzStephen's warriors disengaged and followed his lead, screaming 'panic' and fleeing back across the river. A roar of elation came from the vengeful Ostmen and they plunged en masse into the water in pursuit of the escaping enemy whose horses vaulted up the opposite bank and into the trees, throwing fearful glances over their shoulders at their pursuers.

On the bank of the river, Eirik Mac Amlaibh found that he was almost alone, apart from the wounded who screamed in pain. He watched his fellow Norse struggle up the far bank or through the river, but something kept him from following. It was not fear but a foreboding of disaster and he was paralysed as he prayed that he was wrong.

'Come back,' he whispered. Eirik suddenly felt ludicrous in his armour, with his enormous circular shield propped against his thigh, a helmet on his head, and an undrawn sword at his side. More and more men were crawling up the steep bank after the horsemen with the oddly shaped shields.

Eirik held his breath in anticipation.

Sleipnir was breathing heavily as he vaulted from the river and took FitzStephen up the bank between the sycamores. The Norman nodded his helmeted head to Richard de la Roche as he and his conrois thundered past the Fleming's position amongst the tight deciduous trees.

'Regroup at the top of the ravine,' FitzStephen shouted to the cavalry who followed him further up the ravine. At the lip of the hill he turned Sleipnir and calmed him with a rub to his shoulder. Walter de Ridlesford ran over to FitzStephen and demanded information about the battle.

'Do you need my men to help out?' he demanded as FitzStephen threw his legs over the side of his courser and jumped to the ground, pulling off his helmet and working his shield onto his back where it hung from the guige.

'Gather your men, Walter,' the knight panted as he stabbed his lance into the long grass. Ridlesford whooped and shouted to his sergeants to organise the two hundred infantrymen under his command. As he did this, FitzStephen signalled Hugh de Caunteton to take control of the cavalry while he pulled his lance from the earth and jogged downhill into the trees. The distinctive twang of bowstrings snapping back into place accompanied by the screams of agony told FitzStephen that Richard de la Roche had unleashed the ambush. He prayed that his ruse had been successful or very soon he would encounter two thousand Norse of Waesfjord charging towards him. The feigned flight was an age-old Norman trick and, coupled with the precision and power of the Welsh archers and Flemish crossbowmen, he believed it capable of destroying this foe. He saw men ahead in the trees, but could not yet tell if they were friend or enemy and he slowed his pace and listened intently at the sound of the battle: splashing, screaming, bowstrings, the clash of arrows on shields and the thump of weaponry striking flesh. To his left he espied Richard de la Roche's surcoat and he made for his friend's side. It was only when he approached the Fleming's side that he saw the slaughter that the archers had wrought. Four and a half thousand arrows and quarrels hammered into the Ostman army every minute. Incredibly, as FitzStephen watched, the men of Waesfjord still struggled into the ravaging rain of arrows, huddling behind the few large trees on the western bank. The Norman captain had only been absent from the riverside for a number of minutes, but there were hundreds of dead and wounded prostrate before him like supplicant slaves.

'Keep giving them hell!' Richard de la Roche shouted, but FitzStephen could already see that the Ostmen were defeated. Then, starting with groups of one and two, more the Norse began to turn and make their escape. And that was when the damage became even more severe. The Ostmen, deprived of the protection of the wooden and leather shields, were open targets for the hawk-eyed archers from the Welsh March. One sensible warrior threw his shield across his back, but its swirling colours drew the eyes and the arrows of the archers and by the time he reached the waterside, twenty arrows were poking from his back like a hedgehog and he had to crawl on his face and slide into the water. Miles Menevensis and Richard de la Roche knew their trade well so FitzStephen left them to their work. He watched with pity as they ordered their companies forward to the bank of the river where they targeted the men wading back to the eastern shore. Walter de Ridlesford's men had taken up a position between Miles's crossbowmen and Roche's archers but his cousin had found himself surplus to requirement and was extremely unhappy at that state of affairs.

'God's teeth,' Ridlesford cursed as he joined FitzStephen. 'May a pox rot off their balls! They've gone, the cowards!' He then pointed an accusatory finger at Richard de la Roche's mailed chest. 'You couldn't have left something for us to do?'

'Of course we left you something to do,' the grizzled old warrior laughed from behind his beard and pointed to the bodies which lay strewn around the forest. 'You can collect the arrows from the bodies. It wouldn't do to lose those, they were bloody expensive.'

Walter hummed and nodded his head seriously. 'And how about I take those same arrows and shove them up your arse?'

FitzStephen knew that the war of words would continue for some time between the two men so he left them to it and went to stand beside the river and watch the Waesfjord army flee through the woods on the opposite bank.

'Walter,' he interrupted his cousin mid-profanity. 'Take your men across the stream and secure the far bank and woods.' As he turned, he sighted Diarmait Mac Murchada, Domhnall Caomhánach, and Sir Hervey de Montmorency walking through the wood towards him. Diarmait's son seemed shocked at the destruction visited upon the Ostmen who he had believed invincible. His father had a look of wicked triumph plastered across his face as he walked amongst the bodies peppered with arrows. He congratulated young archers as they stooped to cut the valuable projectiles from the flesh of dead men. The wounded were finished off with the same knives with barely a hint of emotion.

Sir Hervey looked nonplussed by the horror. 'Easy pickings,' he sniffed.

Diarmait ignored him and issued a huge laugh. 'Fifteen minutes,' the King announced in his native language. 'Just fifteen minutes and he defeated them.' He shook his head disbelievingly.

His son, Domhnall nodded as he knelt beside a wounded

Ostman and held his hand. The man was dying, his intestines piled in his lap as he sat propped against a tree. The man appealed for help and Domhnall gave him the quick death he needed, plunging his knife expertly into his armpit where it punctured his heart. He cleaned his knife of blood and climbed to his feet after the man had drifted away.

'They had an army twice the size of ours,' Domhnall told his father with a stunned shake of his head. 'The Ostmen were in a place of strategic strength and they were ready for us. Yet he destroyed them.' He shook his head and nodded his head in FitzStephen's direction. 'Tell me, Father, have we done the right thing bringing this Norman to Laighin?'

Mac Murchada's eyes glowed white-blue and his son could see that the King was no longer listening to his words. 'Our enemies will beg for mercy,' Diarmait murmured as Walter de Ridlesford's troops jogged loudly past the two men. He watched as they clambered into the river before disappearing into the trees on the opposite bank. Diarmait began laughing again and slapped a hand on his son's shoulder. 'Come on, boy,' he said and nodded his head towards FitzStephen who was talking to Richard de la Roche and Miles Menevensis. 'Let's go and congratulate our all-conquering heroes.'

FitzStephen watched as the King of Laighin and his son approached the riverside, but he ignored them and turned towards his two lieutenants, awaiting their reports.

'We had no losses amongst the archers,' Miles told his uncle. 'A well-performed manoeuvre, I would say.'

Richard de la Roche nodded his agreement. 'I would guess five hundred Ostmen dead and as many wounded, perhaps more.'

'If every battle is this easy we will have Diarmait back on his throne before Yuletide,' FitzStephen said with a hint of relief.

'Forget Diarmait,' Miles laughed. 'If every battle is this easy we could put you on the throne, uncle.'

FitzStephen did not answer and held up a hand to quiet Miles as the King of Laighin came within earshot. 'Take your men across the river and scout ahead of Walter – harry the

Ostmen as far as you can, but do not engage them in battle,' he told his nephew. 'You can take Prendergast with you and I will follow with the Irish and my milites.' Miles nodded and jogged back through the trees to deliver the message to the Flemish commander.

'A marvel – that is what you are, my boy,' Diarmait announced with a huge smile and hugged the Norman.

FitzStephen returned his grin, embarrassed but happy at the histrionic show of emotion. 'It will take more than that old trick to take Waesfjord,' he said, 'and more than well placed arrows to put you back on the throne of Laighin.'

Diarmait nodded, but he was barely listening to his warlord's measured assessment. FitzStephen saw the passion in those blue eyes, but the appearance of Maurice de Prendergast and his light horsemen made him forget any worries in his new ally.

Prendergast, tall and stoic in the saddle, nodded to both knight and king as he passed by. 'Yes, yes, do not engage,' the Fleming pre-empted FitzStephen's order with a grimace and without stopping. His horse splashed into the river. 'We'll not take Waesfjord until you get there. But you had better not take too long,' he warned.

FitzStephen turned towards his king. 'It is time to cross the stream, Lord.'

'No, Sir Robert, it is time for some vengeance.'

Eirik Mac Amlaibh had barely spoken a word since the disaster had befallen his army at Dun Cormaic. All down the long road through the low hills, more of the army of Waesfjord had re-joined the column as they retreated towards their longfort home. Helmeted men, many with horrific wounds, walked with great effort in varying degrees of disorder. Most had thrown away their weapons so that they would not be weighed down and caught by the enemy scouts who stalked them through the hills of Forthairt, yet their progress was desperately slow. Every few miles the Ostmen would hear the outriders' hooves thumping on the mountain turf and they would be forced to stop and turn, form a hurried shield wall, and make ready to defend themselves against the devilish horsemen.

No such attack had been forced home yet. It was as if the enemy were herding the Ostmen back to a pen. But the Norse of Waesfjord were not sheep, they were wolves. Ingólfur Andersson had proved this when he captured one horseman who strayed too close to the retreating warriors. The youngster had spilled a lot of information before Ingólfur had savagely spilled his guts on the mountainside. Normans – that was who the enemy were according to the dead boy. Eirik prayed that those vicious men had not set their sights on Ireland. The stories of their massacres among the Danish peoples around Jorvik were still told by traders who frequently visited Waesfjord. It was rumoured that there were still swathes of uninhabited land in northern England, empty since William the Conqueror had savaged those who had supported the King of Denmark's invasion a hundred years before.

Eirik could see the line of torches as Diarmait Mac Murchada's army came down from the mountainside on the Ostmen's tail. The curling line of fire looked like a great fiery dragon straight from the old sagas and it sent a shiver down Eirik's spine. The dead Norman outrider had divulged the full scale of their army and Eirik, who had seen for himself the destructive power of their archers and cavalry, could not believe that his mighty army had been shattered by such a small number of warriors. He would not make that mistake again.

'How far to Waesfjord?' asked Eirik of an axeman who walked in front of him. He had lost his bearings in the dusk and his voice was hoarse from the effort of walking without water or rest.

'Just over the next ridge,' the man said gruffly. Noticing the Norman torches on the hillside behind for the first time, he picked up his pace.

'Don't worry,' Eirik told the man, loud enough for everyone around him to hear, 'we will regroup back in Waesfjord. Their horses won't be able to climb our strong walls and their arrows cannot go through solid timber.' The men around him seemed to consider this as they trudged on in silence through the cold boggy hills. 'No one has ever taken Waesfjord,' Eirik shouted.

It was still and cold in Forthairt and he mightily desired to get back behind the safe walls and the warmth of his longhouse rather than trudging through the hills on already wet feet. Presently the land began to slope downwards, and the evergreens began to thin, and Eirik was able to see the town which was bathed in the light of the large full moon. Wax torches burned at points all along the walls while whale fat lamps smouldered in some of the longhouses belonging to the richer traders. As they crept towards the walls of the longfort, Eirik and his men were greeted by the Gaels whose homes huddled around the five Celtic churches outside the town walls. Thirty people had come out of their houses asking for news and offering help to the injured.

'Are you alright?' one old woman asked in the Irish tongue as she came out of her hovel.

'Yes, my dear,' Eirik answered but, as he stared at the woman, he had a thought that made his blood run cold and backed away from the woman's care. 'You there,' he flapped a hand at a soldier called Óttar Mac Óttar, 'you have men?'

'I do,' the warrior nodded.

'You must take them and get those torches,' Eirik told him, flapping his fat hand towards the town walls, 'and then you must burn the churches outside the walls.'

'You want me to burn the churches?' Óttar was shocked at the command and could not believe that he had possibly heard correctly. 'Burn a church?' He repeated the statement disbelieving and shaking his shaggy long-haired head.

'Only the ones outside the town,' Eirik snapped. 'The Norman archers will use the high towers against us, you fool. We must burn them ... and the homes ...'

'Burn out the Gaels?' an outraged Óttar asked again.

'Yes of course,' Eirik told him. 'Can you not see that they cannot be trusted? Then we must expel any Vestman inside the town. Yes, that would be best.' Eirik could not believe the stupidity of Óttar in not understanding his plan.

'My mother is a Gael,' Óttar said angrily, 'and his wife is one too,' he pointed to a warrior walking ahead of them in the column. 'What do we do about them?'

'Alright,' Eirik replied nervously, surprised to have his orders questioned, 'we can eject their men from the town, though.' He waited for a reluctant nod from Óttar who collected his troops and ran off towards the gate of Waesfjord.

'Ingólfur,' he called to the warrior who had fought so furiously at Dun Cormaic. 'We have a problem,' he said, 'one that requires your attention.' He repeated his fears about the Gaels to the tall warrior.

'You are right,' Ingólfur said with relish, 'we should drive out any Vestman, whether they be man, woman, or child. Beggars and vagrants, that is all they are,' Ingólfur said. 'We cannot trust Óttar to do this,' he said. 'I will begin the fires myself.'

'Thank you, finally someone who understands,' Eirik said, suddenly confident now that he had a great warrior's support.

Ingólfur nodded and began shouting orders to his men.

'Sir?' The old Irish woman came back towards Eirik, casting a nervous eye at the armoured warriors gathering just outside her home in the light cast by the burning torches. 'Would you like some water?' She held a skin up to the rich merchant.

Eirik waited until Ingólfur threw the first fiery torch onto the woman's house before he answered. 'Yes, that would be lovely, my dear,' Eirik said with a smile. 'I am so dreadfully parched.'

He grabbed the heavy skin while around him the shouting began as the first flames licked the thatched roof. Irishtown would burn so that Waesfjord could live.

Smoke filled the lungs of the three men who stared down from the hill and onto the longfort of Waesfjord. The Ostmen had set the houses outside the earth and timber walls alight and the menacing glow of the fires reached even to the trio of warriors.

'Well,' FitzStephen told Walter de Ridlesford, 'at least the smoke keeps the damn flies away from our camp. Bloody bogland,' he said as he slapped another insect from his arm. The two Normans, joined by Diarmait Mac Murchada, had crossed a small river on foot and made their way beyond the outlying pickets to the edge of the hills to get a better look at their target. It was cloudless and with the moon at its zenith the men had been able to get a great view of the Ostman town. They had been quietly studying it for weaknesses when fire had begun to spread amongst the thatched houses. It had started slowly in the north around the Irish corn market, hardly noticeable even to the three men up on their vantage point, but it had spread south with great speed, borne by torches thrown by more Ostman warriors. Churches, inns, shops, and homes went up in flames; none were spared in Irishtown. Some of those living outside the walls had come out to try and stop the blaze, but unarmed and unprepared for the attack they stood no chance and were hacked down by the marauding Ostmen. The rest screamed and ran, abandoning all their possessions to the fire. The flames lit up the earth mound, the glacis topped with a heavy wooden fence, five times as tall as a man, which surrounded Waesfjord.

A seething Diarmait had pointed out the five Celtic churches which stood outside the five gates to the longfort. Four of the churches burned, flames licking the inside of their high stone towers, gutting the wooden stairs and floors and leaving them uninhabitable and useless to the Normans, just as the Ostmen had hoped. As they watched, the northernmost church buckled in the heat and collapsed in on itself with a creaking crash which resonated around the hills and over the water.

As he stared down on the longfort, FitzStephen could see people as they spewed out of the town gates, ejected by the Ostmen. Screaming children, men and women, slave and freeman alike, ran for their lives from warriors carrying fiery brands and unsheathed weapons. Fully armed and filled with fury, the townsmen were unable to stay their hands and began hacking down the Gaelsas they fled past their burning homes. Only St Michael's Church, far to the south, was left untouched by the Ostmen.

Diarmait was inconsolable with rage. Even Walter de Ridlesford, who had seen his share of carnage and horror, was aghast as the Ostmen continued to burn and murder. It somehow seemed more calculating and cold to the Norman because they were not taking the Gaels' belongings; they just inflicted wanton destruction upon the fleeing folk.

FitzStephen crouched on one knee in front of the other two

men at the edge of a small spinney of trees. 'Well, that was incredibly silly of them,' he said.

'Silly?' Diarmait ground his teeth, clenching and re-clenching his jaw angrily. 'That is all you can say?' The fires of the town reflected in his eyes. 'You think burning people's homes to the ground is *silly*?'

'Irishtown is not Fearna,' FitzStephen said calmly and, with one eye closed, traced the shape of the walls of the town with his finger in the air. It was easily distinguishable under the bright moonlight; a long thin rectangle with walls on three sides and the bay lapping at the muddy beach at its back. 'How many men can they have left to defend their walls?' he asked.

'A thousand?' answered Ridlesford with a shrug.

'Indeed. The survivors from Dun Cormaic and maybe a few more besides, but there is over two thousand feet of wall to defend and they have absolutely no idea from where our attack will come.' He turned to Diarmait again. 'So when I say "silly" I mean that they could have brought every Irishman, their friends and neighbours, strapped a spear, blade, or even a stick to their hands and put them on the wall to fight us. Instead they chase them into the hills. Very silly,' he repeated.

Diarmait nodded, angry at his outburst and at the massacre of his people. 'Domhnall will round them up and they will fight in the kern.'

FitzStephen nodded and went quiet for many seconds.

'So how the hell do we get in?' Walter asked curtly.

FitzStephen did not answer as he studied the land below him which ran downwards in the direction of Waesfjord. The hills sloped slowly down towards the walls of the town through twelve hundred feet of soft marshy ground, sparsely populated by trees, bushes, and smallholdings. It was horrible terrain for cavalry and the lack of cover, after the destruction of the Irishtown, would make his troops nervous. Every town had people capable of using hunting bows and he imagined them on the walls, sniping at his unprotected troops. The height advantage provided by the high wall, in conjunction with the lack of cover for FitzStephen's men, would give the Ostmen a distinct advantage over his own archers, no matter how much more skilled his men. Two rivers sparkled in the moonlight to the southern end of the walled town. His eye followed them as they streamed under two great wooden barbicans, through the middle of the town and into the bay beyond. It was a weakness, a small one, but a weakness nonetheless.

He estimated that the longfort of Waesfjord was about five hundred yards long and just two hundred feet across. The defenders would be hard pushed to protect it all, especially the main wall which faced westwards. Over the houses in the town, he could see the Norse longboats, differing in size, some with snarling dragon carvings magnificent at the bows. Around twenty were tied to the heavy stakes which followed the bend of the town wall into the bay, acting as a harbour from which the crews could ferry to the mainland. Ten or fifteen more boats were anchored in the bay. He whistled. Archambaud had been right to ignore the possibility of storming the longfort by sea; his small flotilla would quickly have been overcome by the mighty force of ships available to the Norse.

'Well,' Diarmait began, 'any thoughts? What new tricks do you Normans have at your disposal? Can you bring down fire like rain or cause their walls to quake and collapse?'

Walter and FitzStephen looked at each other without saying anything, raising their eyebrows and smiling secretly at Diarmait's words. They did have a plan which would make the walls 'quake and collapse', though they had not told Mac Murchada of it.

'Can we lure them out?' Walter asked his cousin who grimaced, twisting a piece of long, coarse grass between his fingers before throwing it away.

'Lure them out to where? The ground is uneven, there is nowhere to hide – if they are totally insane they may come out by themselves and come far enough away from their walls so that we can ambush them,' FitzStephen shook his head and grimaced as to the likelihood of that.

'We could scour their territory,' Walter said. 'Kill everybody and burn everything in sight. That might encourage them out for a fight.'

'No, they will stay behind their walls and hope that we

cannot break in.' *Nor*, FitzStephen thought, *do I want to devastate the land that I hope to rule*.

'They did the same to me,' Diarmait spoke for the first time about his one and only attempt to subdue the town. 'They waited behind their walls until we ran out of food. Not one person died on their side.' He dragged his hands through his mane of hair as he watched the burning embers float away from the blaze. The soaring cinders reflected in the bay like a field of stars. 'Why do you think they came out and attacked us at Dun Cormaic?'

FitzStephen shook his head rustling the links of his chainmail hood. He had no idea why the Ostmen would have chosen to sortie out of their unassailable longfort. But he knew for certain that they would not make the same mistake again. As he considered the tactics for the fight ahead and where he would attack, he watched the town. The Ostmen, seemingly pleased with their ferocious work in Irishtown, had retreated back through the burning houses and inside their walls. His victory at Dun Cormaic had eased his anxiety about his leadership, but the longfort posed a far more difficult problem for his men. He steeled himself and made his decision. In the light of the burning churches FitzStephen sketched a rudimentary outline of the ramparts on a patch of dry earth.

'Here's the plan,' he told Diarmait and Ridlesford. 'Three hundred years of independence in Waesfjord is about to come to an abrupt end.'

Before first light the Norman scouts under Maurice de Prendergast descended down the shoulder of the valley alongside the small river to take control of St Michael the Archangel's Church. The hilly marshland transformed into grassy paths and then into a stony road the closer the horsemen got to the church. They were armed to the teeth, prepared for a hard fight, and in no mood to banter with the lone priest who met them in the road.

'Any assault on this place is an assault on God himself,' the bearded priest said in Latin to Prendergast at the head of the horsemen. How the priest had known that the Normans were coming, Maurice could not tell. They carried no brands or torches nor had they encountered any scouts on their way down the mountain. Even the wind was with them, blowing as it was off Lough Garman back towards Banabh. Still, here the priest was, tonsured and standing in the middle of the road in a heavy woollen shift, blocking their passage.

'Luckily, Father,' Prendergast replied without giving away his shock at the man's sudden appearance, 'we are good Christian men, unlike the Norse, and here only to stable our coursers. I promise that nothing will be stolen, if you promise to assist us,' he said, waving his grinning men forward around the priest. 'But if you do not then I am afraid I will not be able to stop my men taking control using force.' Prendergast gave the priest a grimace which said that he would not enjoy destroying the church but that he would do it nonetheless, say his prayers, and beg forgiveness of the Lord afterwards.

The priest screwed up one eye as he considered the threat, but he was a practical man who had watched four other churches burnt to the ground in the darkness of the night before. He knew that he had to protect St Michael's and almost immediately he assented to Prendergast's request and moved out of the horsemen's way. The Fleming nodded in appreciation and shouted orders to his sergeants. Within minutes they had taken the holy ground around St Michael's despite the obvious grumblings of the priests therein.

The burning of the suburbs had left a multitude of displaced people searching for shelter during the night, and St Michael's had provided a haven. The terrified people saw the armed Flemings and again made a move to flee but Prendergast would not allow the men to leave and kept his horsemen circling the church compound, threatening violence on anyone who made a break for it. He also watched the road which wound its way from Waesfjord, and the two roads which stretched away to the south and east.

'Give them the signal,' Prendergast told Herluin Synad once the church and the fugitive Irish had been secured. The rest of the army made their way down the hill now that the scouts had achieved their objective. FitzStephen's main force kept the small river on their left in the unlikely event that the Norse would sortie out to attack their flank, but the five gates of Waesfjord remained firmly shut. Quickly, the Normans took possession of the small church with the tall stone tower beside it. They forced the seven priests into a small anteroom with little delicacy and locked them in. Everyone else was herded outside where the men and older boys were divided from the women and children. Young teenagers cried as spears were thrust into their hands and they were immersed into the ranks of Diarmait's kern. Unwilling to feed the rest, the Normans pointed down the grassy road to the east and told the women and children not to come back. The scouts were required to prod the screaming and crying refugees down the road for half a mile before returning to stable their horses inside the church. Just ten men, injured at Dun Cormaic, would be left to protect those beasts, vital as they were to the conquest of Laighin. With their horses stored safely the army fanned out into the street around St Michael's and went a little way down the south road until they found a place where they could ford the river. Fifty archers crossed first and then covered the milites and the kern as they splashed through the shallow river. Two draught-horses were the only beasts to be taken on the march and they dragged a device made of thick timbers. It had been assembled by Meiler FitzHenry during the night while a number of Diarmait's derb-fine had looked on in confusion, wondering what the bucketed instrument, made of thick shaped wood and rope, did.

On the far bank of the river, the commanders marshalled the army into battle order, raising the standards of those knights who carried their own colours. Steel armour and colourful surcoats were dramatic against the dull backdrop of the muddy grass and dark walls of Waesfjord. They then moved forward on the road which ran parallel to the long wall of the fortress-town, passing close to the ruined remnants of St Bride's Church. Burnt timber and scorched stones were all which remained of the former building and several of the Normans crossed their chests at the unchristian behaviour of the heathen Ostmen. The majority of the army would gladly have cut the throat of the Pope if he thought he could get away with his jewels, but to a man they still believed in the power of the Church and swore vengeance on the despicable Ostmen.

'Why did God not stop this carnage?' a superstitious young archer asked his mate.

'God got chased away from these lands a long time ago, boy,' replied his commander in a blue surcoat with a silver star without turning around to face the boy.

St Bride's stood over four hundred feet from the walls of Waesfjord, but every man could see the sullen Norse warriors who stood on the palisade watching the enemy parade their strength in front of their walls. Many showed their scorn by shouting at the army, delivering disdainful hand signals and derisive songs at the Normans while others shook their fists and weapons, urging them to attack their walls so that they could test their blades against Norman steel. The path continued to close on the walls of town as Diarmait's army approached St Peter's Church, again slighted by the fire of the Ostmen. The stone tower of the church, once used to store and protect the riches of the parish from raids by Norse or the other tribes, had collapsed during the night due to the overwhelming heat of the fire which had scorched through the church beside it. Surely no good could come from so much carnage against Holy Mother Church?

FitzStephen's timber device was left behind the lone standing wall of St Peter's with Meiler FitzHenry and twenty of the kern who began labouring under the Norman's orders. If the men of Waesfjord could see the work going on under the shadow of the church, they obviously did not understand it as they did nothing to stop the work. Beyond the wrecked church the army continued as the road bent sharply towards the town before it again followed the wall northwards at a distance of two hundred feet. They crossed another stream which barely came over the Normans' sabatons before the warrior in the blue surcoat with a white star stopped the army and turned them to face the town. Ahead of them was a massive gate made out of heavy wood with a strong barbican above it. Up and down the wall the Ostmen shouted their defiance at the Normans. They knew that their longfort had never fallen to any invader and they were confident. But there was still a small air of doubt; they were facing the Normans, a tricky enemy who every man assumed would have some ruse up their sleeves to throw against their walls. The standoff continued for a long time – the silent Norman army staring balefully at the now frenzied performance of the Ostmen on the walls of Waesfjord. On and on it went for minutes until a trumpet blast sounded suddenly from amongst the attackers and quieted the defiance of the townsfolk.

Máelmáedoc Ua Riagain stepped out of the line and walked forward with Diarmait Mac Murchada towards the walls of Waesfjord. The two men were just a hundred feet from the town now and within bowshot, but neither showed any fear at the danger.

'Behold, your rightful lord, Diarmait Mac Murchada of the Uí Ceinnselaig, King of Laighin and the Ostmen,' Máelmáedoc shouted at the vast walls in Irish and then French. Waesfjord was a trader's town and he knew that most would understand the one or other of the languages. His words were answered with a din of boos and shouts which Máelmáedoc waited to subside before continuing. 'But he is a good lord and will forgive your disloyalty if you set down your arms, open your gates, and swear fealty to him once again.' In answer the Ostmen began rhythmically rapping their steel weapons on the timber wall making a huge rumpus which drowned out everything else. Stomp, stomp, stomp went the weapons' against the wooden walls. It seemed to go on for an eternity, preventing Máelmáedoc from delivering the rest of his terms for their surrender.

'So be it,' Máelmáedoc said, but only Diarmait could hear and he turned around and waved his hand in the air, signalling back towards his army. The trumpeter sounded three distinct blasts which punctured the clamour coming from Waesfjord. Inside the walls Eirik and the Ostmen heard the trumpet and prepared themselves for the full-frontal attack. But the Normans simply stared at the walls.

'Why do they wait?' Eirik asked Ingólfur, having to shout to make his voice heard. 'What are they planning?'

'I do not know,' Ingólfur replied. 'Perhaps they are scared?'

Unexpectedly there was a thud of wood whipped against wood from the direction of St Peter's Church, a brutal whistle, and a huge piece of stone made of carved rock and masonry suddenly smashed into the wall ten paces from the barbican where Eirik stood. Four men were thrown backwards over the parapet, dead on impact, by the projectile thrown by Meiler FitzHenry's machine – a trebuchet. The stone projectile sent splinters spewing in every direction, slicing into another three men on either side of the impact point. The Ostmen were silenced and Meiler was dancing in excitement at the effect of the trebuchet, its sling arm still swinging from the recoil. Meiler began issuing orders to reload the machine and the Ostmen watched, suddenly frightened, as the men of the kern reloaded the weapon. They pulled on ropes which hauled back the massive arm from vertical to horizontal. At one end of the sling arm was a huge bucket containing stones taken from the ruined church and which acted as a counter-weight. The taut ropes of the trebuchet were held in place by the notched iron cog which stopped the weapon firing prematurely. A single iron bar held the whole mechanism in place when the hauling ropes were removed. Then, under Meiler's careful direction, the sling bag was positioned directly under the counter-weight while two men manhandled a huge boulder as big as a man's head into place. The weapon was ready to be unleashed on the Ostman town. It had taken just three minutes to load.

'Out of the way,' Meiler shouted, taking a length of rope connected to the triggering pin in his hand. He checked the aim once more before planting his feet alongside the weapon and tugged on the pin. It snapped away with force, releasing the ropes which coiled back under the counter-weight. The main arm whipped upwards, dragging the long sling with it in a wide semi-circle which released the projectile at the very apex. The whole of the machine leapt in the air and thudded to ground as the trebuchet's sling arm bashed into the timber cross-arm at its front and the counter-weight crashed downwards. Meiler's second shot was better directed than the first and it smashed into the barbican, ripping off its roof and throwing the debris into the town behind the walls. Two of the beams holding the roof shattered blinding men in a flurry of splinters and sending Eirik to his knees where he screamed like a woman in labour.

'Ingólfur, Óttar,' he exclaimed and groaned when he found blood on his hands. 'Oh, Holy Bride, save me! I am hurt, I am hurt,' he screeched. 'Help me!' His pudgy hands fumbled to find the wound.

'Shut up,' Ingólfur snarled at his chief as he pulled a splinter of wood as big as a dagger from his forearm. 'We need to bring more men to the main wall,' Ingólfur said as he threw the wooden shard over the wall at the Normans and grabbed another man by his shoulder. 'Bring fifty men from the south and north walls,' he told him, pushing the warrior towards the edge of the ruined barbican. 'This is where the attack will fall,' Ingólfur said, nodding his head profusely. It was obvious, he thought. The Normans would not unleash the terror of the trebuchet unless they would follow it up with an assault, he told himself. Around him the shrieks of injured men continued and haunted the minds of the Ostmen on the unaffected parts of the allure. The songs had finished, replaced with the sound of shuffling feet as the living took the place of the dead on the wall. Those who found themselves on the barbican stood in the warm blood of the injured and the dead. Their eyes darted to the trebuchet which was again going through the process to release horror on the walls of Waesfjord.

'Leave no gaps in the line,' Óttar Mac Óttar shouted from his place on the barbican. 'Prepare for their attack,' he screamed, 'and protect our homes. Remember that you are men of Waesfjord!'

But what the Ostmen did not know was that everything that they observed, the trebuchet and the vast marshalling of the gaudily-dressed Normans, was a mere display planned to draw their attention towards the main gate. Elsewhere Norman mischief was already afoot and their walls had already been breached.

# Chapter Nine

At the northern end of the longfort, a man crouched low and, concealed from the defenders' sight, stared over the ruined remains of the Irish corn market from the top of the Selskar Rock. Through the heavy gnarled grass of the rocky outcropping, he watched the northern extreme of Waesfjord and counted the men milling around on the palisade.

'Sixty-three,' he said with a smile. Far fewer, he thought, than he had dared hope. Three blasts of a trumpet emanated from St Peter's Gate but the man just grinned and ignored it.

Behind the warrior, Gilbert de Brienne coughed.

'Err, Sir Robert,' he said gingerly, 'that was the signal. Three blasts.'

FitzStephen paid no heed to the young man. Gilbert was just nineteen but was still the next most senior officer of the fifty-strong mixture of Irish and Norman troops. The knight had led them across the Forthairt hills above Waesfjord in the darkness of the night before, a journey which had taken many hours of effort to get to Selskar. Each man had held the cloak of the warrior ahead of him and had bound their spear tips so as the reflected light of the full moon did not betray their battle plan to the vigilant Ostmen in the city below. Just three hours before, as the first rays of the new day had broken through the gloom, the Norman force had dumped their gear at the back of the Selskar Rock. There they had tried to sleep and waited for the signal to attack the longfort. Hidden from the Ostmen, FitzStephen had stopped the men from lighting any fires and he alone seemed to be unaffected by the cold under the cloudless morning sky. Everyone else had shivered beneath cloaks, quilted gambeson, and leather armour.

Still staring at the vast walls of Waesfjord, FitzStephen felt nervous; he told himself that it was because he was bereft of his

263

armour and surcoat for almost the first time since he had landed in Ireland, but he knew that was not the reason. It was pressure for it was here in the north that his real attack would land. To aid the deception, Fionntán Ua Donnchaidh, as tall if not as broad as the Norman, had dressed in FitzStephen's armour and surcoat and had led the army to before the main wall of the longfort. The Irishman had been embarrassed at the gaudy robes and uncomfortable in the heavy armour and helmet but he had acquiesced. Instead of armour, FitzStephen wore a simple leather jerkin over his gambeson jacket. Dropping onto his belly he crawled forward to the lip of the hill where, chin resting on his flat palms, he continued to study the defences.

'Why are we waiting, Sir Robert?' Gilbert de Brienne asked. He had crawled after him and again began whispering to him from close to his heels. 'The plan was to attack on the three trumpet blasts.'

FitzStephen ignored his subaltern. 'When the time comes, we hit the Ostmen where it hurts them worst: their purses,' he said.

'Of course,' Gilbert replied.

The plan was a good one but still the knight's nerves would not go away. He knew the fear was born of his failure in Ceredigion but even this realisation could not shake his hesitation. With effort he put the memories to the back of his mind and continued to watch the walls for weakness. He believed that it was this attack which would be the most important. As such it was better to let the unimaginative Fleming, Prendergast, attract the brunt of the defenders to the south of the town and give his plan a better chance of success. Thus, FitzStephen had ignored the triple trumpet call from the front of the longfort which called him to war. Minutes later he was able to see some Ostman warriors on the northern wall turn away and begin running through the town streets towards the south where Prendergast's attack was taking place. FitzStephen could even see that some men from the long western wall, which faced the main portion of the Norman army, were climbing down from the allure and were joining the exodus of warriors moving towards the new southern threat. He grinned and rolled onto his back on the grass which covered Selskar. Gilbert de Brienne was again whispering advice.

'Shut up and listen,' FitzStephen said brusquely as he brushed the thick grass out of his eyes. 'There are only fifty Ostmen on the wall now. We go fast and we go low around the side of the rock beside the estuary. We do not stop until we are in the town. Understood?'

Gilbert nodded and FitzStephen rolled back onto his stomach to look at the fortress-town. Speed was everything now. He knew that his attackers would be spotted from the wall even though the burnt out ruins of the Irish marketplace would provide significant cover. The plan to capture Waesfjord appealed to FitzStephen, combating the straightforward defensive strength of the Ostmen with a wily attack strategy which would confuse the enemy and force them to spread their troops too thinly across their walls.

'Light the fires,' FitzStephen told Gilbert de Brienne. The Norman youth crawled low and scrambled down to where the rest of the men waited unseen behind the rock. FitzStephen gave him a two-minute head start before following down the side of the hill, loose earth tumbling down to mark his approach. The Normans nodded proudly as he walked amongst them while the Uí Ceinnselaig looked on critically at the warrior who, despite proving a success at Dun Cormaic, was still a stranger.

'They know the plan?' he asked of Brienne who nodded back. A fire was gathering ferocity at his side. FitzStephen pointed at the blaze. 'Take a brand, light it, and then run like you have never run before,' he told them in French. 'Don't stop until you get to the wall.'

His Normans grinned and nodded their assent as FitzStephen slung his sword over his shoulder. He then stooped to pick up his short axe and took a flaming brand from Gilbert de Brienne. 'You come last, keep them moving onwards. Do not stop for the wounded,' he said it loud enough for all to hear. 'Now, follow me.' He broke into a jog towards the brown lapping water of the shore, following the slope of the hill, filled with leafy weeds and sparse grassy clumps. Behind him the thud of feet trailed his own as he rounded the outcropping. On the shoreline FitzStephen picked up the road which led through the burnt Irishtown to St Ivar's Gate. He increased his pace and urged his men onwards, crouched over with his eyes on the corner of the wall. It was fully six hundred feet from Selskar to the walls of Waesfjord but he had already scouted the area through the smoking ruins just before the dawn, to clear any debris from his intended path.

FitzStephen doubted if the Ostmen would expect any force to come from the north without being seen well in advance. He chanced another look up at the walls but the rising sun was pouring over the longfort directly into his eyes, hiding everything from him. Shadows moved there but he could not identify what it meant. It was too late to stop the attack anyway and all that was left for him to do was to pick up the pace and trust that Prendergast's attack and Fionntán's display had shrunk the defenders on the wall ahead to a minimum.

Behind him the men ran between the drifting silhouettes from the wrecked buildings. Smouldering fires in the husk of Irishtown still sent small strips of smoke towards the sky and perhaps this was the reason that the Ostmen of Waesfjord did not see the fifty-strong force carrying fiery brands towards their walls. They were just two hundred feet from the walls and still no one challenged their progress. FitzStephen could not believe that his force had remained undiscovered this far and as he pumped his legs he waved some of the younger, faster men forward and pointed them towards their target. He had to capitalise on the Ostmen's inaction. The younger men, Diarmait's tribesmen mostly, sprinted ahead with a whoop as FitzStephen slowed to a fast trot.

'Go, go, go,' he said in French.

Finally, from above, the shout came from the Ostmen that their northern extreme was under attack. Arrows started falling amongst the attackers shot by archers on the walls with bows more used to hunting birds and small game than in war. Three men fell to those weapons as the ever-more-stretched group of warriors under FitzStephen burst from between the timber and stone skeleton of Irishtown and into the former marketplace before the walls of Waesfjord.

Gilbert de Brienne, who had been at the back of the group, now pulled up beside his commander and gave him a grin which FitzStephen ignored. Ahead of them the first of their troops vaulted the small bank filled with spiky weeds and landed on the mud and shingle beach. It was all happening so fast that the defenders, who had prepared themselves to meet another escalade against their walls, could only watch, heavy boulders and timbers above their heads, as the lightly armed men arced away from their position towards the harbour, where wall and water met. It was only when they splashed into the muddy shallows that they understood the Norman plan and the shouts of warning began.

The attackers' progress seemed to stop as they hit the shore of Lough Garman. More than one stumbled and went under the water, extinguishing their brands, but more of the attackers slowly waded out beyond the wall, up to their chests in the freezing water. FitzStephen was the last man into the bay. He had been correct about the tide, it was about to turn but right now it was low enough for his men to fight through weed and sludge and get into the longfort. A spear from the palisade above splashed into the water beside him, but FitzStephen was more concerned by the excrement which floated around than the weaponry; the Ostmen obviously emptied their soil into the flooded ditch at the foot of their walls which then slowly made its way into the lough. He tried not to think about it further and waded onwards. Ahead he could already see the ships in the harbour – ten unmanned longships tethered to the wide curving arc of massive wooden trunks driven deep into the bay floor.

'Leave the ships,' FitzStephen shouted in French. There were no guards and the young Irishmen, who did not understand his native tongue, could wreak havoc on the vessels while the Normans and Flemings formed up inside the town wall.

'Follow me. Shield wall,' he shouted, again in French, as he pushed between the wooden trunks. Mussel shells clung to the wood beneath the surface and sliced at FitzStephen's leg bindings, leaving small cuts up and down his limbs. An arrow thudded into the standing timber beside his head and remained there quivering. Another pumped into the stomach of a Norman warrior whose spear got struck as he pushed between the posts.

'Come on,' FitzStephen shouted, 'form wall.'

Just three Ostmen were on the beach, older men who were untangling fishing nets beside two short boats. Two of the men scrambled away as FitzStephen appeared but the oldest lifted a boat hook and charged at the man of Ceredigion. He splashed out of the shallow water to meet him, side-stepping at the last moment, letting the shaft of the weapon fall past him before smashing his short axe into the back of the old fisherman's head. Blood spilled up his arm as the Norman dislodged the weapon from the man's skull. To his right, more armoured Ostmen tumbled down the steep glacis to meet the threat of the man coming out of the depths of the lough like the ghost of Garman Garbh.

Gilbert de Brienne was the next man through the posts behind his leader. 'Beware right,' he shouted to those following. Soon there were ten, twelve, twenty men facing a handful of townspeople who rushed down the muddy bank towards them. They were bloodily despatched in just a few minutes of vicious hand-to-hand fighting. The Normans had their foothold in Waesfjord, but it was tenuous.

FitzStephen left Gilbert to organise the forces into a shield wall as he quickly surveyed the scene inside the town. There was a small stretch of open, muddy beach between the waterfront and the first houses which stretched away to the south. He ignored that direction and looked to his right where the wall stretched away from Lough Garman, curling inland and southwards. He could see the backs of the Ostmen still gathered around the barbican above St Ivar's Gate preparing for a frontal assault. Above him there were still Ostmen on the north wall looking down on the invaders and awaiting orders. FitzStephen smiled; indecision, as he knew well himself, was a dangerous adversary.

'Archers,' the Norman shouted as yet more men poured between the stakes, 'clear that wall.' He pointed up to the top of the embankment. 'And for St Maurice's sake, kill that bloody bowman,' he said calmly as another arrow streaked by him, burying itself in the mud to his left. Immediately six bowmen notched arrows on bowstrings and began shooting at the Ostmen on the wall, forcing them away from the sea and behind their circular shields. FitzStephen knew that he had to get control of the allure or they would be able to outflank the Normans and destroy them.

'You,' he said to two of the archers, 'climb that bank and make sure they don't get around us.' He had only allowed six archers to accompany him in his attack but they would be enough. The Norse bowman was already down, an arrow in his armpit as he reached for his arrow bag. More Ostmen were falling with the feathered shafts protruding from their chests while injured men crawled back along the allure towards shelter. Ten yards of the wall was already clear and the two archers who he had selected were already on their hands and knees climbing up the embankment towards the palisade where they could hold back the Ostmen from a safe distance.

Suddenly FitzStephen noticed thin pumping smoke drifting over his head and turned back towards the sea front. The Irish had done their job and four longboats were in flames on the water. Diarmait's Gaels came through the smoke, grins plastered across their sooty faces and wet from head to toe from their efforts. FitzStephen nodded at them as they ran by towards the rest of the men gathering at a small garden wall parallel to the water line, twenty yards up the muddy beach. He stared momentarily at the smoke which he knew would draw a frenzied Ostman counterattack onto his shield wall. Two Normans crashed through a longhouse door at the end of the garden wall, skewering a woman who attacked them with a skillet. A flurry of screaming children burst from the door at the other end and into the town beyond.

'Gilbert,' FitzStephen shouted back on the beach. 'Get these up on our flank,' he kicked the side of one of two short wooden boats, probably used by the Ostmen for fishing in the River Sláine. 'And set those houses on fire,' he indicated to the knot of houses across the small road from the garden. He wanted the Ostmen to come at his men through the garden and the fire would force them to do just that rather than have to circle around the blaze. If they did the boats could be used to impair their attack on FitzStephen's bridgehead within Waesfjord.

Torches flew through the air on Gilbert de Brienne's order and landed on the thatched roofs, made of barley straw attached to a layer of turves on a mesh of wattle. Soon they, like the longships in the harbour, were on fire, blocking the road and defending the Norman left flank. The wind was whipping off the bay now, driving the fire towards the rest of the town and beyond the cracking thatch FitzStephen could hear the inhabitants' terror at the sudden discovery of the fire and the Norman intrusion into their town. He fancied that he could almost hear the stomp of feet and the shout of angry voices as a large number of men ran towards the Norman position along gravel, timber, and stone streets covered in wattle mats. They came to save their beloved ships and their town.

'They are coming,' FitzStephen shouted, 'be ready.' He walked up towards the garden fence where Gilbert de Brienne had organised his men to oppose the expected attack. The fence would act as a barrier between the Normans and the Ostmen's attack, disrupting the enemy's shield wall and protecting the Normans. Or so FitzStephen hoped. Beyond the smoke, he could see the Ostmen were gathering, their colourfully painted shields locked below bearded faces crowned in steel. Swords, spears, and axes waved at the Normans while Norse insults hissed through teeth bared in anger.

'Gilbert, take five men and watch our flank.' He received a look of pure dismay as Gilbert de Brienne held his eye for several seconds before reluctantly calling five of his friends out of the line and stomping off to his new post. FitzStephen smiled, respecting the young man's desire to fight the Ostmen rather than guard the flank, but he needed a man he could trust if they came from further down the beach and Gilbert had performed well during the initial attack. He would not let him down.

A crunch and a cheer sounded from the other end of the garden. He watched the Ostmen push over the fence at the far end of the garden without a moment's hesitation. These men did not need any added encouragement to press the attack; their home had been successfully invaded, their fortress threatened with being overrun, and their families killed. The Ostmen came forward at a march, urging their brothers to great deeds in the face of the cursed Normans. He turned his back on Gilbert's small group and took his place in the centre of the defensive wall to face the hundred or so warriors who threatened his small force.

'Do your families proud,' one man shouted in the Norse midst. 'Kill them all in St Ivar's name.'

'Let them get entangled in the fence and then knock them back,' FitzStephen shouted, louder than any other voice on the battlefield. He watched the swirling colours on circular shields advance on the Norman-Irish position and he felt his heart race in anticipation of the fight ahead. This was the sight that had terrified Europe for three hundred years – the attack of the Ostmen. He breathed harshly through his nose, ignoring the acrid smoke. Then suddenly, without any prompting, he was calm.

The Norse shield wall was just thirty men wide because that was all the small garden could contain while the fire roared on the Ostmen's right. But three ranks more of warriors filled the space behind and followed the shield wall forward, which would add their weight to the impact with the very lightweight Norman line.

'They don't even have shields or armour,' one Ostman shouted gleefully as he crushed herbs and vegetables below his feet as the townsfolk advanced towards their enemy.

Above, the succinct twang of the Norman bows began from the palisade as the six archers were trying to take out as many warriors as possible before the impact with FitzStephen's small force. The shields caught many of the arrows but some shafts found gaps and at close range crashed through the mail shirts to mangle the flesh of the Ostmen. Then the archers began shooting desperately at the unprotected legs of the Waesfjord warriors and FitzStephen watched as more than one collapsed with an arrow piercing his knee. The archers then began shooting indiscriminately into the mass of men, not even bothering to aim, just concentrating on notching arrow after arrow and pulling the bowstring to its greatest extent. The distance was such that the devastating missiles even powered through the wood shields and into forearms, faces, and chests.

'Steady,' FitzStephen shouted, his breath short as he waited for the heavily armed enemy to strike his lightly armed raiders. The Ostmen sped up over the last few steps and their shield wall rammed into the fence. However, rather than coming up against another shield wall that would meet their charge in the crunch of the frontline, they stumbled, tripping over the flimsy fence with their comrades pushing on their backs. Two ranks of men went down on their faces or hands. Those who stayed on their feet fell forward and found themselves perilously out of the line and alone.

'Take them,' FitzStephen screamed and his men went forward with spears and swords stabbing at the stricken Ostmen. The mail shirts would not stop a strong stroke from a spear and FitzStephen's troops snarled with glee as they killed the first rank of the Ostmen. Brave men fell in the opening scuffle. As the first two ranks struggled to survive, the next rank tried to step forward and engage but the men before them hindered their axes and the only bite came from the Normans and Irish who brought death to the trading outpost.

FitzStephen's first strike of his short axe cleaved into a bearded warrior's spine, spilling blood and a yellow liquid onto the inside of the man's shield. He had abandoned his torch long before and had drawn a mace from his belt. He now used the weapon to deflect strikes while using the hand axe to grind up their bodies. He backhanded another Ostman who had struggled to his knees and cleaved off his jaw bone which was left grizzly hanging by bearded flesh and sinew.

He began keening: 'St Maurice!'

Up and down the line the Ostmen struggled to get over their dead comrades and use their weight and numbers to kill the Norman-Irish, but they were climbing over slick bodies and into a thick smoke which plumed off the burning ships in the harbour. Against all the odds, FitzStephen's raiders were winning, but then suddenly it all changed. Over the angry shouts and screams, burning timbers and clash of steel on steel,

272

he heard a new sound – a sharp intake of dread and panic, and it came from the left hand side of his battle line close to the burning buildings. FitzStephen, in the middle of the shield wall, was pulling his short axe from the face of an enemy teenager when he felt the men to his immediate left bump into him sharply. It took him a few seconds to appreciate what had happened but when he did he realised that he and his force were in very grave danger indeed.

FitzStephen swung on his heels and ran towards his left flank, which was under attack by twenty bearded and snarling Ostmen. Four of his men were already down and another five were fighting the enemy who came at them from three sides. He assessed his position and knew that his left flank were dead men.

'Retreat to the harbour,' he shouted, abandoning those men embroiled in the losing fight on the left. 'Retreat,' he added in Irish learned from Fionntán. There was no point trying to fight now. His flank would fail at any second but they could not disengage the fighting unless the rout was to take the whole of the incursion force.

Why had Gilbert de Brienne not warned him that the Ostmen had gone around the burning buildings, FitzStephen wondered angrily? He looked at the flank where he had posted the young man. One of the two boats he had assigned to the area for use as a crude wall was gone, as was his young lieutenant. FitzStephen searched through the smoke and caught a glimpse of six milites in the fishing boat pulling their way out towards a merchant vessel in the bay.

'Bloody pirates,' he spat in their direction. 'Let's get out of here,' he shouted to his remaining warriors inside Waesfjord. It was now a footrace between the Normans and the vengeful Ostmen. FitzStephen stuffed his mace into his belt and launched himself into the smoke.

Confusion was king inside Waesfjord. That much FitzStephen could tell as he watched another trebuchet shot soar above his head and smash into the torn walls. Warriors from above St Peter's Gate continued to flee from their positions to reinforce their compatriots facing attack on their longfort from the north and south. But little did the Ostmen realise that the attacks on the extremes of the city had already been forced to retreat.

'Get the men ready,' he said calmly to William the Welshman. FitzStephen had never led an attack on a fortress so big, but his plan was working. Coldness descended on him before battle when other men were overcome with fear or fury. It was difficult for him to describe but somehow stillness took him, allowing him to transcend the natural passions that took most men when faced with the danger of battle. Where others lost sight of the greater battle, FitzStephen found a cold, hard, and murderous intent flowed through his veins. It gave him the added advantage of a clear head to command his men.

Another of Meiler's projectiles crashed into the wooden barbican with horrific force, spilling shards of timber and tearing several heavy wooden stakes from their place before the gates. Just minutes later another stone struck the earthen bank, throwing a vast wave of dry soil out towards the Norman army. FitzStephen nodded again, believing that the defenders would be suitably confused so that his main assault could begin.

Now wrapped in his armour and splendid in his surcoat, he lifted his spear and looked eastwards where Richard de la Roche had moved his archers to the flank of the army on a rocky terrace. The Fleming responded with a wave in the air and began shouting at his troops. The archers, a hundred feet from the walls of Waesfjord, notched their first arrows and dug in their heels into the soft, wet mud. As one they drew back their bows and held the enormous weight with quivering arms. Richard de la Roche raised his sword arm and slashed it down in the direction of St Peter's Gate.

'Loose,' he shouted. Two hundred arrows soared like a swarm of stinging wasps against the clouds. Before they had even landed another two hundred were whistling their way towards the gates and the archers were notching a third arrow on their bowstrings. As they did this, the first arrows clattered against the wooden barricade. But many also found the gaps between the defences and caused carnage beneath the shields held high by the Ostmen. Arrows struck into crouched thighs and feet, shoulders and chests. They punched through the weak points in the circular shields and scored across the left arms which held them aloft. They ricocheted and rebounded off iron and steel, slashing across faces and hands.

Again Meiler's trebuchet smashed a heavy stone into the base of the barbican, shaking the whole structure and sending spouts of dust high into the air. Arrows kept falling and blood could even be seen seeping between the gaps in the wooden barbican and down the front of gates. The Ostmen inside had no way to stop the bombardment on their walls and those outside the target area continued to shout and scream defiance at the Norman army as their fellows on the barbican were dying in a rain of death from Richard de la Roche's bows. In the first few minutes nearly ten thousand arrows had landed on the small wooden structure which was bereft of cover thanks to Meiler's earlier sharpshooting. However, he had yet to bring down the main gate. Defended by many pointed wooden stakes dug into the mud, Meiler had been unable to get a direct hit. The problem was compounded by the earth and shale glacis, twice as tall as a man, sloping away from the gate on either side which served to defend the entrance from Meiler's position. He was obviously angry at his failure to bring down the gate and he shouted directions in ever more stretched tones at his men. Miniscule changes in his aim improved the next trebuchet shot but again it failed to break down the gate and allow FitzStephen to send forward his warriors. Presently, Meiler came trotting across to his commander who stood in the middle of the battle line parallel to the long walls of Waesfjord watching the aerial offensive.

'Uncle,' Meiler greeted his commander cordially. 'I can't bring down that gate from where we are now,' he said indicating back towards his men who continued to reload the weapon. 'We have done all the damage we can from there.'

FitzStephen nodded and looked around for a good place to move the trebuchet. A sudden crash of wood on wood, followed by the whip of rope, made both men turn. As if to mock Meiler, a piece of masonry from the weapon slung low on a direct course for the gate. It was an impossible shot but it buckled the gate upon impact, peeling the wooden doors back on its hinges in a splintering cacophony. The defiant shouts and songs of the Ostmen faded immediately. A wound more savage than that which had seen their ships fired had struck their town; they were speechless. Slowly, the Norman and Flemish warriors began to cheer the success. Meiler was the only one who did not cheer the achievement but puffed up his chest and stomped off to deride the Uí Ceinnselaig trebuchet operators for shooting without his command.

'I turn my back for one bloody minute …' he began as he approached the whooping Gaels.

FitzStephen smiled and hefted his spear. It was time for the Normans to seize Waesfjord. Scaling ladders had already been dispersed amongst the men as Richard de la Roche's kept up their arrow storm. But FitzStephen did not order the attack. Instead he turned to Diarmait Mac Murchada. The king had realised that even his vast experiences had not prepared him for planning an attack on the settlement. FitzStephen empathised with his feeling of helplessness but there was one honour that could still be Diarmait's.

'Would you like to the order the attack?' the Norman asked the King of Laighin.

Diarmait smiled and stepped out in front of the army, his arms in the air. His army cheered him and he encouraged them until they quieted down. He drew his short sword. Diarmait's facial expression changed suddenly from smiling to fury as he uttered a single word.

'Attack!'

His sword swept down as if he could cleave Waesfjord in two and his army, led by Sir Robert FitzStephen, swept forward.

Diarmait's army fought long and they fought hard and many men made their names for the bravery which they showed in the fight by the gates of Waesfjord. Some lived and some went to their deaths, but the army of Mac Murchada and FitzStephen was still repulsed. The Ostmen of Waesfjord had battled with a fanatical zeal to defend their homes, families, and livelihood from the invaders and eventually, despite the bravery of many men, FitzStephen was forced to concede that he could not break into the town.

'Not today anyway,' he whispered, gritting his teeth as he pulled back from the charnel house that was the remains of the gate. Blood flooded footprints in the mud as he stepped backwards from the bodies that crowded the gate. He noticed that the Fleming who had stood at his side as they assaulted the gate was dead; an abandoned spear impaled in his chest and still held him on his feet. A battle axe was buried in his brains.

'Slowly,' FitzStephen shouted to his retreating men, his voice carrying over even the jeers of the Ostmen on the wall. Beside him an Irishman screamed defiance at the longfort in his own language. Blood covered his face and bare torso.

'We'll be back tomorrow, you bastards!'

Surveying the damage FitzStephen could see only about ten Norman and Irish dead. If his army had suffered then the Ostmen must have lost ten times that number, he thought. He had killed three men outright in the muddy maul that had been the battle by the gates, but not even he could force his way into the longfort. He could not force victory. Pain issued from his back and he blanched as his mailed handed scored across a painful bruise forming close to his spine. He remembered sweeping his shield onto his back so that he could use both sword and mace after losing his spear. It had not been more than a second later that he had felt a bolt smash into the wooden planks, knocking him forwards into the mud. Sweeping his shield onto his left arm FitzStephen saw a bolt standing in the middle of his silver star.

'That was lucky,' William the Welshman said as he examined the protruding shaft.

'An inch deeper and it would have killed me.' FitzStephen shook his head as if trying not to consider that piece of fortune. 'It came from behind me.'

'Are you sure?' his brother asked, eyes wrinkled in concentration. 'Someone tried to kill you? Who have you been annoying now?'

'A good question,' FitzStephen said, pulling the bolt from

his shield. 'It must have been shot from distance,' he said, 'or I would be dead in the mud.' He pushed his forefinger into the hole in the shield. It disappeared up to the first joint. He cast his eyes over his army who were gathering back at the trebuchet throwing scorn, rather than projectiles, at the walls of Waesfjord.

'Surely not one of Miles's men,' he deemed.

'One of the Flemings?' William considered. 'They are still sore about you bringing them back from Cluainmín.'

'Keep your eyes open, and your mouth closed,' FitzStephen said, pointing the crossbow bolt at his brother's chest.

Richard de la Roche shook his head as he advanced towards the sons of Stephen. 'These Ostmen are stubborn. What more can we do?' he asked. The archers, like Meiler's men, had stopped loosing arrows. The sun was setting behind them over the Forthairt hills, shading the fortress and the defenders in shadows, providing cover from the sharp-eyed attackers.

FitzStephen greeted Richard gruffly. 'We can do it all again tomorrow. They cannot keep this up,' he answered. He turned to look back at the town walls which had resisted him, cracked a smile and slapped Roche on the back. 'Tomorrow,' he said. Turning to William he said, 'Get the tents unfurled and get some pickets out there. Make sure the trebuchet is defended in case they sortie out.' William nodded curtly and wandered off to carry out his brother's orders.

'Uh oh,' Roche said, 'here's trouble.' Beyond the Fleming, Diarmait Mac Murchada approached the two men with Hervey de Montmorency at his side.

'You survived then?' asked Hervey.

FitzStephen nodded, noticing that the Frenchman had a crossbow slung across his back. 'You didn't get involved, I see,' the captain replied. 'Perhaps you had some other job to keep you busy?' he asked as he innocently examined the crossbow bolt which had almost killed him. If Sir Hervey recognised what FitzStephen was insinuating, he did not react to it.

'What a day,' Diarmait said jovially, seemingly unaffected by the horror which lay within sight and unaware of the enmity between his two allies. The King stepped over a Norman who had been dragged back for treatment but had died before receiving any care. He handed FitzStephen a wooden mug filled with water. 'So what now, north to Fearna?' he asked. 'Toirdelbach Mac Diarmait of Cualann needs to be taught a lesson in loyalty. And he is not the only one.'

FitzStephen and Roche swapped disbelieving glances.

'You want us to abandon the siege?' asked the Norman commander.

'You have lost,' Sir Hervey stepped in front of King Diarmait. 'Waesfjord is as strong as ever.'

FitzStephen ignored Hervey. If he did not claim this prize he could not reward his troops and he would be forced to return to England where King Henry would surely hang him for his disobedience. His future was entirely dependent on capturing the longfort of Waesfjord.

'What else can we do?' Diarmait questioned the two foreign warriors. 'The Ostmen have resisted everything you have thrown against them. Have we not lost enough men on their walls?'

'No,' FitzStephen said stubbornly, 'we will attack again at first light. And I will beat them.'

The King's eyes flashed as the Norman again argued against his orders, but as usual the anger subsided quickly and he let his warlord defend his position. Hervey whispered in his ear and pointed a gnarly finger at FitzStephen's chest.

'Waesfjord is like a wounded boar with his back to a great oak,' FitzStephen interrupted Hervey's intrigues. 'One well-placed strike and they will be finished,' he explained. 'I have burnt their ships and there is nowhere for them to flee. We have breached their walls twice already. When Ireland hears that we have captured this impregnable fortress they will fear even our approach,' he said. 'Even Dubhlinn will surrender before our might.'

The name of Diarmait's most hated enemy stopped the King in his tracks and he shook his head as if to clear his mind of his quest for vengeance.

'We should leave, Lord King,' urged Hervey, sending a

toothy and triumphant grin towards FitzStephen. 'We should send a letter to my nephew, the earl, encouraging him to come to Ireland immediately. He will take this miniscule town himself.' Hervey had taken Diarmait by the shoulders and tried to gently steer him away from FitzStephen and Richard as if the frontiersmen were a danger to the King's wellbeing.

'We aren't going anywhere, Diarmait,' FitzStephen said bluntly. 'Waesfjord is ready to fall. All we need to do is extend our hands and take it. My men are staying here.'

Hervey laughed haughtily.

'I agree with you, Sir Robert,' said Diarmait finally, stopping Montmorency's cackle in an instant. 'We cannot leave them at our backs.'

FitzStephen grinned from ear to ear as Diarmait continued, holding up his hands. 'And I have not been totally honest with you, Sir Robert,' he said. 'I did not believe that you and your men could take the longfort and so, before I met you in Banabh, I made my own arrangements to make sure that the fortress falls.'

'An agent?' FitzStephen asked.

'An eminent friend,' the King of Laighin said. 'He will open their gates for us after we give him the signal – a Mass before their walls.'

'A Mass?' questioned FitzStephen. 'He has a taste for the theatrics. Who is this warrior?' He did not know how he felt about the King of Laighin keeping secrets from him. It made him feel uneasy.

Diarmait simply smiled. 'A friend,' he repeated. 'As to how he will open their gates,' he continued, 'well, that is the easy part.'

Inside Waesfjord was carnage. Wounded and dying men lay everywhere and screams pulverised the stockade. Blood puddled and flowed away from the red-splashed gates, soaking and staining everything in its path. The air inside the fortress was thick with steam, which mingled with smoke from the burning fleet in the harbour.

A dying Ostmen warrior, not yet out of his teens, reached

towards Bishop Oisin Ua Bruaideodha and begged for help, grabbing hold of the folds of his clerical robes. The man of the Osraighe could only blink at the boy, whose intestines were folded neatly on his lap, and pull his robe out of his grasp with a snap. He signalled to one of the priests from his entourage to attend to the young warrior and quickly made the shape of the cross in front of the boy who rewarded him with a grisly smile. Bishop Oisin scampered away, gathering his pace to catch up with his travelling companion.

'Bishop, please wait,' he shouted. Ahead the limping figure of Seosamh Ua hAodha, Bishop of Fearna, was easy to pick out as he ignored the shouts of the wounded and pressed on towards the centre of town. The two churchmen had watched the horrific events of the day from the safety of St Mary's Church. They had been making a routine ecclesiastical trip to Waesfjord, Bishop Oisin thought, and had never believed that they would be caught up in a war. The burning of the churches outside the walls had left him aghast as he watched from the safety of St Mary's. Buildings had collapsed, Irishmen had died, Ostmen had screamed pagan curses at Christian Normans, and an invader threatened to overcome the defences. It was all very trying.

'Wait, Bishop Seosamh, please,' he exclaimed again to the older man who stomped along the timber street ahead. Oisin had only inherited the bishopric from his uncle a few months before and he hoped that it would not always be this distasteful. He had believed the bishopric to be a position of comfort and riches rather than the horror that he was presented with in Waesfjord. He felt distinctly angry at Seosamh Ua hAodha as he caught up with him.

'Bishop,' he appealed, 'where are we going? Should we not go back to St Mary's, await the end of this fighting?'

'And what will we do there,' the older churchman asked, 'pray?'

Bishop Oisin was about to suggest exactly that but held his tongue. What he really wanted was a large mug of ale while sitting out the horrid barbarity.

'Ha!' Bishop Seosamh sounded disdainful to the extreme at

his fellow bishop's timidity. 'No, my Lord Bishop, we will do God's work this day and stop this wanton bloodshed.'

Oisin Ua Bruaideodha swallowed. His experiences of doing God's work had all led him towards one place – danger. And, even worse, it sometimes led to effort and exertion without profit. 'What can we do?' he asked. 'What we need is a ship to take us to Veðrarfjord or Dubhlinn,' Bishop Oisin said hopefully.

'There is work to be done in those towns for sure,' Bishop Seosamh said, 'but the need here is far more pressing, do you not think?'

Bishop Oisin certainly did not but he did not dare to nail his colours to the mast in the company of his rival. 'Yes, of course,' he said angrily. 'So where are we headed, to tend to the wounded?'

The Bishop of Fearna laughed deeply. 'If you want to do that I will not stop you, but I think our talents would be best used in other areas. In the meantime, we are here.' He nodded his head towards a longhouse – the biggest in Waesfjord. Seosamh did not even bother knocking as he hobbled through the small garden and up to the door of the building. Darkness was beginning to fall and flame light poured from between the spaces of the door frame.

'God save all here,' the older bishop said pleasantly as he entered the house. Eirik Mac Amlaibh got to his feet unsteadily. He had obviously been drinking and he was covered in blood from a wound on his left shoulder where an arrow shaft was still lodged.

'Bishops,' Eirik slurred a greeting, 'what do you want?'

'Simply the peace of Our Lord to return to these sorrowful shores,' Bishop Seosamh said with a sympathetic smile.

Eirik grimaced but behind him there was a grunt and a curse from Ingólfur Andersson, who lay in a bed by the wall covered in blood.

'Forget peace and give me a sword to get revenge on these Normans.' Blood sprayed from his mouth as he fought to speak.

Waesfjord's chief just shook his head. 'Why would they make peace? They have us on our knees!'

Ingólfur screamed and snarled both at the obvious pain of his wounds and Eirik's words. The Bishop of Fearna identified Ingólfur's defiance and the power which he held over Eirik. The older bishop called his fellow churchman forward.

'Tend to this poor man, Lord Bishop,' he pointed at the wild-eyed Ingólfur. 'He is a good Christian and has fought well and he deserves the loving peace of Holy Mother Church.' Just a moment's glance at the wound told Bishop Seosamh that Ingólfur had no chance of survival and Oisin could encumber the man while he conversed privately with Eirik.

'They are not men,' Eirik Mac Amlaibh continued, visibly shaking as Bishop Oisin passed by him, 'they are ghouls wrapped in steel. They attack everywhere at once. They come from the smoke and the depths.' He sank what remained in his cup, wiping his hairy chin as liquid spilled down it. He looked up into Bishop Seosamh's eyes. 'The Vestmen say this place is haunted but I did not believe it until today,' he said. 'The Normans have brought darkness to our town today. God help us.'

Bishop Seosamh shook his head. 'I fear it is worse than that, Eirik. It seems God is on the side of these Normans,' he put a hand on Eirik's shoulder examining his wound.

Eirik dropped silent, dismayed by the bishop's words. 'But why would God abandon us?'

'You burned the churches outside the walls,' Bishop Seosamh continued with an understanding frown. 'What did you think was going to happen? That God would be pleased with the desecration of his houses?'

The Norse leader swayed even more and fell to his knees, keening and grabbing at the cleric's clothes. 'It was not me, bishop, but Ingólfur. He said the Norman archers would use the watch towers against us.' He began crying. 'Forgive me, Lord, forgive me.' He wept like a beaten child.

'Forgiveness is mine to give,' the bishop said, making Eirik squirm, 'but if God is on the side of the Normans then there is no resistance that can keep them out of this fortress.'

'Are you saying we should surrender?' he looked up at the churchman with hopeful eyes.

Bishop Seosamh placed a hand on Eirik's head. 'Tomorrow is Sunday. We will pray together for absolution and for guidance. We will see whose prayers God will hear.' He looked over Eirik's head to where a much-flustered Bishop Oisin closed Ingólfur's eyes with a soft hand over his face. 'Is that brave warrior dead?' the older man asked. He received a curt nod and Seosamh Ua hAodha smiled secretly. He knew that Waesfjord's defiance had died with him.

The Normans were in rapture as they entreated God's power to give them the strength to take the heathen town whose inhabitants had burned His churches. Some of the warriors seemed to sway as they felt His spirit descend upon them.

Bishop Oisin pleaded with Eirik. 'Do you see how they appeal for God's help?' he said as he pointed over the stockade at the Normans who were holding a morning Mass in front of St Peter's Gate. 'They appeal for help to bring the Lord Jesus' wrath on those who burned His houses,' the bishop continued into Eirik's ear, 'and against God's vengeance there is no defence. With His help these Normans will surely swarm across our defences and slaughter everyone in Waesfjord.' The bishop was a timid man and wanted little other than to climb into a ship and sail away from the town which he thought was doomed to fall. It had taken little for Bishop Seosamh's words to work him into a desperate frenzy of fear.

Below Bishop Oisin, the Norman army was arrayed in all its splendour. They snarled and shouted God's praise, spat God's wrath, and spewed a maelstrom of religious fury on the walls of Waesfjord. They invoked His power and promised to use it for His benefit.

Eirik felt weak from his wounded shoulder and his stomach churned, whether through the amount which he had drunk the night before or from the fear he now felt, he could not tell. Probably both, he thought self-mockingly. The Ostman leader knew the decision to surrender had to come from him but he still hoped that his town could hold out against the invaders. Would Veðrarfjord or Dubhlinn come to help them? Diarmait was their enemy too, he thought, but his heart told him their rival trading towns would rather see Waesfjord in flames than taking valuable trade from their shores. Bastards, he thought. What he would do for Ingólfur's confidant council now?

He fiddled with a frayed piece of bark which had come loose from the wooden stake of the wall, whilst behind him a number of warriors shuffled their feet nervously, waiting for orders. All fight had gone out of the Ostmen. Each one bore a wound from the day before and few had slept through the night. They had all expected another attack in the darkness and so many had seen out a cold night on the palisade, body jerking into action at the smallest noise from beyond the wall. Many, like Eirik, had drunk heavily until deep into the night and then, intoxicated, they had passed out asleep. In their dreams they had relived moments from the battle the day before. Now they stood on the palisade waiting to soak up yet another attack with little hope of success. Outside the walls of Waesfjord, the Normans' Mass reached a crescendo as a priest appealed skywards for victory over the pagan inhabitants of the longfort.

The Ostmen could equal any enemy when they thought God was at their side but now most truly believed that they were abandoned to the despair of hell. The story of Eirik's tearful supplication the night before had reached many ears and set tongues wagging, mostly through the careful endeavours of Bishop Seosamh Ua hAodha. The townspeople had been scared before the Norman attack, having heard the exaggerated stories of the foreigners' victory at Dun Cormaic and the superhuman powers that the warriors of the small army seemed to possess. Now, following the three attacks on the walls, the people of Waesfjord were downright terrified, believing that the Normans had priests capable of sorcery that meant that their warriors could fly over the walls. How else could they have burned their beautiful and precious ships in the harbour? The townsfolk expected death at any time from the bows, trebuchets, and spears and the whimpering of the wounded, women, and children from the town reached even to the Ostmen warriors' ears, mingling with their own fears and exacerbating their terror.

'We are traders, not warriors,' a Waesfjord bigwig called

Harkan whispered to Eirik, 'so get out there and barter with the Normans. Make a deal or buy them off.' Eirik belched and nodded but did nothing else.

Across the wasteland in front of the fortress the entire Norman army were on their knees pleading to the heavens for the strength and fortitude to take Waesfjord by storm. The priest handed out the sacraments to the ranks of men in their battle lines. The ominous and effervescent murmur from the army before their walls was intimidating, the slight morning drizzle and silent ranks of Ostmen stifling. Steam rose from the whispering mouths of the Norman ranks on the cold morning air accompanied by the hum of massed voices.

'St Ivar save us,' a warrior called Eystein repeated again and again behind Eirik, who wiped his brow despite the morning chill. Bishop Seosamh remained silent, letting the fears of the Ostmen and the trepidation of the Bishop of the Osraighe further damage Eirik's faltering courage. The Irishman could sense the mood of the people and revelled in it. This is why he had been sent to Waesfjord by King Diarmait: to instil fear.

The Normans stood up and dusted off their tunics, signalling the end of their entreaty towards the heavens. The walls of Waesfjord seemed to breathe in as the defenders anticipated a renewal of the attack. Shouts sounded up and down the Norman line as their leaders marshalled their army to scale the entrenched wall.

Beside Bishop Seosamh, Eirik began issuing panicked orders to the Waesfjord captains beside him on the palisade.

'You ... you there, take half your men and enforce the southern wall beside St Doologue's Church,' he told one man.

Óttar Mac Óttar, the commander of that part of the wall, looked on aghast. 'You want to lose men from the main wall? We have not enough to defend it as it is.'

'They attacked the north and the south yesterday. What is to stop them doing it again?' Eirik shouted suddenly and angrily. He stopped himself, eyes blurry with thought as they darted from side to side. 'Wait, they are cleverer than that,' he licked his lips, turning on his heels and surveying the town from the height of the wall anxiously. 'Our ships are gone, they could attack the beach. Do they have ships?' he asked another of his captains who looked from face to face for an answer. Eirik ignored him. 'Take another fifty men to guard the beaches,' he ordered another man called Morten.

Óttar and several others looked on disbelievingly as their leader seemed to lose all sense of the reality of their predicament. 'Do not divide our force,' Óttar appealed again but his voice was lost as a din emanated from the Norman lines. They were shouting and yelling, beating their shields and stamping their mailed feet. Colourfully clothed knights were the only men on horseback and they charged up and down the line encouraging their men and working them into frenzy with encouragement, calls for great deeds and battle-tales of their forefathers. The Ostmen on the walls were silenced, awed by the Norman onslaught of noise.

'Holy St Ivar save us all,' Eystein began repeating again for everybody on the barbican to hear.

Eirik stood shaking his head. He turned on Óttar beside him. 'Why haven't you moved your men?' he shouted, stumbling over his words. His eyes locked with those of Bishop Seosamh Ua hAodha and he desperately searched them for answers. He found none as the Irishman bowed his head, seemingly to the inevitable. Eirik stuttered something towards the bishop which Seosamh could not hear beneath the clamour coming from the Normans.

'What?' the churchman shouted, leaning towards Waesfjord's commander. Eirik grabbed Bishop Seosamh by the shoulder of his woollen shift and dragged him close, wild-eyed.

'God has abandoned us! Save us, Lord Bishop. Save us, we repent!' Eirik was frantic now and he fell to his knees, begging Seosamh to make his plea to God on his, and his town's behalf. 'God is protecting the Normans,' he shouted, loud enough for many to hear. All eyes fell on the army threatening their town. Sure enough there were no injured or dead men outside the walls wearing Norman clothes. If anything, there were more men facing the walls than there had been the day before. The intensity continued to build.

'Do you want me to go out and talk to Diarmait?' Bishop

Seosamh asked Eirik. The Norse leader looked like he did not know what to do but nodded his head violently. 'Send out a herald,' the churchman screamed. 'Quickly, before they attack.'

Bishop Seosamh Ua hAodha could not hide his smile. He had served his king and pride swelled his chest. He had also served God by bringing peace to the confrontation between the two armies. It had been a good day. He had fulfilled his task and he would be rewarded.

'Bishop,' Diarmait Mac Murchada greeted Bishop Seosamh with a massive smile, 'how good it is to see you, my friend.' He planted an enormous hug across the old man's shoulders before doing the same to a shocked and nervous-looking Bishop Oisin. The younger man had heard the stories of this great enemy of the Osraighe as he grew up and involuntarily cringed as Diarmait grabbed him. Domhnall Caomhánach and Robert FitzStephen stepped forward to greet the two envoys from Waesfjord and Diarmait introduced them. They stood in front of the walls of the town where every man could see the encounter.

'So the Ostmen are pissing themselves or what?' Diarmait asked with a laugh. 'Well done, Robert, well done indeed.' He threw an arm over FitzStephen's shoulders and presented him to the two bishops with pride. 'This is the man who planned our assault, how did you find it?' he asked in Irish.

'Terrifying,' Bishop Oisin said honestly in the same language. He giggled momentarily before revisiting the horror inside the walls in his memory.

FitzStephen grimaced as it was translated. 'It would have been better to have captured the town rather than have them come out and surrender. Next time it will be different.'

Diarmait cackled. 'You are too hard on yourself, my boy. It was well done. Well done.' He turned towards his two visitors who he directed towards a large tent erected behind the Norman lines.

'So what are their demands?' Diarmait asked seriously of Bishop Seosamh when the group of men went through the curtain doors of the tent. Fionntán Ua Donnchaidh and Hervey de Montmorency were already there sitting at opposite ends, the old Frenchman with his back to the Irish warrior who FitzStephen had tasked with watching his rival. Robert nodded a greeting to Fionntán and sat down beside him. He pointedly ignored the French nobleman who, he was sure, had tried to murder him during the fight for Waesfjord.

'They want peace, that is all,' Bishop Seosamh accepted a chair and a trencher of stew from a pot steaming in the centre of the room. 'And their chief man will accept any terms to obtain it.'

Fionntán translated the conversation for FitzStephen. The Norman interrupted the dialogue just as Mac Murchada was about to speak. 'Tell them to open the gates, throw down their arms, and swear fealty to King Diarmait. If they refuse we attack,' he said and shrugged suggesting that it would not cost him a second thought to burn the fortress-town to the murky ground upon which it stood.

Bishop Seosamh was stopped for a second as he listened to the translation but the churchman was unmoved. 'I agree with Sir Robert's demands. Dead and dying lie in the streets and their headman whimpers like a child. He will agree to whatever I tell him,' he continued eating his food.

'My only demand is that they submit fully to my sovereignty and rule. If they refuse we will slaughter their men, take their cattle, and sell their wives and children as slaves,' Diarmait calmly spoke to the bishop. 'So eat your fill, my friend, and then get back to the town. I will expect their representatives' submission by midday.'

The bishop nodded and began talking quietly to Bishop Oisin who seemed amazed at the ease of the negotiations to save Waesfjord. He had thought that there would be more raised voices, more arguments, more bartering. He was not so stupid as to believe that he was not being manipulated. But what could he do? There was no profit in rocking the boat. Not for the first time he wished that he had his warriors to hand.

King Diarmait joined FitzStephen and Fionntán at the other end of the wooden table. It had been removed from St Michael's Church the night before, much to the derision of the priests. 'So the day is ours,' the Irishman said with a smile as he sat, 'and now it is time for a little revenge.' He meant his business with Dubhlinn.

'Not yet,' FitzStephen said holding Mac Murchada's stare. 'First we must consolidate our gains, heal our wounds,' he said, 'and reward our men.'

Hervey de Montmorency sidled over towards the three men but addressed only the King, 'Lord, as the deputy of Earl Richard, I will accept vassalage and fealty for Waesfjord in his name. This will be in part payment for his future support in returning your crown,' Hervey dropped to one knee in front of Diarmait expecting him to place his hand on his head and grant his claim.

FitzStephen jumped to his feet and shouted at the Frenchman. 'You greedy old bastard,' he said. 'Waesfjord is mine.' His hand dropped to his waist but he had no weapon at his side.

Like a scrawny old cat, Hervey was on his feet in a second, a long dagger in his right hand ready to kill. 'The King knows that my nephew's support is worth a hundred times that of your little band of ruffians! This great act of generosity will convince Earl Richard to come to Ireland. If Waesfjord is not given to me, Strongbow will not come.'

FitzStephen was furious at Montmorency's insistence and nervous that Diarmait might give in to the nobleman's demand for the town. He chanced a glance at the Irishman who seemed to be considering the request. Hervey saw Diarmait's hesitancy too and he dropped the dagger's guard just an inch with a dirty-toothed grin.

FitzStephen laughed. 'How would that starving rat of a man hold Waesfjord?' he asked Diarmait. 'He doesn't even have any troops. He cannot even afford armour. I know of no man who would follow his ragged banner.'

Hervey gasped that he would hire Irish troops to garrison the fortress. Diarmait barely even contemplated Hervey's reasoning. He looked down at the Frenchman.

'Waesfjord was the price for Robert's help, Sir Hervey, and I mean to be true to him,' he held up his hands as the old man began to argue. 'But do not worry. You too will receive extensive lands in Earl Richard's name.' Hervey's noble upbringing forced him to bow to the King's grace while FitzStephen just stared balefully at the Frenchman who had tried to appropriate his prize. He would never trust this deceitful man. And the feeling of hatred was obviously mutual.

'You will have two full cantreds of land, Sir Hervey,' Mac Murchada continued. 'We travelled through the country of the Uí Bairrche on our way to Waesfjord while Siol Bhroin is across the bay from Banabh towards Veðrarfjord. Those lands are yours as my gift.' He said it with a smile.

Sir Hervey, a poor man with a great name, wiped his hands through his greasy grey and fading long hair. Two hundred thousand acres was an unbelievable amount of land and Hervey was tempted.

'Lord King, Earl Richard will be appeased by your generous gift of this land,' he said finally and with a final scathing look at FitzStephen, left the tent.

'Robert FitzStephen,' Diarmait announced. 'You and your brothers will take Waesfjord and rule it in my name as long as you have the strength to hold it. All the country to the south and west is yours also, Siol Maoluir and Forthairt to Carn tSóir Point. Will you accept this charge from the King of Laighin?'

'I will, King Diarmait,' FitzStephen said as he went on his knee and bowed his head.

Diarmait laughed and turned back to his food. 'Good.'

That was it. With a few words Diarmait had fulfilled his pledge and Sir Robert FitzStephen – the failure, the prisoner, the bastard son of a lowborn Norman spearman and his royal Welsh lover – was now the ruler of one of the three most important commercial citadels in Ireland. He ruled his own realm! He had achieved the greatness of which many men dreamed and few ever succeeded in capturing. But there was work to be done to hold his new demense. And there was still a king to put on his throne.

# Chapter Ten

The sails of Maurice FitzGerald's ships were spotted off the coast just two weeks after Waesfjord had opened its gates to Diarmait Mac Murchada and Robert FitzStephen. Two Norman vessels were cheered as they made their way up the last mile of the bay guarded by the sandy headland. But this was nothing to the joy felt by the two half-brothers as they greeted each other amongst the mud and reeds on the beach of the town. A throng of Norman and Flemish warriors swarmed around august old Maurice as he embraced his younger brother, Robert, Lord of Waesfjord.

All around were stumbling accounts of the battle for the Ostman town, exaggerated events and boasts about every great deed. Best of all were the stories of the bravery of Philip de Barri during attack upon the southern palisade, and the stupidity of Gilbert de Brienne. He and his five friends had successfully stormed an English ship in the bay when they should have been defending FitzStephen's flank, but, having tied up all the crew, they had been unable to control the vessel and had been blown far out to sea. The humiliated Normans had been forced to release the English crew and then row the whole way back to land where they had been severely reprimanded by Walter de Ridlesford.

Robert FitzStephen's name was on every Norman's tongue and the newcomers heard varying accounts of his prowess in the fight for Waesfjord. The legend of the man who had defied the King of England and had taken the Viking city was growing.

'He must have killed ten Ostmen in the fight below the barbican,' Philip de Barri told Maurice's sons. 'I wetted my blade too, of course, but Robert ...' He faded off and shook his head in awe of his cousin.

It was already getting late by the time FitzStephen and Meiler finally left the fire-scarred harbour to join Maurice and the other leaders at a feast to celebrate the coming of the reinforcements. The two men made their way through the slave market towards the stockade behind which the Normans had made their camp. At the rear of the rudimentary wall the new lords of the longfort had thrown up their tents with their backs to the massive escarpment. Their untrusting eyes were firmly fixed on the Ostmen town and the angry townsfolk whom they had conquered FitzStephen let his small bodyguard go and get some food while he and his nephew made their way towards the noisiest tent where Diarmait hosted Maurice and his milites. Most of the chief men from the army were there and most were already getting bawdy as the alcohol began to flow.

Miles Menevensis was the worst off as he, completely out of character, drunkenly made fun of the four Ostmen hostages who sat in the corner trying not to draw attention to their presence. The men were part of Diarmait's conditions for Waesfjord's surrender, but FitzStephen doubted that the possibility of the four men's deaths would keep the Ostmen honest to his rule. He, for one, did not leave the stockade without a bodyguard to defend him against a sudden attack by a fuming relative of a dead Norse soldier. He had seen the impotent rage in the eyes of the townsfolk and their desire for vengeance, and knew that at some point it would manifest itself in violence against the Normans.

'So where are you going to put the castle?' Maurice asked his brother after they had swapped news from both sides of the sea. FitzStephen was most pleased to hear that King Henry was suffering on several fronts, primarily from his growing brood of gloomy sons, his jealous wife, a demanding mistress, an interfering King of France, as well as a pious and plotting Archbishop of Canterbury.

'We have been scouting the area in every direction for a good place for a stronghold,' FitzStephen replied Maurice's question. 'There is a rocky outcropping two miles north-west above the ferry crossing. If we hold that, we hold Waesfjord.

From there we can wring their necks should we feel the need. We'll keep a garrison within the walls too.' He began tucking into a mutton stew, flavoured with honey.

'More milites will come from England when they hear of Waesfjord's fall,' Maurice said quietly. 'We will need to put them all under oath. Then, when the castle is finished, and Diarmait is back in control of Laighin, we will use them to fortify Dun Cormaic and take control of the crossing there. A couple more castles will make sure the Irish and Norse get along, and then we take Cluainmín.'

'That would put us within reach of Veðrarfjord?'

'*You fight a battle, then you build a castle,*' Maurice repeated FitzStephen's father's mantra. '*Then you ride for a day and fight another battle.* Stephen wasn't wrong, Robert, and as long as we have Normans to occupy the castles we will keep going west.'

FitzStephen shook his head in disbelief. He had not realised the depth and farsightedness that Maurice had put into the expedition. While he had allowed himself to think no farther than the walls of Waesfjord, for Maurice it was only the beginning. He could see an empire where control of all the Ostman cities of the south coast would be secured by Norman castles, loyal only to the Geraldines. From these fortifications, the Normans could sally out on horseback for thirty miles in every direction, secure in the knowledge that they would have a safe place to return at night. Brilliant white donjons atop earthen mounds would be scattered across the south ready to raise hell in FitzStephen and Maurice's names. Swords and spears would cross in war.

Swordland; that was what the Danes had called land ready for conquest and for Maurice, FitzStephen realised, the whole of Ireland was there for the taking. He had grown up believing his half-brother to be quiet and modest, but he now saw the ambition of Maurice FitzGerald. He wanted a kingdom to rival that of King Henry himself. Waesfjord was just the beginning and the west was the future.

FitzStephen breathed out slowly as he considered the magnitude of his brother's plans. His heart pounded within his chest at the sheer daring and scope of Maurice's aspirations for their future in Ireland. His own dreams were so small in comparison. 'But first,' he replied, 'we fulfil our promise to Diarmait.' It was not the King's face which came to FitzStephen's mind but that of his daughter, Aoife.

Maurice grunted an agreement and turned back to his plate. Up and down the table, all the men were eating various mixed dishes of beef, pork, fish, cheese, fruit, nuts, and vegetables. The Ostmen had intermarried with Gaelic women for generations and as such their cooking had become influenced by that of Ireland. However, they also held some secrets from Scandinavia and FitzStephen feasted on a delicious mix of mussels, cod, ling, hake, whiting, plaice, and herring all stewed in French wine. He left the dark meat, which he was sure was made from seal, to the side. The women had put on a good spread but despite that the men from the varying cultures of England, Normandy, Wales, Flanders, and Ireland complained that the feast did not match their own personal tastes. All boasted that their people made the greatest cooks, and thereafter that every other facet of life was better in their homeland. No one complained about the Gascon wine brought from Wales by Maurice until it ran out and the party had to change to drinking a heavy Irish brew. But the chat was festive and when one of Maurice's pages picked up a lyre and strummed a jovial tune everyone joined in. Later a drunken warrior from Diarmait's household joined the youngster and, despite the language gap, stationed himself at the page's shoulder and began singing in his hoarse Irish tongue to the Norman tune. FitzStephen could not understand the words but knew that it was a raunchy piece as it kept on being interrupted by roars of laughter from the Uí Ceinnselaig in the room who joined in at certain moments with a cheer. Soon others were sent to join in with songs of their own people; a Fleming was left disappointed as he was booed into silence just a few seconds into his sad song of his flooded homeland, while a second rendition was demanded of a Norman drinking song about a knight whose only conquests took place in noblewomen's bedchamber.

FitzStephen was bone-weary and quiet but thoroughly

contented amongst the unrefined group of men who were enclosed in the tent. He laughed as a tall, lithe Irishman and a short, stocky Norman jumped to their feet and started smashing each other in the faces with their fists. God alone knew how they had managed to start the fight, as neither spoke the other's language, but soon enough they were back on their backsides swearing brotherhood in French and Irish, blood pouring from their swollen noses and blackened eyes.

The absence of Hervey de Montmorency was comforting for almost everyone in the camp. The Frenchman had returned to Wales to inform Strongbow of the success of the first adventure, or more likely, go back to his master's side to whisper that FitzStephen meant to supplant him in Diarmait's favour. Most of the men had become nervous of Sir Hervey's connections and his nobility, and were aware that he and Robert FitzStephen hated each other. Of FitzStephen's belief that Hervey had attempted to murder him, they knew nothing.

If Hervey's leaving was a pleasure, that which took Maurice de Prendergast away from Waesfjord was a necessity. The Fleming believed that FitzStephen had deceived him during the attack on the walls of Waesfjord and felt that his men had been put at great risk because of his tactics. Richard de la Roche had managed to calm down the Flemish warlord but the relationship had quickly soured again over the payment of Prendergast's men. The mercenary had wanted bounty and money to pay his army, many of whom desired nothing more than to return to Wales to their wives and families now that they had captured the major sea port. FitzStephen had no money to give them and he had resisted Maurice's demands to pillage the town and the surrounding cantreds. It had almost come to blows until FitzStephen had bribed two of Prendergast's lieutenants with large estates in the extreme south-west of his new-won dominion, lands around the cursed Carn tSóir Point. They in turn had convinced Prendergast to accept over ten thousand acres in the same region. The Fleming had been angry at that, desiring payment in money rather than lands, but had accepted due to the pressures of his bannermen. But in the aftermath of their argument, bad feeling had led to several scuffles between the Normans and the Flemings. One of FitzStephen's archers had ended up dead while the offender was hidden and protected by his kinsmen. The Welsh and Normans, usually the worst of enemies, had begun plotting to get vengeance on the descendants of Flanders and in the end FitzStephen had only prevented further bloodshed by ordering Maurice de Prendergast and his Flemings to visit their new lands in Forthairt.

A gust of wind heralded the entrance of Eirik Mac Amlaibh, followed by an angry looking Walter de Ridlesford, through the flaps of the tent.

'Lord Eirik,' FitzStephen nodded his head to the Norse leader. He had kept him in his position to give the Norman seizure of power more credibility in the eyes of the townsfolk. When FitzStephen had suggested moving his army into the camp built on the embers of the harbour, Eirik had sought and obtained the permission of the town council and had even gone so far as to organise the townsfolk to chop the timber and build the simple palisade. When he wasn't on official business, Eirik remained in his longhouse under guard by Ridlesford – a duty the Norman did not enjoy. Despite their leaders' collaboration, there had still been problems following the Norman takeover. Meiler and Miles had almost incited a full-scale rebellion when they had tried to empty the grave of a recently deceased hauld. FitzStephen's nephews had heard rumours that the graves of the Ostmen concealed huge riches owned in life and sent with the dead to the afterlife in the old style. The young men had been interrupted during their night-time excavation by an armed band of the dead man's relatives, and chased back to their fort by the harbour. FitzStephen had quickly quelled the disturbance by leading a troop of Normans to the dead man's late residence where, buoyed by the sight of twenty armed Norman warriors, he had talked the hauld's family into accepting a paltry sum of silver as recompense for the disorder.

Diarmait Mac Murchada sidled over, pointedly ignoring Eirik, and pulled a stool between the two Norman brothers. 'So have we consolidated our gains? Healed our wounds?' he asked, recalling his conversation with FitzStephen a few weeks before as they had watched the walls of Waesfjord.

'I think we are ready to move,' he replied and leant back in his chair. 'We will stay here for one more week and start to build our castle – the walls of Waesfjord are too long for so few men to hold – and then we will take back Laighin for its rightful king.'

Diarmait slapped the Norman hard on the shoulder with a roar of laughter. 'And we can deal out a little revenge at the same time?'

'Of course,' FitzStephen replied with a hint of hesitation.

Mac Murchada ignored his tentativeness and laughed loudly, crashing his mug of beer into FitzStephen's cup of wine.

'Then drink up, my boy, for it is time to celebrate.'

As he sank what was left in his cup, FitzStephen prayed that the King of Laighin did not see his uncertainty. He had taken his reward and now it was time to win a kingdom for his lord.

The young man struggled out of the cold River Bearú. His crossing over the stony ford had taken much longer than it should have and several times he had disappeared below the stiff current before he had struggled to his feet again. The water only reached to his knees but he looked like he might never make it to the far bank. If he had a tongue he might have cried out for help. If he had eyes he certainly would have wept. And he might have ruled a nation before he had been castrated. But without those body parts he had no hope and he howled dumbly as he tried to feel a path out of the river and onto the bank with his hands.

Blood streamed down the youngster's face and soaked through his trousers before being lost in the river which marked the boundary between the lands of the Osraighe and the Uí Ceinnselaig. The man had been Eanna, heir of Diarmait Mac Murchada and hostage of the Osraighe, but now he was nothing, less than a beggar; less than a slave. His life was over as much as if it had been snuffed out by his tormentors. But his corpse remained as a living warning from the Osraighe to their enemy.

'Get a frigging move on, you stupid bastard.' Donnchadh

Mac Giolla Phádraig laughed loudly from the far shore. 'Make sure you get home to Fearna and tell Diarmait who spoiled your good looks, boy.' His jeers were joined in by five of his derbfine, who threw stones and sticks at the blinded figure as he fumbled pitifully amongst the reeds. The dagger which had been used to perpetrate the mutilation was still bloody in Donnchadh's grasp. The King of the Osraighe snorted another laugh at the pitiful youth before wiping the blade clean on the grass beside Eanna's eyeballs and testicles. Eanna groaned a shout of pain as a stone crashed into the side of his head. He curled into a ball where his muffled cries could still be heard by the men in the shallows.

'He will frigging bleed or freeze to death if he stays where his is,' Donnchadh complained to his half-brother Cian. 'Not much of a frigging message if he dies and gets washed down river to frigging Banabh.' Donnchadh, head crowned with a savage pair of stag's antlers, spat a long stream of spit which cartwheeled in Eanna's direction before splattering into the River Bearú.

'Fearna is that way, stupid,' Cian shouted at the Meic Murchada tánaiste, and waved in the direction of the mountains which rose to the east. Two of his men splashed into the river at Cian's command and pulled the young man to his feet, dragging him up towards the small monastery which stood half a mile up river. The monks had seen the gruesome scene on the far bank, but they had done nothing except hide behind their stone walls. Cian's men quickly hauled a terrified Eanna up the bank and dumped him at the monastery gates, not bothering to wait and see if they came out to claim him or not; they were in enemy territory and death would fetch them if they lingered there too long.

Eanna Mac Murchada groaned and slobbered as the two Osraighe warriors scarpered back to the ford. He swung his fists in the direction of their footsteps, but it only caused him to fall to the wet grass. Already the wounds to his eyes were beginning to scab over, but he remained in a great deal of pain. Beneath it all was the realisation that all his dreams of leading his people after his father's death were gone. No warrior would accept a king who had been disabled by even one of his injuries, never mind three. His life was over. Despite the pain, Eanna thought back to his youth when Amlaibh Ua Cinnéide had joined his father's household. Blinded by his Ua Briain rivals, the King of Oirmumhain had been expelled by his own people. Only Diarmait had shown him compassion and had fed and clothed him in his distress. Would anyone care for Eanna now that he had been mutilated? That word spun around his spinning head. He was in so much pain that he did not even feel the hands of the Augustinian monks slip under his armpits and drag him into the monastery compound.

'Amlaibh,' he cried, but it came out inaudibly, causing a monk to soothe him with calming words.

'Take him to the hospital,' a stern voice broke into Eanna's dark and pain-fuelled world. 'Wait,' the man said abruptly and with fear in his voice. 'My Lord Jesus, it is King Diarmait's son. The Meic Giolla Phádraig have maimed Diarmait's tánaiste!'

Eanna, aware of the conversation around him for the first time, gurgled blood around his mouth as he tried to speak. It stung like vinegar and he tried to spit but ended up choking. He was ruined and the blood loss was beginning to make him feel cold, but he managed to finally shout a command at the monk's which he knew would be understand, and he knew would be followed.

'Fearna,' he tried to shout before he passed out.


Thuds of wooden shovels on wet earth, the scrape of metal tools on timber, and the grunt physical effort filled the air around the place called *Carraig*. Hundreds of men worked and hewed and heaved lumber and stone, and steam from their backs wrapped itself around the high rocky mound where the castle was beginning to take shape. Almost five hundred Gaels and Ostmen from the surrounding countryside had been rounded up by the Normans and had been put to work digging ditches, carrying earth, and shaping wood. Everywhere there was activity and noise. Golden wooden chips littered the muddy ground and the distinctive smell of carved timber and sap wafted around the high outcropping.

The bailey was already finished, thanks to Maurice FitzGerald's preparations in Wales. Pre-cut, shaped, and numbered, FitzStephen's brother had brought over much of the timber needed for the outer wall. Following its completion, twenty archers and the conrois of cavalry had taken up residence inside the crude fortress while the donjon took shape atop the rock. His other warriors still maintained their uneasy hold over Waesfjord which stood a mile and a half to the south-west along the course of the River Sláine.

'Get your arses moving,' FitzStephen shouted at three Ostmen who had stopped to chat halfway up the high rocky hill. The three idlers looked at him and signalled that they did not understand, flapping hands around their ears. FitzStephen grinned as he approached before slamming a fist into the closest man's stomach and repeating his command. They jumped at the sudden violence and began hauling their burden of two massive tree trunks towards the peak. FitzStephen watched the trio move slowly uphill. If there were more reluctant people than the Ostmen of Waesfjord, FitzStephen could not think of them. They seemed not to realise that they were a conquered people. The castle would go somewhat to shifting that misconception, he considered.

It was the perfect position for a motte, FitzStephen thought as he looked upwards. The rocky knoll rose impressively for forty feet, dominating the landscape as far as the eye could see. It stood above the wide river which curled around its base, guarding three sides from attack. From its top the Normans would control the river as well as the best ferry crossing from the north. They could strangle the Ostmen or allow them to live.

FitzStephen was already beginning to sweat from the walk up the face of the motte and could not imagine having to force home an attack up the stiff slope into a cloud of Norman arrows. He waited until the three timewasters had got to the top before turning to look at his new structure taking shape beneath. The axe-wielding Ostmen had done well clearing the trees from the face of the hill and all over the land below small stumps poked out of the soil. Directly below him, Miles Menevensis directed ten Ostmen as they split short thick logs to make a set of steps. Another larger group placed the logs on the hillside. Eventually FitzStephen would send a flying bridge to the bailey but the split-log path would do just as well for now.

As he watched the men another trunk was prepared to be divided. Miles had already found the grain of the wood and forced a flat-headed peg into a gap close to one end. A bearded Ostman bashed the end of the peg with a mallet, ripping the wood along the grain and allowing the Norman to force another peg into the split further towards the closed end. Within a few minutes another trunk would be ready to add to the defences. Beyond the tents of the Norman soldiers, the palisade ran in an oblong for almost a hundred feet and was surrounded on its entire course by a deep ditch which was already filling with water redirected from the Sláine. Swans, ducks, and herons had replaced the black-headed gulls, redshanks, and oystercatchers found on the mud flats around Waesfjord and if anything the river provided a more wholesome air than that back in the longfort. Soon the tents would be swapped for wooden kitchens, houses, and stables for houses and cattle – everything a castle needed to survive.

The Irish and Norse had never seen anything like the fortifications. The nearest thing they had encountered was the walled towns of Waesfjord and Veðrarfjord but they, like the English burghs, were built to protect rather than subdue the population. The castle, carved out of raw earth and hard wood, was profoundly alien, and the natives laughed that a southerly breeze would tear down the small and flimsy construction. But FitzStephen knew that the castle was strong.

As he surveyed the landscape, he noticed a horseman racing towards the newly built fortress from the south, and he had to shield his eyes to get a clear view of the rider. The horseman was still a mile away, but he was travelling at top speed, jabbing his heels into the flanks of his small cob. FitzStephen's trained eye immediately saw that it was an Irishman who rode towards the castle because of his unconventional seat bereft of proper saddle or stirrup. He quickly scanned the skyline for any sight of an approaching army behind the rider but could not see any sign. It did not mean one was not hidden beyond the trees and panic rose in his chest as he began running down the steep hill towards the bailey. He jarred his right knee as he landed on the top step but it held in its place and FitzStephen proceeded slower down the newly carved timber stair. Had Waesfjord rebelled, he wondered? He tried not to imagine the worst but he could think of no other reason that an Irish horseman would exhaust his horse on such an arduous ride.

FitzStephen landed on the bailey beside a confused Miles, but did not hang around to explain himself. Ahead of him he saw Diarmait Mac Murchada burst out of his tent and begin running towards the gates to discover the reason for the appearance of the Irish horseman. He had a good head start on FitzStephen and the King got to the open gate just as the rider pulled his sweaty beast to a stop and leapt down nimbly. He put his head down and ran, reaching the group of men just as Diarmait Mac Murchada, unseen amongst the mulleted warriors, began keening loudly. It was a sound of sorrow that FitzStephen had heard many times during his life as a raider in Wales and England. It was anger infused with grief and its force scared the tired and sweaty horse into a panic so that it reared up amongst the group of Gaels. Even before he muscled his way through the crowd knew that there would no escape from Diarmait's need for vengeance. Someone he loved had been killed or worse.

FitzStephen shoved his way through the group gathering around their distraught king, but stopped short as the rider pulled a leather cap from his head. A head of wavy dark red hair tinted with gold burst from beneath and fell below the shoulders of the rider who FitzStephen had taken for a young man. It was the same figure who had haunted his memory since he had met her in Wales – Aoife, Diarmait's daughter. Her arms were bare and brown from spending time outside while her body was supple and slender. A familiar sense of desire exploded in his stomach as he looked at the princess. Even dressed in a long cloak and rough woollen trousers, he saw her beauty, her wildness, so different to the noblewomen of England. Aoife's eyes flicked angrily to FitzStephen as he approached her father as he raged.

The Irish warriors moved out of the tall Norman's path and that deference did not escape the eyes of the observant girl. She saw how her father's warriors respected the foreigner and she slowly studied the Norman warrior from his feet to his face. FitzStephen was immediately torn between his desire to greet Aoife and his desperation to know what had happened to cause Diarmait's anguish. His curiosity won out in the end and he turned away from the red-headed princess towards her distraught father.

'Diarmait?' he asked.

The King of Laighin turned on the Norman with madness imprinted on his face. For a second FitzStephen thought his ally would attack him. But then Aoife was at his side and she drew the grey-haired man into an embrace, whispering soothing words into his ear. Diarmait nodded and sobbed, dropping his head to his chest.

'Eanna!' he howled as he was led away.

'We march straight into the Osraighe's territory, we find Donnchadh Mac Giolla Phádraig, and we cut off his head, his children's heads, his wives' heads, and the head of every man who fights for him.' Diarmait wailed and swept aside a table's contents in his fury. 'Don't you dare countermand this order, Norman,' Diarmait warned FitzStephen, 'or I will strike off your troublesome head and send your body back to Rhys.' He broke down into Irish curse words, kicking a chicken carcass across the tent and into the linen wall where the derb-fine stood like silent sentinels of stone.

Aoife had left to change from her sweaty riding clothes and Diarmait snarled his way around the tent, ordering his captains to prepare for war before again turning on FitzStephen, and daring him to contest his command. His sorrow at the attack on Eanna had been defeated. Now there was nothing but anger. Just the day before, Mac Murchada had been trying to convince the Norman to hurry his attack on the mighty walls of Dubhlinn. Everything had changed since then.

'We will slaughter every living soul of the Osraighe,' he

screeched.

'I agree,' FitzStephen calmly told the King, who baulked at his taoiseach's accord. 'We need several days to finish the castle. Then we will go and I will kill your enemies.'

'You surprise me, Robert,' Diarmait said through narrowing and suspicious eyes. 'Why do you always make me feel like you are not telling me everything?'

'Probably because I am not telling you everything,' the Norman replied with a small smile. 'You have been saddened and I didn't want to trouble you with my thoughts on top of your own grief.'

'My grief will be sated with the blood of the Osraighe.'

FitzStephen nodded briefly. 'Yet to put you back in power we have to do two things: defeat the Osraighe to protect the Uí Ceinnselaig,' he held up a single finger, 'and beat the army of Ruaidhrí Ua Conchobair to win back Laighin.' He held up a second digit. 'Attack, as always, is the best form of defence,' he said dropping his fingers into a fist. 'So we go north.'

'North then,' Diarmait repeated gloomily, and turned his back on the Norman warlord.

Dismissed, FitzStephen turned to leave. He knew that Diarmait's mind was on his vengeance so it was best not to tell the King that he first meant to force the surrender of the tribes on the Uí Ceinnselaig's northern border before the Osraighe could be targeted. Fearna would never be safe if the other lords of Laighin were against Diarmait. But he could break the news to Mac Murchada when they neared their target. He felt a huge surge of sympathy for the Irishman. In similar circumstances his reaction would have been the same: guilt, anger, confusion, and sorrow. Turning in the doorway he opened his mouth to speak but could not find the words for his grieving master. A man did not want another warrior to see him at his weakest, FitzStephen thought, and he threw the flap of the tent open and squinted as he made his way into the sunlight. His overriding feeling was of relief that Waesfjord was still his and had not been overrun. FitzStephen yawned widely and made for his tent. His twisted knee was hurting him and he struggled through the bailey on the soft re-laid soil and stone taken from the newly dug ditch. As he pushed through into his tent, FitzStephen pulled off his surcoat and shirt in one swift move.

'Hello, Sir Robert,' Princess Aoife said from the corner of the room.

'My Lady Aoife,' FitzStephen swept into a bow despite his shock. He had been well trained as a child by the Countess of Gloucester and his manners kicked in automatically before he even realised he had performed the small courtesy.

Diarmait's daughter laughed sweetly, either at his bow or at FitzStephen's obvious surprise at her presence in his tent.

'You should not be here alone,' he said, suddenly very aware that he was not wearing his shirt.

'Why?' Aoife demanded. Her sudden anger at the question confused the Norman, but as soon as it appeared her irritation disappeared into a smile. 'Why … when I just want to talk to you?'

FitzStephen wondered why he had said something stupid like that to Aoife. He had dreamed to be within this small tent with this woman, and never once had he asked her if she should be elsewhere. She had found one of FitzStephen's long white shirts which she'd bound at her middle with a coil of rope and it reached to her knees. Her legs and feet were bare. Somehow she made the ridiculous-looking clothes striking. He regarded her as the most beautiful woman he had ever seen – alive and untouchable like none he had seen before.

'Thank you for your shirt, Sir Robert,' she said.

The Norman realised that he was staring and he turned away so that he could throw the tent door open to its widest. It was better not to annoy Diarmait by being caught alone with his daughter. Not after the news the Gael had got just that day.

'Are you happy to be back home?' he asked, recalling their conversation in Llandovery.

'Yes and no,' she said, screwed up her nose. 'My herds and slaves are mine again, but I miss the hustle and bustle of Bristol. It was a smelly place, but with so many lovely knights.'

FitzStephen was again taken aback. He had never heard a woman give her opinion so freely and confidently as if she was talking to her equal. Norman women belonged to their father until they were married and then they became the property of their husband. Even a widow was the property of her son. As such they were schooled to be shy and sedate, and expected to be pale, slim, and ready to bear children. But this girl was something new and he was enraptured. He was also intrigued and said, 'Lovely knights?'

'Not smelly like our men,' she laughed. 'They danced and fought each other and asked me for my favour at tournaments. They had exquisite clothes of many colours.'

'Knights are two a penny in England and all dress too gaudily,' FitzStephen said, jealous of those warriors who had caught her fancy and wishing he had his star-spangled surcoat on. He hastily threw his plain shirt over his head, dirty from work, and quickly changed his tack. 'It must have been dangerous for you to come all the way from Fearna to tell your father about Eanna.'

She screwed up her eyes again and seemed to check his statement for sarcasm. Finding none she again became all-sweetness to FitzStephen. 'Perhaps it was dangerous, not for a brave knight who climbed the mighty walls of Waesfjord ...'

He did not correct her small mistake.

'... but for a simple woman ...' she tailed off with a sly grin. She laughed again and pushed closely past him. Her hips had rubbed against FitzStephen's as she left and a final whip of loose red hair struck his face. 'Would you show me your horses, Sir Robert?' she asked as she turned and stretched her back, revealing more of her bare legs to the Norman.

'Of course,' he stumbled, and indicated towards the temporary structure in the corner of the bailey where a mottle of horses roamed in small separated stables.

'They are geldings?' she asked as they made the short walk.

'Some are,' FitzStephen confirmed, 'but most are still whole. It makes them better for fighting,' he said.

'Which is yours?'

He pointed out three of the beasts, two coursers and a palfrey. 'And this is Sleipnir,' he slapped his favourite horse on the shoulder and invited Aoife to do the same.

'He is clever,' Aoife said.

'Unlike most stallions,' he added with a smile. 'He is fast too.' For many minutes neither spoke, but simply enjoyed the attentions of Sleipnir.

'You Normans are strange,' she said suddenly. 'Why are you in Ireland?' she asked without taking her eyes or hand from the stallion.

FitzStephen might have lied, told her grandly that he was in Ireland to fulfil his oath to put her father on his throne, or that he was there for money and land. But he did not. 'I am here for glory,' he said.

'Glory?' she asked.

He shrugged his shoulders. 'I am bastard born to a Welsh princess and a simple spearman,' he said. 'Back home they call me a murderer and a thief. In England and Wales I am nothing, but here in Ireland ...' He shook his head.

'You could be a king,' Aoife finished his sentence with a smile, the end of her tongue appearing for just an instant to lick her front teeth.

'I was going to say a success.'

'And I tell you again,' she told him, 'a king.' She held his gaze and it was all FitzStephen could do not to take her in his arms and embrace her. She was not beautiful, not in the conventional sense, but she was striking; she piqued his interest and played on his mind rather than merely arousing his desires. Not that she was undesirable, he thought, but her intelligent eyes impressed just as much as her svelte body, her words and demeanour as much as her exquisiteness.

'Poor Eanna,' Aoife continued without taking her eyes off FitzStephen, 'he won't be able to rule after Father now that he has been ... hurt. And my other brother Conchobair is being held by the High King. What will happen to my Uí Ceinnselaig after my father is gone?' She smiled innocently with a shake of her head. 'They will need somebody brave to hold my tribe together.'

'I thought your father had promised Laighin to Strongbow?' FitzStephen said suddenly. 'And you too.' He hated that he said it, did not know why, and expected anger in return.

Aoife just laughed sweetly. 'Perhaps I will become queen,

like Meahbh of Connacht? Rule the Uí Ceinnselaig and all the men of Ireland by myself.'

'You wouldn't want a man to fight your battles?' he asked. 'To keep you warm at night?' Embarrassment burned his ears as he heard the words issue from his mouth.

Aoife swirled her red hair as she laughed.

'I can fight as well as any man.'

She held his gaze for a brief second with a grin dancing at either side of her lips.

'I'll wager you can,' he replied.

'But even a queen needs someone to take care of her horses.' She smiled and said goodbye to Sleipnir with a rub to his flank. 'Goodbye, Sir Robert FitzStephen. Do not forget me when you obtain your glory.' With a final swirl of red hair she walked away from the Norman knight.

Aoife was the most alluring woman he had ever met, he thought, but a dangerous one. He felt that he knew the truth about her, that she wanted to use him to win a kingdom. But he also realised that it would not stop him jumping gladly into her clutches whenever the moment presented itself. He was utterly beguiled with a woman whom he had spoken to only twice.

Across the bailey, Miles Menevensis watched the encounter between the princess and the Norman warlord.

'There is a man who is falling in love,' he said seriously to Amalric Scurlock and nodded in FitzStephen's direction.

'Poor, stupid bastard,' laughed Scurlock.

## Chapter Eleven

### *August 1169*

All Laighin suffered; Cualann burned, the Uí Muiredaig lands lay spiked below a field arrows while the Uí Conchobair Failge were pummelled beneath the hooves of the Norman war horses. All submitted to the power of Diarmait Mac Murchada and the lances of Robert FitzStephen. The rebellious Uí Faoláin, the haughty Uí Tuathail, proud old Mathgamain Ua Dimmussaig, and every minor tuath in between, all yielded. Even the powerful Uí Mael Sechlainn of Mide bowed to the alliance, gave hostages, and promised to send tribute in recognition of the growing power of Diarmait Mac Murchada and his Norman mercenaries. All that stood between Diarmait and the undisputed rule of Laighin was the Osraighe and their king who had tortured and maimed his son. By the time Diarmait's army came back down from the flatlands of the north, they were laden with cattle, jewellery, and numerous other pieces of precious plunder that would enrich Fearna and the Norman mercenaries' coffers. Yet many were haunted by what they had seen in the petty-kingdoms of northern Laighin.

'I swear on St Nicholas' white beard,' blunt-nosed warrior Ranulph FitzRalph chattered to FitzStephen as they rode south, 'a mist-wreathed army of wraiths attacked me and old Hugh de Caunteton as we camped in a rath we took from the Uí Drona. These are strange lands, Sir Robert,' he said gravely. Behind him, other men corroborated FitzRalph's strange story of a shadow army near a monastery called Ceatharlach. Worst was Miles Menevensis, who refused to speak of what had occurred when he had led a mixed force of Normans and Irish into the mountains against the savage Uí Morda clan of Laoighis. He had lost few men during the campaign and the chieftain had

311

submitted, but Miles refused to elaborate on the story, implying horrors untold in the forested northern reaches of Diarmait's kingdom.

Behind the Norman army a vast swathe of land lay in ruin. Cries still rose towards the heavens, questioning God's plan and cursing his failure to protect his poor children. For the King who would rather have been feared than loved, it had been a successful campaign. But Diarmait was not content. The Osraighe and Donnchadh Mac Giolla Phádraig still existed and his was a revenge that would not be sated until the one of them was destroyed. It was the type of hatred that could rip an army apart; a deep loathing that valued no opinion which threatened his retribution. FitzStephen had been only too happy to use the anger to his benefit, to secure the north so that they would be free to attack the Osraighe. But Diarmait's Irish troops had become impatient to get their vengeance on the Osraighe for their violation of the King's son. To that end they were moving westwards through the mountains towards a pass that would take them straight into the heart of Osraighe territory.

'This is tough going,' Fionntán Ua Donnchaidh told FitzStephen as the cold, windy, wet weather swept over the army in the boggy lands in the mountains.

FitzStephen snorted a laugh as the rainwater spat off the end of his nose. 'Just a bit of drizzle,' he said. They were headed towards the pass of Gabhrán. This ran between the peaks of Slieve Margy and the Freagh Hill in the extreme north-east of the petty kingdom. Beyond the gap were the lands called Mag Mail where Fionntán's clan were settled. It was a six-mile opening between the two peaks, but the forest had deliberately been allowed to flourish to provide a natural boundary between the enemy kingdoms of the Osraighe and that of the Uí Ceinnselaig.

'It is a land without bog,' Fionntán told FitzStephen of his homeland. 'Fire burns without smoke in the kingdom of the Osraighe ...' As the taciturn Irishman uncharacteristically babbled about the loveliness of his homeland, FitzStephen nodded along barely listening. '... of course, the name means the People of the Deer,' Fionntán said causing FitzStephen's ears to prick up. He had missed the hunt during his time in Ireland and much desired the amusement of the pursuit to take his mind off more serious matters.

'It is an appropriate name,' he told the Irishman, 'for I intent to bring down the mighty stag of the Osraighe using one solid thrust into the heart of their territory.'

'My people will have spies and pickets watching all the passes,' the Irishman told him.

'Then we must push through the gap before word filters down that we are approaching,' FitzStephen replied. He had enough problems without being stopped in the mountains by a force of the Osraighe. The loudest grumbles came from the most reluctant of his allies – the thousand-strong company of Ostmen from Waesfjord. Diarmait, as their sovereign king, had insisted that they should send a thousand warriors to support his assault on the Osraighe and, with Eirik's support, the townsfolk had grudgingly agreed. With them came a number of women and other camp followers who had attached themselves to the army and who further slowed their passage through the mountains. There would always be bad feeling between the Ostmen and Diarmait's army; too many friends, comrades, and relatives had been lost on both sides in the fight for the fortress-town. However, the Ostmen knew what it meant to be an enemy of the Normans and most would do almost anything to avoid fighting them again. Not until they became stronger or the Normans were weakened by defeat. In any case most whispered that the four hundred Normans were too few and that as soon as winter came they would sail away to England with their plunder, leaving Waesfjord to recover her independence again. But not one was willing to lift their hand against them while Maurice FitzGerald lay in wait at the new castle at Carraig.

The quiet moans of the unenthusiastic Ostmen was one thing but the bad feeling which came from the Flemings bordered on perilous. Maurice de Prendergast had returned to Waesfjord still bearing a grudge against FitzStephen and had insisted that his two hundred and forty-strong contingent would march together rather than intermingle with the Normans, Irish, Norse, and Welsh in the same battle formation employed on the march to

Waesfjord from Banabh. They, perhaps more than anyone else, were on constant vigilance, fearing attack by the Osraighe at every hillock and thicket of tangled tree. The stress on the Flemings' faces was immense.

'Bloody moaners,' Walter de Ridlesford, now in command of the Ostmen, said. 'I value the Flemings as much as I value spit.' He coughed disgustingly and spat on the ground in the direction of Prendergast's men who were marching past FitzStephen's column towards Miles' vanguard. 'The Flemings give me *phlegm*, I will tell you that for nothing,' FitzStephen joked back to his cousin. 'No offence meant, Richard,' he said quickly to Roche who waved his remark away. FitzStephen might have been angry or fearful at the mood of his army but the dark spirit which had taken their dazed king was of just as a serious nature. Over the last few weeks a void had formed between Diarmait and every man outside his immediate family. The army had left Waesfjord and spent a week at Fearna before moving towards the land of the Uí Drona through the great tangled forest of Dubh-Tir; the Dark Country of mountains, bog, and tangled trees on the Osraighe's eastern border. In that time FitzStephen had begun to notice Diarmait distance himself from his allies. He could only guess that it was the King's reunion with the disfigured Eanna that had done the damage. As the young man had bumbled around his father's home, struggling to adapt to his new disabilities, Mac Murchada had become quiet and reserved. FitzStephen had expected a gush of fiery vitriol at his son's sad plight but no outburst had come, only a quiet daze as Diarmait had watched his former tánaiste lurch around the stone house unable to call for help or keep his food down. Richard de la Roche and Miles Menevensis reckoned that the Irishman was simply consumed by desire for revenge and guilt, and that this left little room for him to think about anything else. FitzStephen was concerned that Diarmait had perhaps caught him staring at Aoife during their all-too-brief meetings in the Uí Ceinnselaig's capital but he could not share those private concerns with his compatriots. Too often his mind imagined Aoife's lithe figure. He remembered their flirtatious talk in his tent at Carraig, prayed that she felt the same as he, and dreamed that they would somehow end up as lovers. FitzStephen had even thought about writing a song in her honour, as a nobleman in the English court might have done, and he had cursed himself for his softness.

In spite of the problems within the six-nation army, he and the Norman troops were in good spirits. They sniggered at the grumbles of the other men, teasing them that they moaned like women. Even in the rain and cold they laughed, each trying to outdo the other with bombastic mirth. In the filthy bogs they pushed on ahead and taunted the stragglers, throwing mud at them and saying that even the worst of days in the mountains reminded them of the most pleasant day on the Welsh frontier. They were hard men and they were bad men, but they were also robust soldiers and FitzStephen would not have changed the Norman heart of his army for any troops in the world. In truth, their experiences in Wales had prepared them perfectly for war in Ireland and they revelled in the downcast misery of the other warriors. FitzStephen knew that his horsemen and archers would be largely ineffective in this tough mountain terrain, where open ground was sparse and the jumble of vegetation gave ample cover from the deadly accuracy of his bowmen. It was a landscape for light infantry like that which the Osraighe could field. If they were attacked up here in the cold wastes they could not afford to become separated, of that he was certain. The army had to stay together until they got into the flat lowlands beyond the Meic Giolla Phádraig capital at Gabhrán; then they could unfurl their banners and stretch their horses' legs. Until then they had to be on their guard and scout every knoll from where a surprise attack could be launched. They had to keep their spirits up and they had to carry on into enemy territory. In the lowlands there would be nowhere for the Osraighe to hide and the enemy would have to stand and fight.

Blood sullied the stream that searched its way through the Pass of Gabhrán, out of the mountains and into the land of the Osraighe beyond, but the Norman warhorses did not mind. They drank their fill and nibbled at grass as they nervously watched the strange scene which took place on the opposite river bank. Two hundred men of the Osraighe on their knees stared up into the haggard face of Diarmait Mac Murchada. Behind each of them was a man of the Uí Ceinnselaig and at their throats was a blade.

Diarmait looked at the men through tired eyes and with slumped shoulders. 'You have committed treason against your king,' he said quietly, almost to himself. 'You have sinned against God and defied his anointed. There can be only one sentence for that great crime.'

FitzStephen, Fionntán, and Miles sat a little way off under a tree where the Osraighe had made their last stand. The trio were surrounded by arrows which sprouted from bodies and turf alike. The battle had been short and severe, but for their Gaelic allies, the violence was not yet over.

It had been two days since the warriors of the Osraighe had begun their attacks on Diarmait and FitzStephen's column as they passed through the mountains. Across high woodland, wet fen, and festering bog, FitzStephen's army had fought against an enemy who attacked at every opportunity, be it day or night. They came through the rain and the cold, through the trees and the low cloud. They came as a screaming mass of men who slashed and stabbed and melted back into the hills, daring small groups to pursue them. Like the flies which ate at their horses' skin, the Osraighe nibbled at Diarmait's army, ambushing, waylaying, and infuriating them to the point of collapse, and many had died in ill-advised attempts to catch the attackers as they fled. Every mile had taken half a day to complete and it had seemed that the landscape and the natives were working in tandem to defeat them. But it was only when the invaders had reached the valley mouth – their route into the territory of the Osraighe – that they understood that their predicament was only just beginning. Five thousand of the enemy's best warriors, protected behind a double wall of twisted hazel and oak branches and filled with mud and stones, blocked the path and dared the invaders to attack.

They had dared and they had won.

'Is it usual for the Irish to defend their lands like the Meic Giolla Phádraig did?' FitzStephen asked of Fionntán. 'Find a valley and build a wall across it?'

Fionntán's eyes were locked on the two hundred men across the river. 'Yes, mostly we defend a river crossing, attack from a forest, or defend a tight valley – use the terrain to our advantage. It didn't work this time.' Fionntán grimaced suddenly and his eyes tightened as he focused on one man amongst the enemy masses. 'I knew his father,' he exclaimed and signalled towards a young man at one end of the line of doomed warriors. 'His name is Tadhg and his father took my woman from me many years ago. Maybe she was his mother …'

'The one that made you leave your people?' FitzStephen asked of the Irishman.

Fionntán nodded. 'He took my cattle and slaves, and killed two of my people. I only escaped with my life because I had a coracle close by and was able to paddle into the deep water of the river. A week later I became a crewman with a trader out of Veðrarfjord.' He paused as he searched the area close to where Tadhg knelt. 'I don't see the father …' he said before Diarmait raised his voice, interrupting Fionntán who stood watching his enemy's son.

'Can you tell us what Diarmait is saying?' Miles asked of the Irishman.

Fionntán acquiesced and began translating for the benefit of the two foreigners: 'God would have me forgive you,' he began, clearing his voice, 'but I cannot forgive and your families and farms will burn.' Diarmait's voice gathered impetus. 'Your children will be slaves.'

The King of Laighin stopped suddenly as his gaze drifted over the same section of kneeling men that Fionntán had noticed. Diarmait suddenly laughed hysterically and barked a victorious acclamation towards the sky: 'God has been merciful to his good servant Diarmait,' he shouted as he stomped towards a figure with his hands bound and head down. The King slammed his fist into the boy's face and kicked him hard in the stomach. 'Isn't that right – Mac Giolla Phádraig?' he accused the man who lay on the ground, blood at his mouth and terrified. It was Tadhg, the King of the Osraighe's cousin, and the man who Fionntán had identified. Diarmait screamed and attacked, grabbing a dagger from the nearest of his soldier's belt and dragging it across Tadhg's neck. Blood was everywhere but the King kept sawing until the man's head fell back across his shoulders. And he did not stop there, hacking at the spine with the knife and his fingers, tearing away the last shreds of flesh until the head came away from the torso.

Maurice de Prendergast joined FitzStephen, Miles, and Fionntán who observed the frenzy from afar. 'God Almighty and his holy saints, he is mad,' the Fleming said and crossed his chest.

'They maimed his son,' Miles replied, quieting only when he saw that FitzStephen was equally shocked at the rage with which the King had struck. But Diarmait was not to be sated by just killing his enemy, and he attacked the head with his teeth like an animal. He tore at Tadhg's lips, ears and nose. He ripped his eyelids, he shredded his cheeks. All eyes were on the King who stopped his attack and breathed heavily, casting the lifeless head aside as if he did not care. It rolled slowly and unevenly towards the riverside but Diarmait stood blankly staring at the sky, blood masking the lower half of his face. Slowly he raised his hand and dropped it to his side. Up and down the riverbank more blood was spilled as two hundred men were beheaded. It happened slowly in ones and twos as the young men steadied themselves for the murderous act.

'We must stop this,' Prendergast said to his companions.

Fionntán bowed his head and said nothing while Miles looked to FitzStephen for a decision.

'I don't like it any more than you do, Maurice,' their captain replied. 'But if a few hundred die here, then the next time we approach the Irish will surrender,' the captain said, 'or they will fight and they will know fear. You know how this works,' he told Prendergast.

The Fleming was disgusted. He had seen bloodshed during his life on the Welsh march but this was different, even to the seasoned campaigner who had eventually smashed the Osraighe's resistance in the mountains with his cavalry charge.

'Look at them,' he pointed at the few men of the Osraighe

who still lived. 'There is no fear in them, only anger.'

Miles Menevensis shrugged away Prendergast's reservations. 'The dead cannot harm the living,' he said with hint of a smile.

'Don't you see that it will not matter how many times you defeat them, no matter how many you slaughter,' Prendergast replied, 'the Irish will fight on regardless, murder you in your bed, or attack you in these wet hills and woods. They will never forgive and we will never have peace on this island.' He waved a hand towards the growing pile of heads. Each executioner had dropped a head at Diarmait's feet after the deed was performed. The horror seemed so much worse in the idyllic setting, with the mid-afternoon sunny haze following the rain. Diarmait still stared at the sky, blood-drenched beard dripping down his saffron robes.

FitzStephen bit his lip. 'The Irish are no different to what we faced in Wales,' he told Prendergast. 'Except here we are great lords in our own right. We will rule this land, not bow our heads to an unjust and jealous king.'

Prendergast shook his head. 'You put the good standing of your purse over that of your soul,' he told FitzStephen and without another word he stomped away, turning his back on his Norman allies.

The Fleming already had an argument with FitzStephen following the siege of Waesfjord; he had been promised plunder and payment, but instead he had been forced to accept a scraggy piece of land which no-one else wanted. But more than that, the Fleming could not condone being a part of Diarmait's revenge over the Osraighe, Dubhlinn, and all the others who had contributed to his downfall. His soul could not take it and, more importantly, Prendergast could see no honour or reward in it for his men. God would surely damn the Normans for their support of such a man, and life would not reward them. He would not be a part of it. That he promised.

# Chapter Twelve

## *Tuaim dá Ghuabainn, Connacht*
## *September 1169*

Ruaidhrí Ua Conchobair considered the news brought to him by a haggard Donnchadh Mac Giolla Phádraig. According to the King of the Osraighe, Diarmait Mac Murchada was back and had been declared King of Laighin again. Ruaidhrí's puppet, Muirchertach Mac Murchada, had disappeared, assumed dead, and all of the tribes who had declared their support for the High King when Diarmait had been exiled had either been defeated, dispersed, or pacified. A quarter of the island had fallen to the Uí Ceinnselaig and Ruaidhrí had done nothing, Donnchadh accused.

'So he is back,' one-eyed Tigernán Ua Ruairc, King of Breifne, spat with delight. Of all the kings present at Ua Conchobair's chief residence at Tuaim dá Ghuabainn, Tigernán alone was happy that Diarmait had returned to face them. The old warrior scented battle and a chance to kill his enemy. 'We must take our armies south and crush him, once and for all.'

Donnchadh Mac Giolla Phádraig, whose lands had been torn asunder by Diarmait and his foreign allies, nodded his antler-crowned head in agreement at Tigernán's sentiment. And soon all were in accord; they would attack the Uí Ceinnselaig with all haste, kill Diarmait and anyone who stood beside him. All wanted war. All, that was, except Ruaidhrí Ua Conchobair.

'Why should we worry that Diarmait Mac Murchada is back among us?' the High King asked the men who crouched on stools around the central fire in his gigantic stone house. No-one answered him immediately.

'He has some frigging foreigners with him,' Donnchadh Mac Giolla Phádraig finally replied. 'Frigging Flemings, or some such, and they are as sly as frigging foxes.'

'How many of these *Flemings* does he have?' Ruaidhrí enquired almost innocently of the man of the Osraighe. 'I am no chick in a coop and it would take a lot of *frigging* foxes to scare me,' he giggled and leant back on his chair. Behind him was some of the most beautiful artwork that Ireland had to offer: golden ornaments showing intertwining circles, the lives of Celtic saints, animals and crosses.

'There are frigging thousands of them,' Donnchadh said of the Norman-led army. 'Some were on horseback, most in armour; all have frigging bows.'

Breandán Ua Gadhra, a local chieftain from the shores of Lough Ree, sniffed dismissively. 'We have slingers, and we have horsemen,' he said. 'To hell with these Flemings, we will send them back over the sea – come summer.'

Ruaidhrí nodded his balding grey head, pondering over his under-king's words. He agreed with his appraisal but said nothing for a few moments, deep in thought. 'I have reports saying that there are only four hundred foreigners with him.' He shuffled through a number of leaves of vellum which lay on a table beside him.

'They did,' Donnchadh admitted, 'but the Ostmen of Waesfjord are with them now.' The gathered men began chattering as this piece of news was discussed. All the men in the house were from the western reaches of Ireland, the furthest part of the land from Diarmait's territory, and many had not even heard of Waesfjord's capture. But Ruaidhrí Ua Conchobair had heard a reliable report of the longfort's fall from a Corcach merchant, who had heard it from a Scot who had actually been in the fortress when it fell. By his account the Ostmen had given up far too easily after their boats in the harbour had been burned by the enemy.

Ruaidhrí's hatred of Diarmait had cooled in the years since he had expelled the troublesome King of the Uí Ceinnselaig from his seat of power. After Mac Murchada's fall all Ireland had accepted his rule without question and two fighting seasons had passed without the Uí Conchobair clan mobilising for war. But just before the start of the summer, Domhnall Ua Briain of

Tuadhmumhain had risen in rebellion, slaughtered some relatives of Domhnall Mac Cartaigh in Deasmumhain before coming north to raid Connacht. The High King was sure that the most pressing danger lay with the Uí Briain, not in the east in the lands of the Uí Ceinnselaig.

'We must stop Tuadhmumhain first,' one chieftain told the room. 'Then we can move against Diarmait.' As his under-kings argued about what was to be done, Ruaidhrí looked out the door of his stone fortress. It had been positioned to look out over the vast plain to the east almost to the River tSionainn. Though it was only mid-afternoon it was already getting murky and dark. The harvest had been late this year but it would soon be collected into all the small houses in his kingdom. That meant that soon, very soon, the *creach* could begin again – the thievery, killing, rape, and raiding season just before the fall of winter. The chief families of his tribe had been brought inside the vast timber walled fortress of Tuaim dá Ghuabainn in preparation to defend them from the savagery of their neighbours. Ruaidhrí sighed long and mournfully. Every year he had to collect the most important of his people into the fortress and every year the raiders came back to trouble him, no matter how many he killed. Just like Diarmait Mac Murchada they returned no matter how badly they had been defeated.

'Forget the Uí Briain,' Tigernán Ua Ruairc shouted at a chieftain from Ruaidhrí's left. 'They are like children having a tantrum. Diarmait is the real threat. He will never stop until he has murdered us all in our beds.' Spittle sizzled in the fire as it flew from Tigernán's angry, bearded face. His one good eye mirrored the blaze in the centre of the room. His opponent looked like he would make a fight of it but stopped as Ruaidhrí Ua Conchobair took to his feet.

'I have made my decision,' Ruaidhrí said, pausing to gather his thoughts. 'Muster the tribes at Teamhair na Ri,' he exclaimed. 'We will march on the Uí Ceinnselaig when the new moon rises. Diarmait Mac Murchada is a threat that must either be cowered or killed before I can take on the Uí Briain,' he said. 'I cannot allow one man to challenge my rule.'

'Which of the tribes do you want to fight with us?' Tigernán

Ua Ruairc asked, obviously delighted at Ruaidhrí's choice. He suspected that Connacht, Breifne, and the Danes of Dubhlinn would be enough to crush Mac Murchada and his little army of mercenaries, but perhaps Ruaidhrí would want the King of the Ulaidh to also take part and show their support.

'All of them,' Ruaidhrí replied. 'Make sure every taoiseach knows, no matter if he rules over just ten men, that he is to meet me at Teamhair,' he said.

Ruaidhrí Ua Conchobair was a tall, thin man with a balding brow but he held more power than any man in Ireland and when he talked men listened. 'I will know who my enemies are,' he continued. 'Anyone who does not assemble at the Hill of the King in Mide will be considered an ally of Diarmait Mac Murchada and will not be offered terms or mercy. They will be destroyed.'

The riders were sent out that day. They went to all the corners of Ireland with one message: Diarmait Mac Murchada and all who collaborated with him were doomed, for the High King was going to war.

Diarmait Mac Murchada was not, to Domhnall Caomhánach's mind, an evil man. His father loved his family and had even forgiven his traitorous brother Muirchertach, allowing him to retire to a monastery in Aírgialla rather than face death or disfigurement, as was his right to mete out. He played with his grandson and namesake, Domhnall's boy, and was always good and loving to his wives, his cousins, nephews, nieces and extended family. But his reaction when he found out that Maurice de Prendergast had fled Fearna was surprising even to his son. The King of Laighin had torn at his clothes and hair, cursed at anyone who came near him, and demanded that every remaining Fleming left at his stronghold be massacred.

'You will not touch these men,' Sir Robert FitzStephen calmly told Diarmait as Domhnall watched. The big Norman stood in front of his father as he had raged at Richard de la Roche and his men.

'Domhnall,' King Diarmait started to snarl an order and Caomhánach prayed that his father would not go through with his command to kill the Flemings, 'on my order you will charge these foreigners …' Whatever the King's directive had been, it was never finished. Diarmait tailed off his order in the face of the steely determination in FitzStephen's eyes.

Domhnall breathed a sigh of relief. Once again his father's ambition had exceeded his wrath and he had realised that he could not afford to lose the Norman's support by killing Flemings. Diarmait cursed impotently at FitzStephen before storming off towards his new stone house, ranting and raving about treason and loyalty. Domhnall Caomhánach held his hands up to FitzStephen, who nodded at him to show that he understood despite the language barrier. Domhnall then took off behind his father who had gone into the circular house in centre of the half-finished rath of Fearna.

FitzStephen watched father and son disappear before turning to face Richard de la Roche and his men. 'I think it would be best for you to take yourselves across the river, Richard. We need to scout the great forest of Dubh-Tir anyway.' With another look at Diarmait's house he turned back towards his friend. 'It would be sensible that you should leave as soon as possible.'

Roche raised a grey eyebrow and nodded. 'Don't worry. I am not hanging around here in case that lunatic changes his mind and fillets us in our sleep. Perhaps Prendergast was correct?'

'You know my plans, Richard,' FitzStephen continued, ignoring his mention of his departed second-in-command, 'and at least up in the mountains you will be out of our host's sight.'

Grey-haired Richard responded with a nod. 'You really think that this is the best course of action, Robert?'

'If what Mac Diarmait said is true, then there is no way that we can take on the High King's army. Not in a fair fight anyway,' he added with a broad grin. FitzStephen and Diarmait had been told of Ruaidhrí Ua Conchobair's muster at Teamhair na Ri by a rebellious nephew of Toirdelbach Mac Diarmait. Both men knew that it would take a long time for the mighty host to make their way to Fearna, but FitzStephen was not going to wait for Ua Conchobair to attack Diarmait's capital.

Neither was he willing to retreat southwards and invite an assault on newly won Waesfjord. What he had to do was find a way to make Ruaidhrí's superior numbers irrelevant and he already believed that he knew the best place to do just that.

'I hope you know what you are doing,' Roche told him.

'It's a gamble, my friend,' FitzStephen said, staring to the mountains to the west. 'Make sure everything is ready for our arrival.'

Diarmait Mac Murchada seethed as he watched the Flemings march out of the rath of Fearna. He mumbled distant curses as he stared through the sandstone-lined doorway at the leather and steel armoured foreigners as they departed. It was not a question of loyalty, though the King was fast running out of people he could trust; all the tribes of northern Laighin had again betrayed him and flocked to Ruaidhrí's banner at the Hill of the King. No, it was not a matter of loyalty. It was a question of ambition, Diarmait's ambition, and Prendergast's betrayal, along with the High King's impending crusade against him, had put his new objective at risk. For Diarmait Mac Murchada, Chieftain of the Uí Ceinnselaig and sometime King of Laighin, no longer dreamed solely of revenge on his numerous enemies, or even retaking his place on his provincial throne. He now desired Teamhair na Ri and the high kingship, and he wanted the skills of Robert FitzStephen to take him to that goal. He had not forgotten the slighting of his son or all those other wrongs done against him, but ever since he had watched the small number of Normans in action at Dun Cormaic he had been unable to stop the wild horses of his ambition and his imagination from running amok. Every night since he had been exiled he had prayed to God for the chance for vengeance, his prayers all the more impassioned because he had believed them so farfetched. That was until Robert FitzStephen had shown himself to be a brilliant soldier. Since then the man of the Uí Ceinnselaig had prayed only for supreme rule of Ireland. But the loss of two hundred Flemings put all that at risk and so he fumed and prayed and promised God that he would endow churches and monasteries to His glory if only he granted his loyal servant Diarmait his heart's desire.

From the darkness, behind the low doorway of his new house, he watched the Flemings ride through the settlement and out of the thick wood and stone stockade which encircled Fearna. Soon they were out of sight amongst the alder trees which surrounded the fortress. The new building had been erected on the highest point on the ruins of the palace which he had been forced to burn three long years before. A new stockade, twice as big as the last and made from stone, surrounded a handful of domed thatch houses on three sides.

'This changes nothing,' FitzStephen told the King as he stomped noisily into the main room. As always, the house was stuffed with old men who stared at the Norman, suspicious and silent. Diarmait's derb-fine, his bard, and his brehon crouched around the curling stone walls, barely visible through the heavy smoke that circled from the centre of the room towards the roof. Animal carcasses adorned the walls as trophies and herbs burned limply in silver plates.

'Diarmait,' he said again, ignoring the narrow-eyed stares from the men thereabouts, 'this changes nothing.'

Diarmait snorted. 'We cannot defend Fearna without Prendergast's men, and if we can't defend here, we certainly cannot defend the walls of Waesfjord. And if we cannot hold that place,' he shook his head, 'we are finished. All my friends have abandoned me,' he snarled suddenly, not even looking at FitzStephen. 'I have nowhere to run. It is finished.' He referred to his dream of Teamhair na Ri, but the Norman did not know it. 'How long will it be before you leave me?' he asked. 'How long before I am left to the cruel fate of my father?'

'It is true, we are too few to defend Fearna or Waesfjord,' FitzStephen replied. Mac Murchada's head dropped towards his chest as if he had not truly realised the extent of their predicament until the Norman had confirmed it. 'However, we are anything but finished,' FitzStephen said and flashed a massive grin. 'You forget that you have the indomitable Normans of Wales at your side!' He threw his hand onto the King's shoulder. Diarmait looked at the spot which FitzStephen touched and for several moments he stared at the Norman's hand. In the darkness the derb-fine stirred. Long beards and angry mouths beyond the smoke caught FitzStephen's attention.

'Ruaidhrí is marshalling a multitude of warriors,' Diarmait said and reached up to pull FitzStephen's hand away. He turned his back on the Norman and sat down amongst his tribesmen.

'Fionntán told me an old Irish saying,' FitzStephen said suddenly, his voice rebounding off the heavy stone walls. '*It is essential for the man who is not strong to be cunning*. Do you know the verse, Diarmait?' he asked.

The King smiled grimly, remembering the old proverb. 'It is true, but what can we do against such a horde? We would need walls as big as trees, a ditch as wide as a river, and a keep like a mountain,' he said with an ironic shake of the head.

FitzStephen smiled widely. 'It's funny you should say that, Diarmait,' he said, 'for I know a place where we can find all those things.' Mac Murchada turned to look at him. His face was full of confusion. 'Dubh-Tir,' the Norman told him. 'I will turn it into a bastion that cannot be breached by any horde that Ruaidhrí can muster.' Diarmait did not look convinced but the Norman continued. 'I have dispatched Richard de la Roche to dig pits, fell trees, and other dark arts which your enemies will not foresee. The Dark Country is already almost impenetrable but we will use that to our advantage! Winter is already approaching and Ruaidhrí will starve before our mighty wall of trees while we watch him from the comfort of a donjon made from mountains. I once told you, Diarmait,' FitzStephen said, 'that to win Laighin we will have to fight Ruaidhrí Ua Conchobair. I would fight him in a battle site of our choosing rather than chase him back to Connacht for him to choose the place. Dubh-Tir is a trap which he will enter willingly and we shall close it around him.'

'Was that not your plan when you killed the warlord Einion back in Wales,' Diarmait asked, 'to force one all-out battle with all your enemies at once? Was that not what turned you into the pitiful prisoner that I found in Llandovery?'

At one time FitzStephen might have lost his temper at the King's slur. Even amongst his loyal bannermen he would not have let the insult stand. But Robert FitzStephen was a changed man; more thankful and thoughtful if no less ambitious.

'What I did in Wales was the right course of action, then as now we must draw them out,' he said. 'All I can do is trust that God is on my side and that my allies are as brave and honourable as I had hoped, and they had promised they would be. I am a different man than the one you freed from prison, Diarmait. I have learned from my disappointments and this time I will not fail.'

Diarmait laughed. 'Máelmáedoc Ua Riagain believes that you are a gambler, Robert. He says that you will risk everything on a last roll of the dice ...'

'I –' FitzStephen began to object but the King interrupted.

'... and what of that bastard Prendergast, what do we do about him?' Behind Diarmait his derb-fine murmured their agreement.

'We let him go. His archers would have come in handy, but we will still win. And there will be more glory left for those of us who remain.' FitzStephen lied easily; he had been devastated by Prendergast's betrayal but, he knew that all that stood between his army and annihilation was his self-assurance. If he lost anyone else as he had Prendergast there would be no hope, but for the moment he held onto the small sliver of optimism that he could withstand the onslaught using the great wood of Dubh-Tir to his advantage. He was a hunter, after all, and that forest was a hunter's terrain.

'We shall see.'

Diarmait dismissed FitzStephen with a wave of his hand and watched him as he left his house.

'The Norman does not tell you things that make you feel better?' his brehon, Ua Deoradáin, asked Diarmait.

The King shook his head. 'He has been betrayed again and that is an affront I cannot let stand.'

'It is a weak man who would,' the brehon replied. 'The Fleming has to pay.'

Diarmait ground his teeth loudly. 'Damn FitzStephen,' he said. He was just a mercenary, a pirate, and Diarmait was the King. 'Domhnall, get in here!' he shouted.

His eldest son entered the house at a gallop, keen as ever to please his father. He searched the house for possible threats before greeting his father.

'I have a task for you in Waesfjord, my son,' Diarmait told him.

The Ostman town looked just as intimidating to Maurice de Prendergast as it had when he had attacked the walls alongside Robert FitzStephen. That was despite approaching it as a friend rather than a foe on this occasion. His tired troops trudged down the boggy hillside towards Waesfjord where he was impressed to see that St Peter's Gate, broken down by Meiler FitzHenry's trebuchet during the Norman attack, had been rebuilt and strengthened in stone by Maurice FitzGerald. The Geraldine red saltaire flew over the new taller earthworks and Prendergast quickly suppressed a sudden surge of pride as he thought of the great victory that he had been a part of alongside Diarmait and FitzStephen.

'They aren't my people,' Prendergast mumbled and chanced one final look over his shoulder to check the skyline for any sign of a rider racing towards the town to stop him and his men taking ship back to Wales. Thankfully there was no indication of a pursuit across the snow-sprinkled hills. He allowed himself to relax. The worst was surely over and he could not imagine that the placid Ostmen would deny him entry to their town when they knew he was bound for Wales.

The Flemings had forded the Sláine to the north of Carraig, a difficult crossing where one archer had died, but Prendergast was sure that if he had tried to cross the river at the ferry below FitzStephen's fort, he would have been stopped by the distrustful Normans under Sir Maurice FitzGerald.

The last time Prendergast had seen the fortress-town, he had been going north to Fearna with Robert FitzStephen intending to raid all across northern Laighin. Prendergast had been angry then, angry with Diarmait for paying him with the lands of the Uí Bhairrche rather than money, and angry with FitzStephen for not allowing him to pillage the town and surrounding cantreds. For a fleeting second the Fleming considered unleashing his men on the town when they opened the gates, carrying all they could back to Wales with them. It would make up for the meagre pickings from among the Uí Failge and the Osraighe. But as quickly as the thought came he dismissed it; best not to antagonise the dangerous clan of brothers led by FitzGerald and FitzStephen more than he already had.

'How good does Haverford seem after this god-forsaken place?' his younger brother Philip laughed.

'I can't wait to put my feet up,' Prendergast grinned. Winter was almost upon them; the European fighting season was already over, and the Flemings could regroup in Rhos, ready to hire their services to some rich lord in the New Year. Better that, Prendergast thought, than here on this ungodly island where there was no season laid aside for war. The constant state of alert had been punishing even on the Flemish leader who was no wet-behind-the-ears campaigner.

'Bloody hell,' Philip said beside him, 'they haven't got around to rebuilding the churches yet?' The burned remnants of the Celtic churches still littered the area in front of St Peter's Gate. Broken and burned timbers, scorched stone and ruined lintel still poked out of ground. Several of the Flemings, including the Prendergast brothers, crossed themselves as they came to a halt outside the town gates.

'Who are you and what do you buggering want?' shouted an angry voice from above.

'Is it not bloody obvious who we are?' Philip whispered under his breath as he puffed out his surcoat and the indicated to the armaments carried by his troops. It should have been enough for anyone to recognize who the large group of men were.

'Well?' asked Maurice FitzGerald's man, Robert de St Michel, as his head appeared over the newly carved tips of the wooden stockade. He was fully armoured, ready for trouble, and obviously angry.

Prendergast quickly scanned the length of the walls for danger before adopting a friendly tone: 'Robert! How are you my good friend? It is I, Maurice de Prendergast, and I have come to talk to Eirik of Waesfjord,' he finished with a broad smile. Behind him the men stirred. They had been unprepared

331

for a shut gate at the only port friendly to them in Ireland; their only way home.

'Eirik isn't here anymore,' St Michel shouted down brusquely and without greeting the Fleming formally, 'he is up at the Ferry Carraig,' he said, using the name that the Normans had adopted for FitzStephen's new castle.

'With Maurice FitzGerald?' asked Prendergast. So the Normans had taken their puppet-king to their fortress on the Sláine? He wondered what it meant.

'Who else? I suggest you go up there to ... talk,' Robert de St Michel said bluntly, following it up with a broad smile. It was something Prendergast doubted that St Michel did all that often.

'It is late,' Prendergast said, 'and we need shelter in the town tonight. We can go up to the Ferry Carraig tomorrow?'

Robert de St Michel was a short, squat man with a broken nose and crossed eyes which seemed constantly fixed on the nasal guard of his conical helmet. Those same eyes narrowed suspiciously on the Fleming as he agreed to his demands. Prendergast may as well have asked him to move the heavens as open the gates. More men joined St Michel on the wall. They were all fully armed like their leader.

'I'm afraid not,' he said, 'we got word from Sir Maurice this afternoon to deny access to Waesfjord to anyone coming from the north unless they were accompanied by FitzGerald himself,' he stressed. But St Michel wasn't finished. 'He says he will be here by tomorrow morning,' he told him.

'Oh, shit,' Philip whispered behind Prendergast who in turn told his brother to be quiet. He wondered if Robert de St Michel had given the information as a warning or a threat. Either way, FitzGerald had been alerted to his presence in the south by Diarmait and St Michel was not going to open the gates of Waesfjord to his warband.

The barbican now had fifteen Norman crossbowmen with their weapons spanned and ready to loose bolts upon his men who, though they outnumbered the Normans, had no advantage of cover as they stood in the killing zone below St Peter's Gate. Prendergast knew that one wrong word or stupid move could flare up into a fight that neither side could be positive of winning. Both sides eyed each other up and patted their weapons, ready for the fight if it came.

The usually grim Prendergast forced a friendly grin onto his face. 'That's fine, Robert,' he said, pretending to yawn. 'Orders are orders. I think we will await Sir Maurice here after all,' he said happily, almost lazily. 'We shall camp at St Michael's.' He nodded to the Church to the south-west of the town, the only one left standing after the Ostmen had burned Irishtown.

'Fine,' St Michel replied, 'he will see you at first light.' He looked positively disappointed that the Flemings were not going to make a fight of it.

The Flemings quickly extricated themselves from crossbow range and began the long walk south towards St Michael the Archangel's Church. Many grumbled about the Normans who had barred their way though they quietened when Prendergast's lieutenants, Jean de Chievres and Osbert de Cusac, re-joined the Flemish column from their scouting mission to the north.

'There is an Irish army behind us,' Jean shouted as he thundered in beside Prendergast.

His captain almost cursed. 'Who are they?'

Chievres shook his head. 'It is Diarmait's son, Captain Domhnall, with five hundred troops from Fearna.' He chewed his lip nervously. 'They have joined up with Maurice FitzGerald at the castle,' he said.

'What the blazes are we going to do now?' Osbert panted as he asked his question. 'Go back to Fearna?'

'No. I will not give in to threats from Diarmait Mac Murchada and there is no profit in revenge,' Prendergast said with determination. 'At the moment we outnumber Maurice FitzGerald so unless he is stupid, which we know he is not, we are safe from him for the time being. But these Irish worry me greatly …'

'Could we assault Waesfjord?' said a young archer called Thomas le Fleming.

Prendergast threw Thomas a dirty look for eavesdropping on his conversation but answered his question anyway.

'We have not enough warriors to assault,' he said, thinking

out loud and waiting for his lieutenants to bring some ideas to the table.

'Go south to Banabh,' de Chievres suggested, 'and wait for a passing ship?'

'We could sit out there for months without anyone stopping to offer passage,' Prendergast dismissed the idea with a wave of his hand. 'That damned Irishman doesn't know the meaning of forgiveness,' he said, meaning Diarmait. 'His friends, if he has any left, would set upon us within days.'

'So if we can't cross the sea, and we can't go back to Diarmait, and we can't stay here ... where is there left to go?' Osbert de Cusac wondered with slight foreboding in his voice.

'We find a new employer,' Prendergast said, looking westwards towards the mountains.

# Chapter Thirteen

A horde approached the dark-forested mountains. Like the snow which clung to their shoulders, they came from the north. They came with destruction in their hearts. They came to kill.

Their leaders had marshalled a multitude at Teamhair na Rí, and knew that the trees of Dubh-Tir hid just a small band of brigands ready to be wiped from the face of the earth. There was not a moment of doubt in any of their minds that this great army would rid their land of the threat of the foreigners, and of the hated Diarmait Mac Murchada. They were a host from Connacht, Mide, Breifne, Airgialla, Tir Eóghain, Ulaidh, and beyond. All of Diarmait's enemies, Irish and Norse alike, had united to eject the High King's great foe from Ireland.

A lone figure stood beneath twin fluttering banners at the bounds of the forest and watched the army approach. Like the man's surcoat, the great flags showed a white star on a blue field and the standards flickered like fire vapour at their tapered points. Snow swirled angrily on the wicked wind as it whipped at Sir Robert FitzStephen's woollen cloak to reveal his richly coloured surcoat and tough mail armour beneath. FitzStephen considered the long road he had ventured upon to get him to this point: the fight at Ewloe and his investment as a knight; the defeat at Aberteifi and his dismal life in the cells of Llandovery; burning the ships at Waesfjord. Yet the image that remained clearest in his mind was that of Aoife of the Uí Ceinnselaig. He raised his spear in salute to the distant enemy. *Come on*, he thought, *come into the Dark Country. I know its secrets. Here, I am the hunter and you are the prey.*

He wished he could dispel the many lingering worries which inundated his attention. The enemy were many, his allies few. But all his preparations had been made and everything was poised for a momentous clash between the two armies.

He remembered his eldest brother William's words on the shore at Melrfjord just a few months before. He had spoken grandly about some Greeks who had stopped the host of Persia with just a handful of warriors. Well, Robert FitzStephen's challenge was no less great: eighteen thousand warriors under the High King threatened to destroy everything that the Norman knight and his band of four hundred had won. He still had a thousand warriors from Waesfjord and five hundred infantry of the Uí Ceinnselaig, but his real force was that central core of mercenary cavalry and archers. Diarmait Mac Murchada and Richard de la Roche were silently waiting for him upon the small path cut through the trees.

'So they have come,' Diarmait said. His dejection was obvious. No man had been able to array such power since the days of Brian Bóruma and his grand offensive against the Ostmen of Hlymrik and Dubhlinn. Yet here was Ruaidhrí Ua Conchobair showing that his grip on ultimate power in Ireland was almost complete.

'Ruaidhrí won't attack our position today,' FitzStephen told his master. 'They will come in the morning.' He turned around and again stared at the vast multitude of warriors waiting to tear his army apart. A small group was coming over the river accompanied by a number of tonsured priests. 'They want to parley with us,' FitzStephen noted.

'Not scouts?' Diarmait asked, doubting that Ruaidhrí would want to talk to him unless it was to taunt and ridicule him. Diarmait's hopes in FitzStephen's defences were disappearing by the minute as the full power of his enemy unfolded below.

FitzStephen nodded away to the south where a number of men on rugged horses had appeared and were skirting the forest below the cliff face on the southern peak. 'They're the scouts.'

'I will send Domhnall to chase them off,' Richard de la Roche started to move away.

'No. Let them alone,' FitzStephen said. 'They won't get far into the trees.' He watched the men on horseback. He was bemused to see that they used neither stirrup nor saddle and so could not fight from horseback – a sword swipe would certainly unseat them – and he took confidence from that.

336

Suddenly there was a flurry of activity amongst the Gaels. A second later the drifting wind brought the sound of bowstrings to FitzStephen's ears. The scouts fled as the Norman archers stepped out of the trees and chased them off.

'Bite,' FitzStephen urged as he turned his head to watch the main army down in the valley. Ruaidhrí's men had kept the Sláine River between them and the highland forest where the Normans waited amongst the knotted and twisted trees. 'Come on,' he murmured, 'bite.' FitzStephen imagined what Dubh-Tir must look like to the tired men who had marched so far from their homes in winter to fight their king's enemy. The forest grew between two high ridges running parallel, two miles apart for as far as the eye could see. Mist clung to the tops of those high hills. It was a place where goblins and evil spirits were said to live, a place where brave men feared to enter, populated by bog and swamp and nightmarish horrors. As if to aid the forboding, a wolf howled in the distance. FitzStephen hoped that the men below had also heard the cry and were reminded of foul stories from their youth. At both sides of the valley mouth, cliffs looked down on the tree tops, as if some great giant had cut out the earth and removed it. The Norman camp sat between two peaks which formed the southern ridge, defended by a huge and impassable swamp to its rear. If all went to ruin, that was where he would make his final stand. Dubh-Tir was a strong position but it was also one which Ruaidhrí Ua Conchobair would not hesitate to assault, such was his advantage through sheer strength of numbers. That huge lumbering beast which was the High King's army would charge the Norman army hidden in the trees and gore it to pieces.

But what Ruaidhrí would find was not a scared, defeated enemy attempting to hide from the inevitable conquest. He would find a hunter, armed to the teeth and ready to fight in the darkness of a wintry Dubh-Tir where he hoped that his ploys would bleed the great beast to death. The highest form of the hunt had eight parts, FitzStephen remembered, and to take down the proud army of the High King he knew that he would have to employ every one. Already the first three parts had been completed and he had set his 'dogs' along the predicted course of their prey. Soon the Normans would take part in the real fight amongst the conifers and soggy tangle of vegetation. First, however, FitzStephen had to meet his prey face to face and provoke him into attack. He had to sniff out their weak spot. For that task he would need a lymer and an alaunt.

'Máelmáedoc Ua Riagain,' he shouted towards the forest where he knew the King's two closest advisers would be hidden, 'Bishop Seosamh, you too. We three are going to visit the High King of Ireland.'

The trio went down from the forest to talk to the men who had exiled their king, and disfigured his son. They walked calmly towards the temporary shelter which had been erected half way between the forest and the river. It was little more than branches holding up a tatty old Norse sail, but it would serve to hold off the sleet and keep the kings of Ireland dry while they met their foe. In the wind the sail pumped and sagged like a heartbeat, short wind-tells whipping and scratching the temporary structure.

'We should just set fire to the tent,' FitzStephen suggested to the Diarmait's secretary, Máelmáedoc Ua Riagain. 'As they come out, I will deal with the warriors, and you two,' he indicated towards his companions, 'can take down the rest.' Bishop Seosamh shook his head with a grin at the Norman's lack of propriety but did not disagree.

'They will have many warriors with them,' Máelmáedoc said seriously, 'and priests.'

'I didn't say that I would enjoy it,' FitzStephen shrugged.

A number of men came out of the temporary structure to meet the entourage coming down the hill. Not one of the men looked nervous at the meeting and all were content that they now looked upon a beaten enemy, ready to sue for their surrender. FitzStephen felt Máelmáedoc tense as he whispered the names of his king's enemies to the Norman:

'Behind Ruaidhrí Ua Conchobair,' he indicated towards a tall man with a pleasant face, 'is Donnchadh Mac Giolla Phádraig with the antlers on his head. It was he who slighted Diarmait's son,' Máelmáedoc said. 'The ugly one with the bad eye is Tigernán Ua Ruairc, and Hasculv Mac Torcaill is the blond whose grandfather killed Diarmait's father …'

'… and that is Maurice de Prendergast who has betrayed us all,' FitzStephen finished the sentence as the Fleming appeared at Mac Giolla Phádraig's side.

'Traitor,' he hissed at his former friend, who looked disappointed at FitzStephen's indictment.

High King Ruaidhrí did not wait for the accusation to be translated and instead greeted the Norman genially like a relative who had fallen on hard times. 'Please come inside out of the cold so that we may talk.' The High King's warm greeting was translated into French by Máelmáedoc. 'Diarmait did not come with you?'

'He feared betrayal,' FitzStephen shot Prendergast a baleful look. He had heard that the Fleming had sold his services to the Osraighe but FitzStephen had not expected him to be facing them at Dubh-Tir. That his former ally would fight against him sent a cold sweat down his back. He knew the skill of the Fleming crossbowmen and feared how this development would affect his plans. As they entered the tent they were stalked by Tigernán Ua Ruairc, who snarled venomously at Diarmait's warlord.

'We have you now, you bastards. You have nowhere to run this time. Maybe we will bury you with a dog.' Tigernán was almost quivering with excitement at FitzStephen's, and through him Diarmait's, vulnerability. He skulked into the corner of the tent when the High King snapped at him to be silent.

FitzStephen was the last man to enter and he lingered outside, casting one final look up at the intimidating forest that looked down from above. The last shard of low cloud gathered above them on the northern ridge, clinging to the mountain and slowly sweeping westwards. Confidant that all his preparations were in order, he ducked his head into the tent as it was buffeted by the wind. A priest was saying a prayer in Irish in the middle of the room and all the kings had followed Ruaidhrí Ua Conchobair's lead by falling to their knees in prayer. FitzStephen joined them in supplication to the heavens, but tuned out most of the foreign entreaties for peace and said his own short prayer in Latin. He then studied High King Ruaidhrí who whispered silent words with closed eyes. He was a slight man, balding, and certainly no warrior if his feeble arms were anything to go by, but FitzStephen sensed strength of a different sort, for he was certainly in control of this vast army which he had collected. He considered that the High King was not a man to be underestimated; a king who used his intellect rather than brute force. And that made him dangerous.

'So,' Ruaidhrí spoke as his priest finished the prayer, 'how are we to solve this problem?' He addressed his question to Bishop Seosamh, who he saw as the most senior of Diarmait's negotiators.

'You are free to attack us,' the bishop said, just as brusquely, 'and then skulk back to Connacht, when King Diarmait beats you, to lick your wounds.' He turned to look at Tigernán, 'Or maybe get your dog to do lick your wounds.'

'What's going on?' FitzStephen said loudly in French. He had been able to pick up some Irish in his time with Diarmait but could not follow what was going on now. No-one answered, ignoring the Norman and continuing to converse in Irish.

'Damn it,' he cursed. Attempting to cross the room to stand beside the bishop he was met by the tall, blond King of Dubhlinn, Hasculv Mac Torcaill, who put a large hand in the middle of his chest.

'They are talking about cattle. Bloody Vestmen,' he said in perfect, if heavily accented, French, 'they are always talking about cattle or the weather or their dead relatives. Nothing else interests them.' The warrior had a braided beard which made him look older than he actually was but FitzStephen guessed that he was not much over twenty-five years. The Norman raised an eyebrow at Hasculv's proficiency in the French tongue but the youngster shrugged.

'I am Konungr in Dyflin,' he said, using his people's name for Dubhlinn, 'and we trade with Bristol and Chester. They speak French,' was his simple explanation.

The Norman swept into a bow and was about to formally introduce himself when Hasculv interrupted.

'So you took Waesfjord then. How?' he asked bluntly.

FitzStephen shrugged. 'God was against them after they burned the churches.'

Hasculv looked on impassively for a better response and the Norman consented. 'The usual way; we battered them into submission,' he said. Hasculv looked like he wanted more answers but Maurice de Prendergast had sauntered over towards the small group of foreigners.

'Robert, what, in the name of all that is holy, do you think you're doing here?' Prendergast frowned at FitzStephen like a priest frustrated at teaching a particularly dense child his letters.

'My duty, as I promised I would,' FitzStephen retorted.

'These Irish have an army of thousands ready to attack you. That is not *duty* but stupidity! You and your men will die, and for what, a wet patch of swamp around Waesfjord?' The Fleming shook his head. 'We should leave the Irish to their wars and words, your men and mine, and fight our way over the river. Then we sail for Wales together.' FitzStephen looked at the King of Dubhlinn who was listening intently to what Prendergast had said. 'Don't worry,' the Fleming whispered, 'I have already worked out a deal with King Hasculv to sail home from his city. But we need your men to help me defeat the Uí Tuathail ...'

FitzStephen grabbed his former ally by the arm and pushed him outside into the snow which was just beginning to lie. He leaned in close, making sure that the Fleming's armour scored hard into his arm as he squeezed it.

'Hasculv is playing you for a fool,' FitzStephen warned his former ally. 'Of course he'll promise you passage if you help to create a rift amongst his enemies. But there will always be a reason to keep you in Ireland, another enemy to defeat. It will not end with the Uí Tuathail.' FitzStephen shook his head. 'I will not abandon Diarmait.'

Prendergast ripped his arm from FitzStephen's grip. 'Then you go up into those woods and die there. I will find another way home.'

FitzStephen nodded along silently. 'I will look out for you in the battle tomorrow, Prendergast. We will sort out our differences then.'

'If you somehow survive the first attack I will certainly look forward to that meeting.'

The Fleming snorted back a sardonic laugh before turning and disappearing back into the tent.

Máelmáedoc Ua Riagain had watched as FitzStephen had taken Prendergast by the arm and forced him out of the temporary shelter. Diarmait's secretary's eyes narrowed suspiciously as he gazed at the two men as they argued before his attention was called back to the conversation at hand. The bishops were still quarrelling about the ownership of some monastical lands north of Fearna when suddenly High King Ruaidhrí stood up and forced them all to be quiet with but a wave of his hand.

'This is immaterial,' he said, 'what we are really here to do is accept Diarmait's surrender.'

'I offered no surrender so I don't know why you think you can accept one,' Máelmáedoc barely concealed his anger at the High King's bold declaration.

Ruaidhrí laughed loudly, 'You have, what, three thousand warriors at the most up in those woods?'

'We have more than enough to send you back over the mountains,' Máelmáedoc warned, unwilling to give away that their numbers were significantly less than the High King had guessed. 'FitzStephen is ready for you.'

Maurice de Prendergast appeared beside Ruaidhrí and whispered loudly to a translator, who passed on his message to the High King that Sir Robert FitzStephen could not be bribed into betrayal as had been his plan. Ruaidhrí frowned at the information, for he did not truly feel the confidence he showed outwardly. While his Gaelic allies had advised swift attack, the Fleming Prendergast had convinced him that the forest above the river could hold any number of surprises for his army. His scouts had been unable to force their way into the deep, dark woodland and had found nothing to report, but it was still the enemy's chosen battlefield and Ruaidhrí did not want to have to lumber into the dark woods without any idea of what faced his army. There were other methods to winning a battle other than fighting, Ruaidhrí decided.

Robert FitzStephen returned from outside and stood beside Máelmáedoc. High King Ruaidhrí gazed at the warrior who had to stoop so that his oddly cut hair did not touch the woollen sail above them all. In his bright blue and silver clothes, and amongst the dull robes of the Irish and Norse, the Norman looked as colourful as a figure from the famous *Book of Colum Cille*. But not gaudy, the High King thought, his clothes spoke of confidence, marking him out in battle and life. *Here I am*, they said, *come and get me if you dare*. And the robes hid circlets of steel armour, Ruaidhrí knew.

'What do you think will happen here?' Ruaidhrí asked Máelmáedoc. 'Do you think that if we leave now, we will not be back here at the start of spring? And then the year after that? Diarmait will die one way or another. You might as well hand him over now.'

Máelmáedoc said nothing. He was desperate to talk his way out of a devastating defeat, truly believing that his silver tongue was all that stood between the High King and Diarmait's defeat. He had been a soldier before joining Diarmait's household, but even he could not understand how the Norman excavations in the woods could possibly help Diarmait's cause. Máelmáedoc knew that they would be overwhelmed if even a quarter of High King Ruaidhrí's army attacked. He could not allow that to happen.

'Four hundred deaths,' Ruaidhrí said suddenly. No-one said anything for a few seconds as they struggled to understand what the High King's statement meant. 'Four hundred deaths,' he repeated, 'and I will leave your king in control of Laighin.' As his translator started to speak, Ruaidhrí stopped him.

Máelmáedoc was stopped in his tracks. 'Four hundred deaths?' he asked quietly. 'Who do you wish dead?'

'Your foreigners, the *Flemings* or whatever they are called, including that big, angry one behind you,' he nodded towards Robert FitzStephen. 'I don't like the look of him at all. Slaughter them, Máelmáedoc, and Diarmait will remain King of Laighin. Kill them, and Diarmait will be my friend forever.'

Máelmáedoc looked around to stare at the Norman who, unaware that the conversation going on in Irish was about him, took a seat at the back of the tent beside a mischievous Hasculv Mac Torcaill who grinned broadly and did not admit what had gone between Máelmáedoc and Ruaidhrí Ua Conchobair. In unison Donnchadh Mac Giolla Phádraig and Tigernán Ua Ruairc jumped to their feet and began shouting their opposition to the plan; that Diarmait Mac Murchada could not be trusted, that he was the High King's real enemy, and that the foreigners did not matter. Ruaidhrí's brehon silenced them both with a sudden, severe shout for silence on behalf of his king. Both men grudgingly sat down again, throwing desperate and impotent glances to each other about how they could proceed.

'How can we trust you?' Máelmáedoc Ua Riagain asked when the furore subsided. To his right Tigernán Ua Ruairc laughed sarcastically about how one of Mac Murchada's men could possibly ask such a question. 'If we do this – and I am not saying that we will,' Máelmáedoc continued, 'then my king will be utterly defenceless. How can we possibly trust that you will not wait until it is done and then finish the job by attacking us?'

Ruaidhrí considered the question. 'Diarmait's son, Conchobair, has been living in my household for a year and I have grown to like him – a smart young man and a good Christian boy,' the High King said. 'If you are true to your word, my youngest daughter Roisin needs a husband …'

Máelmáedoc hesitated. Before him was an unbelievable offer. Not only would he be safe, but Diarmait would bolster his rule of Laighin by tethering his house to that of the High King by marriage. He would be a closer ally than even Tigernán Ua Ruairc was to Ruaidhrí. Máelmáedoc was barely able to keep his relief concealed as he came to terms with what the High King was offering. It was more than for which he could ever have hoped. His people were saved.

But Ruaidhrí Ua Conchobair was not finished: 'Bishop Seosamh, what did you make of Waesfjord?' he asked. 'It is a good town with lots of souls in need of counsel, I hear.' He knew that Diarmait could be swayed by the churchmen who had supported him so fully in his recovery of power. Their appetite would have to be sated too.

FitzStephen sat up straight as he identified that High King

Ruaidhrí had made mention of his prize. He said nothing but listened intently as the Bishop of Fearna answered in his alien tongue.

'It is indeed a flock that is in need of guidance,' the bishop said.

'I can arrange it that you will be named Bishop of Fearna and Waesfjord. How many more churches is that to your flock? Seven? Eight, even?' Ruaidhrí asked but did not allow the bishop to answer, turning to Máelmáedoc instead. 'I am sure I could make it so that the lands I gave to the Osraighe were returned to Diarmait of the Uí Ceinnselaig. So, do we have an accord?'

Máelmáedoc was taken aback by High King Ruaidhrí's generous offer, which promised everything that they had lost before Diarmait's exile; Laighin and the tribal lands of the Uí Ceinnselaig would be theirs and the Meic Murchada would once again be closely allied to a holder of the high kingship. All it would take was to betray the trust of a few mercenaries from Wales in exchange for a kingdom.

'What the hell is going on?' FitzStephen finally asked from his place at the back of the tent.

Máelmáedoc Ua Riagain ignored FitzStephen, eyeing a way out of the stand-off.

'I will need to get my king's agreement before I can approve it,' he said.

'Don't take too long to decide because my armies attack at daybreak,' Ruaidhrí warned casually. 'I want to hear the foreigners scream under the moonlight or we come for you all and there will be no mercy.'

Máelmáedoc stood and nodded. He was paler around the gills after the High King's threat. 'I will tell Diarmait all of this,' he said. 'I will return with your answer,' he said taking a swift glance at Robert FitzStephen. 'I will meet your representatives here in this tent.'

Ruaidhrí nodded and turned to converse with Maurice de Prendergast while Máelmáedoc signalled to a confused FitzStephen to leave. Behind them the bishop bowed to the High King, smiling slyly before following the Norman and his king's secretary out the door. Ruaidhrí held up a hand to stop his allies from questioning his decision and continued to talk quietly and secretly to the Fleming for a few moments.

It was Tigernán Ua Ruairc who predictably broke the silence. 'You promised me I would get vengeance on Diarmait,' he snarled desperately at High King Ruaidhrí. 'But you offer him his life, his kingdom, and your daughter! Why?'

Ruaidhrí calmly got to his feet, fixing his cloak and tunic so that they were straight. 'You do not understand, Tigernán,' he said flippantly. 'I did not offer you vengeance but justice, and you will get it. But I will get what I want first, and that is a man I can trust in Laighin. You will get ample justice for Derbforgaill, I promise.' The King of Breifne looked at Ruaidhrí, struggling to understand what he meant and not for the first time Ruaidhrí questioned how a man of Tigernán's stupidity had got himself onto, never mind kept, the throne of Breifne. Could he not see the bigger picture? If he subdued Laighin then he would control all of Ireland except for Tuadhmumhain, where Domhnall Ua Briain still threatened the southern borders of Connacht. How could the Uí Briain hope to stand against him if Laighin, the second most powerful country in Ireland, was allied against them?

'It hardly matters, Tigernán,' Ruaidhrí told him. 'There is always a chance that Diarmait will not accept, and if he does that we will kill everyone in that dark wood.' Ruaidhrí cast his eyes over every face in the tent. 'If he refuses me we will scour the forests and pursue these rebels until they are all dead.'

There would be blood on the following day. Either his enemies would be destroyed by his sword or they would be murdered by the hand of Diarmait Mac Murchada. Ruaidhrí considered no outcome other than victory, complete and final.

FitzStephen was furious and stomped away from the tented meeting place through the darkening daylight. His long gait meant that he easily outstretched Máelmáedoc Ua Riagain and Bishop Seosamh Ua hAodha who struggled in the ever-worsening conditions. Snow bit high on their ankles as they ploughed upwards towards the tree line. But neither Irishman called for FitzStephen to pause nor, when he turned to catch a glimpse of his allies, did they look up, so deep were they in conversation, secretive and guarded. FitzStephen slowed as he reached the edge of the forest and, allowing the two men to catch up with him, he turned viciously on them.

'What the hell is going on?' he pointed a finger at Máelmáedoc's chest. 'What did Ruaidhrí say? And why was I not permitted to speak?'

If Diarmait's secretary seemed surprised at FitzStephen's questions, he covered it expertly, countering quickly with a question of his own: 'What were you talking to the traitor Maurice de Prendergast about without me?'

FitzStephen snorted back a laugh. 'We were talking about leaving you damn Irish to fight it out amongst yourselves while we made a run for it,' he said truthfully. 'I told him no,' he added, grabbing a hunk of the Máelmáedoc's shirt. 'Now, I have told you the truth, so about what did you talk to the High King?'

The bishop began babbling in Irish at Diarmait's advisor but Máelmáedoc silenced him with a shake of his head. 'We … were … talking about lands that were taken by Donnchadh Mac Giolla Phádraig after Diarmait's fall,' Máelmáedoc said with a forced smile. 'I am dreadfully sorry that I fell into our native tongue, it was force of habit. You can trust me,' he added throwing his hand up onto FitzStephen's wide shoulder.

'Land,' FitzStephen repeated. It was Máelmáedoc's smile that really worried him. 'Land was all you talked about?' he asked again.

Diarmait's secretary hummed an affirmative. 'The bishop and I are going to report our findings to our king now. We will talk again soon. I expect that you have many preparations to make before the battle tomorrow,' he said and walked away with the bishop stomping alongside.

FitzStephen watched them move into the thick foliage, where he knew a contingent of Diarmait's kern waited to shepherd them back to the Irish camp deep in the forest.

'You heard it all?' the Norman said, though he was

seemingly alone.

Fionntán Ua Donnchaidh stepped from the darkness where FitzStephen had asked him to wait. 'Problems?' the Irishman guessed.

FitzStephen nodded, still watching the place where Máelmáedoc Ua Riagain and Bishop Seosamh Ua hAodha had just disappeared. 'Do you still want to revenge yourself on the King of the Osraighe?' he asked Fionntán.

'Of course,' the Irishman said.

'Do you desire it more than you value your loyalty to Diarmait?' the Normans turned to look directly at him.

'I swore to have my vengeance before I swore fidelity to the Meic Murchada,' Fionntán said plainly. 'You think that we are betrayed?'

'Perhaps. Not by Diarmait, I think. Not yet anyway. But by his secretary and the bishop?' he shook his head. 'Those two are out for themselves, I am sure of it.'

'You have proof?' Fionntán asked.

'I do not,' he said, 'but I have been deceived before and I see the same treachery in Máelmáedoc Ua Riagain's eyes.'

'That one is a trickster alright,' Fionntán nodded, 'and Seosamh Ua hAodha is no different to every other greedy bastard bishop in Christendom.' He breathed out, his face shrouded in misted breath. 'So what do you want me to do?'

'Help me follow them and find out what they are up to,' he told him. 'If they are keeping something from me I want to know about it,' he said. 'I need you to translate.'

'You trust me to tell you the truth?' Fionntán asked.

'I trust that you want revenge more than you want to live.'

'And if it turns out that he is planning to deceive you?' the Irishman said without denying FitzStephen's statement. 'What will you do then?'

The Norman breathed out deeply. 'I can beat the enemy in front of us, Fionntán. I truly can, but another behind will certainly bring ruin to our army. Pray that our friends are true.'

Fionntán's sunken eyes were black holes as he held FitzStephen's gaze for a second longer. But then he was gone, crouching low and noiseless as he moved through the frigid forest.

'Are you coming or what?' asked Fionntán without turning.

FitzStephen followed him into the Dark Country.

Fionntán and FitzStephen were but shadows as they stood silently at the back of King Diarmait's small dark hut hidden in the depths of Dubh-Tir. The Norman had abandoned his colourful surcoat and chainmail, donning instead a dull cloak and hood to hide his distinctive hair and lack of beard.

The duo had passed quickly through the trees where they had discovered the path used by Máelmáedoc Ua Riagain and the Bishop of Fearna to return to Diarmait's camp. Hundreds of Irish warriors had descended on their king's secretary and his companions as they entered the snowbound mottle of turf houses. They demanded news. They wanted salvation and the clamour had provided FitzStephen and Fionntán with the perfect opportunity to slip inside the camp, and then to scuttle into the smoky atmosphere of Diarmait's lair, where he and his derb-fine listened to the advisor's account of his talks with High King Ruaidhrí.

'What are they talking about?' FitzStephen quietly asked his accomplice as the room erupted in anger. Twenty Meic Murchada – Diarmait's closest family – as well as his bard and his brehon crowded into the large hut made from roughly cut boughs and sodden turf slabs. In the centre of the room was a large fire dug into the cold earth and ringed with stone and it hissed each time a droplet of melted snow dropped into its midst. The blaze warmed the faces of the men who, like FitzStephen and Fionntán, were cloaked and hooded against the winter cold. Smoke drifted amongst the tribesmen and upwards to the roof.

'Máelmáedoc tells Diarmait which tribes were at the meeting with the High King,' Fionntán replied softly. 'It is a daunting list. Some of those men had promised help to Diarmait,' the Irishman said. 'The derb-fine are not happy.' He nodded towards Diarmait's kinsmen who surrounded the King of Laighin, crouched down on their hunkers before the simple hearth. The oldest and most powerful had long beards which touched almost to their waists while around them their sons and brothers and nephews listened and passed comment on the secretary's report. In the midst of the derb-fine Domhnall Caomhánach, his head shaved to the crown where his hair grew long to his neck, prowled in support of his father.

'Has Máelmáedoc Ua Riagain made any agreement with them?' asked Robert FitzStephen.

'Not yet ... wait,' Fionntán paused and listened in on Máelmáedoc's report. 'He speaks of a pact which the High King suggested ... it would be of benefit to Diarmait's family ...' Fionntán's eyebrows creased as he translated. For many minutes he only listened, ignoring FitzStephen's urging appeals for information. He put a finger to his lips to hush the Norman.

Fionntán's silence made the fury in FitzStephen's soul grow. His imagination ran wild as he listened to the tone of the Irish conversation and the look of utter contempt on Fionntán's face. What could they be saying, he wondered. As his frustration increased, FitzStephen angrily eyed the King of Laighin who crouched soundless in the centre of the room wrapped in smoke and backed by ragged bracken and timber walls. An ornate sword rested on his shoulder while his long, bony forefingers touched to his lips as he listened to the report from his advisor. This was the man who had promised to be true to him when they had met in the great hall of Llandovery so long ago, FitzStephen thought, and now he flirted with treachery. He felt like throwing off his cloak and charging Máelmáedoc Ua Riagain and set his sword to singing through the air. He would kill the poison-tongued scribe and demand that Diarmait tell him exactly what had gone on behind his back between his secretary and Ruaidhrí.

His body must have tensed for Fionntán suddenly reached out and grabbed FitzStephen's arm. The Norman turned angrily on the Irish mariner, shaking his arm from his grip, but this only succeeded in attracting the attention of several men who knelt in front of them by the fire. Fionntán's eyes widened in warning, appealing to FitzStephen to stay quiet lest they be discovered eavesdropping. Two men of the derb-fine eyed the

Norman suspiciously for a second, but then Diarmait climbed to his feet and indicated for the hut to go silent so that he could speak and the two men looked away. The hoarse tones of Mac Murchada's natural tongue rasped around the smoky hut like a pagan ritual. FitzStephen, unable to understand, watched the King's manner intently for any sign of the threat which he believed Máelmáedoc Ua Riagain had advised. Diarmait looked old and grey as he talked, his arms swung by his sides limply, his shoulders loose and low. He looked, to FitzStephen, like a man whose dreams lay in pieces. In front of Diarmait, his secretary nodded along with the King's words obediently and supportively while grizzled Bishop Seosamh Ua hAodha lifted his hands to heaven in prayer, as if the very words which Diarmait spoke were sent from God. Around the room the derb-fine growled agreement at the King's decree.

Fionntán again grabbed the Norman by the arm, this time hauling him through the crowd and out of the turf hut towards the snow. Their exit earned a number of confused glances from the Irish warriors but Fionntán did not stop and the old sailor forced FitzStephen outside where they were immediately faced by a hundred more men wrapped against the weather and straining to hear what had happened when the King's secretary had gone down the mountain. One of the men asked a question of FitzStephen but he could not understand, and shook his head under his heavy cloak.

'This way,' Fionntán said and roughly directed him through the crowd.

'Fionntán,' FitzStephen hissed as they pushed away from the crowd of people towards the forest. Each of the rough-barked trees was painted with a fine surface of white snow on the windward side. 'What has befallen us?' he asked, his lips stinging and peeling because of the cold.

'Keep your voice down!' the Irishman whispered desperately back. 'You are not safe here.'

For many minutes neither man spoke as the worked their way south and east towards the second camp used by the Normans and their foreign allies. When they had been walking for ten minutes Fionntán stopped and turned towards

FitzStephen.

'You were right,' he said. 'I would not believe it if I had not heard it with my own ears.'

FitzStephen threw back his hood. 'I bloody knew it.' He smiled cynically and shook his head. Somehow it felt better now that he knew for sure that his instincts were correct. Now at least he knew who he had to fight. 'What did Máelmáedoc say? Tell me exactly,' he ordered the Irishman.

Fionntán sucked in the cold air. 'He spoke of an agreement between Ruaidhrí and Diarmait, a marriage of their children and a peace accord ...'

'Peace?' FitzStephen fumed. How could Diarmait consider amity with the man who had driven him from his home and into the mountains? The man who had threatened his life and whose allies had slighted his son?

'There is more,' Fionntán interrupted his anger. 'Ruaidhrí's only price for the settlement is your life and that of your men.'

For many minutes FitzStephen was speechless. 'They make peace and there is no need for a few hundred foreigners in their land,' he finally said quietly. 'What else?'

'They want it done by tomorrow morning,' Fionntán replied, 'or they will attack.' He stumbled into a deep hole and sank up to his knee in the drifting snow. Cursing, he righted himself.

'Divide and conquer,' FitzStephen whispered. 'What did Diarmait say?'

'The derb-fine advised Diarmait to take up the offer,' the Irishman replied, 'and the King cannot afford to lose their support. He appealed to them to trust in your defences but,' he paused, 'they do not understand how such fragile-looking fortifications could possibly survive an attack.' Fionntán shook his head. 'Diarmait told them that they had to think of the future,' he described, 'he said that if we defeated them here then all Laighin would be his, Mide would also fall, and Dubhlinn would be subdued. He told them to remember Dun Cormaic and Waesfjord. But ...'

'But?'

'But the derb-fine told him that Ruaidhrí could provide all those things and without the loss of any lives,' Fionntán said.

'Except those of the Normans and Flemings who came to his aid when no one else would,' FitzStephen snarled. He picked up the pace through the frozen forest. 'Diarmait is a traitor.'

'He allowed himself to be convinced,' Fionntán admitted.

With a roar of pure venom, FitzStephen punched an evergreen with all his might. As the thud resounded around the forest, flakes of snow smashed to the ground around the Norman, hitting Fionntán.

'I must stop this,' FitzStephen said as he examined his left fist. It was cut and bleeding

'How can we prevent it?' Fionntán asked. 'Diarmait has made his decision.'

FitzStephen grimaced. 'The same way that Ruaidhrí would drive a wedge between us. Divide and conquer.'

King Donnchadh Mac Giolla Phádraig watched the flames from five fluttering torches as they hovered on the edge of the vastness of Dubh-Tir. Nothing else could be seen in the darkness. He had watched the small group of torchbearers approach and knew what their arrival heralded.

'Diarmait has agreed to the plan,' Donnchadh mused. 'It is about frigging time.' It was beginning to get really cold, but it was not the temperature, the secrecy, and the waiting that annoyed the King of the Osraighe. It was the embarrassment of being despatched back across the river by the High King like some damned messenger to hear Diarmait's answer. He spat in the snow. What made it all the worse was that if all went to plan and Ruaidhrí kept his word to the King of Laighin then all the lands that Donnchadh had taken three years before would revert to the Uí Ceinnselaig and the man he hated most in the world would again become the strongest king in the east. Diarmait would no doubt demand his submission by force of arms.

'What are they frigging doing up there?' he asked one of the warriors, huddled in a robe against the cold. The five torches still burned on the hillside above them. 'Do they expect me to walk the whole way up there to accept their message? They can go frig themselves if they do.'

Hidden in the darkness, his brother Cian laughed. 'They are

probably worried that we will murder them if their answer is the wrong one.'

'It had crossed my mind,' Donnchadh replied pulling his hooded cape closer around his neck. 'If Diarmait is with them I frigging will kill him,' the man of the Osraighe swore and straightened his antler crown on his brow.

The tent where the kings had met earlier in the day had been agreed as the meeting place for Ruaidhrí's intrigues, however, the snow which had fallen since then had collapsed part of the shelter and Donnchadh's men had been forced to huddle a little way from the crumpled tent, unable even to light a fire to warm the small group for fear that the vicious Norman cavalry and archers would discover them and sweep down from the forest. As if to confirm their fears, distant screaming and shouting emanated from the woods above and Cian looked nervously at his brother the King. 'What is that racket?'

'Mischief,' the older man said and listened to the far-off crash of weapons and screeches of the dying. Both brothers still stared up at the torches on the hill though they were unable to see the figures that had borne them through the trees. 'They did say that they would kill the foreigners.'

'Should we get back across the river?' Cian asked nervously. 'We should get back across the river.'

Donnchadh ignored his brother. 'What the hell is frigging happening up there?' As he strained his eyes in an attempt to penetrate the blinding gloom all hell broke loose around him. Spears and swords fell on Osraighe necks from all sides. In the darkness their assailants were like vengeful ghosts that Donnchadh could not see.

'Die!' attackers called in the Gaelic tongue, throwing themselves into the fight like madmen in the darkness. 'Die!'

Donnchadh grabbed his brother and threw him to the ground just as a spear blazed over his head. The King of the Osraighe dealt a savage kick to the assailant's chest, sending him sprawling back towards the tented meeting place shouting something in a language that Donnchadh did not understand. He cursed when he understood that the men had hidden in the half-collapsed temporary shelter.

'Damn it to frigging hell!' Donnchadh cursed and hauled Cian to his feet. 'They are behind us.' He turned around to see the five torches still flickering on the hillside. While the Osraighe had waited patiently for their king's answer the Uí Ceinnselaig had crawled silently towards them in the darkness.

'They are on both sides of us,' Cian shouted. 'Let's get out of here!' he screamed at his men who obeyed their captain's call and ran headlong down the slope.

'Diarmait betrayed us,' Donnchadh stammered as he swept a spear aside with his sword and looked through the darkness for someone to kill.

'Donnchadh, we need to get out of here,' Cian shouted as he grabbed his arm and dragged him into the night.

'We will see you tomorrow,' the King of the Osraighe screamed towards his enemies. 'We'll be back to burn you out of your damn wood.'

A spear sliced out of the shadows and crashed through one of the antlers which adorned his head. Slicing the bone in two, the spear thumped into the snow at Cian's feet. Donnchadh snarled again, in shock and anger and unbalance, and, like his few remaining warriors, ran for his life.

'Bás!'

Sir Robert FitzStephen shouted the Irish word for death again as he watched the King of the Osraighe flee through the gloom. Beside him Gilbert de Brienne began babbling happily to one of his friends. 'Quiet,' FitzStephen hissed, 'or they will realise that we are not Diarmait's men. Get back up the mountain,' he told the youngster. 'Do it quickly.' Gilbert moved to speak again but FitzStephen's growl stopped him and slowly he and his companions began to move back towards Dubh-Tir.

'Sounds like Miles did good work,' Fionntán said as he appeared beside him.

'Let's hope so,' FitzStephen replied. He had despatched his nephew to intercept Diarmait's traitorous delegation. All those men had to die if the plan was to work. 'If he hasn't succeeded,' he continued, 'then we might not live to see the morning.'

Fionntán was quiet for many moments as he considered the

Norman's words, stooping in the darkness to pick up a spear and a piece of antler. 'It was Meic Giolla Phádraig men at the bottom of the hill,' he said with venom. 'I almost killed their king as they fled …'

'It might have been better if you had,' FitzStephen told him with a half-smile and guided him up the hillside. 'But the survivors will report back with Diarmait's *answer*. My guess is Ruaidhrí will not be amused. Let's get back amongst the trees.'

They reached the five torches quickly. A rustle in the forest made the few Normans who had gone down the hillside go quiet and lift their weapons to the ready.

'It is Miles,' Fionntán said confidently as out of the darkness came twenty milites led by FitzStephen's nephew.

'You got them all?' FitzStephen asked.

'We got them all,' Miles replied and waved forward seven men, each bearing a body on his shoulder.

FitzStephen pointed down the hill to where the skirmish had taken place. 'Put the bodies down there and make it look like these men were in a fight with the Osraighe,' he told Miles's men as he stabbed out the torches in the deepening snow. 'Make sure you remove all the arrows from their bodies. Are Máelmáedoc Ua Riagain and Bishop Seosamh amongst the dead?' he asked his nephew.

'Only the bishop was sent to deliver the message,' Miles responded, making a cross over his chest and pointing to a body on the shoulder of Meiler FitzHenry.

'So what's our next move, Robert?' interrupted Fionntán.

'We wait for Diarmait to conclude that he has once again been betrayed,' FitzStephen replied. 'We wait and watch,' he said, 'and one way or another we get ready to battle for our lives.'

Daybreak came in slowly over the southern flatlands of the wintry Uí Ceinnselaig homeland. Hundreds of strips of smoke broke up the grey sky over the forest of Dubh-Tir while out on the windy river valley the Irish army looked up at the smoke and cursed their enemy who had obviously had a more comfortable night than they. Through chattering teeth they cursed the lack of fuel before clustering into whatever hidey-holes they could find to keep out the cruel cold.

Sir Robert FitzStephen stared out at the High King's army from the cliffs above the Norman camp. Below him Dubh-Tir stretched away to the west between the two ridges. It had been a restless night for the Norman but it had been worth it. After interrupting the meeting with Mac Giolla Phádraig, more snowfall had provided cover for FitzStephen to lead a small force down through the trees towards the river. Twenty or thirty Irishmen, who had crossed to find fuel for their fires, had died. As their screams had emanated across the water, Ruaidhrí's army had decided that it was safer to shiver through the night rather than face the precision of the Norman archers on the western bank. But FitzStephen was not done there and he had gone downriver to a ford. Communication lines between the many nations of the vast army opposing him had already started to fail and the Normans had found the crossing unguarded. From there he and Philip de Barri and their troops had crawled northwards until they had found the first line of pickets, who had been quickly and quietly slaughtered, before melting back over the river to safety. They had not lost a single man while behind them the Irish army had been left in uproar as they rallied to meet a night-time foe who had already disappeared. Later in the night Miles Menevensis and Meiler FitzHenry had led more arrow attacks across the river to leave the Irish in turmoil while the Normans had returned to the safety of the forest to sleep through the early hours.

Already in the half-light of the morning FitzStephen had been busy with last-minute preparations. Small fires had been set alight up and down the length of the woods to hide his army's deployments and inflate their numbers in the eyes of their enemy. Each commander had been contacted, his part in the plan discussed, and then he had ridden each path through the forest and had it cleared of snowfall. Nothing was to be left to chance.

'Cousin,' Walter de Ridlesford greeted him, his feet crunching into the snow as he approached. 'What a lovely morning to be alive.'

FitzStephen didn't even notice Walter's sarcasm. His interest was in the activity down by the river where the High King's army was stirring. 'Did you sleep?'

Ridlesford laughed and shook his head. 'And let our damn Ostmen allies slip away in the night? Not bloody likely. I heard some screaming during the night. Was there trouble?'

'Diarmait sent Bishop Seosamh to meet with High King Ruaidhrí's men at the edge of the forest,' FitzStephen replied.

Walter de Ridlesford gripped the lance hard so that his knuckles turned white. 'Are we betrayed?'

'It was a close-run thing,' he told his cousin, 'but I have driven a wedge between the conspirators that will suit our purposes. The bishop is dead, but our enemy will take the blame.'

'That must have been why Diarmait was making such a racket earlier this morning,' Walter replied, trusting that his cousin knew what he was doing.

'I heard,' FitzStephen replied. 'I don't think he will be conspiring with Ruaidhrí any time soon.'

The two men studied the wintery landscape silently for a number of moments. Their future in Ireland, which had seemed so clear after the conquest of Waesfjord, suddenly seemed strained and dangerous. But it was in neither man's nature to baulk before a fight, even when faced with such daunting odds. They were both of the brood of Nest, the Helen of Wales, and her descendants were all champions.

'Are the men ready to move out?' asked FitzStephen.

'They are,' Walter replied as he stared at the army opposing them. 'There are a powerful lot of them down there, cousin,' he said with a hint of concern, 'so you better have a damn good speech ready to fire up our troops. If not I am going to pull someone out of the line, thump the shit out of him, and threaten to do the same to anyone who doesn't fight well.'

FitzStephen laughed heartily. 'Forget the speeches then; I want to see one of the men beat you to within an inch of your life.'

Walter roared a raucous bellow of a laugh and slapped his friend on the back, chainmail rasping with recoil from the hearty strike. The two cousins made their way down the hillock towards their camp. The Gaels and Ostmen had already been moved away and hidden in the forest, fully versed as to FitzStephen's plan.

'I will get the men together,' Walter said as they approached the camp. The Normans and the small number of Flemings had remained in the camp throughout the night, as much for security as for comfort. A huge impassable swamp lay at the back of the camp, defending their rear while two wooden fences guarded the path up from the forest. Between these were tents and rudimentary houses made of felled wood with foliage roofs. And from one of those buildings came Princess Aoife. FitzStephen watched her as she slinked her way towards him, huddled beneath a fox fur cloak. Beneath it he knew was the supple body that he had dreamed about for so long. She stopped at the bottom of the bank and looked up at him. FitzStephen remembered his obligation and immediately jogged the few paces to join her, sweeping into his most dramatic bow.

'My Lady.'

'I have come to wish you luck in the battle today,' she told him. 'Is it not customary that we should embrace?' She held out her hand.

'Yes,' he stumbled, 'but it is not necessary if you do not want to.'

Aoife laughed sweetly and pulled him close to her. The fox fur pelt was soft against his face as he wrapped his arms around her. A single strand of her hair fell across his eye but all too soon she withdrew, brushing her lips across his cheek.

'Will you fight for me today, Sir Robert?' she asked. 'In Bristol, knights offered to fight for me in tourneys. They asked me for my favour, but I was told not to by my father's wife.' Her hand disappeared below her cloak returning with a small embroidered piece of linen used to tie her hair back. But today it was wild. She handed it to him. 'She said it was obscene, but I'd like you to have it if you will fight for me today?'

FitzStephen dropped his eyes to look at the piece of material. His heart was racing, his mind a blur. 'I will not fight for you, Lady,' he said as he stared at Aoife's gift. Immediately

Diarmait's daughter grimaced at the Norman's statement but said nothing as he raised his gaze to meet her eyes.

'I will not fight for you,' he repeated, 'for I fight for your father and my men. But I will win for you,' he said with a nervous smile.

Her steady, suspicious scrutiny made way for a coquettish smirk to break through. 'Make sure that you do,' she told him, 'for I will be greatly indebted to you forever.' With that she turned and walked away from him. He watched the beauty until she disappeared inside her dwelling just, he supposed, as she knew he would.

'Dammit,' he muttered. Dazed again by her presence, he walked back up the hillside to where his quickly forming army could see him. The small army of mercenaries, arrayed in colourful surcoats and brash chainmail, looked up at their leader. Some looked bored, annoyed that they had been asked to listen to FitzStephen's words. More were keen for a bloodcurdling call to arms that would make it known they could win no matter what. The army suddenly found their position in this foreign land unsure and dangerous. Since landing at Banabh they had known nothing except victory but, many wondered, how could they possibly hope to win with such massive odds stacked against them? It seemed like every farm in the land had been emptied to raise the army arrayed against them. What they wanted to see was confidence and fight from their commander. But all FitzStephen could think of was Aoife's words. In his hand he still held her favour. Did she realise his passion for her? Was she returning his interest? Either way FitzStephen was filled with a sudden surge of joy; he almost shouted out in exultation. Lifting his head he looked at his men with a smile plastered across his face. Now the words came to him!

'Men of Wales; Norman and Fleming, Cymri and Englishman, here we are for a proper fight at last!' He grinned at his men. Many looked nervous but a good number of them smiled back. They trusted him, despite everything that had befallen in Wales. He had given them a taste of victory and they still believed that he could provide them with more. 'And a great fight it will have to be – we face a host of the best warriors that Ireland can bring against us.' Beside him Walter de Ridlesford let out a scandalous snort of laughter which was echoed throughout the army. FitzStephen held up his hands. 'They are brave, these Irish, but we derive our descent from braver men still, Danes and Norse, and the Cymri of Wales. More importantly, we are also are bred from smarter men, the Franks and Flemings from the kingdoms across the sea. From one we have our native courage and the use of armour. From the other the skills and professionalism bred of many hardships.' FitzStephen watched as the warriors below him lifted their chins with pride as their various forbearers were mentioned. These were proud men, the cream of the warriors from the Welsh March, descendants of conquerors. 'We have left behind our native land,' he continued, 'not for the sake of pay or plunder, but by the promise of towns and lands to be granted to us and our heirs forever. Be sure that this is a land of promise, but we must also be aware that this is a kingdom of danger too. One of these two armies must die today and yet, if you avoid dishonour, either glory will illuminate your life or the memory of acclaim will follow your death.' Silence echoed amongst the Norman camp and he let it drag. 'A horde opposes us,' he gestured towards the dark wood, 'they are many, my friends, but we stand as one,' he shouted the last four words loudly, raising his fists towards the sky. His long banner, held by Walter de Ridlesford, billowed by his head, cracking loudly like a whip. But it went unheard as his shout was taken up, first by his cousins amongst the army, and then by the rest of the warriors.

'One,' they yelled. 'We stand as one.' They raised their weapons, clashed their shields, shook their banners, and those who had horns put them to their lips and blared them loudly.

Down in the river valley the kings, princes, and chieftains of Ireland heard the echoes of those battle cries and sensed that they were in for a busy day.

Everything was set for battle.

Eight thousand men of the kern were sent forward by Ruaidhrí

Ua Conchobair to sweep aside all opposition in one fell swoop. The men came from every nation in Ireland and they were led by the great warrior-king Donnchadh Mac Giolla Phádraig. The King of the Osraighe had wanted only his own troops to advance into the woods, led by his Flemish mercenaries, but Ruaidhrí had refused, commanding the foreigners to remain behind. *Political* was what the High King had called it.

'Frigging stupid is what I call it,' Donnchadh said out loud as he led his army up the snow-laden hill. 'Sending frigging farmers to fight when we have Flemings to call upon? Frigging westerners,' he said and shook his shaggy head, still adorned with his antler helm. Despite his misgivings Mac Giolla Phádraig stomped and at the head of his army. Ahead was a wall of trees but for two flickering blue banners at the extreme northern corner of the forest. Between them was the path. Everything about that route screamed *trap*, but Mac Giolla Phádraig pushed onwards. To his right, the cliffs of the northern ridge looked down dauntingly, worse perhaps because the King of the Osraighe did not know what to expect in the dark forest ahead.

'Don't worry,' Cian, the King's brother, told him confidently, 'I talked to the Fleming Prendergast last night and he told me what to expect.'

'And what is that, more frigging arrows and horses? Big frigging whoop.' Cian's silence told King Donnchadh that had been exactly what Prendergast had told him.

'He said that they will be sly as weasels and capable of absolutely anything,' Cian confirmed. 'He said to take nothing for granted.'

His lack of knowledge about what lay beyond the tree line made Donnchadh Mac Giolla Phádraig nervous. He had led raids on the tribes neighbouring his lands and he had fought in countless battles, but his memory of the Norman cavalry and archers tearing into his countrymen on the borders of the lands of the Osraighe remained with him.

'The trees are bound to make it too hard for them to shoot arrows, accurately at the least,' he muttered to his brother as they reached the edge of the woods where the foreigners had planted two blue banners with white stars upon them to guard a path into the trees. King Donnchadh made the sign to avert evil and rubbed his finger over the iron guard on his sword. 'And the terrain will make it impossible for them to fight on horseback,' he chewed on his lip and shook his head in uncertainty. 'Those are their main weapons – so why did they choose to make their stand in the trees and nullify them both?' he asked. 'It makes no sense.'

'Maybe they are scared. Maybe they are simply trying to hide from us?' replied Cian.

'They are frigging well up to something,' the King of the Osraighe replied forcefully. But he knew that he had no choice but to go on. To leave Diarmait and his foreigners skulking in the wood was to invite more attacks on the Osraighe. He had to smash them now while he had the support of Dubhlinn and Connacht at his side. God alone knew when he could count on their help again. Eight thousand was a vast army and surely, he thought, devoid of arrow and horse, the foreigners could not resist the High King's army? Taking a deep breath he hefted one of the Norman banners and cast it onto the ground. He then dealt with the other in a similar fashion. The King of the Osraighe then whipped out his member and began pissing on FitzStephen's star banner at his feet as the kern encouraged him. That done, he raised his voice and turned to address his army.

'In those trees is a bunch of foreigners from across the sea.' He gestured with his thumb into the thick, dark woods. 'They want to steal your frigging wives and they want your frigging cattle. They probably want to rape both of them too.' Shouts and yells of scorn and contempt came back from his army. 'And with them is the most detestable traitor that has ever lived – Diarmait Mac Murchada!' The men of the kern began cursing and shouting, booing the hated King of Laighin. 'Shall we kill them?' Mac Giolla Phádraig asked them. 'Shall we drive them back across the sea?' Most of the men shouted an affirmative and it echoed down the hillside. 'Will you help me spill foreign blood this morning?' A resounding *yes* sounded through the ranks. Even the men who could not hear his voice yelled their agreement, hefting their shields and spears, axes and skenes. 'Then follow me,' Mac Giolla Phádraig shouted, but he need not have done so as his inspired men surged past him and into the trees.

Donnchadh smiled and yelled encouragement as they passed him by. It would be a bloodbath, he decided. The foreigners had made a mistake by hiding in the forest and they would pay for it with their lives. His army were too many! King Donnchadh signalled to his derb-fine to join him. They alone were armed with proper weapons and several even had ancient Ostman helmets to protect their long-haired heads. As a group they advanced into the mesh of gnarled branches and boughs. Soon the whole of Donnchadh's eight thousand men were enveloped in the forest invisible to the rest of Ruaidhrí's army in the valley.

Progress in the tangle of trees and the wet, snowy ground was slow, and the noise of men cursing and fumbling could have raised the dead. The one path which the Normans had cut through the forest quickly became too tight for the eight thousand warriors and many left the road and began forcing their way through the web of twisting vegetation and sodden earth. It took nearly an hour for Donnchadh and his derb-fine to fight his way through a mile of undergrowth, and all of his men were having the same problem as they forged their way westwards. Branches seemed to grow from the very floor and intertwine to form formidable fences. Above them the treetops sagged and bent under the weight of snow and everywhere drips of water splattered the shivering warriors. Axes felled branches rather than enemy soldiers. Swords battered paths through undergrowth rather than past shields.

Donnchadh yelled in pain as a branch swept back and struck him, leaving a red mark across his face. He snarled at his mother's sister's great-nephew and stooped to pick up his sword from a soggy pile of moss where it had fallen from his grasp. Brambles tore at his sleeve. The King of the Osraighe was just thinking that he should stop the attack and go back to the river to admit his failure to Ruaidhrí when he spotted hundreds of his men crouching in the shadows ahead.

'What's going on,' he snarled and tripped on a wet root protruding from the ground. 'Why have they frigging stopped?'

Donnchadh, followed by the Mac Giolla Phádraig derb-fine, walked forward to where a group of men skulked in the shadows of the undergrowth. In front of them was a vast open space, otherworldly and out of place in comparison to the suffocating forest through which the army had just passed. Thousands of newly hewn tree stumps jutted out of the snowy ground.

The Normans had been busy, Donnchadh thought, and had cut down a vast swathe of the forest, carting off the timber, to where he could not tell. It was eerie amongst the otherwise heavily forested Dubh-Tir and the effect was increased by the lowered tones of his warriors who stared out at several hundred yards of open ground where wraith-like mist clung close to the cold, uneven floor.

'What are they up to?' asked the suspicious King of the Osraighe, but before he or his derb-fine could assess the danger his warriors began edging out of the forest and into the cleared land. 'What are they doing? Call them frigging back,' he snarled at his brother. 'Get them back!' Donnchadh Mac Giolla Phádraig turned on his derb-fine. 'Get them out of that clearing now,' he shouted, pushing his way to the edge of the trees. 'Come back!' he yelled at the kern ahead of him, waving his arms. The warrior-farmers either could not understand him or refused to believe that there was any reason to be scared. After a few seconds of shouting King Donnchadh conceded that his army would not obey him, and instead looked up and down the length of the bight in the forest, waiting for the appearance of horsemen who he believed would, at any second, tear his army apart. He held his breath in expectation of disaster. All his men were in the open but still no-one attacked. Within a few seconds his apprehension began to fade and he took a few steps to join his men, hesitantly and still eying the land to his left and right.

'Perhaps we surprised them?' Cian shrugged as he read the question which plagued his brother. Donnchadh grimaced, still nervously looking over both shoulders, as he led his derb-fine further into the hewn forest.

'Come on then,' the King said. 'It'll be impossible to stop them now anyway.' He set a quick pace, crunching through the snow, still expecting the sudden thump of horses' hooves to herald an attack. He knew that he had to get back in control of his men who, now that they had found easier terrain, had begun to move in a southerly direction rather than push back amongst the trees on the far side of the clearing.

'Why are they bunching up?' Donnchadh asked one of his derb-fine who simply shrugged in reply. Indeed rather than continue westwards as he had ordered, his army were slowing up and clustering into one group ahead of him. Minutes later he discovered why – they had blundered to the edge of a massive swamp, hidden amongst the trees and blocking their way further into the forest. Trapped between the cliffs to the north and the swamp ahead, they were forced southwards through the cleared forest.

'This is frigging ridiculous,' Donnchadh cursed. 'We need to turn them around …'

'Uh-oh,' interrupted Cian who stared ahead, shielding his eyes from the weak low sun.

'What?' his brother asked angrily.

'There's some sort of fortification to the south,' he replied with an outstretched arm pointing in that direction. 'It doesn't seem to be manned. Why would they leave it without defenders? Do you think they have fled?'

The King of the Osraighe grimaced as he sank up to his knees in marsh. 'I don't know,' he said as he pulled his soaking leg from the deep dark puddle. 'None of this makes any sense and I don't like it. Call them back. We are getting out of here,' he told his derb-fine, but they ignored him, staring open-mouthed towards the northern cliff tops instead. Splashes sounded around Donnchadh Mac Giolla Phádraig and he looked up at the approaching grey clouds.

'More damn sleet,' the King of the Osraighe declared. Or perhaps hail by the heavy sound of the drops falling on the soggy ground, he thought as he covered his eyes to stare into the bright grey sky.

'Donnchadh,' one of his derb-fine shouted, animated and

desperate. 'Get under cover!'

The King turned to look at the man, but his kinsman had fallen to the ground and had begun screaming. Blood was on the snow and hissing filled the air. Donnchadh Mac Giolla Phádraig turned and looked towards the northern ridge and immediately broke into a run for it was not hailstones that were falling from the sky but arrows. The Normans had known they were coming and the kern was trapped in the open.

'Loose,' Richard de la Roche shouted up on the cliffs. The bowmen released and quickly drew more arrows from the arrow bags at their right thighs. Notching the projectiles, they dragged the massive weapons back to their chins, raising the stave towards the sky while simultaneously noting the range and movement of their targets. Quivering arms and fingers held the weapons still as they waited for the order to release from Richard de la Roche. None of the archers really had to aim; the Gaels were so dense in the open ground below that the Normans and Flemings would struggle to miss. Alongside the archers, crossbowmen worked more diligently, finding targets as they presented themselves rather than adding to the arrow cloud that descended upon the kern.

Robert FitzStephen had ridden up to the cliffside to watch the ambush, but trusted his captains, Roche and Miles Menevensis, to destroy the High King's army. Watching the chaos happening below, he nodded appreciatively at their work. The Irish warriors were already fleeing back towards the trees to the south and east, defeated without even being able to fight back. Hungry, cold, and frustrated, the unarmoured men died in droves or fled hurriedly out of range. The archers cheered as Richard de la Roche shouted at them to cease loosing their arrows.

'Well done,' FitzStephen shouted from Sleipnir's back. He was delighted with his archers' work; eight thousand of Ruaidhrí's army were dead or had fled the field in disorder. He hoped that the damage inflicted upon the kern was such that the High King would fear to send any more troops into the trees, but he doubted it. A real king did not raise an army as large as Ruaidhrí had and then flee from four hundred men, not unless he wanted to be a laughing stock and lose the respect of his subjects. From his left, a rider approached, punching through the pine needles from the ridge to the east, hauling his small horse's head around the harsh barked trees at top speed. It was his brother, William the Welshman, pale faced and breathing hard, and he reined in beside him.

'Robert,' William said as he gasped in air, 'the kern are not reforming, but are fleeing back towards the river.'

FitzStephen offered his brother a skin of water and the younger man gratefully accepted the offer. William had been one of two younger men who FitzStephen had sent to the extreme ends of the two rocky ridges at the edge of the forest. Their responsibility was to watch for enemy movements and report back to their commander with information about where the next attack would land. If William's shattered appearance was anything to go by, the High King's army were coming again – and in force. William would not have left his position to alert him for any other reason.

'What approaches us and where?' asked FitzStephen.

'Ostmen of Dubhlinn, brother,' William said, 'a half mile to the south. They entered the forest just after the kern.'

FitzStephen frowned at the information. There were no paths through that part of the forest and it would take some time for the Ostmen to carve a way through. He closed his eyes and pictured where the next attack would fall. 'They will probably come across Walter de Ridlesford and the men of Waesfjord,' he told William who nodded in agreement. 'Go ahead of me and make contact with Walter,' he told his sweaty brother, 'and tell him what you saw. Tell him to keep to the plan. I will follow you soon.'

William nodded and drained the last remnants from the skin. Swiping a sleeve across his wet face, he took off at a trot through the snow-laden trees, urging his mount onwards as he disappeared down the steep mountain path.

Miles Menevensis appeared at FitzStephen's side, perhaps sensing the approaching danger from William the Welshman's manner. 'Robert?' he asked.

'It looks like Hasculv of Dubhlinn is headed for Walter's

position,' FitzStephen told him. 'I suspect your archers will be needed there.'

Miles nodded. 'It will take time to get there,' he said and pointed towards the forest below, 'and we will have to retrieve our arrows and bolts if we are to be of any benefit.'

'It will take time for Hasculv to force his way through the forest.'

Miles chewed on his lower lip. 'Is this their full attack?'

'Not yet, I think,' he told his nephew as he blew hot breath onto his cold hands, 'but there will be so many Ostmen arrayed against us that it will seem like every bastion of hell has been emptied of them.'

'God help us then,' the bishop's son replied.

FitzStephen did not answer, instead urging Sleipnir to turn and head westwards along the ridge away from the river. It was tough terrain but wild goats had walked the landscape for many years and had carved out a small track which, after several hundred yards along the cliff face, wound its way down the mountainside. The track was just wide enough for a horse or for two men walking side by side. However, when the pathway reached the forest floor it kept going westwards so FitzStephen had cut another narrow and secret path through the forest to allow his allies quick and easy movement through the vast expanse of trees that was Dubh-Tir. In a matter of minutes he had covered over a mile, whereas the enemy, bumbling through the dense forest, would be exhausted by the time they crossed swords with Diarmait's forces. FitzStephen urged his horse to a faster pace, turning east at another junction in the path. The trees narrowed so that they scratched his shoulders on both sides. At one stage he had to stop because the shield strapped to his back got tangled in a particularly wiry branch. It was only after fifteen minutes' riding that he finally pushed into a wide bight in the forest where four wooden shelters, complete with stone fires, protected almost ninety Norman cavalrymen, esquires, and milites, and their horses. Several other paths led away from the bight so that the Normans could combat any incursion into Dubh-Tir quickly. In contrast, FitzStephen reckoned that it would take Ruaidhrí's men several hours to hack their way into the part of the forest inhabited by his army.

'Sir Robert, sir,' Philip de Barri stood and waved at his cousin from outside one of the shelters. FitzStephen returned the small gesture. Others nodded their heads or lifted their chins to greet their commander.

FitzStephen jumped down from his courser and greeted his troops. 'Keep your seats,' he added quickly as they stood to receive him.

'I hope you haven't come to tell us that you have a job for us?' asked old Hugh de Caunteton. It had begun snowing again and all his warriors looked reluctant to leave the comfort of their firesides for the cold and wet of the forest.

Grinning, FitzStephen quickly described Richard de la Roche's easy victory of the Irish kern as he crouched by the fire warming his hands and pulling his cloak close around his shoulders. 'We horsemen have not had a great deal to do in Ireland as yet,' he told his men, 'but I think that by nightfall our conrois will have tested our spears and driven our enemy from this place. Swordwork will keep us warm in any event,' he joked and his men murmured their agreement and started milling around, issuing orders, arming themselves, or seeing to their coursers' needs.

FitzStephen smiled proudly as he left them to their preparations. He prayed that his tactics would not let them down. Doubt still assaulted him, but he could think of no other way to prepare his army and so he leapt back into the saddle and trotted out of the bight into more land cleared of trees. Following the curve of the forest northwards, he found the thousand-strong army of Waesfjord Norse gathering behind the fortifications. FitzStephen slowed his horse to a walk as he passed the ranks of bearded warriors from his newly conquered lands far to the south. He nodded to some and grinned at others but few returned the gestures. None of them wanted to be in Dubh-Tir with the Normans, living in mud huts in the depths of winter. They wished to be safe behind the walls of Waesfjord, enjoying the warmth from their own hearths with good food in their bellies and their wives by their sides.

FitzStephen found Walter de Ridlesford below the rampart

shouting expletives at one Ostman warrior, for what he could not tell and, seemingly, nor could the recipient of his cousin's rancour. FitzStephen had created a long wall from the trees and debris which his army had cleared elsewhere in the forest. To the north the five foot-high rampart was defended by bog while the land to its front fell downhill to a small stream. More hewn tree stumps meant that when the exhausted Ostmen of Dubhlinn finally exited the forest they would be faced by intimidating defences manned by a thousand Waesfjord axemen.

Walter de Ridlesford stopped his rant when he saw FitzStephen approach, simultaneously waving the Ostman warrior off to join his compatriots. 'I caught him lying on his arse in the forest,' Walter told his cousin. 'These Ostmen aren't bad lads, they are just bloody lazy.'

'Have you ever seen two sets of these Northmen fight a battle?' FitzStephen asked Walter who shook his head slowly, as if he had never considered it. 'There is nothing lazy about it, believe me: it will be battle-axe against battle-axe. They form a shield wall and cut lumps out of each other until the weaker one breaks,' he continued. 'Even the winner is ruined by the end of one their fights.'

'I have held ramparts against worse than them,' Walter said with an indignant growl.

'In any event, keep your big, bald head safe. Hold them here,' he stressed, 'and let my cavalry do their job.'

Walter nodded. 'As long as they don't have their longships with them we won't be outflanked,' he joked and jerked a thumb towards the deep swamp to the north.

'I had better go.' FitzStephen leant down and shook his cousin's hand. 'We are relying on you, Walter,' he told him as he swept Sleipnir around and trotted him down the ranks of armoured men.

'Proud men of Waesfjord,' he shouted in French, certain that most would have some grasp of the foreign language, 'today we have a great opportunity to dent the arrogant, proud, and haughty noses of the men of Dubhlinn.' Some men pricked up their ears at the statement. FitzStephen knew that the two Ostman towns were trading rivals. In most affairs the more northern of the two longforts was by far more successful. This inferiority had bred a keen dislike of Dubhlinn in the Waesfjord Norse. In the distance drums sounded and more than one warrior's eyes flicked towards the noise emanating through the snowflake-burdened forest. 'We have a chance to send these Danes back to their homes with the knowledge that the men of Waesfjord will no longer roll over in the face of their arrogance,' Robert FitzStephen continued. 'We can show them that the men of Waesfjord are hardier, steadier, and tougher than any man of Dubhlinn, and that any one of our warriors can bring down five of theirs'.' He had not thought that they would cheer, and they did not disappoint, but the Waesfjord Norse did look more motivated to fight as they stood huddling in their cloaks against the cold.

FitzStephen continued his course down the long line of warriors and cantered the last twenty yards back towards the cavalry in the large bight.

The trap was set for Hasculv Mac Torcaill and it was almost time for the men of Dubhlinn to spring it.

'Hold,' FitzStephen shouted down the line of horsemen. The great beasts were excited, sensing that they were going to be permitted to run and to fight. Like their riders they were energized by the thought of battle. They were ready for action and confident, but still FitzStephen held them back. 'Steady!'

'Hold,' his lieutenants echoed his command.

'Remember what you have been taught and keep your discipline,' FitzStephen told the milites. He had lifted his masked helm away from his face so that they could hear him. 'If they come, you keep your horses moving and do not get drawn into a fair fight, we kill then retreat. Understood?' He knew that if his men concentrated on the straightforward tasks of battle they would be victorious – stab, defend, keep your horse shifting, withdraw, attack – it was simple but effective unless the men began to be distracted by thoughts of glory, riches, and personal triumph. Beneath him his bay, Sleipnir, strained against the grip of his legs.

'Why don't they attack?' Philip de Barri asked. 'Look at

them sitting over there,' he complained, pointing his lance at the edge of the forest.

If anything the snow was getting heavier, but through it FitzStephen could see the Konungr of Dubhlinn, Hasculv Mac Torcaill, gesticulating wildly at the fortifications. Up and down the line of trees, bearded men, some with armour but all clothed against the winter cold, peered out and awaited their king's decision.

'Why don't they attack?' Philip moaned again.

'I wouldn't were I in his position,' FitzStephen told his kinsman, who looked aghast at his words. The cavalry had taken up position to the right of the rampart as soon as the enemy scouts had appeared at the edge of the forest. A hundred yards of open land lay between them and Hasculv's army but FitzStephen did not hide, awaiting a moment to ambush. Instead he kept his horsemen circling threateningly in full view of the enemy. Steam rose from the animals' backs in the frigid conditions and FitzStephen fancied that it must seem to the Ostmen like the Devil's wild huntsmen had been let loose to threaten their flank.

'I can't believe they won't fight,' Philip complained as he trotted behind his uncle.

'Hasculv is no fool,' FitzStephen told him as he rose and fell in and out of the saddle. Working the horse kept him and his men warm in the ever-worsening weather. 'If he attacks the wall he leaves his back open to attack by our horsemen. That will force him to bunch up and then he will be helpless to our archers –'

'But we don't have any archers here,' Meiler FitzHenry interrupted from behind Philip.

FitzStephen nodded. 'And hopefully Hasculv will not discover that fact until it is too late.'

Philip grunted irritably. 'I still think he should attack.'

But Hasculv did not attack, and nor did he retreat, merely staying in the trees as the swirling snow gathered on the ground.

FitzStephen soon felt confident enough to send half his men back to their camp to refresh their horses and to get some food and warmth into their bodies. Still the Ostmen did not attack.

Philip de Barri and Meiler FitzHenry, who had become fast friends since landing in Ireland, passed the time by talking about hawking. Their argument about which was the best sporting bird – Philip's prized sparrowhawk or Meiler's father's gyrfalcon – was taken up by all the remaining members of the conrois and led to a similar discussion about which was the best horse in the ranks of the Norman army. They decided that FitzStephen's Sleipnir was certainly the quickest, but that Maurice de Prendergast's Blanchard was unmatched in looks and scope. That neither Prendergast nor his white horse remained in the army was seemingly neither here nor there. FitzStephen had just started to tell his warriors about his favourite courser, Sanglac, when Miles Menevensis and Richard de la Roche finally arrived at the barricade with their troop of archers and crossbowmen, and a full complement of arrows and bolts at their side. FitzStephen, sensing Hasculv's indecisiveness, ordered them to begin shooting indiscriminately into the trees from behind the barricade. Hasculv's worst fears had been realised and, ten minutes later, the entire Ostman army melted back through the trees towards the High King's camp.

'Track them,' FitzStephen told Richard de la Roche. 'They are certain to return.'

Hasculv Mac Torcaill cursed and squirmed as his cousin bound his arm to stop him bleeding to death. A Norman arrow had scored a deep wound in his forearm as he had left the forest.

The Konungr of Dyflin had believed that he had left the enemy behind him at the rampart, but as his army had made their way through the mesh of vegetation and bog, the arrows had fallen again upon his warriors. His axemen had chased off the perpetrators but they had quickly reformed and had dropped another wave of arrows on his rearguard a few minutes later. Each time he had chased them they had darted away from the danger, never staying in the same place for long enough for the Ostmen to adapt and meet them head on.

'How many did we lose?'

Hasculv's question was directed at one of his jarls called Ingjald, but the warrior shook his head dimly and looked around at the men still moving back downhill towards the river camp.

'That bad?' the Konungr of Dyflin replied and bent down and picked up a handful of snow, sucking the moisture from between his fingers as it melted. He was furious and exhausted. It had taken almost an hour of back-breaking effort to reach the clearing where the Norse rampart had awaited them. Then his army had waited in the snow, unable to do anything until the menace of the archers had forced him to withdraw. The outward journey through the forest had been almost as difficult and he had lost many warriors to the enemy's bows.

Hasculv cursed again as the bandage was tightened around his injured limb and he pushed the young man away forcefully. 'Find me some beer,' he demanded of his cousin.

Horse hooves padded up behind the konungr, but he didn't even bother turning around to greet High King Ruaidhrí Ua Conchobair.

'What the hell happened in there?' the High King demanded of him. 'You outnumbered them by four to one!'

Hasculv calmly got to his feet and walked over to Ruaidhrí, throwing away the half-melted handful of snow. He suddenly grabbed the High King's bridle and held it fast, drawing a short sword from his side with his injured arm and placing it under Ruaidhrí's armpit.

'Shut your mouth or I will kill you, you goddamn Vestman bastard.' Hasculv was livid and refused to back down even when Ruaidhrí's derb-fine closed in with drawn swords and sharp threats. Seeing his konungr in peril, Jarl Ingjald and his warriors quickly hefted their arms and moved to their master's side.

Hasculv ignored them all, his eyes locked on the High King of Ireland. 'Fight your own bloody battles, you puppy. I didn't come here to stand and watch Diarmait make a fool of you. My people are going home.' With that Hasculv turned towards Ruaidhrí's six kinsmen and spat at their feet in disdain before walking away.

The High King kicked his horse to cut him off. 'If you leave now and I lose this campaign, be assured that Diarmait will come for you,' he warned Hasculv, 'and if they do I won't be there to stop the Normans from pulling down your walls and killing every person inside your Godless shanty town.' Ruaidhrí raised his eyebrows, waiting for Hasculv's answer, but the Ostman knew as well as Ruaidhrí that Dubhlinn would certainly be on Diarmait's mind, especially after Robert FitzStephen had shown that a city's walls were no barrier to his army's aggression. Diarmait would never forget the violation of his father's body by Hasculv's grandfather. That was a hurt that could only be swabbed by the balm of vengeance, and Mac Torcaill knew it.

'So we go back in there. Everybody at once,' Hasculv insisted, 'and we kill these damned foreigners once and for all.'

'Agreed,' stated Ruaidhrí.

'But this time we go straight for their camp up on the southern ridge. No messing about "scouring the woods",' Hasculv said, remembering Ruaidhrí's instructions of the day before. 'This time we do it my way – a direct assault on the Norman camp. We soak up any damage inflicted by their archers and stay together when threatened by cavalry. If we do that then Diarmait will have no hope of resisting.'

'Agreed,' Ruaidhrí nodded his head.

'And when we capture their fort, I get to kill Robert FitzStephen,' Hasculv snarled. 'Is that understood?'

'Agreed,' High King Ruaidhrí said with not a little pity for the Norman. 'Prendergast's archers will lead.' He wanted this siege over one way or the other. He had developed a runny nose and his back ached from lying on the freezing ground for too many nights. He was sick of being cold all the time. 'When we get to their camp, you may lead the attack,' he told Hasculv. Suddenly motivated, the Konungr of Dyflin began sending orders through his followers who crunched away through the snow.

High King Ruaidhrí looked up at the dark forested walls of Dubh-Tir and feared what would happen if he sent his men back amongst its tight, suffocating environment. Both of his attacks had stumbled into traps laid by Robert FitzStephen. They had faltered and been forced to flee. Ruaidhrí ran his hand through his ever-thinning hair. Worry was his worst enemy and it was affecting him once again. He knew now that he had to be prepared for horsemen and archers in the cleared parts of the forest, and be ready to face fences made from the felled trees. He would lead the army himself and pray that the Fleming's mercenary archers would be enough to hold back the horsemen.

'Prendergast has frigging gone.' Donnchadh Mac Giolla Phádraig of the Osraighe ran up to Ruaidhrí, muck and snow flying everywhere as he stumbled forward. 'That frigging Fleming took my frigging money and has gone.'

The High King did not even bother answering and just shook his head disbelievingly. His whole campaign against Diarmait was unwinding before his eyes – the weather had made it uncomfortable, his enemies had proved unresponsive to bribery, and the Normans were prepared to hunt his army like animals through the depths of the forest. And now the Flemings, his best troops, had fled. Ruaidhrí exhaled strongly and looked around at his army, assembling on the riverbank ready to assault the fastness of Dubh-Tir. He felt the anger rise in his chest. He could not lose face or all his cowed enemies would rise in rebellion again. Ruaidhrí made a sign to avert evil in the direction of Dubh-Tir.

'Get the army ready to assault,' he told his cousin as he stared at Diarmait's forest refuge. His army would soak up all the damage that the Normans would inflict, try to limit it if possible, but forge ahead and take the enemy apart piece by piece, swarming over whatever defences they had prepared. He would kill them all.

There was no other outcome that the Ruaidhrí could imagine, for he was the High King of Ireland and Lord of Teamhair na Ri, and he was leading his army towards victory.

The entire army of the High King was coming into Dubh-Tir. Norman scouts spread throughout the forest raced through the trees by secret routes to tell their commander of their approach.

'Their progress is slow but they are coming straight at our camp,' Richard de la Roche told his captain as he stitched a small wound on Meiler FitzHenry's chin. 'Mixed Ostmen and Gaels from what I saw,' Roche said and raised his eyebrows in a concerned fashion, 'thousands of them.'

The highest form of the hunt had eight parts, FitzStephen reminded himself. The great beast that was Ruaidhrí's army had run out of energy and had turned to face the hunting Normans, he thought. It was time to deliver the killing blow.

'They will pick up one of the paths which we laid?'

'On course,' Richard confirmed. The Normans had cut a maze of paths from the trees of Dubh-Tir. Some of the paths, like those around the swamp, had been designed to allow the archers and cavalry to be used to their best capability while others had been carved to provide rapid response to the High King's incursions. But most had been felled to allow the enemy to enter the forest into areas that the Normans were prepared to defend.

'"It is vital that the man who is not strong should be cunning",' said FitzStephen to no-one in particular. The battlefield would either be their saviour or their grave, he thought as he turned back towards Richard de la Roche. 'Take ten archers and pepper them from distance,' he said. 'Enrage them, Richard, and lead them onto our spears.' The Fleming nodded his head and left the tent, wishing that he had as much confidence in the plan as his commander.

FitzStephen sat back on the crudely made bench in the wooden shelter. He still had concerns, mostly regarding Diarmait and his conniving aide Máelmáedoc Ua Riagain, but he knew those problems were outside his control. All he could do was fight and send the enemy back to their homes to tell horrific stories of what happened when you attacked a Norman knight. The board was set, the pieces were moving, and Robert FitzStephen refused to be ejected from Ireland.

Even the dense forest fought against the High King's army. Straggling vines wound around twisted trees and hedges of weeds to impair the progress of the many nations of Ireland. They forced their way through the undergrowth and banked snow. The Ostmen of Dubhlinn led the way, tearing a path of a sort with their axes while below them the ground was a mixture of frozen earth, which turned many ankles, and squirming, stinking bog which made progress so desperately slow. It took almost an hour to get just a half mile into the forest; thousands of the finest warriors that Ireland had to offer cursed and pushed, slashed and slid into the unknown a yard at a time.

'Good God,' Ruaidhrí Ua Conchobair shouted as he slipped, managing to steady himself by clinging to the nearest tree. He tried to walk, but his feet could find no purchase and slipped below him as if he were dancing a jig. The High King cursed and hugged the trunk all the tighter. Suddenly he felt the whole tree shudder violently. A huge crack rang through the forest as a barrage of arrows flew past, striking six men who had been following the High King. Ruaidhrí let go of the trunk and rolled into a puddle as the wounded men stumbled and screamed in pain. The alarm was raised but not before another volley of arrows pumped into his army. Ruaidhrí was soaked and mucky from head to foot. Blinded, he was unaware of the men who streamed past him to fight the enemy hidden in the trees. More screaming indicated that further injury had been caused to his warriors.

'Stop! Ignore them,' Ruaidhrí shouted at the men who continued to charge off to engage the enemy. 'We push on into the forest.' He wiped the water and muck from his face and watched as, in the distance, colourfully clothed Normans retreated. Ten minutes later screaming at the back of the column told the High King that the Normans had struck again, but he disregarded them and kept the army together, pushing forward towards the Norman bastion. Soon they broke into a large clearing and the men at the vanguard stopped to await Ruaidhrí's orders, fearful of another ambush.

'Get moving,' Tigernán Ua Ruairc shouted, but the army refused to budge, distrustful of their leader's judgement in light of their earlier attempts to scour the woods of their enemies. In the end, Ruaidhrí ordered several men of his derb-fine forward to scout the way ahead, rather than lead the whole army into danger. They nervously scampered into the clearing, crouching behind snowy tree stumps searching the shadows of the enemy. With his own kinsmen scouting the path, Ruaidhrí led his troops forward.

'You actually want to follow their path?' Donnchadh Mac Giolla Phádraig shouted at the High King. 'What about the cavalry, their archers? It's obviously a frigging trap!'

Ruaidhrí did not answer immediately. He was getting ever angrier as the day went on. It was already approaching the late afternoon and the winter sun was struggling to pierce the tree line above them. But if they were going to break Diarmait and his Flemings he wanted it to be today. He could not understand how Diarmait could choose to live in such awful conditions rather than live in peace under his rule. He had extended his hand to the King of Laighin only to have it slapped away.

He had been insulted and he could not allow that to stand.

'It ends today,' Ruaidhrí told the King of the Osraighe. 'We scout ahead, we stay together, and we get this over with, fast and hard.' Donnchadh Mac Giolla Phádraig shook his head but, under pressure from the High King, led his men onto the path ahead. It was at least thirty feet wide but as they slowly crept westwards, the clearing narrowed until it would only allow four men to pass shoulder to shoulder. Progress again became frustratingly slow as a log jam formed as the huge amount of men waited. To the south Ruaidhrí kept his eyes on the forested cliffs which loomed threateningly above his army. Twice he could have sworn he spotted a glint of sunlight on metal and the colourful outline of a Norman surcoat, but as soon as he looked up it was gone. He tried to keep his and his derb-fine's spirits up but it was difficult as he was so uncomfortable. When the High King addressed a member of the kern he found only terror and tiredness in the man's eyes, not the spirit to fight. It did not help when the scouts led them down the wrong path. They had come to a junction in the path and Ruaidhrí, unwilling to split his army, chose the wider of the two paths which led south. Ten minutes later it narrowed and soon after that it came to an abrupt end at a flooded bog formed from a stream redirected by a Norman dam. Men looked at their High King and scowled at his stupidity.

'He does not know what he is doing,' Donnchadh Mac Giolla Phádraig told Tigernán Ua Ruairc with a shake of his head. 'He will lead us all to ruin.'

The King of Breifne did not disagree, but he had other objectives in entering Dubh-Tir. 'Diarmait is close,' Tigernán said. 'He cannot be allowed to escape again. So we press on as Ruaidhrí says.'

The light was already failing and the snow beginning to fall as they turned back to take up the other route through Dubh-Tir. They were climbing now, higher and higher into the Black Mountains and the ascent was also taking its toll on the Gaels and Ostmen.

'Where are they?' Ruaidhrí asked one of his cousins. 'Why do they not attack?' The anticipation of the fight to come was worse than the battle itself. 'We are almost at their gates!'

'I don't know,' the man answered, 'but the path is narrowing again.'

In fact the hewn trail had tapered to such a small gap that it seemed inevitable that they had taken another wrong turn, but Ruaidhrí pressed on nonetheless, his army spilling into the forest on either side of the path, and walking into a wide break in the wood. The coniferous trees had been cleared for two hundred feet in every direction by the Normans. In the snow and the still cold air, the bight in the forest looked otherworldly, reminding Ruaidhrí of the stories of the magic and mythical people who had ruled Ireland before the coming of the Gaels. The other folk had dwelt in such places, raised barrows lived and in the midst of moody bogs, and no good had ever come to anyone who had found themselves in their old haunts. Around him, the High King could see men crossing their chests as they too recognised the danger from inhuman mischief.

The scouts were the first men into the wide bight and they sensibly skirted the edge of the forest in both directions to discover any new threat from their crafty enemy. The Normans had turned this part of the Dubh-Tir into cavalry country and the scouts did not want to be caught out in the open if any new ambush was sprung. Eventually they shouted the all clear and the rest of the army slowly pushed through the gap. Ruaidhrí Ua Conchobair was among the first and he moved southwards towards a one hundred feet gap in the trees beyond which, he saw, lay the Norman fortifications huddled between the cliffs.

Ruaidhrí gaped as he stared at the defences. Two earthen palisades with yawning entrenchments dug before them, and behind them hid warriors who began yelling insults at the newly arrived enemy in their foreign tongue. They screamed defiance and waved their weapons. Horns blared and rattled in the cold air. A war song began to pick up noise as more and more of the foreigners joined in with its rousing foreign tune.

Ruaidhrí blanched, but it was not because of the din emanating from the Norman camp. He had never encountered anything like that which stretched out before him. Deep pits and sharpened wooden stakes split the land and would force his army to divide during an assault on the citadel. The High King of Ireland had seen war of many kinds – barriers guarding a pass or a river crossing, a huge fortified town, warfare on every conceivable terrain – but he had ever seen such a dramatic construction as that which faced him in the depths of Dubh-Tir. Ruaidhrí shivered and not because of the cold. Despite his vast superiority in numbers, he feared defeat. What other surprises did these sly Normans have waiting, the High King wondered?

He did not have to wait long for the answer. Behind him the screaming had already begun.

The screams came not from the dying, but from the wild warriors of the Uí Ceinnselaig who burst from a hidden path to assault the flank of the High King's army. The nervous Ostmen of Dubhlinn had flooded into the wide bight behind the men of Connacht and had formed up to await instructions at the point furthest away from the Norman fortifications. They had suffered at the hands of the enemy already that day and were not willing to put themselves in danger so soon after their mauling. As they had formed up they paid little heed to the small gap in the trees in the western corner of the clearing.

'Normans.' Konungr Hasculv Mac Torcaill of Dyflin had laughed in derision as he and his army had taken up position in the bight. 'They care more about their pretty dresses than their weapons,' he told his jarls as they stared at the defences which heaved with colourful banners and garish surcoats. The whole forest seemed to reverberate with noise.

'That's it,' he shouted in his enemies' direction, 'keep singing, you bloody minstrels! We shall see what song you sing when my axe is at your neck.' As he cocked his head back to laugh, Domhnall Caomhánach launched the attack on the rear of the Ostman army.

The Uí Ceinnselaig had come silently through the heavy ferns and gorse, hidden from their enemy by the bombastic display from the Normans. Then they had risen from the seemingly impenetrable depths of foliage, covered in moss and mud and had attacked suddenly and ferociously. Five hundred men from the Uí Ceinnselaig slashed sadistically through the enemy like a monster from the darkest depths of Dubh-Tir, their feral screams sounding just a split second before the first sword-strokes fell on Ostman necks.

'Vestmen,' Hasculv shouted and began issuing orders to the men nearest to him. Warriors were already down and more were dying as the lightning attack continued to send the Ostmen reeling backwards into the middle of the clearing. 'Get to my standard,' Hasculv shouted and pointed to his black banner bearing the ring of Thorir which stood behind him. 'Form shield wall,' he cried. It would act as a rallying point for his army who ran this way and that in utter chaos. Within seconds Hasculv had locked shields with his subjects and ordered the advance towards the enemy who had attacked them. Usually it took warriors many minutes to work up the courage to advance in a shield wall, but here the enemy were a rabble of disordered kern; easy pickings for the determined Ostmen. The men from Dubhlinn advanced without hesitation, chanting their war songs so that they were in step and encouraging each other to perform great deeds in battle. Ahead the Irish attack had stalled as the Ostmen outside the shield wall regrouped and fought back. The shield wall poured forward inexorably and Hasculv's men shouted warning to their folk to get out of the way lest they be trampled. Soon the Uí Ceinnselaig would feel Dubhlinn's vengeance, and anyone caught between the shield wall and their target would be in peril. But suddenly, before their eyes, the Vestmen began melting back into the western folds of the forest, leaving countless eviscerated bodies behind them. Many of the Gaels took the small path but most simply poured through the trees, splashing through bog and reed, leaping light-footed, laughing and whooping over snowy fern and frozen briar.

'No,' Hasculv screamed in frustration and took off after his enemy in a fit of rage, breaking the stability of the shield wall. But his people were with him. Unlike the Uí Ceinnselaig, the men of Dubhlinn were encumbered by shields, helmets, and heavy chainmail, and this made progress slow as they splashed through the muddy, wet ground and stopped to disentangle themselves from the thick undergrowth. The Ostmen needed blood to sate their anger but the narrow path would allow only one at a time and either side of the track was impassable to the armoured men. They were cold, tired, and frustrated but mostly they were angry that they had been humbled by the tiny army of Norman newcomers and their ragtag band of Gaels and Waesfjord Norse.

The Uí Ceinnselaig tribesmen easily stayed ahead of Dubhlinn vengeance, always just out of their grasp as they ran bare-chested through the forested path where drops of melting snow splashed on sagging ferns and dripped onto Ostman steel.

Hasculv snarled as he followed, his circular shield wrapped on his back and his axe in hand. It could not have been more than a few hundred yards before the path, which curled southwards towards the mountains, opened up again into another clearing under the cliffs. To their left, the ranks of hewn trees ran back towards the western wall of the Norman encampment and Hasculv watched as his prey, the kern of the Uí Ceinnselaig, scampered towards its safety.

The konungr cursed and ground his teeth in fury at their escape. Yet he had the presence of mind to halt his men for fear of an attack by cavalry if he led his men into the open ground before the wall. Again Hasculv was struck by the eerie atmosphere in the areas cleared by the Normans. Small fires burned there, distributed amongst the felled trees, and partially blocked Hasculv's view away to the east. As his men jostled impatiently behind him, Hasculv hesitated and lifted his helmeted head to smell the small breeze. His nostrils burned in the cold air but he sniffed again attempting to get sense of horsemen hidden upwind. The Norman esquires had laid a huge pile of horse dung about twenty paces from where Hasculv stood and he could not identify any sign of the big beasts over its stench, never mind see over it. The small fires also disrupted his sense of smell, however, when he arched his head around the trees he could see right to the timber walls of the fort to his left and, through the strips of smoke, almost for a mile in the other direction. No cavalry was in view and he allowed himself a moment to relax.

Ingjald laid a hand on his back. 'Where are the horsemen?'

'Probably getting ready to attack Ruaidhrí back in the bight,' Hasculv replied, prodding his thumb back over his shoulder. Even so, the konungr was cautious as he led his men out into the open. He quickly ordered a shield wall to be formed, three ranks thick and stretching across the wide clearing from the cliffs to the forest. 'Rear rank turn around and watch our backs,' he called. 'Ingjald is in charge. The rest of you, come with me to assault the Norman position.' Before he turned to join the attack Hasculv had one final look down the clearing away from the wall. He again sniffed the air for the distinctive smell of horseflesh but he could identify none over the strong reek of the dung pile. The long strip of empty countryside could not hide any cavalry, he decided. His Ostmen needed no order from the konungr and advanced as one with a roar, beating their steel weapons on the iron bosses of their shields, and chanting death threats towards their enemy as they stomped through the snow. The wooden stockade which faced them was stoutly built and was protected on one flank by high ground, but there was a small gap which Hasculv had spotted between the two defensive walls, a gap through which the Uí Ceinnselaig taoiseach, who had attacked him, had led his men. Behind the wall, the Norse had fallen back to let the Gaels through and were now struggling to reorder their shield wall to meet the rapidly approaching threat from Hasculv's men. The Konungr of Dyflin knew that his men would never have a better chance of taking the fortified encampment and shouted his men forward.

'Kill them, murder them, and maim them!' Hasculv shouted, and his men reacted to his calls, breaking into a small jog while keeping their shields locked together. The distance between the three lines of men stretched as the braver men, who had automatically taken up a place in the front rank, ran towards the gap. The second and third groups were not so keen to begin the slaughter and they did not commit themselves so easily, hoping that the front rank would deal with the Waesfjord Norse and that they would not have to risk their lives. Konungr Hasculv Mac Torcaill was amongst the brave men in the front rank, pounding the handle of his battle-axe on his circular shield. He summoned up the battle rage as he stomped forward extolling the names of his forefathers and cursing the enemy.

'*Oskilgetinn*,' he hissed through gnashing teeth. '*Gamla lombungr, sugandi toti tik madr.*' His eyes fixed on where the men of Waesfjord still struggled to reform their defensive line. A big bald Norman stood bareheaded in the middle of the line with a pale blue surcoat emblazoned with a silver beast of some kind. He shouted at the Norse and gesticulated wildly to get them into order. A Norman to kill, Hasculv thought with a smile and deliberately aimed at the man. He would prove that the foreigners were not unbeatable. He would take out their leader, whoever he was, himself.

Suddenly two men on Hasculv's left stumbled and fell on their faces. Another man on the Konungr of Dyflin's right cried out as he too collapsed into the snow with but a shout. Up and down the line more men ruined the structure of the shield wall by falling to their faces.

'Shields up,' Hasculv screamed. 'Close the gaps.' He assumed that some of the dreaded Fleming archers had shot from a place unseen. Gaps had appeared in their formation and if that was not remedied before they locked arms with the Normans they would be easy prey for the enemy. The whole shield wall stopped and raised their arms above their heads, anticipating further attack. But none came; there were no tell-tale thuds as arrows pierced flesh or rebounded off armour and wooden shields, no whistles were heard as the arrows scorched through the sky. Hasculv could hear armoured feet coming towards them and he lowered his shield so that he could see. Before him, the Waesfjord Norse had come out of their fortress and were standing just twenty paces away from his shield wall hurling insults at the men of Dubhlinn. He gritted his teeth as he perceived that they were no longer in disorder but had expertly formed their shield wall ready to meet the attack. Why they had left the safety of the stockade, Hasculv could not tell. Seconds later he saw it: the ground between him and his enemy was peppered with pits in every direction, pits that could break a man's ankle if he stepped in the wrong place. Snowfall had aided the deception by partially hiding the deep rents in the ground. It had been these which had caused his men to fall, these which were destroying his shield wall.

'Halt!' Hasculv shouted, holding his battleaxe in the air.

Around him, his men shuffled nervously looking for direction from their konungr. But Hasculv dithered, wondering if he should advance or retreat.

Sir Robert FitzStephen did not hesitate.

'Forward!' he shouted from the front of his cavalry as he led them from their hiding place in a wide tunnel dug deep into the floor of the forest. The manure pile and fires had hidden the smell of the animals from Hasculv, while recent snowfall had concealed the men's footprints. A blizzard fell from the cloaked shoulders of the charging Normans as their horses leapt from their hiding place in line behind the great knight, his shield slung across his back. FitzStephen gripped his crossbow as he kicked Sleipnir's sides and urged him on towards the shields of the Dubhlinn men. All his warriors were similarly armed and with them were those hobiler-archers who had not left with Maurice de Prendergast. Together they trotted forward, more men joining their long line of horseback archers as they advanced towards the rear shield wall of Hasculv's army. They did not stop to unleash their aerial assault but rode on together.

'Prepare,' FitzStephen shouted, dropping his reins and urging Sleipnir on with a squeeze of his knees. He then snorted in a lungful of air and held his breath as he aimed the weapon at the enemy. 'Loose,' he bellowed and squeezed the trigger. All around him he heard the snap of bowstrings and the whistle of arrows as his men shot. Within a minute another wave was in the air and a third was being notched ready to kill. And the Normans kept their horses going forward so that every shower of crossbow bolts fell harder than the one previous. No army in the world could stand under the death cascade, and the Ostmen were already edging backwards.

'Loose,' FitzStephen shouted again as the Ostmen defending Hasculv's back broke and ran for their lives.

'You men,' he pointed at twelve horsemen, 'follow William the Welshman and keep those men running.' His younger brother smiled from ear to ear at being given the responsibility of harrying the retreating Ostmen. With a nod, William dropped his crossbow to the snowy floor and drew his sword. He clipped his heels to his courser's sides as he led his small conrois towards the mass of men who fought each other to get the quickest way off the battlefield and into the safety of the woods. The Normans hooted and whooped as if they were herding sheep and thundered around the periphery of the retreating men, shooting arrows or picking off stragglers with spear and sword.

'The rest of you will follow me. Hobiler-archers, stay with Miles Menevensis,' FitzStephen shouted, trusting his nephew to know what to do, 'Milites, get ready to earn your pay. Spear formation!' A number of esquires ran between the snorting horses, handing out lances and taking crossbows from their masters before disappearing back to a safe distance.

Ahead, through the narrow eyelets of his war helm, FitzStephen viewed the two lines of Dubhlinn men. The first was struggling across the uneven land to take on Walter de Ridlesford and his Waesfjord Norse, while the second shielded themselves from Miles' measly arrow shower in the tight corridor between the trees and the cliffs.

FitzStephen clipped his heels to Sleipnir's sides and trotted forward towards the extreme left-hand side of the Dubhlinn shield wall. His milites fell in behind him in a single line. There were still fifty paces between them when he urged his courser into a canter, and there were just twenty when he kicked Sleipnir into a gallop, driving his spear into the throat of the first warrior before pulling his courser away and assaulting another part of the line. His men whooped like madmen as they neared the point of impact, loving the excitement of a well-executed assault. Each strafed along the front of the shield wall behind their captain, stabbing and striking down on the faces of the immobile enemy, huddled behind their shields. The cavalry were the hammer and the men of Waesfjord the anvil, and between them the Dubhlinn army was dying.

FitzStephen took an axe-blow plum on his shield as he wheeled away and pointed Philip de Barri to circle around and lead the conrois in another pass along the shield wall. 'Keep your horse moving,' he shouted at his nephew. He pulled away from the fighting and raised his helm and watched as, in the distance, the nimble Uí Ceinnselaig flooded across the land perforated with pits to bravely engage the other line of Dubhlinn warriors. The ragged mass of screaming demons was a fearful thing to behold, but they were no match for the Ostmen led by Hasculv Mac Torcaill, who withstood the impact and fought back with equal fury.

FitzStephen dropped his helm and returned to the fight, a death-masked horseman wrapped in shining steel from the worst nightmares of those who stood in his way. His steaming breath shot from the mouth-holes in his helm to add to the effect as he drew his heavy sword. His first strike opened an isolated Ostman's stomach. Perhaps it was FitzStephen's reappearance or perhaps it was just coincidence, but Hasculv's men chose that precise moment to break and run. They were the warriors who had stepped back from leading the assault on the Norman fortification and most were young or increasingly old, the weak and the fearful. They ran for their lives, across the clearing towards the shallow path back through the forest.

'Back,' FitzStephen shouted, and urged his courser to turn and trot away towards a small bluff under the cliffs. He did not want his men to drown in the midst of the stream of warriors. 'Watch out, William,' he called to his brother who waved a response and copied his brother's movement, taking his small band of horsemen out of the way of the retreating Ostmen.

Philip de Barri was the first horseman to reach FitzStephen's side. Out of breath, he was covered in blood and bearing a huge grin across his face.

'Brilliant, isn't it,' he stated. Within a minute the rest of the cavalry had joined the duo on the slopes of the southern ridge. They all panted silently watching the two Ostmen shield walls flee the battlefield. But there was still an enemy left to fight. FitzStephen's lance was broken beyond use, but he spotted a battle-axe buried in the ground and stooped to pull it from the frozen turf. He was shocked at the weight and lack of balance of the large weapon and he grunted as he hefted it onto his shoulder and righted himself in his saddle. Sleipnir stamped his feet impatiently as his rider watched the remaining Ostmen.

Their konungr, Hasculv, obviously knew that the Normans were coming and had sent some of his best warriors to meet their charge, but the men from Dubhlinn were still facing a prolonged attack by the Uí Ceinnselaig and could only permit a small contingent to face the horsemen. The Ostmen had seen the tactics of the Normans earlier in the day and had watched as they slowly advanced before quickening their charge at the last moment.

'Wait for them to slow,' Jarl Ingjald shouted, turning his back on the slow Norman advance to order his troops, ignoring two of his men who lifted their arms and pointed over their leader's shoulder in warning.

One horseman led the charge. FitzStephen's blue surcoat billowed from his sides as he commanded Sleipnir forwarded at a gallop. He crossed his chest, cast his eyes to the sky, and breathed in a massive lungful of cold air, planting his heels into Sleipnir's sides with a yell.

'Waesfjord,' FitzStephen screamed the name of his prize with a bellow full of desperation, ambition, and hope. He did not even have his shield in the correct position. Instead it was strapped across his back. The Norman stood in his stirrups and launched the battle-axe at the Ostmen. The weapon was usually wielded two-handed by a man with his feet firmly planted on the ground, but all of FitzStephen's strength, his determination to defeat Diarmait's enemies, and his resolve to secure his lands in the south; his future and the prestige of his name, everything went into the throw.

It was a terrible effort. But it had fate behind it and not a little bit of luck and, as it nose-dived towards the hard ground, it skidded under the line of shields and mangled the unprotected legs of a single enemy warrior. The man went down under the axe blow and in ear-piercing agony grabbed for the support of the man alongside. Both were felled, allowing a gasping FitzStephen to crash through the small gap in the shield wall, even though Sleipnir tried to pull away. Together, man and beast trampled the wounded soldier and his compatriot. Seconds later, the rest of his men, who had fallen into line behind their commander, impacted the shattered remnants of the shield wall. FitzStephen drew his sword and sliced down on an enemy axeman. He kept his horse swirling and suddenly Nicholas de Caunteton, Randolph FitzRalph, and Nigel le Brun were beside him, and the enemy were breaking, running to the east in front of the two barricades which defended the Norman camp.

It was too much for the rest of Hasculv's men and they also ran for their lives. They couldn't have remained with the Gaels to their front and the Normans behind and, first in ones and twos, they broke and made their way through the stakes and pits with the devilish Uí Ceinnselaig on their heels. Domhnall Caomhánach's troops were like wolves with the scent of blood in their nostrils and they flayed any Ostmen that they caught.

Hasculv Mac Torcaill lofted his shield to take a strike from an enemy spear and grabbed the shaft, pulling the man towards him and felling him by butting his helmeted head into the Irishman's face. His brother Hamund stabbed low into the man's torso then turned tail and ran. Immediately two more Gaels came at Hasculv and he roared his challenge, throwing one man over his shoulder with his shield arm before ramming his mailed fist into the other warrior's bearded chin. The man slumped to the ground immediately. The Konungr of Dyflin picked up a fallen spear and looked up for the next man to kill. He snarled from beneath his nasal guard and thumped his shield to his chest. He was ready to die but no one ran at him. In fact the closest enemy was a single horseman in a blue surcoat emblazoned with a silver star whose horse circled in front of the Waesfjord Norse as they marched back behind their defences. It was the Norman, Sir Robert FitzStephen, and he had spotted Hasculv.

'Fight me,' FitzStephen shouted at the Konungr of Dyflin, gesticulating with his sword. 'Come on, fight me.' His horse was as wild-eyed as its master and skittered around dramatically, head fighting against the bit.

Hasculv watched the Norman for a split second, a malevolent gaze that chilled FitzStephen worse than the winter cold. But the konungr simply spat on the ground and then ran for it through the field of pits and stakes with those that remained of his folk. The majority of his army were not so lucky and FitzStephen watched as the manic Uí Ceinnselaig tore into them from all sides.

'Leave them to Diarmait's people,' he called to his conrois.

Signalled by Miles Menevensis, a number of esquires ran from the fortifications and the conrois dismounted and gave over command of the snorting and sweaty coursers to their apprentices.

'That was brilliant,' said Ralph as he grabbed the bridle of his father's courser.

'You are right,' FitzStephen replied stiffly. 'This is a proud day for our family.' It seemed to be enough for the boy, who beamed at his father and ran off towards the fortification dragging the sweaty courser behind him like a massive toy.

'Job done,' William the Welshman said as he and all of FitzStephen's warriors joined their leader before the western wall.

'No,' FitzStephen replied, 'not yet.' He broke into a jog back towards the defences, his men breaking into a run to catch up with him. Sweat ran down from Nigel le Brun's head over his broken nose and mingled with the blood from a cut across his cheek.

'Are we beaten?' Brun shouted at FitzStephen, but received no answer. His captain was running and seemed not to hear. Now that they were clear of the trees and away from the battle in the west, FitzStephen could hear the screams of fear and the shouts of anger, the noise of warfare, wafting across the battlefield from the east. But who was winning? Had the mass of Gaels left in the east finally overcome the few Normans left in defence? He could not tell as he put his head down and ran towards the frontline. FitzStephen dashed between the two fences, sliding in snow and mud, just in time to see one king's dream die and another's come alive.

While the Ostmen of Dubhlinn had gone to their doom before the western wall, the allied Irish kingdoms had pushed forward towards the eastern defences. Ruaidhrí had gone into the fight calmly, sensibly sending out scouts to check the land for any hint of cavalry. The High King of Ireland, the most powerful man since Brian Bóruma had ruled Teamhair na Ri, had sent his men forward with all the confidence that he had once again beaten Diarmait Mac Murchada. He had beaten these much-vaunted foreigners and he would rule Ireland without opposition. There would be peace.

'Loose,' Richard de la Roche screamed from the high cliffs. The bowmen had waited patiently, hidden in the thick pine trees. Even when it looked like Sir Robert FitzStephen would be overcome by Hasculv of Dubhlinn, they had kept their position. As the first of the High King's forces had come forward, tentatively to begin with, they had unleashed their bombardment. Arrows, bolts, and spears fell amongst the attackers. Then the tree trunks, stones, and rocks rained down upon the ground before the eastern wall. Only a few of Ruaidhrí's men had died beneath the cliffs, arrows whistling down from above, projectiles thumping into frozen turf and bodies alike.

FitzStephen and his conrois arrived at the palisade just in time to watch Ruaidhrí's derb-fine come forward to stop any more men charging into the archers' range.

'Come on,' FitzStephen murmured as the High King dithered. He could see Ruaidhrí Ua Conchobair, surrounded by the kings and princes of Ireland, staring at the cliffs and surveying the killing ground in front of the palisade, trying to find a weakness. FitzStephen turned to the men who gathered behind him: Gaels, Norman, Welsh, Ostman, Englishman, and Fleming. No-one who had survived the battle had done so without an injury. Famous faces were missing from the crowd. Friends and kinsmen had died so that the rest could take the spoils in a fight where life had become the milites' only reward. That and the hope of a future struggle to maintain their fragile bridgehead in Ireland.

'Come on,' FitzStephen muttered again as he turned his back on his troops. He alone welcomed the chance to prove himself. He coveted the glory that would be attached to his name after beating the High King of Ireland. A man was nothing without a proud name and heritage, and in that moment Robert FitzStephen felt the old pride rise in him again. It rose to quash the fear of death.

'Come on,' he murmured.

A single mass charge by every man at Ruaidhrí Ua Conchobair's disposal would surely overwhelm his small garrison, FitzStephen knew. Richard de la Roche's archers could not stop them all and the warriors behind the barrier were too few to hold them back. With so few warriors left to him, it would be impossible for Maurice FitzGerald to defend Waesfjord and the garrison at the Ferry Carraig would be isolated and surrounded. All it would take for the Normans to be thrown out of Ireland forever was for Ruaidhrí Ua Conchobair to raise his hand, signal his loyal warriors forward, and overrun the defenders. Never again would anyone from the Kingdom of England dare to set foot on Irish soil when the stories of the massacre of FitzStephen's men reached across the sea.

'Come on,' FitzStephen shouted at the enemy. He imagined Henry FitzEmpress's bellow of mirth as was told of the death of the rebel knight, the man who had defied his edict.

'Come and kill us,' FitzStephen yelled as the sleet began falling again, turning the ground to mud and settling momentarily on the timber framed defences before melting to nothing.

FitzStephen's fellow invaders knew as well as he that the High King should attack and overwhelm them and so many were behind him were praying, holding the crosses bound at their necks, promising their God many things if He would get them through this day alive. Their enemy was still a mighty host and was being reinforced by the minute by the men from the retreating Ostmen of Dubhlinn. All eyes were on High King Ruaidhrí, who still dawdled over his decision to attack.

'Have you heard the one about the knight's daughter from Sweynsey?' Walter de Ridlesford asked suddenly and loudly at FitzStephen's side. Nervous, not one of the conrois attempted an answer, but all turned to stare at their compatriot who had obviously lost his nerve. 'She was so ugly that not even the tide would take her out,' Walter finished the joke.

For a couple of seconds no-one said anything. Then Robert FitzStephen began laughing. Slowly his laugh was taken up by his friends and then suddenly all the Normans, Welsh, and Flemings were sharing the joke and laughing with them, translating it into the different languages for the benefit of the rest of the army. Even the venerable Hugh de Caunteton, bleeding profusely from where his ear had been hacked off, was amused and recanted an irreverent joke of his own about the slutty English girls of Somerset. It was ludicrous. They stood on the edge of destruction but they were laughing. The amusement spread, firing defiance in the bellies of the small army. And why should they not laugh, thought FitzStephen? It had been a huge gamble for the Normans to stand their ground and take the fight to the High King, and now it seemed that they would lose having exhausted every trick at their disposal.

'You Normans are out of your minds,' Diarmait Mac Murchada said grimly as he came and stood beside his chuckling warlord. His family had walked down to the fence with him from their huts and FitzStephen once again locked eyes with Princess Aoife. She refused to drop her gaze and with her eyes seemed to challenge him to once again make something happen to save her father, and her future prospects, from the doom which faced them.

FitzStephen grinned confidently at her. 'If you leave now you can get through the mountains, cross the River Bearú, and make your way to Domhnall Ua Briain,' he said to her father.

'And what then?' asked Diarmait. 'You think that my enemies will not find us there as sure as here? No, we will stay

here, fight and die amongst the Uí Ceinnselaig in our own land.'
He was resigned to his fate but determined to throw one last
punch so that men would remember that he was defiant to the
very end. 'If you live, Sir Robert, may fortune smile on you.'
He drew his sword in preparation for the attack and began
kissing each of his wives, children, and grandchildren.

FitzStephen slapped a hand onto Diarmait's shoulder but
could not find anything to say to the man who had promised
him redemption and glory in Ireland, the King who had sprung
him from the damp cells of Llandovery. The King of Laighin
had taken a chance on a poor warrior from Wales and turned
him back into the proud warlord that he had been born to
become. But there was only one thing left to do in the depths of
the forest of Dubh-Tir. They had to die.

Then suddenly from above came a cheer. It hung around the
ravine and echoed around the forest. It was followed by a joyful
shout from the front.

'They are retreating!'

It was Meiler FitzHenry, and he hopped on the spot and
pointed north to where the army of the High King pulled back
from the battlefield. FitzStephen could not believe it. They were
leaving without any of their number even laying a hand on the
poorly defended barricade, the last refuge of their enemy.

A huge cheer came from the small number of desperate men
behind the fortification. More applause came from the archers
on the cliffs above them. Even the Ostmen of Waesfjord raised
a tired ovation. They were prompted by a victorious snarl from
Walter de Ridlesford, who planted a teary bear-hug on one of
their number and then bawled his eyes out on the terrified
man's shoulder.

Diarmait Mac Murchada, almost despondent just seconds
before, howled in happiness at the sight of the retreat of the
High King's army. 'So this is where Ireland was won,' he
smiled at the Norman. 'That is what they will say when the
bards sing of this moment, FitzStephen. This is where I won
Ireland!'

'You mean Laighin?' the knight asked him.

'Yes,' Diarmait countered quickly. 'Of course that's what I

meant. A new power had risen in Laighin.' He paused, unsure if he should make FitzStephen aware of his ambitions. 'But think on this, with more men from Wales we can subdue every tuath on the island. I could rule Ireland and you with me,' Diarmait said breathlessly, his voice fading away. Ten seconds before, the King of Laighin had seen his survival as a success, but now an assault on Teamhair na Ri was unfolding in his mind.

'To hell with Strongbow,' Diarmait said suddenly and turned to grip him by his chainmailed shoulders. 'It is customary for an alliance to be sealed by a marriage, Sir Robert.' His sharp blue eyes bore into the knight. 'For a thousand more of your archers and horsemen, I will give you Aoife,' Diarmait encouraged him with desperation and passion in his eyes. 'I have seen you staring at her, FitzStephen,' the King warned. 'You will take Strongbow's place and we will unite the five kingdoms of Ireland under my rule. Do you want Dubhlinn? Veðrarfjord? They will be yours, and all you have to do is bring me victory!'

Anyone within earshot of the conversation stared at the two men and awaited FitzStephen's answer. Would this mean that the Norman knight would be king after Diarmait? That was the offer that the Irishman had made to Strongbow – the same deal which had seen the baleful Sir Hervey de Montmorency join the adventure to Irish shores.

FitzStephen could barely believe his ears, but his first reaction was to look at Aoife. She wanted a powerful husband, a man with aspirations to match her own, and she saw one in FitzStephen. It did not matter that he was a foreigner, he was, it seemed, the future and a way for her to rule Ireland. She smiled at him and it was all that FitzStephen could do not to accept Diarmait's offer there and then. Images came to him quickly: he saw himself with Aoife on his arm, a crown on his head, and an army of mercenaries who would surely flock to his banner when they heard of his success and the vast kingdom with swordland to be won. He saw himself as ruler of a Norman kingdom to rival Sicily, Antioch, and even Henry's England. Had the founders of those nations not gambled everything to take those realms? Why should it be any different for FitzStephen?

But then his father's face came to him. He remembered the lessons, lessons his father had learned the hard way on the Welsh March and had imparted to his son with the threat of violence should he forget them.

'You win a battle,' Stephen had told his young son, 'then you build a castle and impose your will as far as your horses can carry you in a day. Then you fight and build again, and keep doing it as long as you can afford the men to garrison them.' Never, ever over extend your reach; that was his father's lesson. Consolidate.

It had taken four hundred Normans to secure the tribal lands of the Uí Ceinnselaig for this fighting season – nothing more had been done, in FitzStephen's opinion, despite the victory in Dubh-Tir. How many more warriors would it take to conquer Laighin and the other kingdoms of Ireland? Connacht, Aírgialla, Tir Eóghain, Deasmumhain, Mide, Tuadhmumhain, and Ulaidh – there were so many kingdoms with the strength to rival that of Diarmait's country. It would take a thousand archers and a hundred knights ... and then there was Earl Strongbow, his anger at FitzStephen's usurpation would be terrible and unending. Why else would he have sent an emissary as eminent as Sir Hervey to Ireland in the first place if his intention was not to follow in the near future? He was sure that Sir Hervey had already tried to kill him once, simply because he had crossed the sea before the earl and showed some promise of success. What would he try if FitzStephen took his master's intended wife and throne?

'Well, Sir Robert?' It was Aoife who had spoken. She was not smiling at him any longer, embarrassed perhaps that FitzStephen had not agreed to the offer immediately.

Consolidate, he thought and pursed his lips.

'I cannot accept your offer, Lord,' he turned and addressed Diarmait. He had Waesfjord and two hundred thousand acres and would not risk all that, even for a crown. Not even for that which he wanted most, Aoife. 'We have won an incredible victory and we have, at the very least, secured the lands of the Uí Ceinnselaig and Waesfjord. But I and my family have given everything we have for that victory. We have fulfilled our pledge to you Diarmait.' FitzStephen met the King of Laighin's angry gaze with an innocent stare.

'You do me great dishonour, Robert FitzStephen,' Diarmait's eyes flashed and his long beard quivered. His rage was barely concealed. Beside him Aoife matched his fury.

'No,' FitzStephen told his master, 'I have done you great service – exactly what I promised – but I can risk no more. Go now and talk to Ruaidhrí, be sensible and tell him that you will hold Laighin for him in return for peace and tribute. If he doesn't like that then tell him that he can come back into Dubh-Tir tomorrow. Tell him that Sir Robert FitzStephen, Lord of Waesfjord, will still be here to oppose him in the name of Diarmait Mac Murchada.'

FitzStephen turned to walk away, stopping momentarily to mumble an apology in Aoife's direction. She looked so beautiful, wrapped in a massive fur cloak against the cold which brought colour to her cheeks, her long red hair loose and wild across her back, but she would not accept his apologies, her fuming anger fuelled by embarrassment at being refused marriage. He marched on through the sleet ordering six men to follow him to man a picket line far out in the forest. It was hardly needed. He knew that Diarmait and Ruaidhrí would come to an accord and the High King's invaders would go home.

He had succeeded. FitzStephen had beaten the Irish horde of eighteen thousand with just four hundred Normans, a thousand unmotivated Ostmen, and five hundred unarmoured warriors from Fearna. Surely now his name would be remembered in song. No-one would ever forget his great deeds just as they remembered those of William the Conqueror, Robert Guiscard, and Bohemond of Antioch. They would sing about the great deeds of Sir Robert FitzStephen, he thought, the bastard frontiersman who became a knight, the knight who became a prisoner, the prisoner who became a warlord, and the warlord who had won a kingdom.

# Chapter Fourteen

*Waesfjord*
*April 1170*

He warmed his hands over the fire in the longhouse and wrapped his cloak around him tightly. Rain slanted across the grey bay which he could see through the longhouse door and over the roofs of the nearby houses. It had been a warm start to the year, but the last week had been simply dreadful and Sir Robert FitzStephen shivered as the wind made the hearth glow red. Thankfully the longhouse's previous resident had been rich enough to build a luxurious bathhouse and it had become a welcome haven from the worsening weather outdoors for the Norman. FitzStephen wrapped his heavy catskin cloak even tighter against the cold and wished he could be back in the steam.

The efforts of the last few months had taken its toll on the army. It had been four months since the withdrawal of High King Ruaidhrí from Dubh-Tir and his forces were finally starting approach full strength again. Several warriors had arrived in Waesfjord in merchantmen from Bristol, and those injured during the fighting had recuperated and recovered in the care of a wise woman employed by Fionntán Ua Donnchaidh.

Five days after his scouts had confirmed that Ruaidhrí had retreated across the River tSionainn, FitzStephen and Diarmait had abandoned their position in the mountains for Fearna. It had been sacked and partially destroyed by the High King's allies, but the stone walls still stood and a few days' hard work had made it defensible again. The Normans had then journeyed south to Waesfjord, leaving Diarmait and the Uí Ceinnselaig to bring their plundered capital back to life.

Back in the Ostman longfort, FitzStephen had found the

marketplace full of trade, the harbour full of wintering ships, and his brother's coffers packed with coin. The first four months of 1170 had brought a flurry of commerce to Waesfjord. Maurice FitzGerald had used his extensive influence to encourage traders from as far as Flanders and Aquitaine to bring their wares across the sea in greater numbers than ever before. It was as if the battles in the north had never occurred. Even the rebellious Ostmen remaining in the town had been dazzled by the wealth that had flooded in at the expense of Veðrarfjord and Dubhlinn, and the townsfolk had grudgingly tipped their caps to their new Norman overlords' mercantile acumen. They might never forgive or forget but they had at least agreed on a reluctant peace for the time being.

Elsewhere in Ireland the fighting continued, or so it was said. Tigernán Ua Ruairc had sent men against Domhnall Ua Briain and Tuadhmumhain, Hasculv Mac Torcaill had led his longship fleet to attack the coast of Mide and Ulaidh, and every chieftain between fought their neighbour for dominance, wealth, and slaves. All, that was, except Ruaidhrí and Diarmait who were at peace. They had made a settlement after the standoff in Dubh-Tir, just as FitzStephen had predicted. The High King of Ireland could ill afford to sit in the snow and wait for the well-supplied Normans to starve, but conversely, he could not allow Diarmait to insolently flaunt his victory. So they had come to an agreement that suited them both – Diarmait would rule Laighin and offer homage and tribute to the High King, and Ruaidhrí would go home. Their rivalry could wait and simmer until both thought themselves strong. Conchobair, Diarmait's son, would remain a hostage in Connacht to make sure that his father kept his word. Eventually he would marry Ruaidhrí's young daughter Roisin. But for the time being Conchobair Mac Murchada would be nothing more than a pawn in the power struggle between the two kings. Diarmait was disturbed at that part of the agreement – after Eanna's mutilation it was understandable – but his aspirations had won out in the end and their treaty had been sealed by solemn promises under the eyes of bishops and churchmen from both sides.

Aoife had pointedly ignored FitzStephen during the short period he had spent at Fearna. She was unwilling to forgive or forget the slight to her pride, but nor would FitzStephen ask her to relent. The decision had been made and he would have to live with it. FitzStephen had hoped that work improving Waesfjord would allow him to forget Diarmait's daughter, but Maurice had been very busy in his absence and few things required his attention.

He had wanted to improve the defences to the landward approaches to the city, but Maurice had beaten him to it. Then he had planned the rebuilding of two churches to replace those burned by the Ostmen, but that had been largely beyond his capability and finances. He had finally found a task in organising drainage of the fields around the town, but after a month of digging that chore had been completed and FitzStephen had found himself again without occupation. To pass the time he had hunted wolves and big, rough local deer and this had proved a marvellous, demanding distraction. But even the hunt had lost its pleasure after a few weeks.

Nevertheless, his enforced indolence had provided him with an opportunity to think over the successful venture which he had led. He considered his half-brother William FitzGerald's risk at offering Carew Castle to Yossi of Gloucester, the long sea journey, and Fionntán Ua Donnchaidh who had stayed with him after Dubh-Tir. He proudly remembered the fights at Dun Cormaic and Waesfjord, and considered the lessons taken from the bloody campaign across northern Laighin. It had been a momentous few months since he had been sprung from Llandovery's cells by Diarmait Mac Murchada. Never again would the Normans be so weak, that he promised. As soon as the weather became more favourable he would send Meiler and Miles back to Wales to recruit more warriors. He had faced an entire nation in arms intent on his destruction, but by his steadfastness and courage he had forced his enemies to falter and lose faith. The moment of crisis had passed and news of the glory won by the small warband would already have travelled beyond Ireland's shores thanks to Maurice's merchants.

Out of the door he watched as a number of local craftsmen

worked on the skeleton of a new longship on the banks of the bay under the watchful eye of Nigel le Brun. With Norman leadership Waesfjord would grow and it would need a bigger fleet to support the number of tradesmen that would spread throughout the isles of Britain and even to Frisia, Flanders, and France across the sea. And all the profits would find its way back to Waesfjord and into the pockets of FitzStephen and his brothers. Pembroke would prosper too, and with it the sons of Nest would found a cross-sea empire built on trade and conquest in Ireland.

He smiled as Maurice FitzGerald joined him in the longhouse which had belonged to the late leader of Waesfjord's assembly. Eirik's collusion with the Normans had ended abruptly and painfully while FitzStephen and the army were fighting the High King. In the culture of the Ostmen an honourable man was expected to take revenge on his enemies, not conspire on bended knee with those who had defeated him. As such Eirik had become a disgrace amongst his people, and his wife, distraught at his shame, had divorced him and proclaimed her decision, which was her legal right, in front of all the people of Waesfjord. The act had precipitated Eirik's loss of control of the Waesfjord Thing and Maurice, disgusted with his henchman, had acted to end the political standoff. First, Eirik had disappeared to the Ferry Carraig while Maurice had rooted out the worst dissenters. Through intimidation and coercion, burnings and beatings, he had forced the members of the Thing to again follow his orders. But Eirik had never reappeared in Waesfjord, and nor would he as he was buried in an unmarked grave beneath the herb garden in FitzStephen's new castle.

Maurice greeted his brother with a curt nod. He spied a piece of bracken, used for insulation on the roof, which had become loose and he stuffed it back into place. 'Did you hear the news?' he asked.

His half-brother nodded. 'I heard. Prendergast finally got passage back to Wales in Veðrarfjord,' he said. 'It probably cost him an arm and a leg, but better that than to have Diarmait or Donnchadh Mac Giolla Phádraig catch up with him and actually take an arm and leg,' FitzStephen replied with a small giggle.

'He is here,' Maurice whispered.

'Prendergast?'

Maurice made a scornful face, 'No, Diarmait.'

'In Waesfjord?' he asked. He scattered a number of woodchips, strewn on the floor for heat retention, as he stood to his feet. 'Why is he here?'

'I will tell you myself,' said Diarmait Mac Murchada loudly as he stomped into the longhouse and crossed the room to embrace FitzStephen. 'How are you, Sir Robert?' There was no hint of the anger and distance that had grown between the two men in the last days spent in Dubh-Tir. No sign of the resentment caused by his turning down Aoife's hand in marriage.

'I am well, Lord,' FitzStephen said haltingly. 'What brings you to Waesfjord?'

'For a favour, Sir Robert,' said Diarmait. He dominated the room by his sheer size. 'It involves a stiff fight against massive odds so naturally I thought of you.' The King laughed heartily as FitzStephen called for servants to prepare so food for his guest. 'I want you to go into the west to help my son-in-law Domhnall Ua Briain to secure Tuadhmumhain,' Diarmait explained. 'You will have heard that Ruaidhrí Ua Conchobair is bringing his army down from Connacht.'

'I had heard Tigernán Ua Ruairc was fighting but not Ruaidhrí,' the Norman replied. 'Will this not make your treaty with the High King void?'

Diarmait laughed and shook his head. 'There will be much plunder, especially from Hlymrik, and it will open up another front against our enemy,' he said, ignoring FitzStephen's misgivings.

Maurice saw his brother's hesitation. 'You think that helping the Uí Briain will assist you to hold Laighin?' he asked.

'Yes, indeed,' Diarmait said quickly. 'The best thing to do right now is to keep Ruaidhrí interested in Mhumhain and away from us. So will you do it?'

FitzStephen was bored in Waesfjord, superfluous even,

thanks to Maurice's hard work. 'We will leave within the month,' he told his liege lord. 'A hundred archers and thirty warriors will accompany me.' There was a fight in the west, plunder to be had, and pillaging to be done. Of course Robert FitzStephen would go.

The three men talked late into the night, ate and drank well and it was much later that Diarmait walked back to the church of St Patrick where he was staying during his stay in Waesfjord. The stone walls of the church would keep out the cold winds better than the wood and wattle walls of the Ostman longhouses, he thought. He did not like the alien-looking buildings anyway, they reminded him that he was not amongst his own people. It was dark and Diarmait's head was hazy from the wine which he had drunk in the company of FitzStephen and Maurice. But there were enough burning torches to light his and his bodyguard's way as he journeyed through the streets towards the church. The tall building stood out dark against the night sky and Diarmait waved to a novice monk who guarded the entrance to the church compound.

The church stood on top of a small bluff. Unlike most churches in Ireland it did not have a tall tower beside it as these clerics did not need a place to flee and hide their treasures from the Ostmen. Below lay all the outbuildings required to run and feed the small monastery while in the centre of the compound was a huge carved stone cross, circle around the cross point, resplendent with Celtic designs and Nordic runes.

'Lord King,' a voice like murder came from beyond the intricately carved cross. Diarmait Mac Murchada jumped in fright at its power.

'Sir Hervey,' he said, and waved away his bodyguard. 'I thought you were going to stay hidden. Robert FitzStephen cannot know that you are here in Waesfjord.'

Sir Hervey de Montmorency, looking as decrepit and downtrodden as ever, appeared from the shadows behind the Celtic cross, grinning balefully over decayed teeth.

'He has no idea that I am here.' Hervey walked across the cut mud and reeds thrown on the courtyard but they made no noise beneath his feet.

'Robert doesn't like you,' the King said, taking the French nobleman by the arm and leading him towards the main cell which the priest had vacated to make way for his royal visitor. Diarmait chanced a look over his shoulder to see if anyone was around to identify Hervey. He could make out no-one in the gloom.

'FitzStephen would kill me if he got the chance,' said Montmorency as he bared his horror of a smile again.

'And you wouldn't do the same to him?'

The French nobleman dragged his fingers through his thin and greasy long hair. 'Just give me another opportunity and a crossbow. So you sent him to help Ua Briain?'

'How did you …' Diarmait began before stopping. 'You have been roaming through the town,' he accused Hervey, who had indeed been eavesdropping on his conversation with FitzStephen.

Diarmait shook his head, realising that he should not have been surprised by his ally's underhandedness. 'I did as you asked. He will be in the west when Strongbow lands. Robert will not make trouble for your nephew.'

'Good, good, and so to our main business. You know why I am here. Does the offer still stand?' Montmorency asked Diarmait as they passed into the dark building.

'It does,' Diarmait said, 'but the crown that I want has changed. FitzStephen has given me Laighin. Now I want Teamhair na Ri. I want Ruaidhrí's throne.'

Hervey de Montmorency shrugged. 'Strongbow will sit on whatever throne you occupy so the bigger the better.' He didn't say that the bigger his nephew's victory, the larger the riches that would come to him. 'We should send a letter to England to bring Strongbow here soon. We should formalise the agreement.'

Diarmait nodded and called for Máelmáedoc Ua Riagain to attend him in his quarters. His secretary was with them in a few minutes. He questioned Sir Hervey's presence with a raised eyebrow but that was all.

'I bring news from Strongbow,' Hervey told him.

'You will take a letter to him in Striguil,' Diarmait said as

Máelmáedoc got ready to write. 'I trust no one else with this task.'

'I will not fail,' his secretary replied.

'Diarmait, son of Donnchadh Mac Murchada, King of Laighin, to Richard of Clare, Lord of Striguil,' Mac Murchada began, 'greetings.' He stopped talking. His hesitation continued for many seconds, so many that Máelmáedoc and Hervey swapped glances of confusion.

'My King?' encouraged Máelmáedoc.

Diarmait Mac Murchada said nothing. Was this the right course of action, he wondered? By committing to bringing more foreigners to his homeland was he inviting disaster as his son Domhnall believed? He could barely control Robert FitzStephen and the small number of Normans that he had already brought to his shores. They were so few but had defeated the united powers of every king in Ireland. Despite his fears, he smiled with pride as he remembered the great victory and he imagined how powerful he would be with ten times the number of Normans at his command. No-one would be able to stand in his way and he would be High King of Ireland. In the seal fat candlelight his eyes flashed.

'Diarmait?' asked Sir Hervey, wondering if the Irishman was having second thoughts about bringing Strongbow to his new kingdom. The Frenchman ground his teeth. Had the upstart FitzStephen finally turned the King of Laighin against the earl just as he had always feared?

Mac Murchada cleared his throat. 'My friend, the swallows have come and gone, yet you are tarrying still,' he continued, dictating the letter after a short pause. 'Neither winds from the east nor the west have brought us your much desired and long expected presence. Let your present activity make up for this delay and prove by your deeds that you have not forgotten your engagements but only deferred their performance. Our friend Sir Robert, son of Stephen, has led our forces to victory over the High King and our position in Laighin is now secure. If you come in time with a strong force the other four parts of the kingdom will be easily united to this the fifth. You will add to the flavour of your coming if it be speedy; it will turn out famous if it is not delayed, and the sooner the coming, the better the welcome. The wound in our regards which has been partly caused by neglect will be healed by your presence; firm friendship is secured by good offices and grows by benefits to greater strength. For I hold to the provisions of our original agreement and upon the speedy embarkation of your armies will marry you to my daughter, the Lady Aoife, and name you my son, tánaiste, and heir. The kingdom of Ireland is now your prize and it is ripe for the taking. I will look long for your sails on the eastern horizon,' Diarmait signed off his letter. Máelmáedoc Ua Riagain would spice it up and Mac Murchada trusted him to do it with customary skill.

Hervey smiled malevolently. He was about to come into a vast fortune perched on the coat tails of his nephew.

'I see that you have employed a number of men-at-arms and brought them with you to Ireland,' Diarmait said to the grimly grinning Montmorency, who had indeed employed ten ragged milites – murderers, brigands, and landless Normans – ready to do his bidding however repugnant. 'Will they be sitting around your new estates in Siol Bhroin taking your money or do they need some work while you are in Wales?'

'That depends on two things,' Hervey said quickly, holding up two bony fingers, 'how much it pays,' he retracted one of his talons, 'and who you need dead. I assume that is what you want?'

Diarmait grinned and pursed his lips. 'I need your men to have a quiet word,' he raised an eyebrow, 'with King Diarmait Ua Mael Sechlainn of Mide about how we are to proceed as good neighbours. He has lands that belong to Donnchadh Ua Ceallaigh and my friend, his cousin, Domhnall Ua Mael Sechlainn of Brega. He should return them or face the consequences.'

Hervey's lip curled into a smile. 'What type of devil would kill a king? It could destabilise the whole kingdom, even bring about a civil war. It would leave it open to conquest.'

'I'm glad that you think so,' the King of Laighin smiled. 'Tell your men to enjoy it and to say hello to Diarmait Ua Mael

Sechlainn from me before he dies. Tell him that all his line will join him soon in hell.'

# Epilogue

## *Forthairt – July 1170*

A ship out at sea pitched and splashed through the grey, rolling waves. She was a Norman-built warship, that much FitzStephen could make out from his viewpoint on the cursed Carn tSóir Point, and she was sailing south to avoid the dangerous passage just as had FitzStephen when he invaded Ireland a year before. Wind lashed the warriors who watched the ship's progress high up on the point, as it did the untold numbers of soldiers hidden beneath the dark sail out to sea. On her mast was a long-tailed banner, flicking evilly in the wind and showing the crimson and gold of the Clare family. The top of the flag was adorned with the distinctive blue band indicating a cadet branch of the family.

'Strongbow,' FitzStephen hissed. Annoyance flickered in his mind as he watched the ship smash through another bank of water. Red-headed Aoife appeared in his mind's eye and he again wondered if he had made a mistake by not marrying the beautiful princess. The arrival of Strongbow made it likely that the opportunity had evaporated. He sighed as he let the image of Aoife fade.

Was he nervous or excited by the coming of more of his warlike people? The Normans had been relatively weak but now they were a force that no-one could contain. FitzStephen knew that before the year was out, Ireland would again be in flames. It was the same in every land where the Normans rode.

'Are you sure it is Strongbow?' Maurice FitzGerald asked his brother. 'Surely he would have more ships to claim his bride and the throne.'

His half-brother nodded. 'It may just be his vanguard, a landing party to prepare the way for more to come.' What did it matter how many warriors Strongbow brought to Laighin, he thought. FitzStephen already had his prize and no mere baron from the English borders would take it from him. FitzStephen may have been considered nothing more than a troublemaker and brigand in Henry's kingdom but here on the edge of the world he was so much more. He was a lord of battles and it was the Norman nobility that were nothing. He smiled and turned to his elder brother. 'Diarmait doesn't know what he has invited to Laighin,' he told his brother. 'Strongbow will bring a hundred knights the equal of Robert FitzStephen.'

Maurice returned his grin but doubted his companion's self-effacing words. He had never met a man of FitzStephen's qualities and doubted that Strongbow would be able to rustle up a single man to equal him, never mind a hundred. He watched as his half-brother slung his shield over his shoulder and leapt onto his horse in a single bound.

'We will follow the coast and see where they land. Then we will pick up the River Siúire through Oirmumhain towards the Uí Briain kingdom,' FitzStephen fumbled over the awkward Gaelic words. 'From there we can work our way to Hlymrik.'

'Take care of yourself, brother.' Maurice held out his hand to FitzStephen. 'St Maurice will protect you.'

'He has done so this far. Keep Waesfjord safe,' FitzStephen grinned as his troops fanned out westwards.

Maurice FitzGerald let go of his hand and watched the younger man trot his horse away. His lance was propped against his esquire's shoulder and its blue and white pennant flapped violently in the wind which surged inland. His troopers fell in behind their lord and captain.

Few men, if any, could have done what his incredible younger brother had achieved, Maurice thought as he watched him leave for yet another battle. From a pitiful prisoner to the power behind the throne of Laighin in just a matter of months – Strongbow could bring a thousand knights to Laighin but none would ever rival Sir Robert FitzStephen, Warlord of Waesfjord, or the deeds which he had performed.

Maurice snorted back a laugh. Not that the newcomers would not try, he thought as he turned to look out to sea. The men in the rolling ship were Normans after all and every one of that race were champions. And in Ireland they had found a new land to conquer. Each would search for his own piece of swordland.

# Historical Note

The invasion of Ireland was not a conquest like that made by the Normans after their victory in 1066. Unlike England, Ireland was not a nation state but a motley group of petty kingdoms and chiefdoms, of warring neighbours and brittle alliances. Ireland could not be conquered by killing a single king in battle or by taking a major city. The Norman adventurers would go on to inflict defeat after defeat on the Irish over the next century and a half without ever getting close to conquering the Emerald Isle. The ability of the natives to absorb these defeats was just one reason why these first invaders – who became known as the *Old English* – would eventually become absorbed into the fabric and culture of Ireland. By Tudor times they would be described as 'more Irish than the Irish themselves'.

The Normans from the March of Wales were far from unknown to the people of Ireland. Trade across the Irish Sea was a profitable one for both parties, and there is no doubt that news, fashion, and tastes would have crossed the waves as easily as did people and their wares. That it took a century for the Normans to land an army in Ireland is perhaps most surprising, and demonstrates just how successful the rebellious Anglo-Saxons, Danes, Scots, and Welsh were at keeping the newcomers busy! When they finally did arrive, in the company of Diarmait Mac Murchada, the first invaders were incredibly successful in a very short period of time, the tactics picked up in Wales transferring perfectly to the Irish theatre. The invasion was famously chronicled by Gerald de Barri, more famously known as Giraldus Cambrensis. He visited his siblings, Robert and Philip de Barri (later Barry), in 1185 during their invasion of eastern Munster and his account forms the basis for

415

*Swordland*, though anyone interested in the period would do well to read *The Norman Invasion of Ireland* by Richard Roche, *Diarmait, King of Leinster* by Nicholas Furlong, and *Strongbow: The Norman Invasion of Ireland* by Conor Kostick for a superb overview.

In *Swordland* I have deviated from the historical accounts at several points, not least on Robert FitzStephen's age which in real life was probably ten or fifteen years greater than the character's. As described here, he was Constable of Aberteifi (today's Cardigan) and son of Princess Nest of Deheubarth. Einion ab Anarawd was actually murdered as he slept, in 1163, by his servant Walter ap Llywarch, and on the orders of the Earl of Hertford rather than by FitzStephen's hand – though as the Earl's chief man in the region it is possible that the real-life FitzStephen may have been involved in some capacity. Rhys of Deheubarth did besiege Aberteifi in 1164, though it was chiefly due to the treachery of the clerk Rhygewarch that the castle fell. Rhys actually permitted the inhabitants of the town to flee with 'half their possessions' before he destroyed the castle and imprisoned Robert FitzStephen.

The Lord Rhys is one of the great men of Welsh history though his triumphs were largely undone by the squabbles of his four sons following his death in 1197. Rhys was younger than FitzStephen and had no son called Tewdwr. The Irish annals talk of a son of the King of the Britons who was killed at Cill Osnadh, but his identity is unknown. It seems unlikely that this unnamed warrior was Rhys' son, but it is possible that he was the offspring of one of Rhys' elder brothers or a scion of the Gwynedd or Powys dynasties. Unlike the description in *Swordland*, Cill Osnadh was actually a major engagement when the old alliance of Tigernán Ua Ruairc, Ruaidhrí Ua Conchobair, Diarmait Ua Mael Sechlainn, and Hasculv Mac Torcaill again joined forces and invaded Diarmait's territory, forcing him into an embarrassing submission. They also extracted a huge honour price from Diarmait in revenge for his abduction of Tigernán's wife fifteen years before. This battle took place in 1167, as did FitzStephen's release from Rhys' custody, though it was almost two years before our protagonist ventured across the sea to Ireland.

Hervey de Montmorency was not the brother of the powerful French nobleman, Bouchard, but was almost certainly a distant cousin, whose family came to England around 1066. Similarly, Máelmáedoc Ua Riagain's role has been changed somewhat. He was Diarmait's secretary and translator not, as portrayed in *Swordland*, his chief advisor. That role would likely have been taken up by a number of Diarmait's close relatives or even the hereditary brehons from the O'Doran family.

The historical FitzStephen did fight a battle at Duncormick in southern County Wexford, though perhaps not against the Ostmen, and then crossed the hills of Forth to storm the walls of Wexford which he thereafter claimed as his own. It is not known whether this was with feudal obligations to Diarmait, or by right of the sword, though he did build a castle at Ferrycarrig. The site is now part of the Irish National Heritage Park, which is a wonderful place to visit and experience nine millennia of Irish history – including the history of the Norman invasion.

FitzStephen's attack on the Osraighe was in reality a succession of encounters over a number of weeks, but the most vivid occurred near Freshford and was followed by a massacre. This forms the basis for the imagined fight near Gowran in *Swordland*. I must admit that Maurice de Prendergast was far from the duplicitous character as portrayed in this book. History records him as one of the most noble and honourable men in the story of the conquest.

Towards the end of 1169, Ruaidhrí Ua Conchobair (who was actually of a similar age to Diarmait Mac Murchada) did respond to Diarmait's reappearance by leading a large army to take him on in his home territory. The size of Ruaidhrí's army at Dubh-Tir will never be known, but estimates range from 10,000 men to an almost impossible 60,000. Whatever the size of the force that faced them, Robert FitzStephen did lead his men into the mountain fastness and there constructed defences and dug trenches to confuse and disrupt the approaching horde. Ruaidhrí did indeed make offers to both FitzStephen and Diarmait Mac Murchada to betray the other, but both stayed true. The sources say that Ruaidhrí dared not attack the Norman position in Dubh-Tir except to 'scour the forests and pursue the rebels'. I have used this as a pretext to include the fictitious battle at the end of the book. The reality is that Ruaidhrí, seeing no way to defeat Diarmait and his mercenaries, sent a number of churchmen to negotiate a peace and thereafter withdrew to Connacht. History seems to have forgiven Ruaidhrí Ua Conchobair for wasting this opportunity to wipe out the small number of invaders. Had he done so, the later incursions by Strongbow and King Henry II may have been delayed or even prevented and who knows, Ireland may even have developed to a stage where invasion from Britain was unforeseeable. How different would world history be if that had occurred?

Whatever his reasons, Ruaidhrí Ua Conchobair blinked first, and Robert FitzStephen survived to return to his newly conquered lands. More importantly, however, was the effect on Diarmait Mac Murchada who, back on the throne of Laighin (Leinster), set his sights upon nothing less than the High Kingship of Ireland. Within a few months he had invited more Normans from Wales to help him achieve his goal. Primary amongst this second wave of invaders was one man whose name is synonymous with the Norman invasion of Ireland: Strongbow. Unlike Robert FitzStephen, Strongbow did not simply wish for an estate and great wealth. He desired a throne and in Ireland, with his Norman barons alongside him, he believed that he could win one.

I would like to acknowledge a number of people whose kind support and direction throughout the process of writing *Swordland* was invaluable: to my agent, David Riding at MBA, and to my editor Greg Rees and the whole team at Accent Press, my particular thanks for guiding me through the process and bringing the novel to publication. I'd also like to express my appreciation to everyone who read the book through its various stages of development – Ewan Butler, Sandra King, Anthony Quinn, and the late Wallace Clark – and gave their feedback and advice. My thanks also go to my parents, Emma, my family and friends, and my many fellow online historical fiction fanatics for their constant encouragement and belief and without whom this novel would not have been possible.

*Edward Ruadh Butler*
*December 2014*

# The White Ship
## Nicholas Salaman

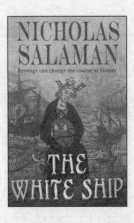

Normandy in 1118 is a hotbed of malcontent barons kept in fragile order by their duke, Henry I, King of England. Fresh from early years in a monastery, Bertold – the bastard son of one of these barons – meets Juliana, a countess and daughter of the King.

He falls in love, or lust (he isn't sure), but sees that his chance could come with work in her small court. Soon, though, he finds himself caught up in a ruthless feud between Juliana and her father. Juliana's daughters are offered as hostages for a strategic castle, and even love is not enough to allay a tragedy that will change the course of history.

# Princes and Peasants
## Catrin Collier

The second volume in Catrin Collier's epic The Tsar's Dragons series, set in the late nineteenth-century Russian Empire. Welsh industrialist John Hughes has built an ironworks on the Russian Steppe – and a city bearing his name has grown up around it.

For people like Hughes' right-hand man, Glyn Edwards, who has found love in a new country, and Anna Parry, a Welsh orphan who has found fulfilment working in Hughesovka's hospital, the city is a chance to build a new life – but fresh arrivals from their hometown have come to cause trouble and threaten the peace and stability of that new existence. Meanwhile, for ambitious Russians like Alexei Beletsky, the city offers a chance to change their homeland for the better – but Alexei still has to deal with the prejudices of the locals as he marries a Jewish girl, Ruth, and the new couple make enemies both Russian and Jewish.

For more information about

**Edward Ruadh Butler**

and other **Accent Press** titles

please visit

**www.accentpress.co.uk**